Emma Blair was born in Glasgow and now lives in Devon. She is the author of twenty-seven bestselling novels including *Scarlet Ribbons* and *Flower of Scotland*, both of which were shortlisted for the Romantic Novel of the Year Award.

For more information about the author, visit www.emmablair.com

Praise for Emma Blair

'Romantic fiction at its best. Pure heart-tugging, page-turning satisfaction'
Bookseller

'An author who so easily gets to grips with everyday life'
Torquay Herald Express

'From start to finish readers will be in the safe hands of an experienced writer of romantic fiction. The characters are beautifully portrayed with a real understanding of their lives'
Historical Novels Review

'[Her] characters . . . are endearing and portray an innocence that befits the period'
Publishing News

'Fascinating characters'
Devon Life

SWEETHEARTS

Emma Blair

SPHERE

First published in Great Britain in 2007 by Sphere
This paperback edition published in 2007 by Sphere
Reprinted 2008

A CIP catalogue record for this book
is available from the British Library.

ISBN 978-0-7515-3800-7

Typeset in Adobe Garamond by Palimpsest Book Production Limited,
Grangemouth, Stirlingshire

Printed and bound in Great Britain by
Clays Ltd, St Ives plc

Sphere
An imprint of
Little, Brown Book Group
100 Victoria Embankment
London EC4Y 0DY

An Hachette Livre UK Company
www.hachettelivre.co.uk

www.littlebrown.co.uk

January 1937

Glasgow

Chapter 1

Lexa Stewart opened her eyes, revelling in the warmth of her bed. She snuggled even further down under the covers, horribly aware that in a few minutes she'd have to get up for work and face a bitter, Scottish, January morning.

A glance at her bedside glass of water confirmed her worst fears: the water was frozen solid. She could hear her mother laying the fire in the front room, a job Alice did every morning before the rest of the family got out of bed, so that when she gave Lexa and her elder daughter Cordelia a shout they could hurry through and get swiftly dressed in front of the grate.

Monday. Lexa inwardly groaned. Her least favourite day of the week. The weekend was gone, and it was back to work again. Not that work was really all that bad – she actually quite enjoyed being behind the counter of her father's fruit and veg shop. It could be quite fun at times when there was a bit of banter going on between her and the customers.

'Lexa! Cordelia!'

Lexa took a deep breath, preparing herself for the massive effort of swinging her legs out of bed, collecting her clothes, laid out the previous night, and making a dash for the front room.

'Lexa! Cordelia! Come along now, the pair of you.'

'Damn!' Lexa muttered. She'd have given anything for an extra half-hour. Or, better still, another hour. But that simply wasn't on. She gasped when her feet slid out from beneath the bedclothes. It wasn't just bitter, it was Arctic. 'Oh, well,' she sighed. It had to be done. There was nothing else for it.

It only took a moment to throw on her somewhat threadbare candlewick dressing gown, scoop up her clothes and rush to the front room, where the fire was already crackling cheerfully. A moment later she was joined by Cordelia, who was chittering with the cold. Neither spoke, being far too intent on getting dressed.

'I'll go and see to your dad,' Alice said. 'He had a bad night, tossing and turning. His indigestion must have been playing up again. Probably the cheese we had for supper.'

Lexa snapped her bra into place, then shrugged into one of the black dresses she wore for the shop. Cordelia was struggling into a similar one, her teeth still chattering.

'It's bloody cold,' she complained, beginning to pull on her stockings. She checked her left leg for ladders, then did the same with her right.

Lexa was reaching for her own stockings when a terrible scream rang out. It was their mother's voice.

'Dear God!' Cordelia exclaimed. 'What's up?'

There was a moment's pause, then the scream was repeated. Cordelia and Lexa jumped to their feet and rushed to their parents' bedroom. The door was ajar, and they hesitated outside.

'Mum?' Lexa queried in alarm.

A wild-eyed Alice, face drained of all colour, appeared. 'It's your father,' she croaked.

'What about him?' Cordelia demanded.

Alice began to shake all over. 'He's . . . he's . . . dead.'

Lexa felt as though she'd been hit on the head by the proverbial hammer.

Cordelia brushed past Alice and went straight to the bed where Jimmy Stewart lay with his eyes closed. Her mother was making a mistake, Cordelia told herself. Had to be. Her dad was as fit and healthy a middle-aged man as you'd find.

'He's dead, I tell you.' Alice joined her at the bedside. 'He isn't breathing and there's no pulse.'

Cordelia bent and listened at her father's nose. Nothing. She pulled the bedclothes back and stared at his chest, which was quite still. There was no sign of movement whatsoever.

She looked at Alice, then at Lexa. Large tears appeared and rolled down her face. 'I think he is,' she said slowly, in a quavering voice.

Lexa reached her mother just as, with a sigh, Alice began sinking to the floor.

Lexa couldn't think straight, unable to take in what had happened. Her dad dead! It . . . it just couldn't be. And yet it was. She was stunned. Like Alice, now sobbing piteously in the wicker chair to which Lexa had guided her, her head in her hands and her long black hair falling forward over her shoulders, Lexa had begun to shake.

'What do we do?' Cordelia asked wildly.

Lexa forced herself to think. 'Go for the doctor, I suppose,' she replied eventually.

That made sense to Cordelia. 'You or me?'

Lexa shrugged. 'I don't mind.'

Cordelia's eyes strayed to the bedside alarm clock. 'The surgery won't be open for a couple of hours yet, so we'll have to wait.'

Lexa nodded her agreement. 'What about the shop?'

Cordelia had forgotten all about that. 'Out of the question. At least for now. It'll have to stay shut.'

'And the deliveries we're expecting?'

Cordelia suddenly felt weary way beyond her years. It was as though a huge responsibility had settled on her shoulders. 'There's nothing we can do about them,' she declared. 'The suppliers involved are bound to understand when they find out why we aren't there.'

Lexa glanced at her father's corpse. How calm he looked. How serene. As if he was merely asleep and having a wonderful dream. Despite herself, she shuddered.

Cordelia went to Alice. 'Would you like a cup of tea, Mum? I know I would.'

'Tea?' Alice repeated, as though she'd never heard the word before.

'That's right, tea. A good strong cuppa.'

'Tea,' Alice repeated again. 'That would be nice.'

'Right then. I'll put the kettle on.'

'I'll do that,' Lexa declared. 'You stay here with Mum.'

6

Alice dropped her head again, but the sobbing had ceased, much to her daughters' relief. 'He was such a good man,' she mumbled after Lexa had left the room. 'I couldn't have asked for a better husband.'

Cordelia gently patted her mother on the back. 'I know, Mum.'

'He was a real gem, that man. Never gave me a moment's grief. Not once. I've always counted myself lucky to have married him.'

'I'm sure he'd have said the same about you.'

'Dead,' Alice said in a hollow voice. 'Why, only last night he . . .' Her voice tailed off, leaving Cordelia wondering what she'd been about to say.

Dr Berryman, the family physician, pulled the bedclothes up over Jimmy's head while Alice, Cordelia and Lexa looked on. 'I'm afraid I have absolutely no idea what the cause of death was, Alice. From what I can make out it could have been any one of a number of things. If I was to make a guess I'd probably say heart attack. But, as I say, that would only be a guess.' He came to his feet from where he had been sitting on the edge of the bed. 'That being the case, I'll have to inform the police.'

Alice's hand went to her mouth. 'The police. Whatever for?'

'That's the rule, Alice. They'll call and ask you a few questions.'

'Is that absolutely necessary?' Cordelia queried, thinking of the extra strain it would put on her mother.

'I'm afraid so. It's procedure.'

'You don't think there's anything untoward, do you?' Lexa demanded.

Berryman shook his head. 'Not at all. It's simply that the cause of death has to be established. After the police have been, Jimmy will be taken to the morgue where a post-mortem will take place. Again, procedure.'

Alice staggered, then sank into the wicker chair she was standing beside. 'Does that mean they'll cut him open?'

'Yes, they will, Alice.'

'Dear God in heaven.'

'Part of the problem is, to my knowledge anyway, Jimmy had no history of illness or anything that might have led to his death. In fact, he was so healthy I hardly ever saw him in the surgery, as you probably well know.'

Alice nodded. Berryman was right about that.

'And what happens after this post-mortem?' Lexa queried.

'The body will be released to the undertaker, at which point everything should be straightforward.'

'You mean we can arrange the funeral?' Cordelia demanded.

'You can start arranging that as soon as you like,' Berryman replied. 'But it might be best to wait till the body's released, then you'll know exactly where you are.' The doctor looked at Alice, aware how hard she was taking all this. However, that was hardly surprising in the circumstances. 'I'll come back early evening, if you don't mind, and give you a sedative, Alice. It'll help you get through the night.'

'Thank you, doctor.'

'Is there anything else I can do for any of you?'

Lexa glanced at Cordelia, who shook her head. 'I don't think so, doctor. But thank you for offering,' she said.

He took a deep breath. 'Then all that's left is for me to say how truly sorry I am.'

'I'll show you out,' said Cordelia.

'Remember, I'll be back early this evening, Alice. In the meantime I'll notify the police.'

Alice ran a hand over her face, then crossed to the bed to sit where the doctor had been. 'If you don't mind I want to be alone with your father for a wee while,' she said to Lexa. 'Just the pair of us.'

Lexa gave her mother a peck on the cheek before following Cordelia out of the room, closing the door firmly behind her.

It was PC Sanderson, the local bobby, who turned up a few hours later. Lexa ushered him through to her parents' bedroom, where Alice was still sitting with Jimmy.

'You have my condolences, Mrs Stewart,' Sanderson sympathised. 'This must have been quite a shock.'

'Just a bit,' Alice replied drily, now fully composed.

'Would you like a cup of tea, constable?' Cordelia asked from the doorway.

'If it wouldn't be any bother.'

'None at all. And you, Mum?'

'Aye, I would.'

Sanderson produced a notebook and pencil. 'I believe Dr Berryman explained I have to ask you a few questions, Mrs Stewart. It's just routine and I'll try to make them as brief as possible.'

'Thank you, constable.'

He cleared his throat. 'Now then.'

He was gone in under fifteen minutes. Some time later an ambulance arrived to take Jimmy's body to the morgue. Alice broke down again and became almost hysterical, both Cordelia and Lexa having to restrain her in case she did herself an injury.

'My poor man. My poor Jimmy!' she wailed.

'I know, Mum. I know,' Cordelia crooned, her arm round her mother's shoulders.

'He was far too young to die. D'you hear? Far too young. He should have had years left in him.'

Cordelia didn't know how to reply to that. Just then there was a knock on the front door. 'You get that, Lexa,' she said.

It was Mrs McAllister from across the landing. 'What's going on?' she asked. 'I saw the police here, and now an ambulance.'

'It's my dad. He died during the night,' Lexa told her. 'The ambulance was taking him away.'

Mrs McAllister shook her head in horror. 'How's your mum?'

'In a terrible way, I'm afraid.'

'Is there anything I can do?'

Lexa considered that for a few seconds. 'I don't think so. Not for the moment anyway.' Then she had a thought. 'You might tell the rest of the neighbours, though. Up and down the close, that is.' The close was the communal stairway which separated the six flats, or houses as Glaswegians tended to call them, in their part of the tenement.

'Aye, right. I'll do that.' Mrs McAllister hesitated. 'If you want me just chap the door. Understand?'

Lexa nodded.

'And tell your mother how sorry I am. She must be in absolute pieces. This is so unexpected, after all.'

'I'll tell her.'

Lexa briefly closed her eyes. What a day. What a nightmare. She'd never have guessed when she'd woken up that morning what was to follow.

A nightmare right enough.

Lexa came into the front room carrying two glasses of whisky. 'Mum's still fast asleep and I can only hope she'll stay so till morning. The sedative Dr Berryman gave her must have been a strong one.' She handed Cordelia one of the glasses.

'Dad's whisky?' Jimmy had always kept a bottle in the house, though he hadn't been all that much of a drinker. He did like a dram on occasions, however – particularly Ne'erday, or Hogmanay.

'What else? I thought we deserved some.'

Cordelia let out a long, heartfelt sigh. 'I can certainly use this. And maybe another one after.'

'Our own type of sedative, eh?' Lexa smiled, attempting a joke which didn't quite come off. She sat down facing her sister. 'I still can't believe it, can you?'

Cordelia shook her head. 'No.'

'It was so sudden. So unexpected. No hint whatsoever.'

Cordelia stared into her glass, seeing a picture of her father in its contents. All sorts of memories flooded through her mind. She felt a choke rise into her throat.

'I'll miss him terribly,' Lexa said softly. 'I mean, he's always been there. Every day of my life he's been there. And now . . .' She trailed off.

'And now he's gone,' Cordelia finished for her.

'Aye, gone.'

'How do you feel, sis?'

'Completely and utterly washed out. Drained. And a bit sick.'

Cordelia nodded her head. 'Me too.'

'And . . . well, grief-stricken I suppose you'd call it. But that's in the mind. My body just feels as if it's taken a terrible battering.'

They sat in silence for a few seconds, each lost in thought.

'I half expect him to come walking through that door and we'll find today's been nothing more than a terrible dream,' Cordelia said eventually.

'Same here.'

'But it isn't a dream. And he'll never walk through that door again. What we've been experiencing is reality. Bloody, awful reality.'

Lexa gazed into the blazing fire. 'The question is, what happens now?'

Cordelia frowned. 'You mean the funeral?'

'No, after that. The shop, for example.'

Cordelia was at a loss. 'I haven't thought that far ahead, Lexa. Dad only died today, after all.'

'Well, it's something we're going to have to think about. And soon. We'll still need money coming into the house. We can't do without it.'

'I suppose . . . I suppose we'll just have to run the shop between us. There's nothing else we can do.'

'Do you think we're up to it?'

'I don't see why not. We've both been working there since leaving school.'

'True enough,' Lexa agreed. 'But only behind the counter serving customers. We've never been involved in the other side of it. Dad did all the ordering, don't forget. And the accounts. I've no idea how either of those two things work.'

'Me neither,' Cordelia admitted.

'Then there's the lifting. Dad never let us carry any boxes, saying they were far too heavy for lassies. He did all that himself.'

'In which case we'll just have to learn the things he did, including the lifting. I'm stronger than I look. And so are you.' She regarded Lexa shrewdly. 'You're the one good at sums and the like, so maybe you can do the accounts.'

'And you?'

'The ordering. I know Dad kept a record of what was ordered, and returned. Presumably I won't go far wrong if I keep to what's gone on before.'

That made sense to Lexa. 'The other thing is, what about money? We'll need to pay deliveries. And our own wages. Have you anything put by?'

Cordelia shook her head. 'I've got a couple of quid in my purse, and that's it. You?'

'The same. I've never seen the need to save.'

'Nor me. Here today, gone tomorrow, so to speak.'

Lexa was beginning to feel more relaxed. 'We're going to have to speak to Mum about the money thing. She must know what the situation is.'

'I only hope she does,' Cordelia mused.

'She's bound to. There must be a bank account some-where, though I've never heard her, or Dad, mention one.'

'Well, we can't speak to her yet. Not while she's the way she is. I doubt we'd get any sense out of her even if we did.'

They continued talking for a while before finally going to bed, where the whisky worked as they'd hoped it would.

Lexa was first up next morning and decided to lay the fire to save Alice a job. She had just got it lit when Cordelia joined her.

'How did you sleep?' Lexa asked.

'Like a top. You?'

'The same.'

'What shall we do about breakfast?' Again, that was normally their mother's province.

'I couldn't eat anything yet. Maybe in half an hour or so. I could murder a cup of tea, though.'

'I'll put the kettle on, then.'

Cordelia was about to head for the kitchen when Alice came through the door into the front room. The girls stared at their mother in shock. Alice's hair, which the previous evening had been a lustrous black, had turned snow white.

'I know,' Alice said huskily. 'I've already seen it.'

'Oh, Mum,' Lexa cried, tears coming into her eyes.

Cordelia could only think that her previously attrac-tive mother now looked old – if not positively ancient.

'Are you ready?' Cordelia asked.

Alice took a deep breath. 'As I'll ever be.'

'Then we'd better be moving.'

The post-mortem had established that Jimmy had died of a massive, and unforeseeable, heart attack. The body had been released to the family for burial, and now the hearse and hired car were downstairs waiting. It was time to go to the cemetery.

There was a good turnout at the funeral, many neighbours and friends, not to mention relatives, coming to pay their respects. To Cordelia and Lexa's surprise Alice remained composed throughout.

Later, during the wake, which Mrs McAllister and other women up the close had organised, Lexa noticed that her mother had disappeared from the gathering. Guessing where she had gone, she looked into her parents' bedroom and saw Alice standing staring at a photograph of her dad taken several years previously, her features contorted into an anguished mask.

Thinking it the best thing to do, Lexa turned round and rejoined the wake.

Chapter 2

The stench that hit Lexa and Cordelia when they opened the door was almost overpowering. It was the first time the shop had been opened in three weeks.

Lexa wrinkled her nose in disgust. 'I never thought it would be this bad.'

Cordelia went inside and flicked a switch, and electric light flooded the interior. Everywhere were boxes of rotting fruit and vegetables, most in an advanced state of decay. 'Bloody hell!' she muttered. This was going to take some cleaning up.

'The whole place stinks,' Lexa declared.

'You can say that again.'

Both girls stared around them in dismay. Where to begin?

'The normal delivery people won't take this lot away,' Cordelia commented. 'And I can't say I blame them either.'

'Well, we'll have to get rid of it somehow.' They puzzled over the problem. 'I've an idea,' Lexa said at last.

'What?'

'Let's get Campbell the carrier to do it for us. That horse and cart of his will be ideal.'

Cordelia couldn't think of any other solution. 'Let's just hope he's free and amenable. Who'll go and enquire, you or me?'

'I'll go. I shouldn't be long.'

'You do that, and I'll look round the back shop to find the accounts and ordering books. You know where his stables are, don't you?'

'Of course. Behind Barry's Garage. Isn't that right?'

'Don't forget to impress on him it's an emergency. We desperately need him.'

'I won't. Ta-ra, then.'

'Ta-ra!'

Cordelia watched her sister hurrying off up the street. What a mess, she thought, turning into the shop again. A lot of work was going to be needed before they opened for business once more.

'Hello! Is anybody there?'

Cordelia came out from the back shop where she'd finally located the ordering book, though so far not the accounts one, to find it was Mr Burnside, their main supplier, who'd shouted. He was an incredibly fat man with a stomach so large it was bigger than many pregnant women's at full term.

She smiled. 'Hello, Mr Burnside.'

'Where in the hell's Jimmy?' he demanded angrily. 'This is the third time I've called with your order. The last two the shop was shut.' He glanced about him. 'What's going on?'

'My father died three weeks ago,' Cordelia informed him. 'The shop has been shut since.'

Burnside was immediately sympathetic. 'I'm terribly sorry to hear that. I had no idea. What did he die of?'

'A heart attack in the middle of the night. There was no warning. He seemed healthy enough going to bed, then simply died. It was a terrible shock to all of us.'

'I can imagine.'

Cordelia spotted his van parked outside. 'I'm afraid I can't take any deliveries for the moment, Mr Burnside. As you can see, we've got this lot to clear away first.'

A look of irritation flashed across Burnside's face. 'Aye, I suppose you have. However, don't for one moment think I'm taking returns. Not on this scale I'm not. This stuff's putrid.'

Cordelia didn't like his tone. So much for the sympathy – that hadn't lasted long. 'We don't expect you to. My sister and I are making other arrangements.'

'Just as well.' He eyed her speculatively. 'Are you and your sister thinking of running this shop yourselves?'

'That's correct.'

He almost laughed, but managed to contain himself. 'A couple of lassies in business? I've never heard the like.'

'Well, you have now,' she replied coldly.

'It'll never work.'

'And why not?' she demanded.

'It just won't, that's all.'

'Lexa and I think otherwise.'

'Think all you want. I tell you straight you'll fall flat on your pretty faces.'

'Our pretty faces, as you call them, have absolutely

nothing to do with it.' She was inwardly raging. How like a man. Or some men, anyway. Her father had never been patronising towards women just because they were female. Quite the contrary.

This time Burnside did laugh. 'A feisty little thing, aren't you?'

She glared at him. 'If I have to be.'

His enormous stomach wobbled as he laughed again. 'Well, good luck to you, hen. You'll need it.'

She had an almost uncontrollable urge to punch him in the belly to see how he liked that.

'If you don't want your order today, then when?' he asked, when he had stopped laughing.

'I don't know yet.'

He raised an eyebrow.

'It depends how long it takes us to clear away this mess.'

'Then I'll wait to hear from you.'

'You do that, Mr Burnside. Now good day.'

'Good day, Miss Stewart.'

She'd show him, Cordelia thought angrily as he waddled from the shop. She and Lexa. By God and they would.

Lexa arrived back a few minutes later. 'Campbell will be here first thing the morn's morn,' she announced.

'Why were you gone so long?'

'He was out on a job so I had to hang around the stables until he returned. His son Billy was there, and he told me that his father was out with the cart, but would be back any time soon. The any time soon turned out to be longer than Billy thought.'

'First thing tomorrow, you say. Was he quite amenable?'

'Not to begin with. Didn't fancy it at all. So I'm afraid I had to offer him a pound more than the going rate to get him to agree. There was no other way.'

'A whole pound!' Cordelia exclaimed.

'It was either that or find someone else. Did I do wrong?'

Cordelia shook her head. 'Probably not. I'd no doubt have done the same thing in your shoes.'

'So what do we do now?'

'Find the accounts book, then lock up and go home again. There's nothing else we can do here until tomorrow.'

Cordelia and Lexa were exhausted. Campbell had arrived as promised, with his son Billy, and together all four of them had loaded the rotten fruit and vegatables on to his cart. It was back-breaking work, at least for the girls, and had taken far longer than they'd anticipated.

To their surprise they'd found they couldn't move a full box on their own. Jimmy had been right about how heavy they were, so it had been a case of the pair of them moving one box at a time. Even then it had been a struggle. Cordelia might have said they were stronger than they looked, but neither of them was strong enough to move one of those boxes on her own.

After Campbell had gone they'd set to with buckets and mops to clean up the shop, which in itself had taken quite a while.

'I'm starving,' Lexa declared, slumping into a chair in front of the fire.

'Me too,' Cordelia agreed. 'I was going to have a look at the ordering book tonight, but I doubt I'm up to it. It'll be an early bed for me.'

'And me. I'm completely done in.'

Their kitchen was a small one, so they ate in the front room where there was a substantial table and chairs. The table was already laid.

Alice appeared carrying two steaming plates. 'Here you are,' she said, putting their meals down in front of them before disappearing off to get her own plate.

Lexa stared in dismay at what Alice had cooked for them. Mince and potatoes, yet again. She glanced at Cordelia, who slowly shook her head.

'So, how did today go?' Alice asked breezily when she re-joined them.

'Hard, Mum. Very hard,' Cordelia replied.

'But you managed all right?'

'We managed,' Lexa answered, poking her meal with her fork. 'Mum?'

'What, darling?'

'I don't want to complain or anything, but this is the seventh night on the trot we've had mince and potatoes.'

'Eighth,' Cordelia corrected her.

Alice affected surprise. 'Is it?'

'Yes, it is,' Lexa stated firmly.

Alice dropped her gaze, and didn't reply.

'Mum?' Lexa asked.

There was a long silence. 'It was your father's favourite,' Alice said eventually.

Lexa and Cordelia stared at one another in consternation, both knowing that to be so.

'I just . . .' Alice trailed off, and shook her head. 'I'm sorry,' she mumbled.

'I don't understand?' a frowning Cordelia queried.

'I think about him all day long. And then when it comes to teatime I feel . . . I feel I have to make his favourite. I don't know why, I just do.'

'Oh, Mum,' Lexa said sympathetically.

'You probably both think I'm pathetic . . .'

'No we don't,' Cordelia interjected. 'Do we, Lexa?'

'Not at all. We understand.'

'Of course we do,' Cordelia agreed. 'You can make it as often as you like. We don't mind. Isn't that right, Lexa?'

'Right.'

'I'll try to do something else tomorrow night, I promise. Maybe a steak and kidney pudding. How would that be?'

'Lovely, Mum.' Lexa smiled. 'But it's up to you.'

'With carrot and onions,' Alice muttered. 'That's how Jimmy liked his mince and tatties. With carrot and onions. And occasionally with a dash of Worcestershire sauce. Not every time, but when he was in the mood for it.'

'I remember.' Cordelia nodded.

Alice sighed wistfully. 'I miss him so much.'

'We all do,' said Lexa. To change the subject, she began talking about their day in the shop.

Cordelia picked up her knife and fork and began to eat. Alice was worrying her. Quite a lot, actually. Her mother just wasn't coping well at all.

Cordelia was checking the delivery against the invoice while Burnside waited impatiently to be paid.

It all tallied, as far as Cordelia could tell, apart from three entries she couldn't make out. Burnside's appalling writing didn't help, either.

'What are these?' she queried, showing him the invoice and pointing out the illegible entries with a finger.

He glanced at the invoice, then back at her. 'Charges for the deliveries I tried to make when the shop was shut.'

'But you didn't deliver anything, Mr Burnside.'

'Precisely.'

'So why are you charging us for non-delivery?'

'Wasn't my fault you were shut. I was here in good faith three times. I have to charge for that. It's normal business practice. You never informed me you were shut, you see.'

Cordelia was appalled. 'But our father had just died.'

'And sad I was to hear that, when I was eventually told. Doesn't change matters, though. I was here, you weren't. End of story.'

'This is outrageous!' she protested.

'I should have been informed. I wasn't, so I have to charge you. As I said, normal business practice.'

She regarded him coldly, beginning to loathe this man. Though, in fairness, he and her father had seemed to get on well enough. 'Not very compassionate, are you, Mr Burnside?'

He shrugged. 'Business is business. That's the long and short of it.'

She was tempted to refuse to pay, then decided it would be too much trouble if she didn't, as the shop was shortly to reopen and Burnside was their principal supplier.

'All right,' she conceded reluctantly.

'The whole bill in cash,' he said. 'It was always cash with Jimmy. Cash on the nail.'

Cordelia had been aware of that, and the appropriate money was in the back shop. It had turned out that Jimmy did have a bank account, although transferring it into Alice's name had been a more complicated legal procedure than they'd anticipated. It had taken several visits, but the balance was available at last. 'If you'll just hold on for a few seconds I'll get it for you.'

'A lovely day, if bitter,' Burnside commented to Lexa, who'd been watching the exchange.

She didn't answer.

'Cat got your tongue, lassie?'

She was about to make a caustic reply when Cordelia returned with the money, which Burnside slowly counted before leaving them without even a goodbye.

'I'll put the kettle on, then we can get down to sorting this lot out,' Lexa said.

Cordelia took a deep breath, and heavily exhaled. 'Make the tea strong. I need it.'

Lexa could well understand why. She felt the same way herself.

Right from the word go the reopening was a huge success. Customers who had heard the news came in to buy, and offer condolences; those who hadn't came to buy and hear why the shop had been shut.

'Well, we certainly can't complain about sales today,' Cordelia declared at closing time.

Lexa grinned back at her. 'Let's just hope it continues, eh?'

'Let's hope,' Cordelia agreed.

They were halfway home when they were stopped in their tracks by someone shouting their names. It was Mrs McAllister, their neighbour across the landing, and they waited for her to catch up.

'I've been wanting a quiet word with you two,' she said as she joined them.

'Oh?' Cordelia queried with a frown.

'It's about your mum.'

For some reason Lexa's heart sank. 'What about her?'

'I've been calling in recently for a cup of tea and a chat during the afternoon. To keep her company like.' Cordelia and Lexa nodded. 'Did she mention?'

'No,' said Cordelia.

Mrs McAllister hesitated, biting her lip.

'Well?' Lexa prompted.

'I've dropped by four or five times now, and on each occasion I could distinctly smell alcohol on your mother's breath. I'm sorry to tell you, but that's the God's truth.'

The revelation shook Cordelia. 'Are you sure? Are you absolutely certain?'

'Oh, aye. I know alcohol when I smell it.'

Lexa glanced at her sister. 'I've never smelt anything. Have you?'

Cordelia shook her head.

'Well she's drinking, and I thought you two should know. I'm not criticising, mind – she's just lost her man, after all. But I thought you should know what's going on.'

'Thank you, Mrs McAllister. As Lexa said, we weren't aware.'

'Poor woman.' Mrs McAllister shook her head sympathetically. 'I pity her. I can't imagine what I'd be like if I lost my Gordon. Maybe I'd take to the bottle as well.'

Lexa had a sudden alarming thought. 'Have you told anyone else about this?'

'Of course not,' Mrs McAllister replied quickly, quite put out at the suggestion. 'Alice and I are good chinas. I wouldn't go cliping on her. Only to you two, her daughters. For her own sake.'

'Thank you for telling us,' smiled Cordelia. 'As I said, we had no idea. None at all.'

'Best nipped in the bud before it gets out of hand, eh?'

'We'll see that happens, Mrs McAllister.'

'You can bet on it,' Lexa added.

Together, they continued on their way. Their neighbour had certainly given the girls something to think about.

The first thing Cordelia did on reaching home was go into the kitchen where her mother was busy cooking.

'Oh, hello, dear. Everything go well today?'

'Couldn't have gone better, Mum. We did a roaring trade.'

'That's good. And a relief too. Your dad always said customers could be fickle, and might easily take their allegiance elsewhere if they weren't looked after properly.'

'Well, not in this instance.' As she spoke, Cordelia opened the cupboard where her father's bottle of whisky was kept. When she'd last looked the bottle had been half empty; now it was almost full. It was obviously a new bottle. And she could only wonder how many there had been since the original.

'I'll be dishing up in a few minutes,' said Alice.

Cordelia decided she and Lexa would leave the confrontation until after their tea.

The meal was over, the washing-up done. The three of them settled into chairs in front of the fire. As they did so, Lexa glanced across at Cordelia and gave her an almost imperceptible nod.

'Mum?' Cordelia smiled.

'Yes, dear, what is it?'

'I don't think this drinking helps matters much. Not really.'

Alice matched Cordelia's smile. 'Whatever are you talking about?'

'The whisky you've been drinking in the afternoons. And please don't deny it. We've been watching the bottle. Or should I say bottles?' The latter was a lie, but both she and Lexa had decided not to implicate Mrs McAllister.

'Oh,' Alice said hollowly. 'You've noticed, then.'

'We have.' Lexa was lying too.

'It's only a wee amber sweetie to get me through the day. Nothing more than that.'

'You never used to need a wee amber sweetie, as you call it.'

Alice's face clouded over. 'Maybe not. But that was before your father died. Things are different now.'

'I'm aware of that, Mum,' said Cordelia. 'And how hard things are for you. But taking to the bottle isn't the answer. It never is. All that'll happen is you'll start drinking more and more, and then what?'

Alice dropped her gaze to stare at the floor. 'It's the bedroom, you see.'

Lexa frowned. 'Which bedroom?'

'Ours. Your father's and mine.'

'What about it?'

Alice swallowed hard. 'I can't bear being in there at night. So many memories of your dad and myself. They haunt me. Not only that, it's the bed where Jimmy died. Night after night I'm lying on the bed where he died.'

Cordelia sat back in her chair and sighed. That thought had never crossed her mind. How terrible for her mother. 'And that's why you're drinking?'

Alice nodded. 'It's not the only reason, but it's a large part of it.'

Lexa could only think of one solution. 'Would buying a new bed help?'

'It might. But it would still be the same bedroom.' Alice shivered. 'I dread the evenings, knowing I've got to go in there at night.'

'There is a way round this,' Cordelia declared, after a minute's reflective silence.

'Which is?' Lexa queried.

'Change bedrooms. Mum goes into one of ours, and one of us goes into hers. If Mum doesn't mind changing a double bed for a single, that is.' Even as she made the proposal Cordelia realised that she didn't fancy sleeping in her parents' bed any more than Alice did.

Lexa could see her sister's reluctance. 'I'll change with Mum.'

Relief flooded Alice's face. 'Will you, darling? I'd be ever so grateful.'

Lexa nodded. 'Starting tonight if you like.'

'On one condition,' Cordelia said firmly. 'The drinking stops. Do you agree, Mum?'

'I agree.'

'Swear to it?'

'I swear. Word of honour.'

Lexa wasn't looking forward to this at all. But she'd do it if Alice kept her word and stayed off the whisky.

Chapter 3

Cordelia stared at the invoice a smiling Burnside had just handed her. 'Your prices have gone up,' she stated coldly.

''Fraid so.'

'And why's that?'

He shrugged. 'Nothing to do with me. Prices have just gone up in general, which means I have to pass on the increase. Sometimes prices go up, sometimes they come down. That's simply the way it is.'

She stared at him, wondering if he was telling the truth. She wouldn't have put it past him to be lying.

'They seem to have gone up considerably.'

'Then you'll have to charge more. Pass on the increase, as I've done.'

Cordelia took a deep breath. She hadn't expected this. She glanced over at Lexa, who was watching them.

'Are prices likely to go up again in the near future?' Lexa asked, her voice as cold as her sister's.

Burnside shrugged again. 'Your guess is as good as mine.

It is winter, don't forget. Prices are always higher in winter when fresh produce is scarce. Your father would have told you that.'

Cordelia thought back over the years she'd worked in the shop. The trouble was she hadn't taken much notice of the wholesale side of things, having been happy merely to serve behind the counter. If only she'd paid more attention, she'd know whether Burnside was telling the truth. But she hadn't.

'Well?' Burnside demanded, still smiling.

'I'll get the money for you.'

'That's a good lassie.'

Cordelia turned on him and looked him straight in the eye. 'Miss Stewart to you, Mr Burnside. I don't want any more "lassie". Understand?'

His smile faded. 'If you wish. I was only trying to be friendly.'

'Well, don't. This is a straightforward business trans-action, nothing more. Being friendly, or anything else, doesn't come into it.'

Bully for you, sis, Lexa thought. Put the bugger in his place. Well done.

'Well if you want to take that attitude . . .'

'I do,' Cordelia interjected. 'I'm Miss Stewart, and so is my sister. Remember that in future.'

His eyes glittered, but he didn't reply.

'Now wait here.' Cordelia swept into the back shop, where she put the kettle on before counting out his money.

She couldn't help but reflect that a strong cup of tea seemed to be required after every Burnside visit.

*   *   *

'It's your birthday next week. What do you want?'

Lexa sighed. 'Don't remind me. Nineteen! I'm getting old.'

That amused Cordelia, who was eighteen months older than her sister. 'Hardly that.'

'Well, it seems that way to me. Lots of girls are married at my age. Even more at yours, come to that.'

Cordelia smiled indulgently. 'I don't think we're in the old maid category just yet. There's plenty of time left for marriage and children. Ooodles and boodles of it.'

Lexa, who was stacking leeks, paused to consider her sister's words. There had been several boyfriends in the past, but nothing serious. No one she had considered 'special'.

'Your knight in shining armour will turn up one day,' Cordelia declared. 'Probably when you least expect it. You'll see.'

'I hope so.'

'And one for me as well. It's not as if we're ugly or anything. Nobody could accuse us of that.'

Lexa held up her hands. 'You know the worst thing about this job?'

'What?'

'These. Hands that are permanently dirty – or look it. No matter how long and hard I scrub them they never appear clean.'

'It's ingrained, that's why,' Cordelia said. 'And I agree, it is the worst part of this job. We just have to put up with it, that's all.'

'I wonder if it puts men off?' Lexa mused. 'It probably does.'

'Maybe.'

'They probably think we work down the pits, or something.' Lexa laughed at her own joke.

'Anyway, you still haven't answered my question. What do you want for your birthday?'

Lexa thought about it. 'Do you know what would be really nice?'

'Not until you tell me,' Cordelia replied sarcastically.

'A pair of silk stockings.'

'Silk stockings!' Cordelia exclaimed. 'They cost an absolute fortune.'

'You did ask.'

'I know that, but I didn't expect the answer I got. Talk about delusions of grandeur! What would you want with silk stockings anyway?'

Lexa smiled. 'I've always coveted a pair. It must be pure magic wearing something like that rather than what we normally buy.'

'Lisle?' Cordelia teased.

'I never wear lisle stockings, and well you know it, Cordelia Stewart. Those are for grannies and the like. They're horrible.'

'And if I decide I can't afford silk stockings, what then?'

'A bottle of scent wouldn't go amiss.'

'Any particular one?'

Lexa shook her head. 'As long as it smells nice.'

Then a customer came into the shop, and the conversation ended.

'Oh, it's yourself, Peggy.' Alice smiled as she answered the front door. 'Come on in and I'll put the kettle on.'

Mrs McAllister was paying yet another afternoon call on her neighbour. She'd have done it anyway, but Cordelia and Lexa had asked her to report back to them if she smelt alcohol on their mother's breath. So far, she hadn't. Alice was keeping her word.

'And how are you the day?' Alice asked.

'Not too bad. Yourself?'

'Getting by. You know?'

Peggy McAllister did know. Alice meant that she was gradually coming to terms with Jimmy's death.

'I've no cake or scones to offer you, I'm afraid,' Alice apologised. 'I haven't been out to do the shopping yet as I've been busy cleaning.'

'Don't worry about that.' Peggy smiled. 'A cup of tea will go down nicely.'

'How about I push the boat out and we have coffee instead?' Coffee was expensive.

Peggy's face lit up. 'That would be a real treat.'

'Then that's what we'll have.'

Peggy followed Alice into the kitchen where Alice began laying out cups and saucers.

'I was wondering if you'd like to come to the Labour Hall with me Saturday night?' Peggy enquired.

Alice shook her head. 'Not for me. But thanks anyway for asking.'

'I know you and Jimmy always stayed in Saturday nights, but now he isn't here for company any more it would do you good to have a wee night out. We play housey-housey, which can be great fun. And there's aye the chance you'll win something.'

'As I said the now, not for me, Peggy.'

'Look, Alice, you don't want to be sitting here being a misery to yourself. Learn to have a wee bit fun.' Peggy sighed. 'I've been going for years, as Gordon takes himself off to the pub for a right old session Saturday nights. And when he gets in he falls asleep straight away in the chair. That's why I started going to the Labour Hall in the first place. I don't want to listen to his snoring for hours on end.'

Despite herself, Alice smiled. Jimmy had also snored – and in his case without the benefit of drink. 'I wouldn't know anyone,' she said quietly.

'Of course you would, woman. They're all neighbours from this street and round about. You'll recognise lots of faces.'

Alice simply couldn't imagine going out without Jimmy by her side. It had been so long. She hadn't gone out on her own since the start of their married life. She'd be a fish out of water.

'Maybe some other time,' she prevaricated.

'I can't get you to change your mind? It'll do you good.'

'No, Peggy. It's not for me.'

Peggy decided to give up. Alice clearly wasn't going to budge – this time, anyway.

Lexa blinked awake. It was the morning of her birthday. Nineteen years old! She wasn't sure whether or not she liked the idea.

She wished it wasn't a work day. It would have been nice to celebrate by going into town and having a nose around. Doing some window shopping with Cordelia. But there was no chance of that. Their own shop called.

'Happy birthday!' Alice and Cordelia chorused when she went into the front room, where the fire was already alight.

'For you, lass.' Smiling, Alice handed her an envelope and a small brown parcel.

'Thank you, Mum.'

Alice, eyes shining, kissed her on the cheek.

'And this is from me, sis,' Cordelia declared, also handing over an envelope and a parcel similar to the one Alice had given her. Both parcels were soft and squidgy to the touch.

The envelopes contained birthday cards, as Lexa had presumed they would. But the big surprise was that the parcels, when opened, revealed a pair of silk stockings in each.

'Mum, Cordelia, I can't thank you enough,' Lexa enthused. Such luxury, such wonderful, wonderful luxury.

'And for breakfast I'm going to cook us all bacon and eggs. How about that?' Alice proposed.

'With fried bread?' Lexa queried excitedly.

'If the birthday girl wants fried bread, then that's what she'll have.' Alice hurried off to the kitchen.

Lexa couldn't have been more delighted. It was a lovely start to the day.

'We bumped into Mrs McAllister earlier on, Mum,' Cordelia said when she and Lexa came home from work.

'Oh, aye?'

'Told us she suggested you go to the Labour Hall with her on Saturday night to play housey-housey, and you turned her down flat.'

Alice shrugged. 'Why would I want to play housey-housey? It's not me at all.'

'But it would get you out of the house for a while,' Lexa argued.

'I'm happy to stay in, thank you very much.'

'Are you really, Mum?' Cordelia queried.

'Yes I am.'

'Well, I think you should know Lexa and I discussed the matter and we think you should go with Mrs McAllister. At least give it a try. If you don't like it you don't have to go back again.'

'As I said to Lexa, I'm happy enough to stay in with you two.'

'You won't be. Lexa and I are going out Saturday night ourselves. So you'll be in alone.' This would be their first night out since their father's death.

'You are?'

'To the dancing. We're going to trip the light fantastic. If you can do such a thing in Glasgow.'

'Who knows, we might even get a couple of clicks,' Lexa said with a laugh in her voice.

Alice considered that, not relishing the idea of being by herself. For she knew what would happen: she'd sit there brooding. Thinking of Jimmy, remembering.

'And I doubt we'll be back till late,' Cordelia pointed out.

'Quite late,' Lexa added, turning the screw.

'Oh.'

'That being the case you might want to reconsider Mrs McAllister's offer,' Cordelia said. 'You might surprise your-self and have a right old time of it there. Thoroughly enjoy the experience.'

'Anyway, what's for tea?' Lexa asked, deciding they'd pushed the matter far enough.

'Stew.'

'That sounds nice,' Lexa enthused.

A thoughtful Alice left them to return to the kitchen, and the meal she was preparing.

'How do I look?' Alice demanded nervously. 'Have I got too much powder on?'

'You look fine, Mum,' Cordelia assured her.

'Are you certain?'

'Cross my heart and hope to die.'

'Just fine, Mum,' Lexa added. She glanced at the clock on the mantelpiece. Mrs McAllister should be knocking the door any moment now to take Alice to the Labour Hall. She and Cordelia would be leaving about half an hour later.

'There she is!' Cordelia exclaimed when the expected knock came. 'Have a good time.' She kissed her mother on the cheek. 'And see if you can win some money.'

'I'll do my best.'

Both girls accompanied Alice to the front door to say their goodbyes. 'She'll be all right,' Lexa declared when the door was closed again and their mother and Mrs McAllister had started off down the stairs.

'Of course she will. Probably love it.'

Lexa nodded. 'Let's just hope so.'

When Lexa and Cordelia got home from the dancing, they found Alice still up waiting for them.

'Well, Mum?' Lexa eagerly demanded. 'How was it?'

'Very pleasant.'

Lexa was disappointed. 'Just pleasant?'

Alice's eyes twinkled. 'To be honest, I had a rare time. Peggy was right, there were lots of people there I knew who made me most welcome. It was a good laugh.'

'Will you go again?' Cordelia queried.

'I've said I would. Next Saturday.'

'Did you win anything?'

Alice shook her head. 'But I came close once or twice.'

'The main thing is you enjoyed yourself. That's what matters.'

Lexa looked up from the accounts book in which she'd been doing the weekly figures. She was sitting at the front room table, while Cordelia and Alice talked together by the fire. 'We're down again,' she told them.

A look of anxiety flashed across Cordelia's face. 'By much?'

Lexa told her.

It was five months now since they'd taken over the shop. Initially they'd done well, and then, for some reason, their profits had begun to dip. They were losing customers, and they didn't know why.

'It's worrying,' Lexa said unnecessarily.

Cordelia could only agree. Mystified, she shook her head.

'Did this ever happen to Dad?' Lexa asked Alice.

'I've no idea, darling. He never discussed the shop with me. That was his sole province.'

Lexa sighed and closed the accounts book. 'Things will have to buck up soon or we'll be in trouble.'

She and Cordelia stared grimly at one another.

*   *   *

'This is simply unacceptable, Mr Burnside,' Cordelia declared, absolutely furious.

His expression was one of benign innocence. 'What is, Miss Stewart?'

'The quality of this produce. Just look at those tomatoes, not to mention the apples.'

'What's wrong with them?'

'They're inferior, that's what's wrong with them.'

'I can't agree with you there. They're both A1, top grade.'

Cordelia snorted. 'Pull the other one, Mr Burnside. You're trying to fob us off . . .'

'I am most certainly not,' he interjected firmly. 'This produce is exactly the same as I'm supplying to my other customers. My word on it.'

Cordelia had had enough. Three price rises since the reopening, and now this. 'Well, I can't accept any of it,' she stated hotly.

'As you wish.'

'And from today I'll be looking for a new supplier. One who'll supply me with decent produce.'

Burnside slowly smiled. 'I'm afraid you can't do that, Miss Stewart.'

'And why not?'

He took a deep breath. 'Well, you see, it's like this. Grant you there are many suppliers in Glasgow, yes indeed. But we each cover our own area and don't interfere in each other's territory.'

That rocked Cordelia. 'What exactly are you saying?'

'My area is Mount Florida here, Battlefield, Cathcart and Langside. That's my patch, so to speak. Mine and mine alone. Any other supplier would simply refuse to deal with a shop in those districts. Just as I would refuse, if approached, to do business with any shop outside my patch. It's called live and let live.'

Cordelia was appalled. If this was true then he had her, to borrow an expression her father had occasionally used, by the short and curlies.

'So.' Burnside was smiling now. 'If you want to stay open then you'll have to continue dealing with me. There's no other way.'

Lexa crossed over to stand by her sister's side, thinking what a truly horrible man Burnside was. He was clearly enjoying this.

'Well, what's it to be?' Burnside demanded.

Cordelia swallowed her pride – temporarily, that is. She needed to think about this. Make enquiries. Find out whether or not she was being lied to, being given a big story.

'Are you sure you can't change at least some of these boxes?' she asked in a flat tone. She was damned if she was going to plead. She'd go to hell first.

'Sorry. They're the best I can do.'

Bastard, she thought. Bloody bastard.

'Made up your mind yet, *Miss Stewart*?'

The way he'd spoken her name was insolence person-ified, which certainly wasn't lost on her.

'If there's no alternative then I'll have to accept this lot,' she replied through gritted teeth.

'Good.'

Cordelia swung on her heel and headed for the back shop and his money, which Burnside took with a grunt when she handed it to him.

41

He slowly counted it before wishing them both a cheery good day.

Burnside wasn't their only supplier, though by far and away their main one. There was also Mr Drymen, who supplied them with various types of vinegar and other small items. As chance would have it he called in at the shop the following day.

Telling Lexa to look after things, Cordelia took him into the back shop. 'Can I ask you a question, Mr Drymen?'

'Aye, go ahead.'

She related the conversation she'd had with Burnside. 'Is it true I can't use anyone else?' she finished.

'I'm afraid so. That's the way these people work. Each has his own territory which no one else will interfere with.'

'Damn!'

'I don't say it's right,' Drymen continued. 'But that's how they operate.' He paused, then said, 'I take it you're not getting on very well with Burnside?'

'That's an understatement if ever there was one.'

Drymen shook his head. 'He can be a hard man, and no mistake. Especially if he takes against you as he's obviously done. My advice would be to try to patch matters up between the pair of you. Be nice to him.'

'Do you think that might make a difference?'

Drymen shrugged. 'It might. It's possible.'

Be nice to Burnside! The very idea made her cringe inside.

After Drymen had gone Cordelia recounted what he'd said to Lexa, who was just as dismayed as she was.

Chapter 4

Granny Stewart, Jimmy's mother, was in her seventies, white-haired, frail and wearing a bombazine dress which made Lexa think she looked like a beetle on account of the way the black material could sometimes shimmer metallically green.

'I'm disappointed your mother hasn't been to see me in a long while,' the old lady said reproachfully. 'Is there a reason for that? Have I offended Alice in some way?'

Lexa shook her head. 'You haven't offended her at all, Granny.'

'Then why hasn't she been?'

There was a silence.

'Perhaps you don't know?'

'It would be a guess, Granny. That's all. Nothing's been said.'

'Hm,' Granny Stewart snorted, her piercing blue eyes fastened on Lexa. 'I'm listening, girl.'

Lexa shifted uncomfortably in her chair, wondering if she should say anything or not. Eventually she decided she would. 'I think, Granny – and I only think – it's because you remind her my father. He was so much like you. His face, that is.'

'Aaah!' Granny Stewart breathed. Now she understood. That made sense. Jimmy had been a younger, male version of herself. No one could ever mistake him for other than her son.

'Is she still grieving badly, Alexandra?' Granny never called Lexa by the diminutive.

Lexa nodded.

'It can be hard. Very hard indeed,' Granny Stewart said sympathetically. 'I know what I was like after your grandfather passed on. It was as though the world had come to an end.'

'I'll mention that you asked after her and see what she says,' Lexa volunteered.

'You do that, child. I've always been fond of Alice. A good woman, and a fine wife to Jimmy. I'd hate to lose touch.'

'I'm sure it won't come to that,' Lexa replied, attempting a smile. 'It'll just take time.'

'Let's hope so. Now, would you care for some more cake?'

'I'm stuffed, Granny. I couldn't eat another mouthful. Honestly.'

Granny Stewart regarded Lexa shrewdly. 'So, tell me about yourself.'

'There's nothing to tell, really.'

'No young man in tow?'

Lexa shook her head.

'And Cordelia?'

'She hasn't got one either. Not at the moment, anyway.'

'And how's the shop doing?'

Granny Stewart listened intently as Lexa explained about their problems with Burnside.

'I see,' Granny Stewart murmured after Lexa had finished. 'Doesn't bode well, I shouldn't think. He sounds a right nasty piece of work.'

'He is, Granny. Believe me.'

'You'll find a solution, I've no doubt about that. You'll come up with something.'

'I sincerely hope so. Our takings can't keep going down the way they are. We're only just in profit as it is. Before too long, if things carry on as they are, we'll be in the red. Losing money instead of making it.'

Granny Stewart took a deep breath. 'Tell you what, girl. Would you like me to read the cards for you?'

That surprised Lexa. Granny Stewart was well known to have a rare gift at reading the cards – indeed, some people called her a spaewife, someone with an uncanny ability to forecast the future – but this was the first time she'd ever offered to read them for her.

'I'd like that. Thank you.'

Granny Stewart pointed to a drawer in a free-standing kitchen cupboard. 'They're in there. Will you fetch them for me to save my old legs?'

'Of course, Granny.'

Lexa opened the drawer, and there they were, right at the front: not ordinary playing cards, but ones decorated with weird and wonderful designs. She returned to the table and handed her grandmother the box, then watched in fascination as Granny Stewart took out the cards, stared at them for a few seconds, and then began shuffling. When she had done that to her satisfaction the old lady asked her granddaughter to cut them into three piles and then select one of the piles, which she did.

'Hm,' Granny Stewart murmured, studying the layout she'd placed on the table.

Lexa could only wonder what on earth she was about to be told. She wasn't at all sure she believed in this sort of thing, but had to admit it was exciting. She was also aware that lots of people did believe in it.

'I'm looking at the future, not the present,' Granny Stewart said softly. 'I see a man. Tall for a Glaswegian, if that's what he is. Good-looking. Easy-going personality. You're going to meet him soon, and he will have a lot to do with your future.'

She fell silent and studied the cards some more. 'You'll recognise this man when you come across him as he has different-coloured eyes, and could easily be the one you'll marry. Yes, that's a distinct possibility.'

Lexa was hanging on every word. 'What else can you see?'

'Great happiness in your life. And great sadness too. Things aren't going to be easy for you. Happiness, and unhappiness. Joy and sadness.'

'Will I have children?' Lexa asked eagerly.

'Oh, yes. Two. Both boys, I think, who'll grow up to be successful in whatever career they choose to pursue.'

'Do I have them by this man with the different-coloured eyes?'

'That isn't clear, Alexandra. All I can tell you now is that you will have two children.'

Lexa digested that.

'This man,' Granny Stewart went on, 'has something to do with aeroplanes. Precisely what, I can't see. But there is a bird here which represents aeroplanes to me.'

How would she meet someone connected with aeroplanes? Lexa wondered. It seemed highly unlikely. 'Anything else?'

'Turmoil, enormous turmoil. Confusion. Darkness. Darkness that gives way again to light. A bright shining light filled with love and affection. Love and affection born out of a cruel misunderstanding.' Granny Stewart sighed. 'That's all I can make out from this cut of cards. Now I'll try another. The present.'

When Lexa left her grandmother's house half an hour later all she could think about was what she'd been told. Some of it was highly disturbing. And although she'd generally enjoyed the experience of a reading, there was a part of her that wished it hadn't taken place.

'Mrs McCrindle! Can I have a word?'

Mrs McCrindle stopped and turned to see Cordelia and Lexa hurrying towards her. The two girls were clearly on their way to work. A look of embarrassment crossed Mrs McCrindle's face as she guessed what they wanted.

'Hello, Mrs McCrindle. How are you?' Cordelia smiled.

'Fine. Never better.'

'We haven't seen you in the shop for ages. And you used to be such a regular customer.'

Mrs McCrindle flushed. 'No, I suppose it has been a while.'

'Do you mind if we ask you why?' Lexa queried, also smiling.

Mrs McCrindle looked down at the pavement, her embarrassment now all too obvious. She wished she hadn't run into the Stewart lassies.

'No reason, really,' she lied.

'Oh?' That was Cordelia.

'If there's something wrong we'd like to know,' Lexa prompted. 'That's why we're asking you. If there's something amiss then perhaps we can fix it.'

Mrs McCrindle decided to be honest. They wanted the truth, after all. 'It's your prices,' she said bluntly. 'They're awfully high.'

'Are they?'

'Oh, aye. Compared to other shops, that is. And the quality of your stuff just isn't what it once was. It's pretty poor nowadays, actually.'

'I see,' Cordelia said thoughtfully.

'Now if you don't mind I'd better get on,' Mrs McCrindle declared. 'I've lots to do as it's washing day.'

'Sorry to have held you up,' Lexa apologised.

'That's all right. Bye, then.'

'Bye.'

Cordelia and Lexa stared at one another. 'It's high time we looked into this,' Cordelia said. 'But let's open the shop first before we decide anything.'

Twenty minutes later, having given the matter a lot of thought, Cordelia had made up her mind. 'Right,' she said firmly. 'Here's what we'll do. I want you to go round all the other greengrocers in the areas Burnside mentioned and see what their prices and quality are like so we can compare.'

Lexa nodded. 'Understood.'

'Start with Battlefield, as you can walk there. After you've done that take trams to Langside and Cathcart.'

'Will do.'

'Then we'll know exactly what's what.'

'I'll leave straight away. Is there anything else I should do?'

Cordelia shook her head. 'That's enough for now. Have you got money on you for tram fares?'

'I should have.'

'Then I'll see you later.'

When Lexa returned that afternoon, she hung up her coat and waited until Cordelia had finished dealing with a customer.

'Well?' Cordelia demanded the moment the customer was out the door.

'Mrs McCrindle was right. Without exception every shop was cheaper than us and the quality of the produce better.'

Cordelia's eyes blazed. 'Burnside's been taking us for a couple of mugs all along, hasn't he?'

Lexa nodded. 'So it would seem. Charging us more than everyone else, and dumping his rubbish on us.'

'No wonder we've been losing customers hand over fist. Who can blame them for going elsewhere?'

'It's because we're women, of course,' Lexa declared bitterly. 'That's why he's been taking advantage. Thinks we're soft.'

'Which we aren't.'

'Not in the least.'

Cordelia took a deep breath. How could she have been so stupid as not to realise what was going on? But the truth was, she hadn't.

'So what do we do now?' Lexa queried.

Cordelia shook her head. 'I don't know. Not off the top of my head, anyway.'

Their conversation was interrupted at that point by the arrival of another customer. While serving her Cordelia felt guilty about the prices she was charging and the fact that the vegetables the woman was buying were of such poor quality.

Burnside. She felt like murdering that fat bastard.

'It seems to me we're in a total bind,' Lexa commented that evening after tea.

'If only we could change to another supplier. But we can't.' Cordelia fumed quietly.

'We could try?' Lexa suggested hopefully.

Cordelia shook her head. 'Remember that Mr Drymen confirmed what Burnside told us. No other supplier would touch our business.'

'Well, we can't go on as we are,' Lexa said. 'It won't be long before we start losing money.' She turned to Alice. 'What do you think, Mum?'

'I just wish your father was still here. He'd sort matters out with this Burnside, I'm certain of it.'

'Aye, well, Dad was a man, obviously,' Cordelia said bitterly. 'That's the difference.'

'Perhaps this Burnside is a misogynist,' Alice mused.

Lexa frowned. 'What's one of those when it's at home?'

'A man who dislikes women. Hates them, even. Or certainly thinks them inferior. There are a lot more around than you'd imagine.'

Cordelia clenched her fists. If only she could think

of a way out of this. Find an answer. But she couldn't, no matter how hard she tried. Burnside had them over the proverbial barrel.

There again, Mr Drymen had suggested she might try being nice to the bugger. That that might help. But she knew in her heart of hearts she'd never bring herself to do such a thing. She was far too proud, to her own detriment, to do that.

And what if she did humble herself before him and he just laughed in her face, as he probably would? What then? What a fool she'd feel. A complete and utter idiot.

Alice ran a hand over her face, then looked from daughter to daughter. 'I never thought I'd ever hear myself say this, but if things are as bad as you make out then perhaps we should just chuck in the towel and sell the shop.'

Both Cordelia and Lexa were appalled. 'Mum!' Lexa exclaimed. 'How can you even make such a suggestion!'

Alice shrugged. 'Do you have an alternative?'

Lexa opened her mouth, then shut it again. She didn't. Neither did Cordelia.

'Your dad bought that shop years ago for a song,' Alice went on. 'But nowadays it should be worth a pretty penny. Certainly far more than he paid for it. The money would keep me going for quite a while. And you two shouldn't have too much trouble finding other jobs.'

Sell the shop? If Cordelia had hated Burnside before, she hated him even more now. All this was entirely his doing.

'Granny . . .' Lexa began, then trailed off.

'What is it, dear?' Alice prompted.

'When I went to visit Granny Stewart recently she read my cards and one of the things she said was that I'd be making a move soon. I didn't understand what she meant by that at the time. Now I do.'

'What else did she say?' a curious Cordelia enquired, jealous because Granny Stewart had never offered to read her cards.

'Oh, this and that. Nothing of consequence,' Lexa prevaricated.

'Sell the shop,' Alice mused. She smiled, and as she did so tears crept into her eyes.

'I feel such a failure,' Cordelia said to Lexa the following morning at work. They'd been open for an hour and so far hadn't had a single customer. Not one.

'Me too.'

'But Mum's right. What else can we do?'

'If we don't sell now we'll just go deeper and deeper into the red until we come to the point where we'll have to sell anyway. That being the case, better sooner than later.'

'It still rankles, though,' Cordelia said through gritted teeth. 'We could have made a go of it if it wasn't for Burnside. Look how we started off. Couldn't have been better.'

'If it wasn't to be, it wasn't to be,' Lexa declared philosophically.

Cordelia would never have admitted it, but the unknown lay ahead. And it scared her. She'd never worked anywhere other than the shop. Nor had Lexa. Yes, the unknown scared her all right.

When they get home that evening, Alice met them at the door. 'The shop goes up for sale first thing Monday morning,' she declared without preamble. 'It's all arranged.'

'What are you asking for it, Mum?' Cordelia enquired.

Alice told them. 'That's the price the agent and I agreed on, at his suggestion. I have to admit it's even more than I'd dared hope for. Substantially so.'

Lexa was pleased. 'Did this agent say how long it might take to shift?'

'He was hopeful it would go fairly quickly. But, as he pointed out, you just don't know. A week, a month, or it could still be sitting there next year.'

'And in the meantime we close,' Cordelia said bleakly. 'Before we go into the red.'

'Exactly.' Alice nodded.

'It's the only thing we can do,' Lexa added, unnecessarily. All three of them were only too aware of that.

Burnside strolled into the shop. 'I've brought your order,' he announced.

'We don't want it,' Cordelia retorted harshly.

He blinked at her. 'What do you mean you don't want it?'

'Precisely that. You can take all that rubbish you were about to dump on us and stick it up your fat, repulsive arse.'

Burnside went puce. 'How dare you talk to me like that!'

'Why not?'

'Because . . . because . . .' he spluttered, momentarily lost for words.

'And don't threaten us about refusing to deal with us in future,' Lexa declared. 'That won't get you anywhere.'

'Nowhere at all,' Cordelia added venomously. 'The fact of the matter is we're closing down and selling the shop.'

He stared at them for a few moments, then burst out laughing. 'I told you you'd fall flat on your faces. I told you. Lassies running a business. The very idea!'

Cordelia couldn't control herself. Crossing quickly to him she slapped him hard across the face, a real stinging blow. 'We would have managed fine if it hadn't been for you. You hear? We know what you've been up to. Charging us more than anyone else, unloading third-rate produce on to us. Our closing is all your fault, Burnside, yours and no one else's. So now get out before you get more than a slap.' With that she went over to a box and picked up a long, razor-sharp knife they used for cutting turnips and the like.

Burnside took one look at the knife, paled and fled. He was through the door faster than the girls would have believed was possible for a man of his size.

'I feel better after that,' Cordelia declared, throwing the knife down. She had never intended to do more than frighten him with it.

'Me too,' Lexa agreed.

'It's a crying shame, so it is,' Campbell, the carrier, said to Lexa. 'Your dad's had this shop for years and years, as long as I can remember.'

Campbell and his son Billy were there to take away the remaining stock and dispose of it.

'Don't think we're happy about the situation, because we're not. But unfortunately closing down and selling has become a necessity.'

'Dear me.' He shook his head.

Cordelia stood gazing about her. The shop had become an integral part of her life since she started work there. It surprised her just how much she'd miss it, particularly the banter between herself and customers. That had always been good.

'Almost done,' Billy gave Lexa a broad smile which she wasn't in the mood to appreciate.

'Fine.'

'It's like cutting off an arm, isn't it?' Cordelia said to her sister.

'Worse.'

Cordelia thought about it. 'Aye, maybe you're right.'

Finally Campbell and Billy were finished, and the shop was empty. Cordelia paid Campbell, who wished them all the very best before he and Billy left them to it.

Cordelia jiggled the shop keys in her right hand. 'Shutting up for the last time.'

'The last time,' Lexa repeated, a lump in her throat.

'Will I do the honours, or do you want to?'

Lexa shrugged. 'It doesn't matter. You do it. You're the elder, after all. You've worked here longer.'

True enough, Cordelia reflected. 'My privilege, then.'

They had a final check of the back shop to ensure nothing had been left behind.

'All right?' Cordelia said.

'All right,' Lexa confirmed.

Cordelia locked the front door, stood up straight, then took a deep breath. Lexa hooked an arm round her sister's, and together they walked away.

Neither looked back.

Chapter 5

Lexa stared across the street at a building painted a burgundy colour with the legend *Vins* above the front door. She was here for an interview, having replied to an advertisement in one of the evening papers for a junior clerk in a firm of wine merchants. It was not her usual line of work, but the advertisement had caught her eye and now she was here she was certainly impressed with the building. It was rare to see such a distinctive colour in Glasgow. In fact, she'd never seen anything quite like it.

'Oh, well,' she sighed aloud. 'Here goes.' It was her third interview since the shop closed, and she wasn't very hopeful.

She started off across the road.

'So how did it go?' Alice demanded when her daughter arrived home. Cordelia as well as Alice waited anxiously for Lexa's reply.

'Your guess is as good as mine, Mum.'

'You must have some idea how you got on.'

Lexa considered that. 'It was the owner himself who interviewed me. A Mr McLeod. Nice man. Terribly well spoken.'

'What did he ask you?' Cordelia wanted to know.

'About my previous employment. I explained about the shop, Dad dying and Cordelia and me trying to keep the business running. I also told him how Burnside treated us, and that that was why we failed in the end. I have to say he was most sympathetic – or at least appeared to be.'

'And the job?' Alice prompted.

'A clerk as advertised. There is some accounts work involved and Mr McLeod was impressed that I had experience of that. He asked me a number of questions about the shop's accounts and how I'd handled them. I got the impression my answers were satisfactory.'

'Are there any other lassies up for the job?' Cordelia asked.

'He did mention that there were. Quite a few, I think.'

'What about pay?'

'Salary, Mum. And monthly at that.' Lexa quoted the figure she'd been given.

Cordelia sniffed. 'Hardly a fortune.'

'Well, it is a junior post, after all. Not as much as I was getting when Dad was alive, but enough to survive on. Should I get it, which I doubt.'

'And why's that?' Alice queried.

'He spotted my hands, Mum. Look at them.' Lexa held them out. 'I've scrubbed and scrubbed them and you can hardly see any difference.'

'Aye.' Alice sighed. 'It'll be a while before those marks disappear. But they will, in time.'

Cordelia glanced down at her own hands, the bane of her life, which were just as bad. At least, as her mother had said, the ingrained marks would eventually go. 'So when will he let you know?' she asked.

'He promised to write, whether or not I landed the job. So now all I can do is wait.'

'And answer other adverts while you do, I presume?' Alice said.

'Of course, Mum. Though there doesn't seem to be a lot around at the moment.'

'You can say that again,' Cordelia moaned. 'You've been lucky. Three interviews so far, while I've only had one.'

'It'll all sort itself out, I promise you,' Alice declared.

'Where are you off to tonight, Mum?' Lexa was surprised that evening when Alice appeared wearing her coat and hat.

'Mrs McAllister and I are going to a whist drive in the Labour Hall,' Alice explained.

'A whist drive!' Cordelia exclaimed. 'Since when have you started going to whist drives?'

'As from now. Mrs McAllister has talked me into it. Says I'll enjoy myself, which I will do if it's anything like the housey-housey.'

Lexa shook her head. 'You really are beginning to get out and about, aren't you?'

'Is that a criticism?' Alice snapped.

'No, not at all. I approve. It's far better than you sitting moping here night after night. Isn't that so, Cordelia?'

'I agree.'

'I appreciate it's the middle of the week, but there's

'nothing stopping me going out then, is there?'

'Nothing.'

'It's not as if I . . .' Alice trailed off, a stricken look on her face. 'Have to get up in the morning to get you two and your father off to work,' she added lamely.

'No, you don't,' Lexa agreed, subdued.

Without saying anything more, Alice turned on her heel and left them.

Lexa hurried through to the front door when she heard the early post arrive. To her disappointment there wasn't anything for her, just a letter to her mother with Granny Stewart's handwriting on the envelope.

'No luck?' Cordelia queried when she saw Lexa's expression.

Lexa shook her head. 'It's beginning to look as if I haven't got it.'

'Well, the man did promise to write one way or the other. So there's still hope.'

'Yes, I suppose so.' She glanced sharply at her sister. 'Haven't you got an interview today?'

'Nope. I don't know what gave you that idea. I am going out, though.'

'Oh?'

'Just a notion I've had. It'll probably come to nothing. But it's better than sitting round here twiddling my thumbs.'

'No clues?'

'No clues,' Cordelia replied mysteriously, before vanishing back into her bedroom to get dressed.

* * *

Alice hadn't been to the graveside since she'd decided to sell the shop, too consumed with guilt to do so. Now she'd forced herself.

'I'm sorry, Jimmy,' she said in a low, husky voice. 'But there was nothing else for it. This Burnside had placed the girls in a situation there was no way out of. We simply had to put the shop on the market in the end.' She paused, then went on, 'And I hope you don't mind me going out enjoying myself as I've been doing. It's all harmless fun. Bit of a laugh really. At least it gets me out the house.' Producing a hanky, she blew her nose. 'That's all I have to say. Except I miss you terribly, and always will, to my dying day.'

Pulling herself together, Alice headed for the gate out of the cemetery, and in the direction of the nearest tram stop. She had only been home a few minutes when Cordelia came bursting through the front door.

'I've got a job!' she yelled. 'I start tomorrow.'

'Slow down, slow down!' Alice said, laughing. Cordelia took several deep breaths. She'd been running, desperate to impart the great news.

Lexa joined them. 'What's all this about?' she demanded.

'I've got a job,' Cordelia repeated. 'I start tomorrow morning.'

A pang of jealousy pinged through Lexa. 'Is this to do with what you wouldn't tell me about?'

Cordelia nodded. 'It was just an idea, and it's paid off.'

'What sort of job, dear?' Alice queried, delighted for her daughter.

'In the flower market. I went there and started asking

around and sure enough there was someone looking for help. I spoke to him – his name's Joe – and Bob's your uncle!'

'Will you be selling flowers then?' Lexa frowned.

'That's right. Joe has a stall, and up until last week was assisted by his wife. She's now too pregnant with their first child to continue working, so, as from tomorrow, I'll be taking her place.'

'Oh, Cordelia.' Alice beamed and kissed her on the cheek. 'This is wonderful news.'

'Congratulations, sis,' Lexa said, also kissing her.

'The great thing is it's hardly any different from working in the shop. Instead of selling fruit and vegetables I'll be selling flowers. Lots and lots of lovely ones.'

'Tell us about this Joe,' Lexa prompted.

'Mid-twenties. Reasonably attractive. Seems pleasant enough.'

'Surname?'

'Joe Given.'

'And you begin tomorrow?'

'At the crack of dawn. So it'll be a very early start for me. I can't wait as I'm sick to death of hanging round the house with nothing to do.'

Lexa appreciated the sentiment. So too was she.

'Well, one down and one to go,' Alice declared. 'It'll be your turn soon.' She smiled at Lexa.

Lexa wasn't so sure.

Lexa glanced at the clock on the mantelpiece. The early post must have passed by now, and still no word from Mr McLeod. So much for his promising to write whether or not she got the job. As far as she was concerned he must have reneged on his word. And again there had been nothing in the previous night's newspaper that had interested her. In fact there had been bugger all whether she'd been interested or not.

Patience, she cautioned herself. Something was bound to come up. The only question was when?

'Will you run and get some messages for me, dear?' Alice had come into the room.

'Of course, Mum. What do you want?'

'I'll write it down so you don't forget anything.' Alice had always enjoyed making lists. Jimmy had teased her about it ever since the day she'd given him a so-called list with only a single item on it.

'I'll get my coat,' Lexa said, as her mother busied herself with pencil and paper. A few minutes later she was on her way, pleased to be doing something useful.

When she returned, Alice was waiting for her. 'A letter has come for you in the late post,' she announced.

Lexa's face lit up. 'It has?'

'Your name and address have been typewritten, so I presume it must be from Mr McLeod.'

Lexa put the full shopping bag to one side and took the envelope Alice handed her. She'd done Mr McLeod less than justice in thinking he'd reneged on his word, which made her feel a little ashamed.

'Go on, open it,' Alice urged.

Now she had the letter in her hand she was scared to open it in case it was rejection. There again, she wouldn't know one way or the other unless she did open it. Who wanted to work for a boring wine merchant's anyway? The job was probably dreary as anything.

'Good luck.' Alice smiled encouragingly.

'Here goes,' Lexa murmured, attacking the flap.

The envelope contained a single sheet of paper, which Lexa quickly scanned.

'Well?'

Lexa looked at her mother, then began to grin. 'I've got the job! Start the first Monday of next month.'

Alice grabbed Lexa and hugged her tight. 'Congratulations! I'm ever so pleased for you.'

When she could breathe again Lexa let out a huge sigh of relief. Maybe it wouldn't be so dreary in a wine merchant's after all. 'I really didn't think I was going to get it, Mum. Apart from anything else I was certain my hands would go against me.'

'That just shows how wrong you were.'

Lexa suddenly frowned. 'I'm going to have to buy some new clothes. Things suitable for an office.'

'True enough.' Alice nodded. 'We'll go straight to the bank and take out a bit of cash which I'll lend you until you can pay it back. How does that sound?'

'Ideal, Mum. Thank you.'

'Don't worry. At least we have it to draw on.' She thought about the shop, which remained unsold. Please God it would move soon. Things were beginning to get tight. 'Right! Coats. And off to the bank.'

Lexa glanced again at the letter she was still holding, and silently thanked Mr McLeod for choosing her over the other applicants.

She wouldn't let him down.

*　　*　　*

'Here's a ten bob note. Nip to the stall and get two teas and two bacon sannies, one each,' said Joe Given. 'We need something to warm us up.'

Cordelia accepted the note. She and Joe had become great pals in the two weeks she'd been working for him. He didn't seem like a boss, more a co-worker helping her learn the ropes. 'Two sugars as usual?' she queried.

'Heaped. I like my tea nice and sweet.' He grinned. 'Just like me.'

'You've certainly got a big tip for yourself,' she teased.

'Not at all,' he protested. 'I'm simply telling the truth, that's all.'

Cordelia liked Joe, you couldn't help but like him. He was just that sort of man. 'Sez you.'

He laughed. 'Get on with it. I'm dying for that sannie. I'm so hungry my belly's beginning to think my throat's been cut.'

Cordelia headed for the stall set up at one end of the market where tea, coffee and snacks could be bought. It did a roaring trade.

'Another cuppa, Alice?'

Alice shook her head. 'No thank you, Mary. I'm awash as it is.'

'How about another piece of cake, then?'

'Are you trying to make me fat?'

'A wee bit of what you fancy does you good,' Granny Stewart declared piously.

'A wee bit is one thing, a third slice of your cake would be quite another.'

'Aye, maybe you're right.' Granny Stewart nodded. 'Too

much of a good thing and all that.' She eyed Alice speculatively. 'I'm pleased you accepted my invitation to come and visit. It's been a while.'

Alice glanced away. 'I'm sorry about that.'

'I wouldn't want to lose touch with you, Alice. That would be a pity.'

'There's no fear of that, I can assure you,' Alice protested.

Granny Stewart produced a small packet of cigarettes, and lit up. She allowed herself five a day. 'So, how are you coping?' She'd decided it was time to get down to the nitty-gritty.

'Fine.'

Too quick a reply, Granny Stewart noted. 'I'll ask again, and remember I'm a widow myself and have been through the business of losing my man. How are you coping?'

Alice flushed slightly. 'It's not easy, is it?'

'No, it's not.'

'In fact, to be brutally honest, it's bloody hard. Every single day has to be struggled through. It's like . . . well, walking down a long black tunnel with no prospect of there ever being light at the end.'

Granny Stewart sighed. 'Things do get better, I promise you. You somehow learn to live with what life has become. At least, that's been my experience.'

Alice felt her hands begin to shake, so she placed her cup and saucer on the floor. The linoleum was old and badly cracked in places, but highly polished, as Granny Stewart was extremely houseproud and always had been. She refused to let age get in the way of her daily housework routine.

'I feel terribly guilty,' Alice mumbled.

'Why guilty?'

'About Jimmy dying. For some reason I blame myself for that.'

Granny Stewart shook her head. 'How on earth could you be to blame? That's absolute nonsense, woman. He died of natural causes, plain and simple. It was his time, that's all.'

'A heart attack out of the blue is hardly natural causes,' Alice argued. 'I keep thinking he might have been unhappy, or upset with me, and that's what brought it on.'

Granny Stewart stared intently at her daughter-in-law. 'You two had a wonderful marriage. If anything had been amiss Jimmy would certainly have told me – he used to tell me everything. He came here the week before he died and was as happy as Larry. Couldn't have been more so.'

'Are you sure, Mary? He might have been putting on a front.'

'He wasn't. I could read Jimmy like a book, and there was nothing wrong in his life. Nothing whatsoever. So stop blaming yourself for something which didn't exist.'

A silence fell between the two women. Alice stared at the floor. 'There's more, though,' she said eventually.

'Like what?'

'I've been going out to the Labour Hall with a neighbour. Housey-housey and whist drives. The point is, I've been enjoying myself there. Having a right old laugh, which surely can't be right.'

'And you feel guilty about that as well?'

Alice nodded.

'You've got yourself into a proper state, haven't you? All this guilt washing around inside you. Well, Jimmy would have approved of you getting out and about. The last thing he would have wanted was for you to sit pining at home being a right old misery guts. He would have been the first to say life goes on regardless, so get on with it.'

Alice took a deep breath. 'Thanks,' she whispered.

'Now, you're to stop havering, lassie. Hear?'

'I hear, Mary.'

'No more of this guilt you've been wallowing in. That's done and gone with. Right?'

'Right,' Alice mumbled.

'Say it as though you mean it.'

'Right,' Alice repeated, boldly this time.

'That's better.' Granny Stewart suddenly smiled. 'I haven't commented so far, but white hair suits you.'

Alice was surprised. 'Do you think so?'

'I've just said, haven't I?'

Alice thought for a few seconds, then said, 'It happened the night after Jimmy died. I went to bed my normal colour, and woke up totally white. Caused by the shock, no doubt.'

'At least it didn't all fall out.' Granny Stewart smiled again. 'That happened to a friend of mine years ago. When she woke up in the morning all her hair was there on the pillow beside her.'

'How awful!' Alice exclaimed. 'Did it grow back again?'

'No, it didn't. She was bald as a coot till the day she passed on. She had a grand collection of hats, though. Dozens of the damn things. We never saw her without one on her head. So count yourself lucky.'

Alice laughed. Having heard that, she did.

'Now,' declared Granny Stewart, changing the subject. 'You haven't mentioned my arthritis yet.'

'Oh! Sorry. How is it?'

'I was beginning to think you'd never ask,' Granny Stewart replied, tongue in cheek. 'It's terrible.'

'Let's look at you,' Alice said when Lexa entered the front room, the morning of her first day at *Vins*.

She was wearing a black skirt that came to mid-calf. Her blouse was plain white cotton closed at the neck with three pearl buttons. Its sleeves were long and straight, and the cuffs also sported pearl buttons. 'What do you think?' she demanded.

'You look absolutely terrific. Are you nervous?'

'As a kitten.'

'Only to be expected. But you'll be fine. I'm sure of it.' Alice glanced at the clock on the mantelpiece. 'Now on you go. You can tell me all about it tonight.'

Both girls back working, Alice thought with satisfaction when Lexa had left. Now all she had to do was sell the shop.

In fact she'd go to see the agent later on and try to chivvy him up a bit.

Yes, that's precisely what she'd do.

Chapter 6

'These are for you, Mum.' Cordelia handed Alice a large, mixed bunch of flowers.

'This Joe of yours is certainly very generous,' Alice commented as she accepted them. 'Since you started with him there hasn't been a single day when we haven't had a display in the house.'

He *was* generous, Cordelia reflected. In many ways. He always paid for her tea and whatever she had to eat from the stall. 'Are you complaining?' she teased.

'Not in the least. Make sure you thank him for me.'

'I will. You'll have to stop by sometime and meet him for yourself. You'll like him.'

'I'll do that,' Alice promised. She placed the flowers in the sink, intending to deal with them after tea.

'I met his wife today,' Cordelia said.

'What's she like?'

'Very pleasant. She's called Ellie and is the size of the proverbial barn door. She's huge. Absolutely enormous.'

Alice smiled, her mind filled with memories. 'I was the

same way with you two. I thought I was going to have elephants rather than babies.'

Cordelia laughed. 'Really?'

'And both times I got to the stage where I could only walk very slowly. Your dad used to say it would have been quicker rolling me along.'

Cordelia laughed again at the image that conjured up.

'Had a great sense of humour, your dad. Used to have me in stitches with some of the things he came out with.'

'I remember.' Cordelia smiled.

'Never crude, mind you. Your dad was never that. But funny as all get out when the mood took him. I remember . . .' Alice suddenly stopped, and blushed. 'Never mind what I remember.'

'Was it rude, Mum?' Cordelia teased.

'Well, let's just put it this way: your dad was no saint. Not by a long chalk.' She leaned over the sink and smelt the flowers. 'These really are lovely.'

'I'll sort them out in a vase if you like. I'm becoming a dab hand at arranging. Joe's been teaching me. Strange for a chap to be so good with flowers, but there you are. It's his livelihood, after all.'

'I was going to do them myself, but you can if you want. First, though, how about mashing some spuds for me? I could use a hand.'

There were four of them in the office. The chief clerk was Mrs Sanderson, a formidable-looking middle-aged woman with a somewhat dumpy figure and grey-flecked hair which she always wore pinned back in a bun, who was really a sweetie at heart. The other two girls were Pam, who was a little older than Lexa, and Lily, a typical old maid type. Poor Lily was plain as a pikestaff, with a jaw too big for her face and extremely unattractive glasses. Lexa and Pam had become good pals, but hadn't socialised out of work yet, though they had chatted about going dancing together on Saturday night. Dancing was the favourite way in Glasgow of meeting members of the opposite sex.

Mrs Sanderson glanced at her wristwatch, then over at Lexa. 'I think you can make the morning tea now, Miss Stewart,' she said.

Lexa laid aside the pen she'd been using. 'Yes, Mrs Sanderson.'

Mrs Sanderson nodded her approval, then returned to the file she'd been immersed in.

It was one of Lexa's duties to make the morning and afternoon tea. Every week the four of them in the office contributed threepence each towards a packet of biscuits. Chocolate ones were the favourite, though occasionally they would go for garibaldis, or some other fancy types. Mostly, though, they plumped for chocolate.

Lexa left the office, and as luck would have it almost immediately ran into Mr McLeod. It was the first time she'd seen him since starting.

'Ah, Miss Stewart. How are you?' he asked with a friendly smile.

'Fine, thank you, Mr McLeod.'

'Settling in all right?'

'Very much so. I'm enjoying the work.'

'Splendid.' He beamed. 'That's what I like to hear. Is Mrs Sanderson in her office?'

'She is, sir.'

'Good. I want a word.'

He left her to it, and Lexa went to find the kettle.

A little later, in the ladies' room, where Pam was allowed to smoke and Lexa had taken to joining her for a brief break from her desk, she asked, 'So what's Mr McLeod junior like?'

'Haven't you met him yet?'

Lexa shook her head.

'Well, maybe that isn't so surprising. He's out a lot, "on the road" as they call it.'

'Oh?' Lexa queried, not understanding.

'He's what you call a company rep – representative. It's his job to drop in on customers to chase up orders. That sort of thing.'

'I see.' Lexa nodded.

'He not only travels round Glasgow but further afield as well. The Trossachs, for example, where there are a number of hotels who use us. He's very good at what he does, apparently. A right Mr Smoothie.'

Lexa smiled at that.

'Bit of a dreamboat actually. Tall, dark and, as they say, handsome with it. I fancy him rotten, to tell the truth, but I've no chance there.'

'Why not?' Lexa frowned.

'He's a bit posh, if you know what I mean. Went to a private school and talks with a plum in his mouth. He'd never entertain the likes of me.'

'What's his name?'

'William. No Bill or Billy for him. It's William.'

He sounded intriguing, Lexa mused. 'Is he nice?'

'Oh, aye, very well mannered and easy-going. Though I have heard tell he can have quite a temper if provoked. But I've never witnessed that side of him.' Pam took a deep draw on her cigarette, then blew smoke out through her nose. 'He drives a car, too, provided by *Vins*. Well, he'd have to, to get around like he does. He could hardly go to the Trossachs on a bus to do company business, could he?'

'No,' Lexa agreed, finding the idea amusing.

'You'll run into him soon enough, no doubt,' Pam went on. 'And you'll know him when you see him. He's very broad-shouldered, from rowing, I believe.' She stubbed out her cigarette in the ashtray she herself had provided. 'Anyway, we'd better get back or old pruneface will have a go at me.' Pruneface was Pam's nickname for Mrs Sanderson, albeit the two got on well enough.

It was a Saturday, and the market was packing up for the rest of the weekend. Joe and Cordelia had nearly finished.

'I usually go for a couple of pints at this time of the week,' Joe announced. 'Care to join me?'

That took her by surprise. 'In a pub?'

'Well, I presume you've been in one before?'

Cordelia became flustered. 'No, I haven't,' she confessed.

Now it was his turn to be surprised. 'Then it's high time you did. You do drink, don't you?'

She nodded. 'Occasionally.'

'Then what's the problem?'

'Well . . . I was brought up to believe nice women didn't go into pubs. That they're a men-only sort of thing.'

Joe laughed. 'That's true about many, but not all.' He pointed to the Hielan Laddie across the road. 'And certainly not there on a Saturday afternoon. Lots of people who work in the market go in then, many of them women. I can assure you that you won't be the only female, or feel out of place.'

'Then I accept.' She smiled, thrilled to pieces at the invitation.

They finished tidying up, and then Joe took her across the road and into the pub.

The first thing that struck Cordelia was the distinctive smell: a combination of cigarette smoke and beer. She rather liked it. As Joe had said, there were quite a few people milling around and, as he'd assured her, a number of women present.

'Over here.' Joe escorted her quickly to a vacant table. He smiled. 'Bit of luck, this. Usually you have to stand as the tables are all full. Now, what'll you have?'

Cordelia's mind raced. She didn't want to ask for whisky; it might give the wrong impression. 'Shandy, please.'

'Coming up.' Joe made his way to the bar. Cordelia stared at his retreating back, thinking what a lovely, tight bottom he had. Absolutely scrumptious. The thought made her blush. He's a married man, she scolded herself. She shouldn't be thinking such things. On the other hand, there was nothing wrong with simply admiring it. No harm in that at all.

'There's a question I've been meaning to ask you,' he said, when he returned with their drinks.

'Which is?'

'Your name. It's very unusual.'

Cordelia had a sip of her shandy. 'My mother's to blame for that. Not long before I was born she read it in a magazine, some sloppy love story or other, and liked it so much she decided to give it to me. Apparently it originally comes from some Shakespearean play or other. Don't ask me which one. I've no idea.'

'Shakespearean,' he mused. 'Impressive.'

'It caused me a lot of trouble at school where everyone else had ordinary names. Mine stood out, being so different.'

'Are you saying you were bullied?'

Cordelia shook her head. 'Some of the other pupils tried, but they soon found out I could stand up for myself. I even gave a boy a bloody nose once.'

Joe laughed. 'Did you really?'

'Biffed him hard and he ran away crying his eyes out. Served him right, the sod.'

Joe gazed at her in admiration. 'Sounds like you were quite a tomboy.'

'I was nothing of the sort. But as I said, I could look after myself. My sister's the same. You'd never think to look at her that she's tough as old boots inside.'

'And what's her name?' he asked out of curiosity.

'Alexandra. But she's always been called Lexa for short.'

Joe produced a packet of cigarettes, and lit up. He didn't offer Cordelia one as he knew she didn't smoke. 'Tell me more about yourself,' he prompted.

'No, enough about me. What about you? Where and when did you meet Ellie?'

*   *   *

Alice stared intently into the mirror hanging above the fireplace in the front room. She was definitely looking better, she decided. The drawn look had gone from her face, and many of the lines that had appeared after Jimmy's death had been smoothed away. The sparkle was back in eyes which had been dull for a long time now, and her colour was better.

She nodded at her reflection, approving of what she saw. There could be no doubt she was well on the way to recovery, at least physically. She was becoming her old self again, and that pleased her a lot.

'I've got some wonderful news,' she announced when Lexa and Cordelia got in.

'What's that, Mum?' Lexa asked.

'I've had a letter from the agent telling me he's got someone interested in buying the shop.'

'Oh, that is wonderful!' Cordelia breathed.

'It's not definite or anything, but the agent says the man truly is interested and should be making a decision sometime next week.'

Lexa held up two crossed fingers. 'Let's hope, eh?'

'Let's hope,' a beaming Alice agreed.

Cordelia flopped on to an easy chair. 'Joe and I had a drink after work today,' she declared. 'In a pub.'

'A pub!' Alice exclaimed disapprovingly.

'It's all right, Mum. There were other women from the market there. Apparently it's a sort of tradition that they go after closing for the weekend.'

'Even though,' Alice muttered.

'Did you have a nice time?' Lexa asked.

'Very. Joe and I had a right old natter. I learned a lot

about him and his family. How he met his wife, and so on.'

Alice shook her head. 'I don't think it's a good idea drinking with your boss. It just isn't done.'

'You don't know Joe, Mum.' Cordelia smiled. 'You'd search long and hard to find anyone less like a boss. He simply isn't like that.'

Lexa stared quizzically at her sister. 'You're not getting keen, are you?'

'Don't be daft!' Cordelia snapped in reply. 'He's a married man. A *happily* married man, I might add.'

'That's all right then.'

Cordelia snorted. 'The very idea. And his wife, whom he dearly loves, all set to drop too.'

'Cordelia!' Alice admonished her. 'Don't be so crude.'

'Well, she is, Mum.'

'I appreciate that. Can't you say she's close to her time, or something? About to drop is awful.'

Cordelia was amused. She knew only too well how prudish her mother could be at times. She should have known better than to offend Alice by her choice of language. 'Sorry, Mum.'

'I should think so too.'

'What was the pub like?' Lexa asked. She had never been in one either.

'Cosy. And friendly.'

'What did you have?'

'A shandy. Two, actually.'

'And Joe?'

'Pints and drams. I fancied a dram myself but didn't like to ask in case it was considered unladylike.'

Lexa nodded her agreement, wishing she'd been there.

One of these days she too would go to a pub when the proper opportunity presented itself.

'I'm off to the kitchen,' Alice announced, and left them.

Cordelia leaned forward in her chair when her mother had gone. 'Want to know something?' she said quietly to Lexa.

'What?'

'I couldn't help but notice Joe's got the most fabulous bum. I'm not interested, mind, but it's still the most fabulous bum.'

Both girls giggled.

A young man arrived at the door to *Vins* just ahead of Lexa. 'Good morning,' he said, smiling, holding it open for her.

'Good morning.' She smiled in reply, taking in the strong, pleasant face adorned by a Ronald Colman moustache. A moustache that certainly suited him.

'You must be the new girl, Miss Stewart,' he said once they were inside.

'That's correct, sir.'

'I'm William McLeod. Pleased to meet you.'

Pam hadn't been exaggerating, Lexa thought. He *was* something of a dreamboat. 'Pleased to meet you, sir.'

'Are you enjoying working here?'

'Very much, sir.'

'I know I have. But then wine can be fascinating.'

She couldn't think of a reply to that, never having drunk a glass of wine in her life.

'Goodbye then, Miss Stewart,' he said, turning into a corridor different from the one she would take.

'Goodbye, sir.'

Well well, she thought as she continued on her way. There was certainly nothing wrong with him. She could understand why Pam was attracted.

Pam came across to Lexa at the start of the midday break, and sighed. 'It's so stuffy in here today. Do you fancy going out for a walk and a breath of fresh air?'

'After my sandwich.' Alice made her dinnertime 'piece' for her every working morning with the exception of Saturdays.

'Aye, all right. I'll wait.' Pam never ate at dinnertime. 'I'll just nip off to the lav and have a fag while you do that.'

'Fine.'

Fifteen minutes later found them strolling along the street, coming up to a set of traffic lights just as they turned red. A car passed them, and stopped, waiting for the lights to change. Pam nudged Lexa in the ribs. 'That's him. William McLeod.'

It was a smashing car, Lexa noted. Big too. William looked quite the gentleman sitting in the driver's seat. 'I met him coming in this morning. He held the door open for me.'

'You didn't say,' Pam accused.

Lexa shrugged. 'I didn't think it worth mentioning. We only exchanged a few words, that's all.'

'And what do you think?'

'About him?'

Pam nodded.

'He's a bit of all right. You weren't kidding when you told me that.'

Pam sighed. 'If only . . .' She trailed off, and sighed even more heavily, which made Lexa laugh.

They both watched the car as the lights changed and it sped away.

'Mum, this is a surprise!' Cordelia exclaimed when Alice appeared in front of her.

'I was in town and thought I'd stop by. You did tell me to, remember?'

'Of course I remember.' Cordelia looked across to where Joe was serving a customer. He'd be free in a minute.

'It's years since I've been to the flower market,' Alice declared. 'I'd forgotten how pretty it all is.' She gazed about her, drinking in the heavy aroma that was everywhere. What an agreeable place to work, she thought.

'Joe!' Cordelia called when the customer had gone.

He came over. 'Aye, what is it, Cordelia?'

'Joe, I'd like you to meet my mother. Mum, this is Joe.'

They shook hands. Joe smiled. 'I can see where Cordelia gets her looks from,' he said.

Alice blushed. 'Get away with you.'

'No, I mean it,' he insisted.

What a flatterer, Alice thought, secretly pleased. Absent-mindedly she smoothed back her hair.

'Your daughter's doing terribly well here,' Joe went on. 'I don't know what I'd do without her. Truly.'

Cordelia beamed to hear that.

'I'm told your wife's expecting at any moment,' Alice said.

'Aye, that's right. Next week, we think.'

'What are you hoping for, a boy or a girl?'

Joe shrugged. 'Doesn't matter. As long as it's healthy and Ellie comes through all right I'll be happy.'

Correct answer, Alice reflected, warming to the man. 'Then I'll wish your wife and baby all the very best.'

'That's kind of you, Mrs Stewart. I appreciate it.' He turned to Cordelia. 'Why don't you take your mother to the stall and buy her a cup of tea? On me, of course.'

'Mum?'

'That would be lovely.'

Joe dug in his pocket and produced a two shilling piece which he handed to Cordelia. 'Take as long as you wish. I can easily manage here until you get back.'

'I see what you mean,' Alice said to Cordelia as they headed for the stall. 'A very charming young man. I liked him.'

Chapter 7

'We've sold the shop!' Alice announced when Lexa and Cordelia arrived home from work. She was quite flushed with excitement.

Lexa clapped her hands together. 'Oh, Mum, that's great!'

'For the asking price?' Cordelia queried.

'That's what the agent says in the letter I received this morning. It's now up to the lawyers to do their stuff, which will take about a month, I understand.'

'Well, that's one less thing to worry about,' said Lexa.

Alice nodded her agreement. 'It's such a relief. Money was beginning to get very tight indeed. It would have run out a while back if you two hadn't been in work.'

'I think we should celebrate,' Cordelia declared.

'How?' Lexa demanded.

'A wee nip each from the whisky bottle. What do you say?'

'I'm in favour.' Alice beamed. 'I'll get the bottle. You put out the glasses, Cordelia.'

A few minutes later they were holding up three filled glasses in a toast.

'It was a good shop and did us all proud,' Alice said quietly. 'But sadly, it had to go.'

'Amen,' murmured Cordelia, and they drank.

'What's wrong?' Ginge McPherson asked Cordelia. Ginge was another stallholder in the market and a friend of Joe's, who was called Ginge for the obvious reason, his hair being a somewhat virulent shade of orangey red.

'Joe hasn't shown yet,' Cordelia replied worriedly. 'He's always here setting up when I arrive. I don't know what to do.'

'I expect Ellie's gone into labour.'

'That's the conclusion I came to. Unless something else has happened to make him late.'

'I doubt that.'

'I can set up all right,' Cordelia went on, 'but I can't open for business without a float.'

'That's easily taken care of.' Ginge smiled. 'I'll lend you half of mine.'

'Will you!' Cordelia exclaimed in delight.

'Of course I will. Joe's a china, don't forget. He'd do the same for me. Now, let's get you sorted out here first.'

It was hours later when Joe finally showed up. 'It's a girl!' he declared, beaming from ear to ear. 'Mother and daughter both doing well.'

'Oh, Joe,' Cordelia enthused. 'I'm ever so pleased for you.'

'Everything went off without a hitch. It was a long labour, mind, but Ellie got there in the end.'

'You must be delighted.'

'What do you think?'

Cordelia laughed. 'Have you chosen a name yet?'

'We haven't. Ellie believes it's bad luck to choose the name before the baby's born, though we'll no doubt come up with one before too long. But listen, I didn't really expect you to be here. I thought you'd have gone home again when I didn't put in an appearance.'

'I would have done eventually as I didn't have a float. Then Ginge came over and offered me half his. So it's been business as usual.'

'Good old Ginge,' Joe declared. He ran a hand over his face. 'God, I feel dreadful. And must look it, not having shaved this morning. I was at the hospital all night and until about an hour ago. I'm absolutely knackered.'

She could see he was. His eyes were red-rimmed, his face pasty with bags under the eyes. 'Why don't you nip over to the pub and have a couple?' she suggested. 'That'll buck you up.'

'What a good idea.' He nodded. 'I could certainly use a pint and dram.' He hesitated. 'Are you sure you'll be all right alone?'

'I've managed so far, haven't I?'

'True enough,' he acknowledged. 'And done a splendid job, no doubt.'

'On you go then. And why don't you see if Ginge can get away? I think you owe him a drink.'

'Another good idea. I'll do just that.' Acting on impulse, Joe kissed her on the cheek. 'You're a real sweetheart, so you are.'

When he'd gone she touched the spot he'd kissed, a

strange feeling fluttering through her tummy. But the feeling was quickly forgotten when she had to attend a customer.

'Come on, you've got time for one,' Joe urged as they were packing up for the night.

'I really should get home, Joe. My mother will have the tea ready.'

'She'll understand when you explain the reason for being late. She's a woman, she's bound to.'

Cordelia couldn't see where being a woman came into it.

'Please?' Joe begged. 'Just one to wet the baby's head.'

Cordelia relented. 'All right. But only one, mind.'

'That's my girl.'

In the pub, Joe returned from the bar and placed a large whisky and lemonade in front of Cordelia. 'Are you sure you can handle that?' he asked sceptically.

'I can handle it,' Cordelia assured him.

'It's an awful grown-up drink, you know.'

'I am all grown up, Joe. Or hadn't you noticed?'

That flustered him. 'Of course I had. I'm sorry.'

She hadn't asked for whisky on their previous visit to the pub, not wanting to give the wrong impression, but she knew Joe a lot better now. 'My dad used to give us a dram from time to time,' she explained. 'He wasn't much of a drinker himself, but thought his daughters should be prepared for the ways of the world. He was a smashing man, my dad.'

Joe heard the sadness in her voice. 'You still miss him, don't you?'

'I think about him every single day, and so do my mother and sister. We were all very close.'

Joe raised his pint. 'To the wee lassie, eh?'

'To the wee lassie,' Cordelia repeated, and had a sip of her drink.

'It's funny to think I'm a parent,' Joe mused. 'Of course I knew I was going to be, but now it's actually happened. I'm a father.' He paused, then muttered quietly, 'Bloody Norah!'

'Quite a responsibility.' Cordelia smiled.

'Oh, aye, it is that. And one I'll take very seriously, believe you me.'

Cordelia did believe him. He was that sort of man. 'Are you going back to the hospital later?' she asked.

'Darn tootin'. I'll have to get cleaned up first, then a quick bite to eat and I'll be off.'

'Will you have to cook something yourself?'

He shook his head. 'Ellie's ma will have a meal ready for me. And if it isn't Ellie's ma it'll be her sister Margy.'

'So you'll be well looked after while Ellie's in hospital?'

'Oh, aye. As Ellie will be when she comes home with the baby, until she gets properly back on her feet again.'

Cordelia didn't ask about his side of the family. She knew that both his parents were dead and he was an only child.

'Thanks again for what you did today.' He smiled at her.

'That's all right.'

He patted her on the hand. 'As I said earlier, you're a real sweetheart.'

Despite the temptation to linger Cordelia kept to her

word and only had a single drink, leaving Joe to have another. It might have been the whisky, or something else entirely, but she felt quite elated as she made her way out of the market.

She even began to hum.

Lexa stood at the tram stop shivering as the rain came lashing down in the proverbial stair rods. She'd only been there a couple of minutes and already she was soaked through.

She peered up the street, hoping to spot her tram. But there was no sign of it. Then, to her disgust, the rain, unbelievably, became even heavier. A car came to a halt alongside, and the window was rolled down. William McLeod gazed out at her.

'I thought it was you, Miss Stewart. Where are you off to?'

'Mount Florida.'

He nodded. 'I can go that way. Hop in and I'll give you a lift.'

Lexa didn't hesitate. She hurried round to the other side of the car, opened the door and slid gratefully inside. 'Thank you, Mr McLeod.'

'You're welcome. What a night, eh?'

'Terrible.'

He engaged gear, and the car purred forward. 'We live in Cathcart ourselves, practically next door. A bit of luck, eh?'

She smiled. 'For me, anyway.'

'I was hoping you weren't going to say Springburn, or somewhere like that. Would have meant quite a detour.'

Lexa drank in the smell of well-polished leather, thinking how masculine it was. Like Mr McLeod himself. 'Quite a detour,' she agreed. 'But then if I was going to Springburn, or any other district on the northside, I wouldn't have been standing at that particular tram stop.'

He shot her a surprised look. 'You know, I never thought of that. Simply didn't cross my mind. There again, it's been a long, long time since I last took a tram. In fact it's so long I can't even remember when.'

It's all right for some, she thought wryly. 'Lovely car,' she said aloud.

'You like it?'

'Very much.'

'It's an Austin Twenty and fairly old. Roomy, though, which is ideal for my job as I can get a number of cases of wine in the boot, and more on the back seat. If I'm carrying a really big order we also have a van which I drive. I do all the maintenance myself. It's something of a hobby with me. I've always been fascinated by engines, ever since I was a small lad.'

'Really?'

He laughed. 'In another life I'd probably have been a mechanic. That would have suited me down to the ground. Fiddling around with engines all day long. Sheer bliss.'

'Instead you work for your father?'

'Indeed I do. And thoroughly enjoy it. I seem to have inherited his passion for wine and the wine trade.'

Lexa wondered if she should confess she'd never tasted wine, then thought better of it. There was no need for him to know that.

'Talking of my father,' William went on, 'you impressed him at your interview.'

'Did I?' Lexa was astonished.

'You certainly did.'

'In what way?'

'Two women trying to run their own shop. He thought that terribly ambitious.'

The condescension annoyed Lexa, but she wasn't about to show it. 'Doesn't he consider women capable of such a thing?'

'As a matter of fact he does. My father is quite forward in his thinking, as I hope I am. No, what he meant was having to deal with men on the business side. As you appreciate, many men can be extremely prejudiced, believing women should stay at home and leave the men to go out to work. Isn't that what happened with the chappie who put a spoke in your wheel?'

'Burnside,' Lexa muttered bitterly. 'We'd have done all right if it hadn't been for him.'

'Nasty, eh?'

'Very.'

William flicked his eyes on to her, then back to the road again. 'Still, you did your best. No one can take that away from you.'

'No,' she agreed. 'They can't.'

'And look on the bright side. You've come to work for us. I've no doubt you'll be a positive asset.'

'Thank you. I appreciate that.'

William leaned forward slightly and peered through the windscreen. 'I don't know if it's my imagination but I think the rain is easing slightly.' He was right. A few minutes later it stopped altogether. 'That's better.' William breathed a sigh of relief. 'Now, whereabouts in Mount Florida are you?'

Lexa named the street.

'I don't know it. You'll have to guide me.'

Lexa closed her eyes for a few moments, listening to the sweet purring of the engine. It was a lovely, soothing sound. Like a big cat.

'Here we are,' she told him when they eventually reached her close. 'Thank you ever so much.' She smiled at him in the darkness.

'My pleasure, Miss Stewart. I'm glad I've got to know you.'

And she him, she thought. 'Bye then.'

'Bye.'

Opening the car door, she slipped out, then closed it again. She gave him a cheery wave before vanishing into her close.

Well, she thought. How about that? How about that indeed! She couldn't wait to tell Pam in the morning.

'Engaged!' Pam exclaimed in astonishment, while Mrs Sanderson and Lexa gaped on. What a bombshell!

Lily flashed the ring in front of them. 'What do you think?'

The diamond was minuscule, Lexa noted. But it was a diamond. 'We didn't even know you had a boyfriend,' she declared. 'You've never said.'

'We've been going out for a couple of years now. He's a Sunday school teacher, same as myself.'

He must be a blind Sunday school teacher, Lexa

thought uncharitably. For there was no denying that Lily was plain, if not downright ugly. That chin alone would have sent most men running. Oh well, there was obviously no accounting for taste.

'I think your ring's gorgeous.' Mrs Sanderson had recovered her composure.

'So do I,' Pam lied.

'So when's the big day?' Lexa asked.

'Oh, not for a couple of years yet. We'll have to save up first. And that'll take time.'

'What's the chap's name?' Mrs Sanderson enquired.

'Davey. He works in a bank as a teller.'

'Well well.' Mrs Sanderson smiled. 'Why don't we celebrate the engagement by having two chocolate biscuits each today instead of one. How does that sound?'

'That was a turn-up for the book,' Pam sniggered the moment the ladies' door was shut behind her and Lexa.

'You can say that again!'

Pam produced her cigarettes and lit up. 'I was gasping for that,' she sighed after exhaling.

'Who'd have thought, eh?'

Pam shook her head in amazement. 'I'll tell you this, if Lily can hook a man then there's hope for the rest of us.'

'We shouldn't be too bitchy,' Lexa said. 'We should be wishing her every happiness.'

'But I do,' Pam protested. 'It's just . . .' She trailed off, then said, 'I thought she was destined to be an old maid, that's all. She's spinster material through and through.'

'Obviously not,' Lexa commented wryly.

'I wonder what this Davey looks like?' Pam mused.

'Who knows?'

'Probably as ugly as she is.'

They both laughed.

'Then again, maybe not,' Lexa said lightly.

'Perhaps we'll meet him one day.'

'Perhaps. On the other hand, we could ask Lily if she has a photograph.'

'Oh, yes!' Pam enthused. 'I'd love to see that.'

'Me too.'

Lexa took a deep breath. 'By the way, you'll never guess who gave me a ride home in his motor car last night.'

Pam frowned. 'Who?'

'I was standing at the tram stop in that terrible rain when this car stopped in front of me and Mr McLeod junior told me to jump in.'

Pam's eyes went wide. 'You lucky cow!'

'It seems the family live in Cathcart, which is close to my house. We had quite a natter along the way. He's very nice.'

'Of all the jammy sods! I'm green with envy. Spitting with it!'

Lexa laughed, having guessed this would be her friend's reaction. She went on to tell Pam what they'd talked about, Pam insisting on hearing every last detail.

'Do you mind if I join you?'

It was a Saturday afternoon, and Cordelia was enjoying her now customary drink in the Hielan Laddie.

'Of course not, Ginge. Grab a pew.'

He sat, and eyed the half-drunk pint and empty whisky glass where he presumed Joe must be sitting. 'Joe gone to the cludge?'

Cordelia nodded. 'He should be back in a moment.'

'Unless he's on the throne.'

Cordelia considered his remark distasteful. But market traders were quite a crude lot at times, both the men and the women; it was something she'd had to get used to. She smiled, and sipped her whisky and lemonade.

'Good day?' Ginge queried.

'Not bad. We've had better.'

'Same with us.' Ginge had a partner called John. 'I must say, you're looking even lovelier than ever.'

'Get away with you!'

'No, I mean it,' he protested.

Cordelia gazed at him, wondering if he was after something. It was most unlike Ginge to say such a thing. 'Have you already had a few?'

'No, this is my first,' he replied, indicating the pint in front of him.

Was he taking the mickey? She defied any woman to emerge looking lovely after working in the market. Even a film star couldn't have managed it. So what was he up to?

'Going out tonight?' he asked.

She shook her head. 'Don't think so.'

'It's a shame to stay in on a Saturday night. I'm off to the jigging myself.'

'Oh?'

Ginge opened his mouth to speak further, then shut it again when Joe arrived back at the table.

'You seem to have an admirer there,' Joe commented later when Ginge had left them.

That puzzled her. 'Who do you mean?'

'Old Ginge, of course. I'd say he's quite stricken.'

'Nonsense!' she protested.

'Didn't you see the way he was looking at you? That silly expression plastered all over his face. It was dead obvious.'

It hadn't been to her. 'Well, if that's the case he can forget it. I don't fancy him in the least.'

'Oh, come on, Cordelia, he's not a bad lad. He can be very good company.'

'I'm not interested in good company, Joe. And I'm certainly not interested in Ginge. Nor am I interested in any man at the moment. They're simply not on the agenda.'

He studied her, as puzzled now as she herself had been earlier. 'Why not?'

'Because that's the way it is.'

'Are you saying you don't like men?'

'Of course I like them. It's just that at the moment there's no one special.' For some reason she suddenly found herself blushing, and glanced away.

'I'll have a word in Ginge's shell-like,' Joe said eventually. 'Tell him he's not on.'

'You do that.'

She drained her glass, then produced a ten bob note. 'The next one's on me, and I insist. Will you go up to the bar and get them?'

'You don't have to buy a round, Cordelia. You know that.'

She pushed the note in his direction. 'When you're ready.'

Why had she reacted so aggressively? she wondered.

She hadn't a clue.

Chapter 8

Cordelia worried a nail. This was the second time Joe hadn't turned up. She'd wait another ten minutes, then go and find Ginge. With a bit of luck he'd be able to lend her money for a float, just as he'd done before. Meanwhile, she'd start setting up.

Joe appeared just before noon. 'Sorry about that,' he apologised. 'I've just come from the hospital.'

'Something wrong with Hannah?' Cordelia queried, her voice filled with concern for the baby.

'No, it's Ellie. A female problem. She was bleeding like a stuck pig.'

'Oh, dear!' Cordelia was appalled. 'Is it serious?'

'Serious enough for her to go back into hospital. She was crying her eyes out when I left her.'

'Poor Ellie,' Cordelia sympathised.

'The doctor said he'd know more when I visit this evening. In the meantime she's undergoing a series of tests.'

Cordelia had a sudden thought. 'What about Hannah? Who's looking after her?'

'Margy – Ellie's sister. She's agreed to stay at our house and take care of the bairn until Ellie gets home again. She can do that, you see, because her husband's in the merchant navy and often away for months at a time. He's deep sea at the moment, and won't be returning for a while yet.'

'Does she have children?'

'Margy? No. She's never been blessed. It's a pity, because she'd be a smashing mum. Simply loves kids. Hannah will be well taken care of.' Joe shook his head. 'Christ, I hope nothing happens to Ellie. I just don't know what I'd do if it did.'

'I'm sure everything will be all right,' Cordelia murmured.

'I can only hope and pray.' He shook his head again. 'She lost a lot of blood, Cordelia. Frightened the life out of me.'

'Well, she's in the best place for whatever's wrong with her. The doctors will sort her out. In the meanwhile, why don't you nip over the road and have a drink? That'll make you feel better.'

'No, I won't. But I could murder a cup of tea and a bacon sannie. I haven't had any breakfast.'

'I'll go and get them for you.'

It was a sign of how distraught he was that he failed to give her money as he usually did.

Lexa glanced at Pam, then back at the photograph Lily was proudly showing them. Davey wasn't at all bad-looking. Not handsome, but not bad-looking at all. She could only wonder what on earth he saw in the plain, heavy-jawed Lily.

'He's got a wonderful sense of humour,' Lily declared.

Pam bit her tongue, desperately wanting to say 'He must have, getting engaged to you'.

'He makes me laugh all the time,' Lily went on. 'We get on like a house on fire.'

Lexa wouldn't have said Lily also had a wonderful sense of humour. If anything, she was dour: more likely to scowl than laugh. There again, Lexa only saw her at work. Perhaps she was different outside.

'Excuse me,' Mrs Sanderson muttered. Leaving them, she crossed to her desk, where she produced a hanky from a drawer and proceeded to mop her forehead. 'Is it me or is it particularly hot in here?'

'I don't think it's particularly hot,' Pam replied. It wasn't even stuffy, as it often could be.

'Me neither,' Lexa added.

'So that's my Davey,' Lily said, regaining Pam and Lexa's attention.

'You've done well there. Good luck to you.' Pam smiled.

'Very well,' Lexa agreed. Lily had indeed.

Later, Lexa made a point of going over to the chief clerk's desk. 'Are you all right, Mrs Sanderson?' she asked anxiously. The older woman had been mopping her face and forehead all through the morning.

'I'm feeling somewhat light-headed,' Mrs Sanderson replied in a cracked voice. 'And nauseous.'

'Is there anything I can do?'

'A couple of aspirins might help.'

'I have some here.' Lily reached for her bag. She'd never confided it to the others, considering it none of their business, but she suffered from severe period pains and always kept aspirin to hand to help alleviate them.

'I'll get a glass of water,' Lexa volunteered.

'Thank you, girls,' Mrs Sanderson said, taking two of the tablets. 'I'm sure I'll be better soon.'

But a few hours later Mrs Sanderson laid down her pen. 'It's no use, I can't go on,' she declared. 'I feel absolutely awful and will have to go home.'

'Will you be able to manage the journey?' Pam queried, thinking the older woman looked dreadful.

'I'll take a taxi. Will one of you be so kind as to go out into the street and hail one?'

'I'll do it,' Lexa said.

She was fortunate, being able to flag a taxi down within a few minutes. Asking the driver to wait, she went back to the office where she found Mrs Sanderson already wearing her coat and hat. The three girls assisted the ailing woman out to the cab.

'Hello, Mum. Where are you?' Lexa called out when she got home from work that evening.

'In my bedroom.'

'What are you doing there?'

'Come on in.'

Lexa could tell from her mother's voice that something was wrong. Going into what had once been her bedroom, she found Alice in bed with sweat streaming down her face.

'I've come down with the flu,' Alice croaked. 'The doctor's already been and diagnosed it.'

Lexa immediately thought of Mrs Sanderson and wondered if that was what she had. 'You were fine this morning,' was all she could think of to say.

'Not really. I just didn't let on, that's all. When it started to get bad I chapped Peggy McAllister's door and she fetched the doctor. He's returning tomorrow to see how I'm doing.'

Lexa stared at her mother in concern. Alice really wasn't looking very well at all.

She sighed. 'One minute I'm hot, the next I'm shivering cold.'

'Is there anything I can do, Mum?'

'I don't think so.'

'Are you hungry?'

Alice gave her daughter a wan smile. 'Food's the last thing on my mind. What you can do is fill up that glass there. I've to drink lots of water.'

Lexa was filling the glass at the kitchen tap when Cordelia came in. Quickly she explained the situation. Then both girls sat on the edge of Alice's bed, their expressions worried.

'I'm sorry about this,' Alice apologised. 'I should have your tea waiting for you like always.'

'Don't be daft, Mum,' Cordelia scolded. 'We're quite capable of making our own tea.'

'Peggy, bless her, did a wee bit shopping for me. There are sausages and I thought you could make mashed potatoes and turnip. You know, mash the mixed tats and turnip with butter and black pepper.'

Cordelia turned to Lexa. 'One of us is going to have to stay off work until Mum's better.'

'No,' Alice protested. 'That's all taken care of. Peggy will be seeing to me, so you don't have to bother. She's a good neighbour, right enough.'

'Are you sure?' Lexa asked anxiously.

'Oh, aye, I'll be fine. Peggy has my key and will come in every hour or so during the day.' She started shivering quite violently. 'Here I go again,' she muttered.

'Would you like an extra blanket?' Cordelia asked.

'No. I'll be boiling in a few minutes. That's how it's been going for hours now.'

Lexa and Cordelia couldn't have sympathised more, but at the same time they were desperately hoping they didn't catch it. It would be terrible if all three of them were laid up.

'There is one thing,' Alice said hesitantly.

'What's that, Mum?' Cordelia queried.

'I'd love a hot toddy. Do you think that's possible? I just don't want you thinking I'm going back on the bottle or anything.'

Despite herself, Lexa smiled. 'I'll do that for you right away.'

'Thanks, darling. And you might put some sugar in it if you don't mind.'

'Anything else?' Cordelia asked.

'No. Just the toddy.'

Lexa and Cordelia came to their feet. 'Just shout if you want us,' Lexa said.

'I will.'

'How's Ellie?' Cordelia asked the following morning when she arrived at the market.

'She had the hysterectomy yesterday, but apparently there were complications so she'll be staying in even longer than we thought.'

'Oh, Joe,' Cordelia whispered. This was terrible news.

'I only spoke to her briefly, as that was all the time allowed me. She's in an awful state knowing we can't have any more children.'

'That's understandable.'

'She'd always wanted two or three. Now that'll never happen.'

'At least you have wee Hannah. It would have been a real tragedy for Ellie if that hadn't been the case.'

'Aye,' Joe agreed sadly. 'You're right there.'

'Did they tell you what sort of complications?'

'The doctor did explain, but to be honest I couldn't make head or tail of what he was saying. It was all double Dutch to me.'

'We've had the doctor in as well,' Cordelia told him. 'Mum's come down with flu.'

'I'm sorry to hear that.' It was Joe's turn to be sympathetic. 'I've heard there's quite a lot of it going around.'

'Really?'

'So I was told the other day. Nasty thing, flu. I had it once myself and hardly got out of bed for three weeks. Laid me right low, it did. I had no strength at all. Weak as a kitten.'

Their conversation was terminated by the arrival of the daily delivery.

Lexa glanced at the clock, and frowned. It was most unlike Lily to be late for the office. In fact, Lexa couldn't remember a single occasion when she had been.

'Are you thinking what I'm thinking?' Pam asked.

Lexa nodded. 'The flu.'

Pam sat back and sighed. 'According to the newspaper this morning it's turning into an epidemic. People are dropping like flies.'

Lexa's expression became grim as she wondered if she was going to be next. She certainly felt all right: no raised temperature or headache. She hoped she was going to be fine.

'Do you mind if I nip into the bog for a fly fag?' Pam asked.

'Be my guest.'

'Thanks.' Pam smiled. 'That's one good thing about old pruneface being off – I can have a fag whenever I fancy.'

Later that day word arrived at *Vins* confirming that Lily had indeed come down with flu and would be staying at home until she was well again.

Cordelia came awake with her body still shuddering, and a low moan on her lips. Sitting up, she ran a hand over her forehead.

What a dream she'd had. She recalled it now with a combination of pleasure and horror. She'd been in bed with Joe, the pair of them stark naked, making love. The act had seemed so real to her that she'd actually . . . Her eyes widened at the memory. 'Dear God!' she muttered. A warm glow was radiating throughout her entire body.

And then it hit her: something her conscious mind either hadn't realised, or had been denying, all this time. She was in love with Joe Given.

She couldn't be, she thought. Mustn't be. Joe was a happily married man with a new wee baby.

But married or not, she was in love with him. And the more she thought about it the more clearly it dawned on her how deep that love went.

'Joe,' she whispered. 'Dear Joe.'

She took a deep breath, then another. Lying back again, she stared up at the ceiling, a thousand things flitting through her mind. Then she smiled at the memory of what had wakened her. Surely the genuine article couldn't be even better? There again, perhaps it might be.

But only with Joe.

The office door opened and William McLeod came in. 'I'm told you're the only one left standing.' He smiled at Lexa. 'Or sitting, to be precise.'

'That's right, sir.' Pam had succumbed to flu several days previously.

'Well, I've been sent along to help out.'

That surprised her. 'What about your regular job?'

'Put on hold for a little while. Well, not quite. I'll be doing that Saturdays and Sundays until things return to a semblance of normality.' He smiled again. 'So, it's no rest for the wicked, eh?'

Such a charming smile, she thought. 'I'm sure you're not that, sir. 'You don't strike me as being wicked in the least.'

He laughed. 'Only a joke, Miss Stewart. Only a joke.' He crossed to Mrs Sanderson's desk, and sat down. Picking up an account he began studying it.

'I don't want to sound cheeky, sir,' Lexa said hesitantly, 'but do you know what you're doing?'

'Oh, yes, Miss Stewart. I worked in this office for a

spell during my training. Dad wanted me to be familiar with every aspect of the company.'

Lexa blushed. 'Sorry for asking, sir.'

'No, you did the right thing.'

Lexa, terribly aware of his presence, got on with her work until it was time for the morning break, when she put down her pen. 'We usually have a cup of tea about now,' she said. 'Would you care for one, sir?'

'Oh, yes. Milk and two sugars, please.'

Lexa rose from behind her desk.

'And one of those lovely chocolate biscuits that I know you ladies have. At least you used to in my day.'

Lexa stared into his twinkling eyes, then, embarrassed, glanced away. 'I'll get one for you, sir.'

'Good-oh.'

Lexa hurried off to make the tea and find the biscuits.

Cordelia had a sudden thought which appalled her. What if Ellie didn't come out of hospital? What if she died?

That would leave Joe a widower, and free. A man needing another wife, someone to look after the baby. And help bring Hannah up.

Ellie was extremely ill, after all. Who knew what the outcome might be? Her complications, so far anyway, were not responding to treatment. If she did die Joe would of course be devastated, and rightly so. But time would surely heal his pain and he'd start looking round. That would be Cordelia's opportunity. They got on extremely well, no doubt about that. She already loved him with all her heart. So could she make him fall for her?

She shook her head. She musn't think like this. It was

wicked, pure and simple. Except she wasn't wishing Ellie dead, only contemplating the chance which would present itself should Ellie die.

'Are you constipated?'

Cordelia snapped out of her reverie and focused on her sister. 'No. Why do you ask?'

'Your face is all screwed up as if you're in pain. I just wondered, that's all.'

'I'm merely thinking.' Well, that was true enough.

'About what?'

'None of your business.'

'There's no need to be so snappy about it,' Lexa retorted.

Cordelia was about to reply when Alice called out. 'I'll go,' she said.

'Do that.'

Cordelia paused for a moment. 'Sorry, sis. I didn't mean to be sharp.'

Lexa's expression immediately softened. 'That's all right. No offence taken.' She wondered what Cordelia had been thinking about to make her face so contorted, but a few moments later she'd forgotten all about the incident.

'Do you think you could possibly work late tomorrow night?' William asked Lexa. 'We're absolutely snowed under, as you're well aware. Two of us trying to do the work of four.'

Lexa thought quickly. 'I don't see why not.'

'It'll mean extra pay, of course.' He smiled.

Well, she hadn't intended to do it for nothing. 'Thank you, sir.'

'And I'll run you home in my car. That should make things easier.'

'It certainly would.'

'In fact, perhaps you could do a few late nights this week. I certainly shall.'

'Anything to help, sir,' she replied, thinking that the extra cash would come in handy.

He nodded his appreciation. 'Now tell me, how's your mother doing? Any improvement?'

'When I got home last night she was sitting in the kitchen drinking tea, and nattering away nineteen to the dozen with a neighbour. So she's well on the mend.'

'Good.'

'Knowing Mum she'll be fully back on her feet within a few days. She's got the constitution of a horse.'

William laughed. 'Has she indeed!'

'Oh, aye. Nothing keeps her down for long. Though I have to admit this flu hit her hard.'

'Which makes me wonder how Mrs Sanderson and the others are doing. And when they'll be back.'

'Still no word, sir?'

He shook his head. 'Nothing.'

'I hope they're all right.'

'Oh, I'm sure they are,' he replied breezily. 'Ill, of course, but hopefully recovering like your mother.'

Lexa gazed at the pile of papers stacked on her desk, and prayed the others would return soon.

Working late with William, the two of them the only ones in the building? She rather liked the idea of that. And a lift home would certainly be a treat.

Chapter 9

William studied the front page of that morning's newspaper, his brow furrowed in thought. The headline news was that Herr Hitler, the German Chancellor, had marched into Austria and annexed it. Surely this wasn't a good thing? William mused. If Austria today, who tomorrow? And where would it all end?

He laid his newspaper aside and thought of Lexa, who'd gone out for a lunchtime walk in the spring sunshine. He found her very attractive, which was strange because he was normally attracted to tall, willowy, cool blondes, whereas Lexa had raven-black hair, green eyes, and a full bust. Her legs were shapely, though, and he wondered how tall she was. About five feet four, he'd guess, which wasn't tall at all.

He thought of Helen, his current girlfriend. She was tall, willowy, cool and blonde. And rapidly becoming a pain in the backside. She'd proved to be terribly good in bed, eager to comply with his every suggestion and whim. But outside the bedroom she was troublesome, forever demanding, and wilful. William sighed. Helen had been fun, no doubt about that, but perhaps it was time to move on.

'What's your Christian name?' William asked Lexa that night as he was driving her home.

'Lexa. It's short for Alexandra.'

He glanced at her in surprise, then brought his attention back to the road. 'I've never known a Lexa before. It's very unusual.' He thought for a few moments, then declared, 'I like it. I like it a lot.'

'Thank you, sir.'

'Let's have less of the sir bit.' He smiled. 'At least outside the building. Far too formal. From now on I shall call you Lexa, and you call me William. How does that sound?'

'If you wish . . . William.'

He laughed at her hesitancy. 'Say it again. Get used to it.'

'William,' she repeated.

'That's right, Lexa.' He changed gear. 'Isn't that far nicer?'

She supposed it was. Though would take a little getting used to.

'Well?' he demanded.

'Far nicer, William.' She smiled back at him.

'But only outside the building, mind. My father's very old-fashioned in certain ways. Especially concerning business. At least our business. He'd have a canary on the spot if he heard a member of staff call me by my Christian name at work. I'd get a proper ticking off, and a lecture to boot.'

William? Lexa thought. So they were on first name terms now. Even if only in certain circumstances. That was one thing she wouldn't be confiding to Pam, who no doubt would read all sorts of wrong things into it.

'Penny for them?' Cordelia asked.

Joe had been staring vaguely ahead, clearly lost in thought. He shook his head. 'Nothing.'

'Worrying about Ellie?' His wife still hadn't made any improvement and was causing her doctors grave concern.

'I suppose so,' he lied. For that wasn't what he'd been thinking about at all.

'Listen, why don't you nip over to the Hielan Laddie and have a couple of pints to cheer yourself up a little? I can manage fine here by myself.'

He immediately brightened. 'Are you sure?'

'Of course I'm sure, daftie. On you go.'

To her surprise he pecked her on the cheek. 'You're an angel. An absolute angel.'

She watched him walk away, thinking again what a wonderful sexy bottom he had.

'Mrs Sanderson!' Lexa exclaimed in delight as the older woman entered the office.

'Aye, it's me right enough.'

William immediately got up off his chair, which was Mrs Sanderson's place. 'How are you?'

'A lot better, thanks. Certainly fit enough to return to work.'

Lexa thought the head clerk still looked pale, and noted the heavy bags under the eyes in the slightly haggard face.

'What are you doing here, Mr McLeod?' Mrs Sanderson asked.

'I've been helping out as your office was reduced to Miss Stewart there. We couldn't expect her to cope all on her own.'

Mrs Sanderson crossed to her desk and sat down. Taking a deep breath, she stared at the piles of papers in front of her. 'I see there's a lot of catching up to do.'

'Miss Stewart and I have done our best,' William declared. 'We've been working late to try to come to grips with it all.'

Mrs Sanderson nodded that she understood. 'So what now? Are you staying on, or leaving us to it?'

'I'll have to ask my father about that. It's his decision.'

'I take it then he hasn't had flu?'

'No, I'm happy to say, and I also escaped. As, obviously, did Miss Stewart. So, if you'll excuse me, I'll go and have a word with him.'

To Lexa's dismay William returned later to inform them he was to go back to his old job straight away. She smiled wryly as the door closed behind him.

'Ellie's taken a turn for the better,' a jubilant Joe announced to Cordelia. 'The difference in her between last night and the night before was quite remarkable.'

Cordelia's heart sank. 'That's wonderful.' She tried to sound enthusiastic.

'It most certainly is.' Joe made a fist and jabbed the air. 'Thank God!'

Cordelia watched that with mixed feelings.

'They've told me I can take wee Hannah in a couple

of nights from now,' Joe went on. 'That'll cheer Ellie up no end.'

'How long . . . before you think she'll be allowed home?'

He shook his head. 'The doctors wouldn't commit themselves when I asked them. But I'm hoping fairly soon. And when she does get home there'll still be a period of convalescence for her to get through. Which won't cause any problems as she'll have her mother and Margy to help.' He took out a cigarette and lit up, his eyes sparkling with delight. 'I was beginning to get really worried, you know,' he confessed. 'Really worried. But now everything's going to be hunky dory again.'

Cordelia turned away so he couldn't see her expression.

William stared at the long, lean naked body lying beside him. How could a female be so passionate, yet passionless at the same time? He couldn't understand it at all. It was a mystery as far as he was concerned.

They were in Helen's house. Her parents were away for the weekend, as they often were, at their place in the country. Their absence made it easy for William and Helen to go to bed together, which might otherwise have been difficult.

Helen stared back at him, and smiled. For some reason she always reminded William of a large, blonde cat. 'What are you thinking?' she asked.

'Nothing.'

'I don't believe you.'

'No?'

'No.'

'All right, I was thinking what an incredible shag you are.'

Helen laughed, a deep throaty sound. 'Flattery will get you everywhere.'

'I thought it already had,' he teased in return.

Reaching out she stroked his flank, then ran her long, painted nails along his skin. 'You're not so bad yourself. But then I've told you that before.'

'Many times.'

She regarded him quizzically. 'You really are quite conceited, aren't you?'

'Am I?'

'Oh, yes,' she breathed. 'There are occasions when it simply oozes out of you.'

'And you're not?'

'Women can get away with it, whereas it doesn't sit well on a man.'

'I stand reprimanded.'

'At the moment you're not standing at all,' she teased.

That made him smile. 'True.'

'But perhaps it'll do so again shortly?'

'Perhaps.' He knew it to be his imagination, but to him it seemed she was purring.

'In the meantime, be a good chappie and get me another drink. I'm absolutely parched.'

'When did your last slave die? You're quite capable of getting it yourself.'

'That's not very gentlemanly,' she protested.

'I suppose it isn't. On the other hand, would you deny me the pleasure of watching you walk around in the nude?'

She laughed again, that same deep throaty sound. 'I'll take that as a compliment.'

'It was intended to be.' He was damned if he was going to let her boss him around, which she was forever trying to do. 'And you can give me a top-up while you're at it.'

For a few moments she considered insisting he fetch the drinks, then decided not to. Languorously she slid off the bed. 'By the way, I shan't be seeing you for a few months,' she announced.

William frowned. 'Why's that?'

'Mummy's bronchitis has been playing her up dreadfully, so she's off to Cannes and wants me to go with her for company. I think it's a jolly good idea. Quite spiffing, really. I may love Scotland but its climate does leave a lot to be desired.'

'Cannes?' William mused. 'I'm jealous.'

'Have you ever been there?'

'Once. On wine business. It's very nice.'

Helen turned from pouring drinks to face him. 'You don't mind, darling, do you?'

He didn't mind at all. In fact it would simplify matters. He would give it a while and then send a letter saying he was breaking it off between them. Easier than having to do it face to face. 'Of course not,' he replied.

'I just thought you might be somewhat upset.'

'Naturally I'll miss you.' He smiled. It wasn't entirely a lie. There were certain aspects of her he would miss. But only certain ones.

She did have a beautiful body, he reflected, and knew only too well how to use it. He'd often wondered about that, but had always been too polite to enquire about her previous history. Nor had she ever volunteered information on the subject.

Helen returned to the bed and handed him his top-up, then sat down beside him. 'Can I bring you back a present?'

He hesitated before replying. 'Let me think about that,' he prevaricated. There wouldn't be any present, of course.

Helen extracted a cigarette from a packet on the bedside table, and passed him a gold lighter. Her eyes bored into his as he flicked it alight.

'Thank you,' she said. Taking the lighter from him, she replaced it on the bedside table. 'Can you give me a massage, darling, when I've finished this cigarette? You do it ever so well. Such strong, masculine hands, which know exactly what they're doing.'

William inwardly groaned. He hated giving her a massage, finding the procedure incredibly boring. The first few times he'd done it for her at her request he had quite enjoyed it, but now he found it tedious in the extreme.

'Of course. It'll be my pleasure.'

'And then afterwards . . .' She trailed off and gave a shrug. 'Who knows? If you feel up to it, that is.'

'I'll try to manage,' he answered drily.

'You usually do.'

He took a sip of his drink, and reflected again on her ability to be passionate and passionless at the same time. It was to do with emotion, he suddenly realised. She might get sexually aroused, but that was somehow disconnected from any other feelings, which she successfully kept apart.

In other words, she might be hot in bed, but she was otherwise cold. Beautiful, but manipulating. Oh yes, most certainly that. She would definitely have to go. Such a woman wasn't for him.

Lexa glanced up from her desk as a grim-faced William came into their office and stopped just inside the door.

'Can I help you, Mr McLeod?' Mrs Sanderson politely enquired.

Lexa instinctively knew something was wrong. William's expression told her so. It wasn't simply grim, it was darkly grim.

He cleared his throat. 'I'm afraid I have some rather sad news. We've just learned that Miss Parker passed away yesterday.'

It took a moment for the penny to drop. Miss Parker was Lily. Lexa stared at William in disbelief.

'Bloody hell!' Pam muttered. Normally that would have earned her a severe reprimand from Mrs Sanderson, but not on this occasion.

Mrs Sanderson was blinking at William. 'Dead?' she stuttered at last.

'That's correct. From flu. It can happen, you know.'

Mrs Sanderson knew only too well. She had been horribly aware of the fact when she'd been ill.

'But she was only recently engaged,' Pam said rather stupidly. As if that made any difference.

'So I understand,' William acknowledged.

Lexa was in shock. They all were. Lily dead! It didn't seem possible.

'She was a good worker,' Mrs Sanderson said in a hollow voice. 'I'll say that for her. She'll be missed in here.'

Not so much as by her fiancé, Lexa thought. Poor man. What a state he must be in, not to mention her parents. She didn't know how old Lily had been, but certainly too young to die. God bless her.

'I still can't quite take it in,' Pam declared later in the ladies' room where she was indulging in her usual cigarette.

Lexa shook her head. 'Me neither.'

'And there were times when we were so rotten about her. Remember how we laughed at her getting engaged? Amazed that anyone so plain could land a man?'

'Don't remind me.'

'Now she's gone.'

Lexa felt as if she might cry. 'I wonder how her Davey's taking it?'

'Badly, I should imagine.'

Lexa nodded her agreement. 'I can just picture her, that big jaw jutting out like it did. And now...' She trailed off as tears seeped into her eyes. Going into the single cubicle she tore off a piece of toilet paper and dabbed the tears away.

'That could have been me,' Pam stated, tight-voiced. 'Or Mrs Sanderson.'

Or her mother, Lexa thought. How terrible that would have been. To have lost both her father and mother within such a relatively short space of time. Fortunately, it hadn't happened.

Pam stubbed out the remains of her cigarette and immediately lit another. She was badly shaken.

Lexa gazed at her tea, which remained undrunk. She had simply not been able to face it. Picking up her cup, she threw the contents down the sink. 'I feel a bit sick,' she said quietly.

'Me too. Sick and . . . oh, I don't know. My stomach's churning.'

Lexa ran some cold water and splashed it over her face, which made her feel a little better. 'We'd best be getting back,' she declared, drying her hands on the towel provided.

'No rush,' Pam replied. 'Old pruneface won't be telling anyone off today.'

'No,' Lexa agreed. She didn't suppose Mrs Sanderson would.

'Can you hold the fort while I nip over for a couple of pints?' Joe asked.

Cordelia stared at him, thinking how distracted he'd been all morning, for ever gazing off into space when he should have been busy. 'Is everything still all right with Ellie? I mean, she hasn't had a relapse or anything?'

'No, she's fine. Getting better by the day. If the improvement continues I should have her home by the end of the week.'

So what was bothering him? Cordelia wondered. She had no idea, and he wasn't being forthcoming. 'On you go, Joe. Take as long as you like.'

He beamed at her. 'You're a real pal. One of the best things I ever did was hiring you.'

Her heart leaped to hear that. Glancing up the street she saw that the Hielan Laddie's doors had just opened.

To her surprise, Joe was gone several hours. She could only wonder again what was troubling him. She knew him well enough to know that something certainly was.

'Miss Parker's funeral is on Thursday and my father has asked me to attend to represent the firm,' William announced. 'He's also asked me to take along one of Miss Parker's colleagues from this office. Is there a volunteer?'

Mrs Sanderson shook her head. 'I know I should go, but I would prefer not to, if you don't mind, Mr McLeod.'

'Fully understandable.'

Pam bit her lip, undecided. Lexa could see that her friend didn't want to attend either, so she raised a hand. 'I'll go with you, Mr McLeod.'

'Are you certain, Miss Stewart?'

'I'm certain, sir.'

For a brief moment a strange expression manifested itself on his face, and then was gone. 'I'll collect you from here at eleven o'clock on Thursday,' he declared.

'I'll be ready.'

'Good.'

Mrs Sanderson took a deep breath. 'I think we'll have our tea now, Miss Stewart.'

Lexa rose and went to make it, well aware that it was half an hour before the normal time.

Chapter 10

William glanced sideways at Lexa as his car purred away from the funeral. She was clearly badly shaken, and in distress. 'Wasn't very pleasant, was it?' he said softly.

Lexa shook her head. 'No.'

'Still, I think it went as well as these things can.'

Now it was her turn to glance at him. 'Have you been to many funerals?'

'A few. The last was an elderly aunt. That wasn't quite so bad as she was in her nineties and had led a full life. Very full, actually.'

'Unlike poor Lily.'

'Unlike poor Lily,' he agreed.

'It was her fiancé Davey who got to me. He was near collapse from the look of him, shaking all over and crying.'

'Her father wasn't too clever either. But then what else would you expect when he'd just lost his only child?'

Lexa was remembering Jimmy's funeral, and how awful that had been, recalling it all as if it had been only yesterday.

'I have a suggestion to make,' William said.

'Yes?'

'I don't know about you, but I could use a stiff drink. There's an hotel we pass, the Victoria, which *Vins* supplies. How about going there?'

'Sounds good.'

He smiled. 'Excellent.'

Lexa knew the Victoria Hotel, but had never been inside. The bar area turned out to be very old-fashioned, with dark heavy furniture and faded wallpaper.

'I'm having a large gin and tonic,' William declared when Lexa was seated at a table. 'What about you?'

Lexa had tried gin several times in the past, and liked it. 'Same for me, please,' she replied.

'Coming up in a mo.'

Lexa was more upset than she'd thought she'd be. Although she hadn't been particularly pally with Lily, as she was with Pam, they'd still spent every working day in the same office together. In her mind's eye she could see Lily beavering away at her desk. A good worker, Mrs Sanderson had called her, and so she had been. She'd also been a nice human being.

'There we are.' William placed a drink in front of Lexa.

'Thank you.'

He sat, and had a sip of his. 'I shall take you home after this. You're to have the rest of the day off.'

That took her by surprise as he hadn't mentioned it before. 'I'm quite capable of going back to the office, William. Honestly.'

He gave her a soft smile. 'Perhaps. But I've decreed otherwise. Home you'll go.'

'And you?'

'I've a few calls to make later this afternoon. But I also shall be having an early day. I think we both deserve it.'

How kind, she thought. The more she got to know William McLeod the better she liked him.

'There was an epidemic of flu after the Great War, you know. Millions of people lost their lives on account of it. My father told me it was a terrible time.'

'I have read about that.' Lexa nodded.

'For a few days we thought Mummy was coming down with it this time round,' William went on. 'But fortunately it turned out to be nothing more than a heavy cold. We were much relieved, I can tell you.'

'That was lucky.' How odd it sounded, Lexa reflected, to hear a man of William's age using the word Mummy. It sounded ever so childish coming from him. She had a sip of her gin, which instantly warmed her insides, and relieved some of the strain she was feeling. Another sip relaxed her even more. 'Just what the doctor ordered,' she said, attempting a smile.

William stared at Lexa, again thinking how attractive she was. He couldn't imagine anyone looking more different from Helen, whom he still hadn't written to. He'd do it the following week, he promised himself.

There was a calmness about Lexa which was in striking contrast to the highly strung Helen. A virgin? Probably. Especially as she was from a working-class background. Girls like her, well aware of the shame an out-of-wedlock pregnancy would bring themselves and their families, invariably held on to their virginity till their wedding night.

They stayed chatting at the Victoria longer than either had expected, each totally at ease in the other's company. Lexa thanked him when he eventually dropped her off outside her close. His reply was a dazzling smile, and a thank you of his own for accompanying him to the funeral, before he finally drove away.

She watched his car until it disappeared before turning and going inside.

'What are you doing home so early?' Alice exclaimed.

Lexa explained about being given the rest of the day off.

'That's decent of him,' Alice acknowledged. 'I was just about to put the kettle on. Do you fancy a cup of tea?'

'Lovely, Mum. I'll just get changed first.'

'You do that. And after the tea I've washing to hang out in the back court.'

'I'll help you with that if you like.'

'You're a darling.'

They had a large copper in the kitchen which was used to boil whatever washing they had. Afterwards it was carried down to the so-called back court, a communal area at the rear of the tenement, and hung out to dry on a clothes line supported by a pole with a notch at the end which ensured that the heavily laden line didn't sag, or collapse to the ground.

'I've a question to ask you,' Alice said when Lexa joined her for the promised tea.

'What's that?'

'I'm worried about Cordelia.'

Lexa frowned. 'Why?'

Alice shook her head. 'I don't know, but she just hasn't been herself of late. Haven't you noticed?'

Now Lexa thought about it Cordelia had been acting strangely. Moody, irascible, snappy even. 'Yes, I have,' she admitted. 'Though I didn't think too much of it.'

'Any idea of the reason?'

Lexa thought about that, and came up blank. 'None at all. She certainly hasn't said anything.'

'Hm,' Alice mused.

'Have you asked her?'

'Not yet. Not outright anyway. I have made a few skirting enquiries, with no response on her part. There again, I'm her mother. It may well be something she doesn't want to discuss with me. On the other hand, she might with you, being a sister and close in age.'

Lexa could understand that. 'Do you want me to have a word?'

'If you would, dear. I'd be ever so grateful. You of course would tell me the outcome.'

If she could, Lexa thought. 'I'll wait and choose my moment,' she said. 'I'm more likely to get some answers that way.'

Alice nodded her agreement. 'She's worrying me, that's all.'

'I understand, Mum. Leave it to me.'

Henry McLeod was a tall, slim man with thinning grey hair and a neat grey moustache. When he walked a discernible stoop was evident, acquired from years of desk work.

'Brandy, William?'

'Please, Father.' William had been summoned to the study after dinner.

Henry poured two generous measures into balloon glasses, and handed one to his son. 'I've got a job for you,' he said.

'Oh?'

Henry sat facing William, cradling his glass between his hands. 'I believe war is becoming inevitable,' he stated slowly. 'What's your opinion?'

William shrugged. 'I don't think the situation on the Continent is looking all that rosy. The Germans seem hell bent on expansion.'

Henry nodded his agreement. 'They've never forgiven us for winning the last lot, you know. They might have been beaten, but many of them could never bring themselves to acknowledge the fact. Of course, the worst thing we did was to impose such harsh conditions at Versailles. That was a mistake, and one to be set down to the French who insisted on the total humiliation of their former enemy. Which brings me to what I want to talk to you about tonight.'

'This job you've got for me, Father?'

'Exactly.' Henry paused, had a sip of brandy, then said, 'Let us say war was to break out, and France was to fall. What then?'

William blinked at his father. 'Is the latter likely?'

'The German war machine, from what I understand, is huge and excellently equipped. The French army is not nearly so well equipped, nor as large. So who knows what might happen should war be declared? My idea, at present, is to be prepared for any contingency.'

William was beginning to see what his father was driving at. 'If France did fall then our supply of wine would be cut off,' he said slowly.

'And once we got through our current stock that would be the end of us. No more *Vins*.'

'So what do you propose, Father?'

'Investment, William, to cover all possibilities and ensure we don't get caught short. Over the next few weeks I shall find further storage premises which I intend filling to capacity. Then, no matter what happens, we, as a business, shall continue to survive.'

'What if war doesn't happen and France doesn't fall?'

'It wouldn't really matter. We'd sell everything eventually, so we wouldn't lose out.'

William could see that, and thought his father's plan a most prudent one. As they would say in the vernacular, his father was simply covering the company's arse. 'And how do I fit into all this?'

'I want you to travel to Paris and speak to our suppliers there. I shall set out our orders for you before you leave.'

William nodded that he understood.

'Naturally the orders will be far greater than normal, and the suppliers, for whatever reasons, might baulk at filling them – or be reluctant to do so. You know what the Frogs are like: everything is a problem, usually of their own making and natural intransigence. They're also obsessed with bureaucracy to the point of lunacy. Your job will be to place the orders and facilitate matters.'

'I see.'

'I also wish you to travel to the south of the country. Some areas there grow excellent wines which aren't yet commercially exploited, but mainly only drunk regionally. There you will speak to certain *vignerons*, whose names I will give you, and arrange for quantities of their best products to be bought and shipped back here. Incidentally, they should be a great deal cheaper than those we purchase in Paris, where a third party is involved.'

William allowed a wide smile to light up his face. 'You really have thought this through, haven't you, Pater?'

'Of course.'

'And let me guess. Should it all come to pass as you foresee, when wine starts to run short over here you'll increase your prices to make an even tidier profit?'

'Business is business,' Henry replied with a grin. 'And I am a Scotsman after all. We're renowned for our acumen.'

William took a swallow of brandy, running over the conversation in his mind. 'So when do you want me to leave for France?'

'In a couple of weeks. There are a few preparations still to be made. I'll have Brenda my secretary take care of your travel arrangements.'

William had a thought. 'Who'll do my deliveries while I'm away?'

'Don't you worry about that,' Henry assured him. 'I'll ensure they take place.'

Paris? William reflected. He'd been there before, and enjoyed the experience. Returning would be a pleasure. As for the south of the country, he had no doubt he'd enjoy that as well.

Henry finished his brandy. 'Another?'

William saw off what remained of his drink. 'Please.'

It was a thoughtful William who went to bed that night.

*   *   *

'Are you all right, sis?'

Alice was out at the Labour Hall with Mrs McAllister, and Cordelia glanced over at Lexa, surprised. 'I'm fine. Why do you ask?'

She had to tread carefully here, Lexa warned herself. Be casual, disarming. 'Oh, I don't know. You seem a bit withdrawn of late.'

Cordelia affected surprise. 'Do I?'

'Well, I've noticed it. To begin with I thought it was your monthlies but it's gone on longer than that.'

Cordelia bit her lip. She was desperate to talk to someone about Joe, but hadn't felt able to. There again, if she couldn't speak to Lexa in confidence, whom could she speak to? Certainly not her mother, who'd be outraged that she'd allowed herself to fall in love with a married man.

'Well?' Lexa prompted softly.

Cordelia shook her head, and didn't reply.

'Have you got yourself into some sort of money problem? If so, I can probably help out.'

'No, it isn't that,' Cordelia replied quickly.

'So there is something?'

Cordelia sighed. 'It's very personal, Lexa. And you'd no doubt disapprove.'

Now she definitely had to know, Lexa thought. 'That's all right, sis,' she said in an offhand manner. 'You don't trust me. I can understand that.'

'But I do trust you!' Cordelia protested.

'Obviously not. That seems clear.'

Cordelia rose to her feet. 'I'm going to have a whisky. Want one?'

Lexa nodded. 'I'll keep you company.'

Well well, Lexa thought when Cordelia had left the room. Whatever it was must be bad for her sister to need a drink.

Cordelia returned a few minutes later, handed Lexa a glass, then slumped back into the chair she'd just vacated.

'Better days!' Lexa toasted.

Amen, Cordelia thought, and drank.

'How's work going?' Lexa enquired.

Cordelia started. 'Why do you ask that?'

Lexa knew from Cordelia's tone that she'd hit a nerve. Was it something to do with work, then? 'Just making conversation, that's all.'

'Are you sure?'

Lexa frowned. It definitely was something to do with work. 'Is Joe giving you a hard time, or something?'

Cordelia appeared to shrivel in her chair. 'Oh, Lexa, I've got myself into an awful situation,' she confessed in a tight voice.

'What sort of awful situation?'

Cordelia gulped down a deep breath, then another. 'If I tell you, promise me you won't let on to another soul. And that includes Mum. Promise me?'

'I promise. Cross my heart.' What on earth was about to come out? she wondered.

Cordelia took a large swallow of whisky, and shuddered. She closed her eyes for several seconds, then opened them again, her expression haunted. 'You were right about it being connected with Joe,' she said.

Anger flared in Lexa. 'Has he been harassing you, is that it?'

Cordelia laughed. 'If only it was. That's something I dream about, night and day.'

Lexa was lost. 'I don't understand. Why should you dream of him harassing you?'

'Not harassment exactly. The truth is . . .' She stopped to have another gulp of whisky, then forced herself to continue. 'The truth is I've fallen in love with him. Head over heels. I'm obsessed with Joe Given.'

'Fallen in love?' an astounded Lexa repeated.

'As much as any woman can love a man.'

'But he's married, Cordelia.'

'Happily married, with a wife who's just given him a lovely wee daughter.'

'Oh, Cordelia.' Lexa sighed. 'Does he know about this?'

'Of course not.'

'He hasn't noticed? Picked anything up?'

Cordelia shook her head. 'I don't believe so. If he has, he hasn't said anything.'

Lexa stared at her sister in consternation. 'So what are you going to do?'

'I have absolutely no idea.'

'The obvious thing is to change jobs. Get away from him. It must be terrible for you being in his company day after day.'

'It is,' Cordelia wailed. 'And I can't change jobs. I've considered doing so, and just can't bring myself to leave him. That would break my heart.'

What a mess, Lexa thought. 'How did it happen, sis? You falling in love with him, I mean.'

'Search me,' Cordelia replied grimly. 'It just did. It took me ages to realise it. And then . . .' she had no intention of telling Lexa about the dream she'd had of her and Joe making love, 'it simply dawned one morning that I'd fallen for Joe.'

Lexa shook her head. 'I don't know what to say.'

'There's nothing you can say. But at least I've got it off my chest. It's been bottled up inside me all this while, bursting to get out.'

With tears of sympathy in her eyes Lexa got up, went to her sister and hugged her tight.

'Promise me you won't tell Mum?'

'I won't,' Lexa assured her. Cordelia was right; their mother would go barmy if she were told such a thing. 'Or anyone else. This is strictly our secret.'

'Thanks, sis.'

They remained silent for a few moments, Lexa continuing to hold Cordelia tight.

'Know something?' Cordelia said eventually.

'What?'

'When Ellie had those complications and was forced to stay on in hospital I actually found myself sort of hoping she wouldn't come out.'

'You mean die?'

'Yes,' Cordelia whispered. 'Joe would then have been free and I would have made him fall for me.'

Lexa was shocked. It was a terrible thing to wish someone dead.

'We'd be married and I'd become Mrs Joe Given,' Cordelia added lamely.

She really had it bad, Lexa thought grimly.

'What do you think of your sister now?'

Lexa considered that. 'I've heard it said that love is a

kind of madness, that people aren't in their right minds when they're in love, which in this case would seem to be about right.'

'Aye, I think whoever said so knew what they were talking about. Imagine me wishing someone dead. I'd have to be insane to do that, but I did.'

Lexa released her sister, and stood gazing pityingly at her. 'How about another whisky? It won't solve the problem, but at least it'll make you feel better.'

'Have you managed to have a word with Cordelia yet?' Alice asked anxiously several days later, when she and Lexa were alone.

'I tried, Mum, but I didn't get anywhere,' Lexa lied.

'Damn!' Alice swore softly. 'Not even a clue as to what's bothering her?'

'Not even a clue, Mum. She kept completely shtum.'

Alice shook her head. 'Then I'll simply have to wait and hope she comes out with it in time.'

Pigs would fly first, Lexa thought, and changed the subject.

Chapter 11

Lexa's heart skipped a beat when she saw William's car heading in her direction. She was waiting for a tram. Would or wouldn't he stop? He did.

'Care for a lift, Lexa? I'm on my way home.'

'Please.'

'Then hop in.' He opened the passenger door, and she got inside, the now familiar smell of highly polished leather assailing her nostrils. 'Wonderful day, isn't it?' He smiled as the car pulled away from the kerb.

'It certainly is.'

'An Indian summer. Nothing like it. It's a pleasure to be out, driving or otherwise, in weather like this.' He took one hand from the steering wheel and loosened his tie, undoing his top button. 'I hope you don't mind?'

'Not in the least.'

He effortlessly changed gear. 'How's the new young lady settling in?'

'You mean Miss Quigley? Absolutely fine.'

'Do you all get on together?'

'Oh, yes. She's fitted in well.'

'Good,' William said, nodding.

Angela Quigley had filled the vacancy left by Lily's death, and was as glamorous as Lily had been plain. A real looker.

'At least you don't have to make the tea any more,' William said lightly, that job having fallen to Angela as the newcomer.

Lexa laughed. 'That's right. Not that it bothered me to do so. In fact I rather enjoyed it, to tell the truth. It gave me the chance to nick the odd chocolate biscuit.'

Now William laughed. 'Did you really do that?'

'On occasion when I couldn't resist the temptation. I simply adore chocolate. But then I think most women do. Certainly all the ones I know.'

William again reflected how relaxing it was to be in Lexa's company. It was something he really enjoyed.

'So what have you been up to today?' Lexa asked. 'I didn't see you round the building.'

'I've been out making deliveries and taking orders. Mainly in Glasgow, but I also had to do a run to Largs where we supply several large hotels.'

Lexa sighed. 'I do envy you, William.'

'And why's that?'

'Oh, your travelling round and about. Getting places. Seeing things and meeting people. And all the while I'm stuck in a stuffy office dealing with boring accounts, invoices and the like. Not that I don't enjoy my work, I do. And I'm certainly grateful for the job. But you take my point?'

He glanced sideways at her, a thought forming in his

mind. 'I think you said before you haven't been to many places outside Glasgow?'

'That's right.'

'Why not? You can get a bus or train to all sorts of destinations.'

'True enough,' she agreed. 'It's just never happened, that's all. When we had the fruit and veg shop we didn't finish until Saturday night, which only left Sunday to do things. And you know what it's like in Glasgow on a Sunday: everything's shut up tight. Even the swings in the park are chained and padlocked. It doesn't exactly make you want to get out and about.'

He was only too aware that Scotland was deadly on a Sunday. You couldn't even get a drink unless you went out of your area and could sign in at an hotel as a bona fide traveller. The country was ruled by the Church, and that was how the Church decreed it should be. As Lexa had just said, even the children's swings were chained and padlocked on the Lord's day, the sabbath.

'I've had an idea,' he said.

'Oh?'

'I have some deliveries to make in Balloch and Balmaha, on the banks of Loch Lomond. I wasn't going to do them until next week, but I could go this Sunday instead if I wanted. Presuming the weather keeps up why don't you come with me and we'll have a picnic?'

Lexa was completely taken aback. 'A picnic?'

'Yes, a picnic. I'll ask Mrs Mack, our cook, to put something together and we'll take it with us. What do you say?'

Lexa couldn't think straight. Her mind was whirling. A picnic with William! And at Loch Lomond too.

He sensed her uncertainty. 'Don't worry. I'll be a perfect gentleman, I assure you.'

She didn't know whether she wanted him to be a perfect gentleman. But this was an opportunity she couldn't pass up. She was suddenly seized with excitement at the prospect.

'I'll be delighted to go with you, William.'

'Excellent!'

They were packing up for the day when Joe stopped what he was doing, sat on a box and held his head in his hands.

Cordelia immediately went over, hesitated for a moment or two, then put an arm round his shoulders. 'What is it, Joe? What's wrong?' she asked in concern.

'Nothing. I've got a headache, that's all.'

He hadn't looked well since arriving at work, she reflected. Somewhat white-faced and lethargic. Distracted too, as he'd been only too often of late.

'Do you want me to go to the chemist and get you some aspirin?' she volunteered.

'No thanks.'

'It isn't any trouble.'

He forced a smile on to his face. 'You're a gem, Cordelia. It's not aspirin I need but a couple of pints and whiskies.'

That surprised her. Surely alcohol wasn't the best thing for a headache?

Reaching up, he clasped her hand, and squeezed it, sending a thrill through her. God, how she loved this man. She'd have laid down her life for him. He gazed into her eyes, his own warm and pleading. Beseeching almost. 'If only things were different.' he said quietly. 'But they aren't, I'm afraid.'

She was mystified. What was he going on about? What things was he referring to?

Joe let out a huge sigh and came to his feet. 'Let's finish this lot off,' he declared. 'The sooner we do the sooner I can get to the pub.'

'A picnic with the boss's son!' Alice exclaimed. 'My my, we are coming on in the world.'

Lexa blushed. 'Now don't you go thinking it's anything romantic, Mum. It isn't.'

'No?'

'No,' Lexa replied emphatically. 'We're just friends, nothing more.'

Alice gave a cynical laugh. 'I've never been quite sure there can be such a relationship between a man and woman. Perhaps from the female's point of view, but from the man's? That's a different kettle of fish entirely.'

'Well you're wrong in this instance,' Lexa snapped. 'William would never consider me romantically.'

'Why not?'

'Because our backgrounds are so different. His family are posh, certainly wealthy. And he went to a public school – Kelvinside Academy, I believe. And me? Working class and Queen's Park – a decent enough school I grant you, and a good one, but not a school you have to pay to go to.'

Alice regarded her daughter shrewdly. 'Do you like him?'

'Of course I like him. I wouldn't be going on a picnic with him otherwise.'

'No, that's not what I mean. What if he too was working class. What then?'

Lexa took a deep breath. 'But he isn't, Mum. So there's no point in speculating.'

'None the less,' Alice persisted. 'Answer my question.'

Lexa shrugged. 'He is extremely good-looking. And terribly pleasant to be with.'

'Aha!' Alice exclaimed triumphantly. 'So you do fancy him.'

'I didn't say that,' Lexa retorted sharply.

'You didn't have to. I could see it on your face and hear it in your voice.'

Lexa sighed. 'What if I do? It won't lead to anything. Can't lead to anything. We'll have our picnic on Sunday, if the weather's fine, and that'll be the end of it. He's only being nice, no more.'

Maybe, Alice mused. Maybe. Time would tell.

Cordelia got into bed and closed her eyes, preparing to go to sleep. And in that moment it hit her. 'If only things were different,' Joe had said. 'But they aren't, I'm afraid.'

She gasped and her eyes flew open. Those statements of Joe's suddenly made sense.

She fumbled for her bedside light, snapped it on and sat up while she considered this revelation.

She went over it again carefully. It would certainly explain Joe's peculiar behaviour of late. His continually being distracted, staring off into space. Calling her a gem, and all the other compliments he'd been putting her way. But could it really be true? She'd thought him a happily married man. Wasn't he for ever saying so? Or . . . She frowned. He used to say that. Now she thought about it he hadn't for a while. Not since Ellie had come out of hospital.

Cordelia swallowed hard. Was it really possible Joe had fallen out of love with his wife and into love with her? Dare she hope that to be the case?

'Oh, my God,' she whispered. Had her dream come true? Was Joe as much in love with her as she was with him?

A warm melting feeling washed through her, causing her to bring up her legs and hug them. She then shivered all over, a tremor of sheer happiness. She recalled how he'd clasped her hand earlier that day. And his eyes, warm and pleading. Beseeching almost. As if he was wishing with all his heart that it was she he was married to, and not Ellie.

Joe in love with her! The very thought made her want to jump out of bed and dance with joy. She'd got this right, she was certain of it. Interpreted the signs correctly. Made sense of what had previously been a mystery. Joe was in love with her, and she with him.

So what to do about it? Nothing, she eventually decided. The next move must be his. But in the meantime she'd give him all the encouragement she could. Make it plain she felt the same, and was available.

Flicking off the bedside lamp again she lay back and began to imagine what having an affair with Joe Given would be like. The actual physicality of it.

'Joe,' she whispered in the darkness, a huge smile plastered all over her face. 'Darling Joe.'

'I have a confession to make,' Lexa said. She was sitting on a travelling rug, and William had just that second opened a bottle. To one side was a wicker hamper filled with goodies which Mrs Mack, the McLeod cook, had provided for them.

William picked up a crystal glass and began filling it. 'What's that?'

'I've never had wine before.'

He stopped what he was doing to stare at her in utter amazement. 'You've never had wine?'

She shook her head.

He suddenly burst out laughing. 'And you working for a wine merchant too. That's incredible!'

Lexa felt herself blush. 'Well we don't exactly get free samples just because we're employed there.'

He had to concede that was true enough. He added more wine until the glass was three-quarters full, then passed it across. 'Let's see what you think. That's a Merlot, by the way. One of my own particular favourites.'

Lexa took a tentative sip.

'Well?'

She had another sip. 'It's very nice,' she lied. She wasn't sure at all.

He nodded his approval. 'I'm glad you like it.' He filled a glass for himself, then held it up in a toast. 'Here's to your initiation into the delights of good wines.'

'I'll drink to that,' a cautious Lexa replied. Perhaps it was an acquired taste.

William smiled. 'Hungry yet?'

'A bit.'

'Just a bit?' he teased.

How could he possibly know she was actually ravenous?

Lexa had been so excited at the prospect of the picnic she'd hardly eaten any breakfast. 'Well, perhaps more than that,' she admitted.

William laid his glass aside and opened the hamper. 'Shall we see what Mrs Mack has laid on for us?'

Lexa's reply to that was a smile. She looked out over Loch Lomond, thinking what a splendid setting they were in. She couldn't imagine anything more beautiful. The sky was blue and cloudless, the water a deeper shade of blue and sparkling. Off to her right she could just make out Balmaha, where William had made his second delivery.

'Do you think there really is a monster in the loch?' she asked.

William laughed, but not derisively. 'That's Loch Ness you're talking about. Not here. But in answer to your question, I've absolutely no idea. Though I'd like to think there was.'

'Why's that?'

He thought for a moment. 'Wouldn't it be wonderful if a creature from the dark and distant prehistoric past is alive today? That truly would be something, in my opinion. Against all odds, so to speak.'

Not for the first time she thought what a lovely voice he had, if a little plummy. And how handsome he looked in his grey trousers and the open-necked white shirt which he'd rolled up to the elbows. Nearby was his blazer with his tie on top.

She'd swithered and swithered over what to wear herself. In the end she'd decided to keep it simple – it was a picnic, after all. Her cream cotton blouse with short sleeves, and a fully flared Royal Stewart tartan skirt that came to just below her knees, suited her beautifully.

'If a monster did show up it would probably frighten me to death,' she declared.

'I doubt one will,' William replied drolly. Then, tongue in cheek: 'But in case one does don't faint, just run like hell for the car and I'll show you how fast that machine can go.'

Now she laughed, thoroughly enjoying herself. She watched him keenly as he rummaged in the hamper.

'Ah!' he exclaimed. 'Smoked salmon sandwiches. And chicken ones. Cake, some apple tarts and a cold game pie. How does that lot sound?'

Salmon! Chicken! Talk about the lap of luxury. 'Yummy,' she replied.

'Indeed.' He passed her a china plate which had come with the hamper. There was also a selection of solid silver cutlery. 'Would you care to help yourself?'

'Thank you,' she answered, accepting the plate.

'Dig in. What goes back will just be chucked in the bin, so don't stint yourself. I certainly shan't.'

They ate in silence for a few minutes, then William said, 'The weather is going to change for the worse next week. Just my luck.'

She frowned. 'Why so?'

'I'm off to France on business, which'll probably mean a rough crossing on the boat.'

'France?'

'Paris to begin with, then down to the south where I'm to meet some *vignerons*.'

That stumped her. 'What's a *vigneron*?'

'A man who grows grape vines to make wine. I suppose you'd call him a farmer who specialises in the one product, grapes.'

'I see,' she murmured. 'How long will you be away for?'

'Not certain, Lexa. Probably a month, maybe more.'

She looked away so he didn't see the disappointment on her face. A month was an awfully long time. 'Are you looking forward to your trip?' she asked, her voice suddenly husky.

'Oh, yes. It'll be great fun. Especially Paris, which I've been to before. Incredible city. Makes Glasgow seem like a morgue by comparison.'

That made Lexa laugh. 'Really?'

'Really. Everything's lit up at night. There are cafés and bars galore, not to mention the women. They are exceptional, I can tell you.'

It surprised her how jealous she felt when she heard that. 'Are they so pretty?'

'Not just pretty, Lexa, but stylish with it. Every female you see is a complete knockout.'

'You make Paris sound very exciting,' she said in a low voice.

'It most certainly is that.'

She glanced down at her tartan skirt and thought how woefully inadequate it must be compared to what Parisian women wore. She suddenly hated it and vowed to throw it away once she got home. She looked up at William, and in that moment, as their eyes locked, she got the shock of her life. It was as if she'd been hit on the head by the proverbial sledgehammer.

'What is it?' He frowned. 'You look as though you've seen a ghost.'

Not a ghost, she thought. But something just as stunning.

'I've never noticed before,' she stammered. 'Your eyes.'

'What about them?'

'One is a paler shade of brown than the other.'

William laughed. 'I get that from my mother whose eyes are exactly the same as mine – the left slightly paler than the right. It's not noticeable all the time, especially in darker weather. But in bright sunlight like today it usually is. Quirky, eh?'

Lexa could only think of what Granny Stewart had read in her cards. She'd meet a man with different-coloured eyes who could turn out to be her future husband. The thought made her gulp.

'Lexa?'

'Sorry, William,' she apologised hastily. 'I was miles away.'

'Thinking about my peculiar eyes?' he teased.

It was precisely what she had been thinking about. 'Of course not,' she lied.

'Then what?'

'Oh . . . just wondering what Paris must be like. All those brightly lit cafés and bars you mentioned. Has to be quite a sight.'

'It is indeed.'

Lexa looked down at her glass, trying to come to terms with the jolt she'd just been given. Was William really a possible future husband?

The idea set her heart racing.

*   *   *

'Thank you for a wonderful day out, William. I thoroughly enjoyed myself.' Lexa smiled as his car came to a halt outside his close.

'It was my pleasure, I assure you,' he replied, matching her smile.

'And please tell Mrs Mack her food was delicious.'

'I shall. We must do it again sometime?'

'That would be lovely.'

For one wild moment she thought he was going to lean across and kiss her, but he didn't.

'Goodbye, then.'

'Bye, Lexa.'

Then she was out the car and hurrying upstairs where Alice was waiting to hear how the picnic had gone.

Lexa recounted everything, with the exception of William's eyes. As far as she was concerned that was none of her mother's business.

For now, anyway.

Chapter 12

'Did you have a good weekend? Do anything interesting?' Pam enquired, over her usual cigarette while they drank their tea.

'No, nothing interesting,' Lexa lied. 'Just the usual.'

'I met someone at the jigging,' Pam declared enthusiastically.

'Oh?'

'His name's Bobby.'

'And?' Lexa prompted.

'He walked me home afterwards and we had a good old kiss in the back close.'

'French kissing?'

'Of course. None of your baby stuff. There were times when his tongue was halfway down my throat.'

Lexa laughed. 'Are you seeing him again?'

'The plan is to meet up next Saturday at the same dancing and take it from there, I suppose.'

'What did he look like?'

Pam pulled a face. 'Nothing special. About my height,

and quite burly. He's an apprentice engineer with a couple of years left before he gets his ticket. I have to say we really clicked. At least I thought so, and I got the definite impression he did too.'

Lexa was delighted for her friend, who'd been looking for a steady boyfriend for ages now.

At that point there was a whoosh of water as the lavatory was flushed, and seconds later Angela Quigley came out of the cubicle.

'I met someone too,' she declared.

Despite what she'd said to William, Lexa wasn't sure she liked Angela. There was something about the girl she found off-putting. 'Good for you,' she said coolly.

'Want to see something?'

'Like what?' Pam queried.

Angela undid the scarf round her throat and pulled it off. 'Ta-da!'

Lexa and Pam stared at the vivid purple love bite discolouring Angela's neck.

'Bloody hell!' Pam exclaimed. 'What is he, a vampire?'

Angela laughed. 'He might as well have been, the way he kept sucking on me. An absolute brute. And I'm not kidding either.'

'You'd better not let Mrs Sanderson see that,' Lexa warned her colleague. 'She'd have a fit. Might even get you sacked.'

'Don't worry. I have no intention of letting her see it. This scarf will be staying on until the mark goes.'

'An absolute brute, eh?' Pam smiled.

'From head to toe. It makes me go all funny just thinking about him.'

When Lexa returned to her desk she had trouble regaining her concentration. Then it dawned on her why. She was jealous. Not so much of Angela, but of Pam. She wondered what it would be like to be French kissed by William.

Very pleasant, she decided.

Joe started when Cordelia put a hand on his shoulder. 'Sorry,' he apologised. 'I wasn't expecting that. You gave me a bit of a fright.'

It had been Cordelia's policy of late to touch Joe whenever she could, trying to establish something of a physical, if limited, relationship between the pair of them. 'You're jumpy today?' She smiled.

'Am I?'

'You've been that way all morning.'

'It's lack of sleep. The baby kept us awake for hours on end.'

Cordelia wondered if that was true, or whether it could be his guilty conscience that had kept him awake. There again, perhaps he'd slept perfectly well and it was his feeling for herself that was causing him unease. She moved even closer to him.

'Tell you what,' she said. 'Why don't you go over to the Hielan Laddie and treat yourself to a couple of pints? That'll calm you down.'

'Are you sure?'

'I can manage on my own, you know that. So on you go.'

'Thanks, Cordelia. I shouldn't keep doing this, but you're a class act right enough.'

Class act! she thought. That was a new one. Reaching up, she brushed the tip of a finger across his cheek while mentally willing him to declare his love for her. Sadly, he did no such thing. But he would, Cordelia assured herself. Eventually he would. It was only a matter of time.

She watched his retreating back, the warmest of warm feelings coursing through her.

'Brown eyes, one slightly paler than the other,' Granny Stewart mused.

'That's right.'

Granny Stewart lit her third cigarette of the day while she thought about it. 'What about aeroplanes?' she asked after a while. 'Is the chap connected in any way to those?'

Lexa shook her head. 'Not that I'm aware of. Though, I suppose, there could be a connection I don't know about. He is fond of tinkering with cars, mind you. Told me once he'd have loved to be a mechanic if he hadn't gone into the family business.'

'Hm,' Granny Stewart mused. This was a difficult one. 'You like him, I take it?'

Lexa blushed, and nodded. 'Not that there's much chance. His family are rich and posh, so he would hardly look at the likes of me.'

Granny Stewart gave her granddaughter an affectionate smile. 'Not necessarily. It depends on the man himself, and what feelings he may have for you. Does he have any?'

'Again, I don't know. He certainly hasn't said or done anything that might show he had.'

'I see.'

'He is tall for a Glaswegian, and dark, with a pleasant personality. Things you mentioned when you read my cards.'

'I remember.' Granny Stewart nodded. 'Those attributes would certainly seem to fit. But as for the eyes, that's where I can't be sure. I would have thought different-coloured eyes would have been brown and blue, for example. But both brown, only one a paler shade than the other. That really is quite perplexing.' She took a deep breath. 'I'm afraid I'm going to have to disappoint you, Lexa. I really can't say if he's the one or not.'

'Oh well.' Lexa sighed. 'Coming to ask was worth a try. I just hoped . . .'

'Indeed.'

When Lexa was making her way home, she reflected she was none the wiser about William. He might be the man Granny Stewart had seen in the cards, but then again he probably wasn't. Either way, a relationship between the pair of them was highly unlikely, so she might as well put it out of her mind.

Both Lexa and Cordelia, having met at the close mouth on return from work, came up short in amazement on entering the sitting room, where Alice was standing by the fireplace.

'Well?' a nervous Alice demanded.

'Your hair,' Cordelia said, and shook her head. 'You've had it dyed.'

'Back to its original colour,' Lexa added unnecessarily.

'I had it done in a place in town. Rather a good job, in my opinion. What do you think?'

Lexa knew exactly what she thought now the initial shock was over. 'It takes years off you, Mum. No doubt about it.'

'I agree,' Cordelia concurred, still somewhat open-mouthed.

'It's not too obvious, I hope?'

'Not in the least, Mum,' Lexa assured her. 'Certainly not from this distance.'

Alice was pleased. 'Come and have a closer look.'

They did, and had to admit that even up close the hair wasn't obviously dyed.

'Why did you have it done, Mum?' Lexa asked curiously. 'I thought it looked fine white.'

'It was a whim,' Alice admitted. 'I was walking past the shop when I suddenly decided to go in. And now here I am, just like I used to be before Jimmy passed away.'

'I'm sure he'd have approved,' Cordelia declared, not sure at all but thinking it the right thing to say.

'Do you?'

'Oh yes, Mum. Most definitely. He'd have said, "Good on you, girl!"'

Lexa laughed. That had been a favourite expression of her dad's, only used in relation to Alice.

'Have you shown Mrs McAllister yet?' Cordelia asked.

'No, I haven't. I wanted the pair of you to be the first to see the new me.'

'Then away through and knock her door.' Lexa smiled. 'Just don't give her a heart attack, that's all.'

Alice laughed, and went.

'I think Mum dyeing her hair means something,' Cordelia said when the door had closed behind her.

'Like what?'

'That perhaps she's finally come to terms with losing Dad. That she's making a new beginning for herself.'

Lexa hoped it was true.

William stared at the front of an English paper he'd finally managed to find. The Germans had marched into Czechoslovakia, Hitler at the head of an army which was now occupying the once-Czech Sudetenland.

William read the article through carefully, then laid his paper aside while he drank the coffee he'd ordered, and reflected on what had happened.

One thing was certain, the news wasn't good. The British government had agreed to let Hitler expand his boundaries without a fight, but would the Führer stop there? William felt a cold shiver run through him. What next? Or who next? And then how would Britain react? That was the big question.

Cordelia sighed contentedly. She and Lexa were home alone, Alice having taken herself off to the Labour Hall with Mrs McAllister. 'I'm convinced Joe's in love with me,' she declared.

Lexa frowned. 'What makes you say that?'

'All the signs are there, sis. I can read them like a book.'

'But you told me he's a happily married man.'

'I thought he was. But something's changed. I see it in him daily. The way he looks at me ... oh, a dozen things. He's fallen out of love with Ellie, and into love with me. Isn't that wonderful?'

'But what about Ellie and the baby?'

'I don't care about them,' Cordelia replied coldly. 'All I care about is Joe, and us being together.'

Lexa considered what her sister had said. 'It would be a brave man who walked out on his wife and divorced her for someone else. Particularly when there's a child involved. It just isn't done. You know that.'

'Maybe,' Cordelia replied vaguely. 'But it does happen.'

'And what if he doesn't leave his wife, albeit he's in love with you. What then?'

'He will,' Cordelia stated firmly.

'But what if he doesn't?'

Cordelia stared hard at her sister, then glanced away. 'That's when Plan B comes into action.'

How melodramatic that sounded, Lexa mused. Plan B indeed! It was like something straight out of a corny film. 'Which is?'

'You won't approve,' Cordelia said quietly.

'Does that matter?'

'No, it doesn't if you must know.'

'So what is it? I'm all ears.'

'I'll become his lover. His mistress.'

Lexa literally rocked in her chair. 'You'll do what!' she exclaimed.

'You heard me. Become his mistress. That's the correct word, I believe.'

Lexa was both horrified and flabbergasted. Had her sister really just said what she had? It was unbelievable!

'See,' Cordelia declared defiantly. 'I told you you wouldn't approve.'

'I most certainly don't. I appreciate that there can be sex before marriage, but usually only when a couple are engaged and the date's been set. What you're proposing is something entirely different.'

Cordelia's face seemed to crumple in on itself, her previous defiance disappearing. 'What else can I do, sis? I love him so very much.'

'Even though,' Lexa protested.

Cordelia ran a hand over her face, part of her ashamed of herself. 'I'm hoping it won't come to that. But if it does, so be it. That's how strongly I feel about him.'

'Oh, Cordelia,' Lexa sympathised softly.

Cordelia dissolved into tears.

Pam burst out laughing the moment she and Lexa entered the ladies' on Monday morning. 'You'll never guess what I heard at the jigging Saturday night?'

'What?'

'I ran into an old pal of mine who knows Angela. Apparently she got a nickname given her at school.'

'Which is?'

'Wait for it.' Pam paused for a moment, then said, her voice quaking, 'Angela Tarantula.'

'Ang—' Lexa broke off and also burst out laughing.

'Isn't it terrific?'

'But why tarantula?' Lexa queried when she'd finally stopped laughing.

'It's to do with the way she moved as a youngster. According to my pal she used to sort of scuttle round the playground, just like a spider.'

Angela Tarantula! Lexa shook her head, delighted. The nickname was hilarious, in her opinion.

That night, on leaving work, Lexa and Pam made sure

they did so with Angela, then pretended to stop and talk while Angela walked away.

It was true, Angela did sort of scuttle. Much to their amusement.

Ginge sauntered over to the stall where Cordelia was busy arranging a show of flowers. 'How's it going?' he asked.

'Fine.'

He glanced up at the sky. 'Do you think it's going to rain?'

Cordelia also glanced up. 'It might. Hard to say.'

'Been busy?'

'So-so.'

'Same with us. Fewer customers. But –' he shrugged '– that's the way it goes sometimes.'

She smiled, but didn't reply.

'I was wondering, if you'd care to come for a drink after we pack up tonight?'

Cordelia shook her head. 'Sorry, no can do.'

'Have to hurry off home?'

'That's it.'

'Tea on the table, eh?'

'Right again.'

Ginge stuck his hands in his trouser pockets. 'Listen, Cordelia, I know you don't fancy me. Joe made that clear. But that doesn't mean we can't be friends, does it?'

She hesitated. It sounded reasonable enough. 'No,' she said slowly.

'I'm not trying to get off with you or anything, I swear. So a drink wouldn't do any harm. It's simply a way of us getting to know one another better.'

Cordelia couldn't see anything wrong with that. Just as long as he knew not to try anything on. 'Tell you what,' she said. 'Not tonight. But how about tomorrow night? That gives me a chance to tell my mum I'm going to be late.'

'Done!' he enthused. 'Straight after work?'

'Straight after work,' she agreed.

Cordelia was in stitches. She couldn't remember the last time she'd laughed so much. Ginge just kept coming out with joke after joke, some of them pretty near the knuckle, each funnier than the last.

'Stop it!' she pleaded, tears streaming down her face. 'I'll wet myself in a minute.'

Ginge grinned at her. 'Enjoying yourself?'

'Not half.'

'Good.'

Cordelia sucked in a deep breath, then attempted to wipe the tears away. God, but he was a hoot!

'Another drink?' Ginge asked.

She glanced at the clock behind the bar, realising with a start that she'd stayed far longer than she'd intended. 'I really must go, Ginge. Honestly.'

'Oh, come on, have another. If you're late then the damage has already been done.'

'No, I really must go,' she protested.

'Well, you can't.'

That surprised her. 'Why not?'

'Because it's your round, lady. I insist you not only pay for it, but stay and drink it with me.'

The way he said it made her want to laugh again. 'Oh, all right then. But this is the last.'

What a character, she thought as he made his way to the bar with her money. This was a side of Ginge she'd never suspected existed.

Henry McLeod, sitting behind the desk in his study, pushed away the several sheets of paper he'd been intently studying. 'Excellent, William. Excellent. A tremendous job.'

'Thank you, Father.'

'You've even managed to acquire a dozen cases of Château d'Yquem. I'm delighted. As you know, it's been terribly difficult to come by in recent years.' Château d'Yquem was considered by many connoisseurs to be the finest sweet white wine produced.

'At a price. But it'll still sell, despite our mark-up, if somewhat slowly.'

Henry nodded his agreement.

'I hope the new storage premises are ready. The first shipment should be arriving in a few weeks' time.'

'Everything's in train, William. I've seen to that.'

'I must say,' William went on, 'it was strange buying in such large quantities. I rather liked it.'

'And the wines from down south?'

'Terrific, Father. And such good value. Cutting out the Parisian middlemen made a huge difference. The arrangement I've made with the *vignerons* is that we shall be buying direct from now on, which means more profit for us.'

Henry's face suddenly clouded over. '*If* we can buy direct,' he said meaningfully. 'Tell me, what's the general feeling over there about the German situation?'

William's expression became grave. 'Lots of them think war is inevitable if Hitler keeps on as he has. There's a feeling of nervousness everywhere, and apprehension. But they're extremely positive too as they have a great belief in their defence systems, convinced they'll halt Hitler in his tracks should he attempt to invade.'

'I wonder?'

'Wonder what, Father?'

'If these defence systems would stop Herr Hitler. Perhaps, perhaps not.'

'And what about us?'

'We have the English Channel, William. We're safe as long as we control that. Mr Chamberlain also sets great store by the peace accord he signed with Herr Hitler. Too much store in my opinion. The man's no fool, but in this instance he might be somewhat naive. I personally wouldn't trust Herr Hitler as far as I could throw him.'

'He does seem a particularly nasty piece of work.'

Henry McLeod shook his head in despair. 'God help this country if we have to go through again what we did last time. God help us.'

'Amen,' William said quietly.

Chapter 13

'I have something for you.' William was giving Lexa a lift home. She glanced at him in surprise. 'Something for me?'

He laughed. 'A present from France, actually.'

She was thrilled. 'Really?'

'Really.' He nodded. 'Nothing much, mind you. But I thought you'd like it.' Reaching into his door pocket he extracted a gaily wrapped, slim parcel. 'There you are,' he said, handing it over.

Lexa stared at what she'd been given. It was hard to the touch. 'Can I open it now?'

'Of course.'

Eagerly she undid the ribbon and paper to discover a glossy book inside titled *Paris*.

'I remembered you saying how you'd love to see Paris, particularly the nightlife. Well, that's the next best thing, a book full of pictures. I thought of you the moment I saw it.'

Lexa couldn't have been more delighted as she hurriedly

flicked through the pages. 'Why, thank you,' she stuttered.

'You won't be able to read it as it's in French. But that doesn't stop you looking at the pictures, or making out what they're of from the captions.'

'I don't know what to say,' she confessed.

'Thank you was enough. Pleased?'

'What do you think?'

He laughed again, pleased because she was.

Lexa marvelled at the book, the first gift she'd ever received from a man. It was something she'd treasure. Her eyes shone with gratitude.

William congratulated himself on bringing back an item she clearly appreciated. Mentally he gave himself a pat on the back.

'So how was the trip?' she asked, clutching the book to her bosom.

He told her where he'd been, what he'd seen, and what he'd done, and she listened enraptured.

Later that evening Alice closed the book, which she'd been leafing through. 'He brought you this back from Paris and you say there's nothing between the pair of you?' she said sceptically.

Lexa shook her head. 'There isn't, Mum. I've explained all that.'

'Hm!' Alice snorted.

'I'm sure he brought back a book for all his employees.' Cordelia commented innocently, trying to get a rise out of her sister.

'Now don't you start!' Lexa snapped, beginning to get cross.

'Sorry, I'm sure.'

'It does seem odd though,' Alice went on in the same disbelieving tone.

'He's just a nice man, Mum. That's all there is to it.'

Alice raised an eyebrow. 'A nice man who keeps giving you a lift home in his car?'

'It's on his way.'

'I think he's after you.' Cordelia smiled, continuing to stir, and enjoying every moment of it.

'I doubt that very much.'

'Has he got a girlfriend?'

Lexa frowned. 'I've absolutely no idea. It's not the sort of question I can ask him. Far too personal.'

'So he's never said one way or the other?' Cordelia went on.

Lexa was beginning to wish she'd never shown them the book, or said where she'd got it from. 'No, he hasn't,' she snapped again.

Cordelia was enjoying herself. She hadn't been able to have a go at her sister for a long time. It was great sport. 'If he hasn't then perhaps you're under consideration?'

'This is ridiculous!' Lexa exploded. 'And I'm not listening to any more idle speculation. I'll tell you both for the last time, there's no romance, or potential romance. Now please get that into your heads.'

Alice gazed consideringly at her. 'There's no need to fly off the handle, young lady. We're only talking, that's all.'

'You're not just talking, you're trying to make me feel embarrassed. And you're bloody well succeeding.'

'Language, Lexa,' Alice admonished her. 'None of that in here. Your father never allowed it, and neither will I.'

'That's not so. Dad used to swear on occasion, though rarely, I admit. But he did. You've just chosen to forget that.'

Fuming now, Lexa snatched the book from Alice and stamped her way to her bedroom, where she slammed the door.

As she sat on her bed she could distinctly hear Cordelia laughing, which infuriated her even further.

Why wouldn't they believe her!

Cordelia, bending over a box of flowers on the ground, yelped in surprise when her bottom was resoundingly smacked. Coming bolt upright she turned to face the culprit to find it was a grinning Joe.

'Sorry, darling. I simply couldn't resist that,' he slurred.

'You're drunk,' she accused him mildly.

'Quite right. I'm steamboats. Drunk as the proverbial skunk.'

This was happening more and more often of late, she reflected. She was convinced that Joe's feelings towards her were the cause of it. When was he going to face facts and declare his love?

'That hurt,' she complained, though she was secretly delighted at his having taken the liberty.

'Sorry. I didn't mean to hit you so hard.' He winked salaciously. 'But what man could resist such a gorgeous bum, eh?'

She flushed. 'Is it really?'

'A cracker, Cordelia. Take my word for it.'

She went all gooey inside. 'You've got a lovely one your-self,' she told him shyly. Dear God, had she actually said that?

'Well, it's the first time a woman's ever told me so.'

Cordelia couldn't help herself. 'Not even Ellie?'

'Not even Ellie,' he replied, shaking his head.

'I'm surprised.'

'Maybe she doesn't think it's as nice as you do.'

Cordelia could have commented on that, but didn't, considering Ellie to be a fool. 'Are you fit to work?' she asked.

'Of course I am.'

'You don't look it. You're swaying all over the place.'

Joe stared down at his legs. 'Are you sure it isn't the ground that's moving?'

'No, Joe, it isn't the ground, I can assure you.'

He gave her another wink. 'I'll manage. Don't you worry.'

'You can't serve customers while stinking of booze, Joe. It's just not on.'

He thought about that. 'No, I suppose not,' he admitted. 'So what'll I do?'

Cordelia had an inspiration. 'Ginge has that place at the rear of his stall which he uses for all sorts. Have a word and I'm sure he'll let you kip in there for a couple of hours.'

Joe gave her a foolish grin. 'Good thinking, girl. Good thinking. That's a terrific idea.'

She watched him stagger away. What she didn't know was that he went to another nearby pub for a few more whiskies before speaking to Ginge, who was only too happy to oblige. She didn't see him again that afternoon, and by the time she had finished the packing up when the market closed he still had not reappeared. Taking the well-worn brown leather satchel they kept the float and takings in she headed in Ginge's direction.

It was dark inside the wooden construction behind his stall, and she had to wait for several seconds to adjust her eyesight. Then she saw Joe, lying on an old blanket over to one side. Going to him, she squatted and shook him by the shoulder.

'Joe,' she said quietly. 'It's time to go home.' He snorted, but didn't waken. 'Joe,' she tried again, with a further shake.

He rolled on to his back, and what happened next caught her completely by surprise. It all seemed to take place in a split second. Joe snorted again, and suddenly she'd been pulled to the ground and on to her side. Her eyes went wide as he started to kiss her, muttering something she couldn't catch and clutching her so tightly she could scarcely breathe.

It didn't last long. Almost before she realised what was heppening Joe grunted and turned away. A stunned Cordelia felt him settle himself into a more comfortable position, and then he began to snore.

Still disbelieving, Cordelia came to her feet and did her best to brush herself down. Not in a million years would she ever have thought her first kiss with Joe would be like that. She was shaking inside, though, thankfully, there weren't any outward signs of what had happened.

She stared at Joe in the darkness. He was fast asleep,

and still snoring. Had he thought she was Ellie, or what? She had absolutely no idea.

Picking up the cash satchel she went outside to find Ginge chatting with his partner John.

'Will you do me a favour, Ginge?'

'Sure. What is it?'

'I can't get Joe to wake up. Can you do it and give him this money when you do?'

Ginge laughed. 'That pissed, is he?'

'So it seems.'

'Well, don't you worry, I'll wake the bugger. It won't be a problem as I'll not be as gentle as you probably were.'

'Thanks, Ginge.'

She handed him the satchel and then, in as dignified a manner as she was able, walked away from the stall and out of the market.

'Damn!' William swore as he cradled the phone. Celia Rutherford had let him down yet again. One thing was certain, he wasn't top of her priority list. Far from it, it seemed.

So what was he to do? He had no intention of going without a partner. That would be boring. Besides, he had a reputation as a ladies' man to uphold.

Yes, this needed thinking about. Chewing on a finger-nail he rejoined his parents in the drawing room, where he sat brooding for the rest of that evening.

Joe was instantly apologetic when Cordelia arrived at work the following morning. 'I'm terribly sorry,' he said contritely. 'I didn't mean to drink so much. It just sort of happened without my realising. Kind of crept up on me like.'

Did he remember what he'd done to her? Cordelia wondered, not replying, waiting for him to go on.

'I'll make it up to you, Cordelia, I promise. There'll be a bonus for you at the end of the week. How's that?'

His eyes told her he didn't remember. There was guilt there, but nothing like the guilt there would have been if he'd recalled kissing her. If he did remember anything he probably thought he'd dreamt it.

'What's wrong with you recently, Joe? You keep drinking like there's no tomorrow. I'm spending more and more time running this stall all by myself while you're getting legless in the pub.' Come on, she mentally urged. Confess it's because of your feelings for me. Now's your perfect chance.

Joe glanced away. 'I've got a lot on my mind, angel. An awful lot.'

'Do you want to tell me about it?' She held her breath, waiting for his answer.

'I can't. It's too personal.'

Tell me! she mentally screamed. 'We're good mates, Joe. Good chinas. There's nothing you can't say, or confide, to me. I want to help if I can.'

For a moment he was tempted. But this was not the time or place.

She scrutinised his face, willing him to unburden himself. 'Joe?'

He shook his head. 'Maybe some other time. But not now.'

She turned away, filled with bitter disappointment, and

not a little disgust that he'd let this golden opportunity slip by. 'We'd better get on with it, then,' she said.

'Yes, let's do that,' he agreed.

It had become a regular thing that William, when he was able to do so, would pick Lexa up at the tram stop and drive her home. Tonight he had a proposition to put to her.

'What are you up to Saturday night?' he asked casually.

'Nothing.'

'Not going out with anyone?'

Lexa frowned. 'No. I just said.'

'Hm.' He drove on in silence.

What had that been all about? Lexa wondered. Why on earth was he interested in what she was doing Saturday night?

'What about you?' she queried tentatively.

'What about me?'

'Are you going out?'

'On Saturday night?'

'That's right.'

'I am, as a matter of fact. My old rowing club has a get-together once a year which I do my best to attend. Meet up with the lads, that sort of thing. It's usually good fun.'

She glanced sideways at him. 'You sound as though you miss the rowing, and your friends.'

He smiled. 'I do, Lexa, very much. But I had to give it all up when I joined the family business. A great deal of training goes with rowing and I simply didn't have the time any more. Regular early morning outings, for example, would have been impossible.'

The term puzzled her. 'Outings?'

'It's a rowing expression. When you go on the water in a boat, by yourself or with others, it's called an outing.'

'I see.'

'It's a grand sport. But, as I said, a demanding mistress. If you're doing it properly, that is.'

He really did miss it, she thought. How sad he'd had to give it up. 'Have you ever seen the Oxford and Cambridge race?' she asked.

He shook his head. 'No, I'm afraid not. Though maybe one day I'll manage to do so. That would be a real treat.'

Lexa glanced out her side window. The leeries had already been round to light the gas street lamps they were passing, and the flames were throwing pools of harsh white light on to the pavement and road.

'Lexa?'

'Yes, William?'

'Would you care to come to the Saturday get-together with me?'

She must have misheard, Lexa thought. 'I beg your pardon?'

'I said, would you care to come to the Saturday get-together with me?'

Her heart started pounding nineteen to the dozen. William was asking her out! She was suddenly beset with confusion, unable to think clearly.

'Well?' he prompted when she didn't reply.

'I, er . . .' She took a deep breath. 'You've caught me a bit by surprise, William. This is so . . . well, out the blue.'

'Does that mean no?'

'Not at all. I mean, what would I wear?'

He was amused. It was just like a woman to ask that. 'It won't be formal. I'll have a lounge suit on. You . . . well, how about a little black dress? That would be appropriate.'

She didn't have a 'little black dress'. But never mind. 'I'd love to go with you, William. I accept.'

He beamed at her. 'Excellent. Shall I pick you up at, say, seven?'

'Seven would be fine. I'll be waiting and ready.' She suddenly frowned. 'Does that mean you'll be coming to my house?'

'Unless you wish me to wait outside in the car?'

'No, come to the house. The nameplate will tell you which is ours.'

Going out with William McLeod! The impossible had somehow become reality. But she was terribly nervous at the prospect, and prayed she wouldn't disgrace herself in any way.

'I knew something like this was going to happen!' Alice exclaimed triumphantly when Lexa told her.

'I'm going to need a new dress, Mum. Will you meet me in town Saturday afternoon after work and help me choose?'

'Of course, dear. I'd be delighted.'

'Is he really as good-looking as you've said?' a curious Cordelia wanted to know.

'Judge for yourself. He's picking me up at seven.'

'You'll naturally ask him in?' Alice said. 'It's only polite to do so.'

Lexa couldn't see why not. She had nothing to be ashamed of, after all. William knew she came from a working-class family so he could hardly expect anything else. Their house might not be the Ritz, but it was as clean as a new pin. Spotless, in fact.

'Of course I'll ask him in, Mum,' she agreed.

Chapter 14

'It's him!' Lexa exclaimed when there was a knock on the front door. 'Are you sure I look all right, Mum?'

'You look fine, Lexa. Now calm down.'

The dress Lexa and her mother had chosen was black, of course, with a softly draped surplice bodice and a gently flared skirt with unpressed pleats across the front. Around the waist was a buckled belt of the same fine alpaca-type fabric. And since Lexa had recently had a pay rise to mark the first anniversary of her starting work at *Vins*, there was enough left of her savings to enable her to buy a black woollen coat to wear over it, slightly waisted and falling to a little below her knees.

'On you go, sis, answer it. Let's have a gander at this dreamboat of yours.'

'Now don't you go spoiling anything,' Lexa warned her.

'Who, me?'

'Yes, you.'

Lexa went through and opened the door to find it was indeed William standing there.

He smiled. 'Hello.'

'Come on in.'

Lexa had already told him he was to be invited to meet her mother and sister, and he'd come armed with a bottle of wine.

'Mum, this is William.'

He shook hands with Alice, then handed her the bottle. 'A little something,' he declared.

Alice looked at the bottle in surprise. Wine! She'd have much preferred whisky. 'Why, thank you, Mr McLeod.'

'William, please.'

Lexa hadn't been exaggerating, Cordelia thought. He really was quite a dish. And what a lovely smile!

'I thought you might care for a dram before you and Lexa leave?' Alice offered after Cordelia had been introduced.

'That's kind of you. I'd love one.' William knew his Glasgow manners. It would have been rude to refuse.

The whisky was already laid out, as were glasses. Alice poured three tots, Lexa having told her she wouldn't have one.

'Slainte!' William toasted.

'Slainte!' Alice and Cordelia responded in unison.

They chatted for a few minutes, and then it was time to leave. Goodbyes were said at the door, and William and Lexa made their way downstairs.

'What do you think?' Alice asked Cordelia when they were back in the front room.

'She's fallen on her feet there. He's gorgeous.'

Alice couldn't have agreed more. She'd taken a real shine to William.

*   *   *

The band stopped playing. Lexa and William applauded along with the other dancers.

'Enjoying youself?' William asked.

'Isn't it obvious?'

He laughed. It was. They made their way off the floor, as the band was taking a break.

'I have to go to the ladies' room,' Lexa whispered when they arrived at their table.

'On you go. But hurry back.'

What a nice thing to say, she thought. Hurry back! That meant he'd miss her. 'I won't be long,' she promised.

Fifteen minutes later William glanced at his wristwatch in concern. What was keeping her? He knew there was sometimes a queue for the ladies' lavatories, but quarter of an hour seemed a long time to wait. Five minutes later, a little worried now, he decided to investigate to ensure nothing was wrong.

Something was. He found a clearly terrified Lexa being pawed by someone he'd never seen before, who had to have been brought along as a guest and was obviously very drunk.

Lexa had been backed into a corner from which there was no escape, and the man was slobbering all over her neck. She'd already been told how pretty she was, and how he wanted to take her outside. She gave a huge sigh of relief when she spotted William running towards them.

William grabbed the drunk by his jacket collar and hauled him off. 'What the hell do you think you're doing?' he demanded, eyes flashing with anger.

'What's it to you, pal?'

'That happens to be my girlfriend you're assaulting.'

The drunk's eyes narrowed. 'Is she indeed?'

'Yes she is. Now apologise and bugger off.'

'And if I don't do either?'

'I'll flatten you here and now.'

The drunk laughed. 'Big words.'

William didn't reply, but just stared hard at the man, who began to realise his antagonist was in deadly earnest. What's more, William was taller and better built than he was. He decided to back down.

'Sorry, miss,' he mumbled. Then he stumbled past William and on up the corridor in the direction of the large room where the function was taking place.

'Are you all right?' a concerned William asked Lexa. She fell into his arms.

'Thank you, William. Thank you.' And with that she dissolved into tears.

'There, there,' William consoled her, patting her on the back. 'It's all over now. No harm's been done.'

'He tore my dress. He grabbed hold of me and when I jerked away part of the top was ripped,' she sobbed.

Damn! William thought. And damn the drunk, whoever he'd been.

'I did my best to get by him, but he had me trapped. He kept touching me. All over.'

William reached for the handkerchief in his breast pocket and handed it to her. 'Here, use this.'

'Thank you.'

He could see the rip now, a large one under the shoulder area.

'I'm sorry, but I want to go home, William.'

'I understand,' he replied. 'We'll go and get our coats.'
Lexa was still sobbing as he led her away.

The car drew up outside Lexa's house, and William killed the engine. They'd hardly said a word to each other during the drive.

'I can't tell you how sorry I am about what happened,' William apologised.

'It was hardly your fault. And you did rescue me from that animal.'

'I know, but . . . well, it was me who took you there. We were having such a good time, too.'

Lexa smiled wanly. 'Yes, we were.' She wondered if he'd kiss her, but he made no attempt to do so. 'Goodnight then, William.'

'Goodnight, Lexa. And again, I'm terribly sorry.'

She watched him drive away, then turned and went indoors. Alice, who was at the table playing patience, looked up in surprise when she opened the door of the front room. Cordelia was sitting reading an old edition of the *Bystander*.

'You're home early!' she exclaimed.

'Oh, Mum, it was a disaster,' Lexa wailed, and promptly burst into fresh tears.

Gradually, over the next few minutes, a sobbing Lexa explained why she was so distraught.

'The bastard,' Alice hissed. 'I wish I'd been there. I'd have smacked him good and proper, so I would.'

'I thought William was going to hit him. And he very nearly did. But in the end it didn't come to that.'

'Would you like a dram?' Cordelia asked, concerned.

'No. But a cup of tea would be lovely.'

Cordelia hurried off to put the kettle on.

'Sit down, dear.' Alice could see how shaken her daughter was, which was hardly surprising in the circumstances. 'Did William ask you out again?'

'No.' Lexa sniffed. 'I think he was too embarrassed.'

Alice bit her lip. 'Did he kiss you goodnight?'

Lexa shook her head.

Not very promising, Alice thought. After seeing Lexa and William together she'd been certain they'd click. And who knew what that might lead to? She'd had high hopes, which this drunk might well have blown apart, the bastard.

'It was all going so well,' Lexa went on. 'And then . . .' She broke off in despair.

If the drunk had walked through the door at that moment Alice would have stuck a knife in him.

Lexa's tram came into view. It was the fourth evening in a row that William had failed to show up and run her home. It was definitely all over, she thought bitterly. Over before it had even begun.

The following evening was the same. No William.

The next day Lexa and Pam decided to go for a walk to get a breath of fresh air, which they sometimes did at dinnertime. Anything to get out of the office where Angela Quigley, who'd taken over Lily's job, was proving to be a right pain in the backside.

'She's really getting on my nerves,' Pam declared roundly.

'Same here.'

'Are you aware she shags?'

Lexa's eyebrows shot up. 'How do you know that?'

'She actually told me one day. Boasted about it. Said it was absolutely fantastic.'

Well well, Lexa thought. Though she wasn't really surprised. Angela had all the hallmarks of a born slut. 'With the same chap?' she queried.

'More than one. She boasted about that too.'

'She'd better be careful she doesn't end up in the family way. For a start she'd lose her job, and then there would be the scandal she and her family would have to cope with.'

'True,' Pam nodded. 'Though I'd hardly cry my eyes out if she did get the sack. Good riddance, I'd say.'

Lexa was about to reply when she suddenly spotted William's car in the heavy traffic. Her heart sank when she saw that there was an extremely attractive young woman sitting beside him. The pair of them appeared to be chatting animatedly.

'What is it?' Pam queried when she saw the look on Lexa's face.

Lexa tore her gaze away from the passing car. 'Nothing.'

'Are you sure?'

'Positive. I just . . .' She broke off, and shook her head. 'It's nothing, Pam. I promise you.'

'Shall we turn back?'

'Yes,' Lexa replied, managing to smile. 'I think we should. That'll give you time to have another ciggy before we start again.'

'Good idea!' Pam enthused. She was gasping for a fag, she realised. But of course she couldn't smoke in the street.

It simply wasn't done for a woman to smoke in the street.

Well, that really was that, Lexa reflected miserably as they started retracing their steps. She'd been a fool to think she had a chance with William.

She could have kicked herself.

Lexa couldn't believe her eyes when William's car halted at the tram stop where she was waiting. He beckoned her to get in.

'How are you?' he asked as they drove off.

'Fine.'

'Sorry I haven't picked you up for a while, but I've been exceptionally busy.'

'Oh?' She was remembering the extremely attractive young woman she'd seen on the very seat she was now occupying.

'I've been overseeing the deliveries we've been receiving from France into our new storage premises. It's been quite a job, I can tell you. Certainly kept me on my toes.'

So that was the excuse, she thought. 'I've seen some of the paperwork that's been coming through our office. Far larger quantities of wine than usual.'

'You can say that again.' William reached into his inside jacket pocket and produced an envelope. 'By the way, this is for you.'

She was taken aback. 'What is it?'

He laughed. 'Don't sound so suspicious. It's money to pay for your dress that got ripped.'

'Money?'

'You're beginning to sound like a parrot. Here, take it.'

Lexa accepted the envelope, which wasn't sealed, and

glanced inside. She gasped at what she saw. Quickly she counted what turned out to be four crisp white notes. 'It's twenty pounds!' she exclaimed.

'That's right.'

'But my dress cost nowhere near that amount. It's far too much.'

'Then use it to buy two dresses. Or there again, a very expensive one.'

That made her smile. She could never, ever, spend twenty pounds on a dress. She simply wouldn't be able to bring herself to do so. 'I really can't take this, William. It's extremely kind of you, but I can't accept it.'

'Of course you can. And will. It's the least I can do after what happened that night.' He glanced sideways at her. 'Please? It'll help ease my guilty conscience.'

'All right then,' she reluctantly agreed. 'And thank you.'

When he dropped her off it was with the promise that he'd be at the tram stop the following evening.

It was getting close to packing-up time when Joe finally made an appearance at the stall. To Cordelia's amazement he was carrying a suitcase, and looking absolutely wretched.

'What's that all about?' she asked, pointing at the suitcase.

'Ellie's thrown me out.'

'What!' This was completely unexpected. 'But why?'

'I can't explain here, Cordelia. I'm going over to the Hielan Laddie to rent a room. Join me there when you've finished.'

She nodded. 'I'll see you after I pay Ginge back the

float I borrowed this morning. Shall I bring him with me?'

'No, don't say anything. I'll explain over a drink. By Christ, I need one, I assure you.'

She watched him trudge away, trying to digest the startling news. Ellie had thrown him out. But why? Could it be Ellie had found out he wasn't in love with her any more? Could that be it?

A smile slowly spread across her face. Joe was available at last.

Cordelia waited impatiently while Joe was up at the bar. He had insisted on buying her a drink, and getting a refill for himself, before telling her why Ellie had thrown him out. When he returned to their table she noticed that his hands were shaking. She was looking forward to this, Cordelia thought gleefully. 'Well?' she demanded as Joe sat.

He produced his cigarettes, and lit up. 'What a mess,' he declared woefully. 'What a fucking bloody mess.'

'So what did you do?'

Joe took a deep breath. 'Something awfully stupid, Cordelia. I bitterly regret it now. In fact, I've never done anything more stupid in my entire life. My only excuse, if it is one, was that the temptation was too great.'

What temptation? What was he on about?

'Do you remember I told you that Margy, Ellie's sister, came to look after me when Ellie was in hospital?'

Cordelia nodded. 'I remember.'

'Well, one night we'd both had a few jars in front of the fire. And, well, Margy has always sort of fancied me like. We've often flirted, but only in fun.'

Cordelia felt a chill beginning to run through her. This wasn't at all what she'd expected to hear.

Joe dropped his gaze. 'I honestly can't remember how it came about. I think I was droning on – don't forget I was half cut – about missing Ellie in bed. How lonely it was sleeping alone when you're not used to it. Then somehow Margy's arms were round me and she was whispering in my ear, saying she was dreadfully lonely too with Big Alec away so long at sea.'

Joe paused to take a gulp from his glass. Cordelia was staring at him in icy fascination, feeling that her entire world was about to explode in her face.

Joe went on. 'Next thing I know we're through in the bedroom going at it hammer and tongs.' His eyes gleamed in memory. 'By God, she was good. I shouldn't say this, but she knocks Ellie into a cocked hat.'

Cordelia felt she might throw her head back and scream. All this while she'd been in love with Joe, believing him to be in love with her, and he'd been shagging someone else!

'Only once?' Cordelia heard herself ask.

Joe shook his head. 'Every night from then on until Ellie came home again. And never since.'

'I take it Ellie's found out?'

'Oh aye, she's found out all right. Margy told her.'

Cordelia sat back in her chair, and studied Joe. That didn't make sense. 'Why would she do such a thing?'

Joe stubbed out his cigarette, and immediately lit another. 'Because she's pregnant, and it shows. A pregnancy that could have nothing to do with Big Alec. It's impossible for it to be his.' Joe swallowed the remainder of his drink. 'Want another?'

'What I do want is to hear the rest of this before you go back to the bar. Now go on.'

Joe sighed. 'Ellie had a right barney with Margy last night, insisting she tell her who the father is. I was out at the time, but I gather the pair of them were pissed as newts. Anyway, eventually Margy, in floods of tears apparently, caved in and told Ellie the truth. All hell broke loose after that.'

Cordelia could well imagine.

'Ellie was beside herself when I finally got home. Not only had I slept with someone else, but the someone was her sister. And to top it all, I'd made Margy pregnant. Something Big Alec had failed to do throughout their married life.'

Cordelia remembered then that Joe had once mentioned that Margy was childless.

'I pleaded with Ellie all day to see sense, for us to try to talk it through. But she wouldn't, and in the end she packed a suitcase for me and told me to get the fuck out and never come back.'

Cordelia frowned. 'Surely she'll eventually come round?'

Joe shook his head. 'You don't know Ellie. Once her mind's made up that's that. And even if she did take me back, I'll have Big Alec to contend with when he gets home. He's not called big for nothing – he's bloody enormous, with hands like shovels. He's a stoker, so you can imagine how strong he is. When he finds out the baby's mine – and he will, even if he has to beat it out of Margy – then he'll be straight after me.'

Joe stopped and gulped, a faint sheen of sweat appearing on his forehead. 'And when he finds me, if he finds me, he's quite capable of murder. I'm not exaggerating. He is.'

'You're in the shit,' Cordelia stated coldly. 'And it's entirely your own fault.'

'What am I to do?' he pleaded, desperate for a solution.

'I've no idea, Joe. That's something you're going to have to figure out for yourself.'

Suddenly Cordelia didn't want to be there any more. Or with Joe. His story sickened her.

She came abruptly to her feet. 'I've got to go. See you in the morning.' She glanced at his empty whisky glass. 'If you're capable, that is.'

The first thing Cordelia did when she got home was go straight into the bathroom and throw up time and time again.

She then informed Alice that she had a splitting headache, didn't want any tea, and was off to bed.

She cried silently for most of the night. And when she woke in the early hours she cried again.

Chapter 15

Henry McLeod led the way into his study, and closed the door behind them. William had requested a private word.

'Brandy?'

'Please.'

Henry headed for the decanter while William sat. 'So, what's this all about?' he queried as he began to pour.

'I need your advice, Father.'

'Oh?' This was unusual. William rarely asked for his advice.

'Actually, it's more of a ruling.'

Henry was intrigued. 'I'm listening.'

'There's a girl I'd like to take out regularly. But it could be a problem.'

'How so?'

'She works for us.'

'Ah!' Henry exclaimed softly. 'I see where the problem lies.' He handed William a balloon glass containing a generous measure.

'I wanted to know how you felt about that,' William went on. 'Am I allowed to go out with someone from work?'

Henry sat facing his son. 'Are you serious about her?'

'I could be. I certainly like her a great deal. She's different, and we seem to get on terribly well.'

'Hm,' Henry mused. 'May I enquire who she is?'

'Lexa Stewart.'

'The lassie with the dirty hands?' Henry smiled.

'They aren't dirty any more, Pater,' William protested. 'They haven't been for a long time.'

'I'm aware of that, William. I was simply teasing, no more.'

William had a sip of his brandy. 'Well?'

'In principle I'm not against you seeing someone from work. That's all fine and well as far as I'm concerned. The trouble is, what happens if you go out with her for a while and then the pair of you split up? That's when it could be difficult. In other words, you could be making a rod for your own back.'

William thought of Lexa, something he'd been doing more and more of late. And very agreeable thoughts they were.

'I hate to say this,' Henry continued, 'but there is also the matter of class. Not that I personally object to you courting a working-class girl, or even marrying one. But if you did the latter could she cope with a whole new way of life – our way of life – and all that that entails?'

'To be honest, Father, I really have no idea. Not yet, anyway. That's something I'd have to find out. But surely we're rushing our fences here, talking about potential marriage. At the moment I hardly know her.'

'But she is special?'

'Could be,' William demurred.

'Then you'd better find out.'

Yes, he had, William thought. Now that he knew his father had no objection to his seeing Lexa.

'The pub's just opened,' Cordelia declared. 'Why don't you go on over?'

'Do you mind?'

'I wouldn't have suggested it if I did,' she replied sarcastically.

'Thanks. You're a doll.'

A doll! she thought as he walked away. Only a few days previously she'd have been thrilled to be called that by Joe Given. Now it seemed like an insult.

She shuddered at the memory of his kissing her while in a drunken stupor. Remembering made her stomach churn and filled her with nausea.

'What's going on?'

Cordelia started, having been completely lost in thought. 'How do you mean, Ginge?'

'His lordship going to the pub at this hour?'

'He needs a drink,' Cordelia stated flatly.

'Must do. He seems to be over there an awful lot nowadays.'

'Of course he is. He's living there.'

Ginge's eyes widened in surprise. 'He hasn't mentioned it to me!'

'Well, he is. Ellie threw him out.'

'Really!'

'Really!' Cordelia echoed, not caring whether or not Joe wanted the fact kept secret.

'But why? I thought those two were right lovebirds.'

'Hm.' Cordelia snorted. 'Some lovebirds when Joe's been screwing his sister-in-law while Ellie was in hospital. Not only that but he's put the sister-in-law up the duff. Something, apparently, her husband has never been able to do.'

'Dear God!' Ginge whispered. This was a turn-up for the book sure enough. 'And what's the husband got to say about all this?'

'He doesn't know . . . *yet*.' Cordelia then went on to give Ginge the whole story.

Ginge whistled when she finally finished. 'I wouldn't like to be in Joe's shoes when this Big Alec catches up with him.'

Nor her, Cordelia thought with grim satisfaction. Joe would get a right pasting. Or even murdered, which Joe was convinced Big Alec was capable of. She doubted it would actually come to that. But this was Glasgow after all, and if it did it was Joe's tough luck.

How callous she'd suddenly become, Cordelia reflected. Where there had once been love, there was now dislike. That, and utter contempt.

'You're very quiet tonight.'

William's eyes flicked sideways. 'Am I?'

'You've hardly said a word since picking me up.'

'Sorry, I didn't mean to be rude.'

'You haven't been. Just quiet, that's all.'

'I've been thinking.' Well, that was true enough.

Lexa nodded. 'Work?'

'No, about you actually. To be frank, I've been thinking a lot about you recently.'

She didn't know what to reply to that, so stayed silent.

'I was wondering,' William said slowly. 'I know of a dinner dance this coming Saturday which should be rather fun. Would you care to go with me?'

That rocked Lexa. The last thing she'd been expecting. William was asking her out again!

'Well, Lexa?'

She took her time in answering. 'What would your girlfriend say?'

'Girlfriend?' He frowned. 'I don't have one.'

'But I saw you with her. At least I presumed she was your girlfriend. I was walking in the street when I spotted you and her in this car together.'

What on earth was she talking about? William wondered. 'When was this?'

Lexa told him.

He shook his head, completely baffled.

'She was very attractive. Still is, I presume. And wearing a nurse's uniform.'

The penny instantly dropped. 'That wasn't a girlfriend,' William said, laughing. 'That was Kirsty, my sister.'

Lexa gaped at him. 'Sister?'

'Twin sister actually. She's a staff nurse at the Western Infirmary, where she has live-in accommodation. She'd had a few days off and I was running her home. She's a real sweetie. You'd like her.'

'I thought . . .' Lexa broke off in confusion. 'Well, you know what I thought.'

'I may have some vices,' William joked lightly, 'but I can assure you incest isn't one of them.'

Lexa blushed bright red. 'I'm sorry I got the wrong end of the stick. But no one has ever mentioned you have a sister, far less a twin.'

'Well, there we are.'

How foolish she'd been to jump to conclusions, Lexa berated herself. But who could blame her?

William laughed again. 'Wait till I tell Kirsty. She'll think it a right hoot. Girlfriend indeed!'

Lexa looked straight into his eyes for the briefest of seconds, and her insides melted.

'Anyway, I take that as a compliment,' he said.

'Why so?'

'You thought her very attractive and she's my twin.' He was teasing now.

'Are you very alike facially?'

'Some people think so. Only she's a blonde whereas I'm dark-haired. You still haven't answered my question.'

The abrupt change of tack lost her. 'What question?'

'About Saturday night.'

'I'd love to go with you,' she smiled, still melting inside. She had no doubts about that.

'Don't take your bad temper out on me, young lady,' Alice admonished Cordelia. 'I don't know what's got up your hump but you've been in a foul mood for days now.'

Cordelia knew that to be only too true. She'd been snapping at everyone. 'Sorry, Mum.'

'I should think so.'

'I don't know what's come over me lately,' she lied.

'Is it that time of month?'

Cordelia considered lying again, then decided not to. She shook her head instead.

'I didn't think it was. Anyway, I'd better get moving as I don't want to keep Peggy McAllister waiting.'

As soon as Alice had left for the Labour Hall Lexa asked, 'Is it Joe that's bothering you?'

Cordelia sighed. 'Aye, it's Joe all right.' This was the first chance she'd had to be alone with Lexa and bring her up to date.

Lexa listened intently as Cordelia told her what had happened.

'His own sister-in-law?' she echoed, appalled.

'Putting her up the duff.'

'Poor you,' Lexa said sympathetically. 'No wonder you've been out of sorts.'

'I just feel such a fool. I was utterly convinced that he was in love with me. How wrong I was!'

'He's got no feelings for you at all?'

Cordelia laughed bitterly. 'How could he when he's been shagging his sister-in-law? It was all in my imagination, Lexa. I've been kidding myself right down the line. Believing he loved me because that's what I wanted to believe.' Tears crept into her eyes. 'If I blame anyone it's me, not him. Thinking back he didn't mislead me. It doesn't stop me thinking him a bastard, though.'

'Are you going to leave the stall?'

'I'm considering doing so. The trouble is I enjoy working there. It can be a good laugh at times.'

'But it does mean seeing Joe on a daily basis. I can't imagine that's a good thing.'

Cordelia wrung her hands, feeling completely wretched. 'You're right, of course, but I don't know if I have the strength to leave. I hate him now, but still want to be there alongside him.' She shook her head. 'I know it doesn't make sense. None at all.'

On a sudden impulse Lexa went over to Cordelia, knelt, and put her arms round her. 'Things will sort themselves out for the best. You'll see.'

Cordelia wasn't convinced.

Pam lit up her mid-morning cigarette, inhaled deeply, and blew smoke at the ceiling. 'I was ready for that,' she declared.

Angela Tarantula came into the ladies' room, closing the door behind her. 'Well well,' she said in a mysterious tone. 'Who'd have thought it.'

'Thought what?' Lexa asked.

'You and Mr McLeod junior. You were seen, you know.'

Lexa's heart sank. 'By whom?'

'Me, of course, silly. You in his car. Bold as brass you were.'

'Is this true?' Pam demanded.

'Yes, it is, as a matter of fact.'

'Well, at least you're not denying it,' Angela said, eyes glittering.

'There's nothing to deny,' Lexa replied. 'He gives me a lift home some evenings as he lives not far from me. That's the long and short of it.'

Angela winked. 'No romance, eh?'

'None whatsoever,' Lexa declared firmly.

'You lucky cow,' breathed Pam, who'd always fancied

William like mad. 'I'd give anything for him to drive me home. He's such a smasher.'

'Come on,' Angela urged. 'There must be more to it than that. You can tell us.'

'I swear there isn't,' Lexa lied. 'It started one night when I was standing at my tram stop in a torrential downpour. He stopped his car and asked where I was going. Ever since then he's given me the occasional lift.'

'Why have you never mentioned it?' Pam demanded.

'Because I didn't want you lot seeing anything in it that simply isn't there. All right?'

'Still interesting though.' Angela smiled.

Lexa felt like slapping her.

'Oh, Christ!' Joe muttered, just loud enough for Cordelia, who was serving a customer a few feet away, to hear.

She glanced across at him and saw that his expression was one of . . . what? She couldn't quite decide. But he certainly didn't look best pleased.

The woman who approached him a few seconds later was somewhat short, and clearly pregnant. 'We have to talk, Joe,' she said.

Margy, Cordelia thought. Had to be.

'Of course,' Joe replied, attempting a smile. Turning to Cordelia, he asked, 'Can you mind the stall for a bit?'

She nodded, but said nothing, and watched the retreating backs of Joe and Margy as they headed for the Hielan Laddie.

They packed up early that afternoon, as it was Saturday, and Cordelia accepted Joe's invitation to join him for a drink. She hadn't intended to go, but curiosity had got the better of her.

'So what was that about?' she asked when they were sitting in the pub.

'The woman was Margy.'

'I guessed that.'

'You'll never believe what Ellie's done?'

'I'm all ears,' Cordelia replied sarcastically.

'Gone and let our house go. Given the keys to the factor and moved in with her parents.'

'Dear me,' Cordelia commented, completely unsympathetic.

'I never thought she'd do such a thing. Not in a million years.' He sagged where he sat. 'I don't know if I'll ever see her or wee Hannah again. Her folks live way over in Shettleston.' He shook his head. 'God alone knows what she's done with our furniture and all the other bits and pieces.'

'Probably sold the lot,' Cordelia said, thoroughly enjoying his misery.

'That's not all,' Joe went on. 'Margy's terrified of Big Alec coming back. She's had a letter from him saying he'll be arriving in Glasgow at the beginning of next month.'

'Dear me,' Cordelia said, repeating herself.

'She wants us to run away together.'

Cordelia had a sip of her drink. 'And will you?'

'Don't you understand? I love Ellie and wee Hannah!' It was almost a wail.

'You should have reminded yourself of that before fucking Margy.' Cordelia smiled, relishing sticking the knife in. She knew the F-word would upset him.

'I never thought it would end up like this,' Joe protested.

'What you did think was that it would just be a bit on the side with no after effects. Right?'

Joe nodded.

'How wrong you were. As a result you've lost your wife and daughter, not to mention gained the prospect of having Big Alec coming after you.'

Joe paled, and nervously reached for his drink.

Cordelia studied him, amused by the fact that he must be going through absolute hell. 'When did you say Big Alec was coming back to Glasgow?'

'The beginning of next month.'

'Not long, is it?' she mused aloud.

Joe gulped. 'No.'

'Maybe you should take Margy up on her offer and the pair of you run away together?'

Joe shook his head. 'I couldn't do that. I simply couldn't.'

'Why not?'

'I told you, I love Ellie and wee Hannah. Margy doesn't come into it.'

No, you just used to come into Margy, Cordelia thought, and sniggered.

'What?' Joe demanded.

'Nothing.'

'So why are you sniggering? There's nothing to snigger at. I'm in deep shite, and that's the truth.'

It certainly was, Cordelia reflected. 'I'm sure you'll think of something,' she declared lightly. 'In the meantime I'm off. Thanks for the drink and see you Monday morning. If you turn up, that is.'

He stared at her as she came to her feet. 'Why are you being so hard on me, doll?'

If only you knew, Cordelia thought. If only you knew. 'Bye then,' she said, and walked away, leaving his question unanswered.

'That's one of the best meals I've ever had,' Lexa declared. 'I've never tasted lamb like it.'

William was delighted. 'More wine?'

'Please.'

How manly he was, Lexa reflected as he topped up her glass. And how good-looking. Not to mention excellent company.

'I must say, I like your dress.'

She flushed slightly at the compliment. The dress was burgundy-coloured crushed velvet which contrasted extremely well with her hair. 'Why, thank you. It's one of the three I bought with the money you gave me.'

'Then you chose well. I'm sure the other two are just as nice.'

For the briefest of moments she saw the slight difference in colour between each eye. Then it was gone. 'Did you and your sister attend the same school?' she asked, making conversation.

'Heavens no. Kelvinside Academy is an all-boys institution. Kirsty went to Laurel Bank, which is exclusively for girls.'

Lexa tried to imagine that, having been used to both boys and girls being mixed up in the same class. 'What about university? Did you go there, William?'

'I had the option, but decided not to as I was joining the family business. What about you?'

She realised he was teasing her, but didn't take offence. 'Same here.'

He raised an eyebrow. 'You had the option of university?'

'Of course not. I meant going straight into the family business. Only in my case it was fruit and veg, not wine.'

Reaching across the table he placed a hand over hers. 'We have a lot in common then.'

'And a lot that isn't,' she reminded him, meaning their backgrounds.

A waiter arrived to remove their plates and the three-piece band struck up.

'Shall we?' William proposed. 'We can order our puddings later.'

'Let's.'

He escorted her on to the floor, and they began to dance. Before the first number was halfway through she was snuggled dreamily against his shoulder.

Would he or wouldn't he? she wondered as they drew up outside her close.

'Will I see you again?' he queried softly.

'If you wish.'

'Next Saturday. I'll pick you up at the same time.'

'Fine.'

And then, leaning over, he kissed her.

Chapter 16

A dark-faced Joe appeared out of the crowd to slip in alongside Cordelia. 'How did you get on?' she asked.

'Terrible. I went all the way to bloody Shettleston, miles on the tram, and when I got there her mother wouldn't let me see either Ellie or wee Hannah. Barred the door and told me to eff off.'

'So you didn't speak to Ellie, then?'

Joe shook his head. 'Not a word. It was a wasted journey.'

'I'm sorry.' She wasn't at all.

'I did think of barging in past the old bat. But what good would that have done me?'

'Business has been quite brisk,' Cordelia stated brightly.

'What?'

She repeated herself.

'Oh, fine.' As if that was important, he thought.

'What are you going to do now?'

He shrugged. 'I haven't the foggiest.'

'You could try again in a few days' time.'

'Naw,' he snarled. 'I'd still be kept standing on the doorstep.' Swearing volubly, he pulled out his cigarettes and lit up. 'Do you mind if I nip to the pub, Cordelia? I'm blazing inside.'

The pub was no more than she'd have expected. 'On you go. Don't worry about me.'

'Thanks, kid. You're a pal.'

A pal? She glared as he walked away. She was hardly that. If anything she was quite the opposite.

'Bastard!' she hissed through gritted teeth.

Lexa lay in bed, having woken early. She began thinking about William and their night out together.

How she'd enjoyed it. A real treat. Lovely food, dancing, and William. Who could possibly ask for more?

And he'd kissed her too. Taking his time, his tongue probing her mouth. And she, being daring, she'd thought, had responded in kind. Something she'd never before done with a man.

How was it he was able to make her melt inside the way he did? Melt, and go all tingly. One thing was certain: she wanted to experience it again. She sighed, thinking she couldn't have been more content. Was she falling in love? She decided it was a distinct possibility.

Cordelia nudged Joe in the ribs. 'She's here again.'

'Who?'

Cordelia nodded in the direction from where Margy was coming towards them. A quick glance at Joe told her he was horrified.

'She won't leave me alone,' he complained bitterly.

Hardly surprising, considering the belly on her. And the fact that the father wasn't her husband. 'I suppose it's the pub again,' Cordelia said.

'I'm sorry. But where else can I take her, doll?'

Far away? Cordelia almost replied, but didn't. Timbuctoo seemed a suitable place to her.

Margy arrived at the stall, her face worn and haggard. Joe had a quick word with her, and then the pair of them headed off for the Hielan Laddie.

He came back an hour later, alone, and lost no time in telling Cordelia how difficult Margy had been.

'It was awful. She started greeting right there in the pub,' he said.

'A full boo hoo?'

Joe nodded. 'It was ever so embarrassing. People kept looking over. One chap in particular kept glaring at me as if I was some bloody wife beater or something.'

Not wife beater, but wife cheater, Cordelia thought grimly. Then she reminded herself that that was unfair. Hadn't she been prepared to sleep with Joe as well? No, she was definitely being unfair. What was really upsetting her was that Joe had betrayed Ellie with Margy, and not herself.

'She still wants the pair of us to run away together before Big Alec gets home,' Joe went on. 'The nearer that gets the more terrified she's becoming.' He stopped and shook his head. 'Quite right too. Big Alec will give her one hell of a hammering. It'll probably be the hospital for her, and no mistake. The man's vicious.'

'Then it'll be the hospital for you too,' Cordelia was unable to resist pointing out.

'If not the morgue,' Joe added, and shuddered. Sweat popped out on his forehead.

For the first time since he had told her about Margy, Cordelia felt some sympathy for him.

Ginge materialised with a coffee in one hand and a bacon sanny in the other. 'I thought you might like these, as being on your own you haven't the chance of getting them for yourself.'

'Thanks, Ginge. Just what the doctor ordered.' She smiled in appreciation.

'Where's his lordship then? As if I couldn't guess.'

'The pub.'

'I thought so. Has he decided what he's going to do yet?'

Cordelia shook her head. 'Nope.'

'He's landed himself in a right pickle, hasn't he?'

'You can say that again. With knobs on.' Cordelia had a sip of coffee, then a bite of the sandwich. 'I'm needing this,' she declared.

Ginge studied her, thinking what a fanciable female she was. If she'd been interested in him he'd have been after her like a shot. As it was, he'd have to settle for having her as a friend. Still, never give up hope, he told himself. Who was to say things might not change?

'Are you winching yet?' he asked casually, wanting to know if she was going out with anyone special.

'Are you?'

'Oh aye, hundreds of lassies,' Ginge replied drily.

'I take it that means you aren't?'

'That's right. And you?'

Pain lanced through Cordelia as she thought of Joe, and what she'd felt for him. She'd really loved that man. The rat.

'Not at the present,' she replied.

'That sounds as if there's been someone recently?' Ginge probed.

'There was. But it's over now.'

'Were you close?'

'What is this, the bloody Spanish Inquisition?' she snapped.

'Sorry,' he apologised, thinking he'd obviously touched a raw nerve.

Cordelia laid down her coffee and sanny as a customer came up to the stall, and Ginge left her to return to his own.

'I thoroughly enjoyed that,' Lexa declared as she and William emerged from the picture house after seeing *Wee Willie Winkie*, starring Shirley Temple and Victor McLaglen.

'I did too.' William smiled. They'd sat in the back row and he'd had his arm round her the whole time. Several times during the programme they'd kissed, as had other couples in the coveted seats.

It was a lovely night, the sky lit with myriad stars, the moon full and pale yellow in colour.

'Do you fancy a coffee before we head home?' he proposed. 'I know a cosy little café nearby.'

'That would hit the spot.' She hooked an arm round his. 'Let's go, then.'

'I'm thinking of buying a new car,' he told her when they were seated in the café.

'Oh? What's wrong with the one you already have?'

'There's nothing wrong with it. And I shall still be using it on company business. No, what I have in mind is something for my own private use. Something sporty.'

She liked the sound of that. 'Anything particular in mind?'

'A Hornet.' He beamed. 'That's the ticket. If I can find one at the right price. And colour.'

She would never have thought of the latter. 'What colour do you prefer?'

'Red. Or green. Either would suit.'

Lexa knew nothing about cars, and had no idea what a Hornet looked like. 'If I was choosing I'd go for green,' she said.

'Why's that?'

Her lips curled into a smile. 'Simple. It's my favourite colour, and always has been.'

'Any shade of green?'

'Preferably the darker ones.'

William was about to reply when a sudden scuffle broke out. Moments later voices were raised, then fists were flying.

'Forget the coffee. Let's get out of here,' he said, getting quickly to his feet. He ushered Lexa to the door and out on to the street. Behind them bedlam had broken out. 'Are you all right?'

Lexa took a deep breath. 'A bit shaken, that's all. It caught me completely by surprise.'

'Me too. It just sort of erupted out of nowhere.' They started walking in the direction of where the car was parked.

'I wonder what it was all about?'

'I think I can guess,' William replied. 'Several of the voices were German.'

'German!' Lexa exclaimed.

'I distinctly heard them as we were heading for the door. There's a lot of anti-German feeling at the moment. So no doubt something was said, either to the Germans or by them, and a fight resulted.'

Lexa was suddenly scared. 'Do you think there is going to be a war, William? The newspapers seem to believe so.'

William took his time in replying. 'It's certainly beginning to look that way. In my opinion, and I hate to say this, it's only a matter of time.'

Lexa shivered with apprehension. 'And we'll be in it?'

'I don't see how we can stay out,' William replied grimly.

War! Lexa thought. How horrible. She'd heard stories about the Great War and how awful that had been. If there was another it would probably be even worse. Taking William's arm she moved closer to him, holding his arm so tightly it was as if she never wanted to let it go.

Joe had been gone for more than an hour when he returned with a grin plastered all over his face. It was the first time Cordelia had seen him smile since the Margy business had blown up.

'It's all been settled,' he informed her after she'd finished dealing with a customer.

'What has?'

'What I'm going to do.'

'And?'

'I'm not staying in Glasgow. That would be suicidal. Big Alec would hunt me down and then I'd be for it. So I've decided to go to London and find work there. That's the sensible thing to do.'

'What sort of work?'

'I've no idea, as I've never even been to London. Or England for that matter. But I'll find something. They're bound to have a flower market and that's where I'll start looking.'

Cordelia glanced away, not wishing Joe to see her expression. 'Are you taking Margy with you?'

'No fear. She can stay and face the music all by herself. I've already told you, I don't feel anything for her. What happened between us just happened, that's all.'

'What about Ellie and Hannah?'

Joe sighed. 'That's the hard bit. I'm going to miss them both like buggery.' He stopped and shook his head. 'There's no point in hanging around when I can't even see either of them. It seems to me Ellie has made it crystal clear it's over between the pair of us, and I just have to accept it.'

Cordelia wanted to be sick. Joe going away! She'd never really believed it would actually come to that. Not deep down. And now it had.

'I've done a deal with Ginge,' Joe went on. 'I've sold him this pitch, which puts money in my pocket. He'll be running this stall from now on.'

Cordelia was stunned. 'How will that affect me?' she asked.

'Ginge wants you to meet him in the pub after work. He'll talk to you then.'

'And you, Joe. When are you off?'

He smiled broadly. 'Right now, darling. I'll get my things together and catch the late night train to Euston.'

Her mind was reeling from all this information. 'Tonight?' she stuttered.

'That's right. I'm getting the hell out while the going's good. When I have an address I'll let Ginge know and he can forward on the money he owes me.'

'So this is . . . goodbye then?'

'It is indeed, darling. It is indeed. And I have to say I can't thank you enough for all the hard graft you've put in for me. I couldn't have found a better assistant. You're a real diamond.' Joe pulled out his wallet and extracted several notes. 'That's your pay till the end of the week plus a wee bonus thrown in for good measure. All right?'

She accepted the money while fighting the almost over-whelming urge to slap his face. 'Thank you,' she muttered.

He pecked her on the cheek. 'I'm off then. Wish me luck.'

'Good luck, Joe. All the best,' she somehow managed to reply.

Tears formed in her eyes as she watched him head for the Hielan Laddie and out of her life for ever. She instinctively knew she'd never see Joe Given again.

'I got you a drink in,' Ginge declared when Cordelia joined him in the pub later. She sat and immediately had a large gulp of whisky and lemonade, which made her feel better. Then she took another gulp, draining her glass.

'Steady on,' Ginge admonished her. 'You'll be pished as a fart if you carry on like that.'

'Can I have another, Ginge?' She fumbled in a pocket. 'Here, I'll pay. And another for yourself.'

Ginge stared at her. It was obvious how upset she was. 'You won't be losing your job, Cordelia, if that's what you're worried about. I want to keep you on.'

'Thanks, Ginge,' she replied, attempting a smile. 'Now how about that drink? And I insist I pay.'

He took the ten bob note from her and headed for the bar. He'd expected her to be a bit put out by Joe's departure, but nothing like this.

Cordelia had managed to compose herself by the time he returned. 'So what's the score?' she asked.

'As I said, I want you to stay on and work for me. Do you agree?'

'What's the wage?'

'Same as you're getting now. Though I could up it a little.'

'Then up it.'

Ginge smiled. 'How does another seven and six sound?'

Cordelia nodded. 'It's a deal.'

'It's a deal then,' Ginge repeated. 'I'm somewhat relieved, I have to say. I wasn't at all sure you'd want to stay on and work for me.'

That surprised her. 'Why not?'

He shrugged. 'I just wasn't, that's all.'

Cordelia realised what he was getting at. 'Listen, just because I don't fancy you doesn't mean I don't like you, or consider you a pal.'

'Thanks, Cordelia.' He smiled.

'Now let's get down to the nitty-gritty. I've been left on my own on that stall far too often. I really do need someone to help me. Especially for the heavy work. Humping boxes isn't easy for a woman.'

'I agree. In fact, I couldn't agree more. I considered it scandalous the way Joe treated you.'

'So?'

'I've already thought about that. I've a young cousin who's looking for a job at the moment. I'm sure he'll jump at the chance if I was to offer him one. What do you say?'

'Sounds all right to me.'

'That's settled then.' Ginge beamed. 'I'll have a word with him later on tonight, and he can start on Monday.'

Cordelia stared into her drink, thinking of Joe.

'Cordelia?'

She sniffed, and had a sip of her second dram. 'Life sure does play tricks on you, doesn't it, Ginge?'

He hadn't a clue what she was talking about.

'Go away!' Cordelia said huskily when Lexa tapped on her bedroom door. She had finished her second whisky with Ginge and then excused herself, saying her tea would be on the table, but when she got home she had been unable to fancy any food and had fled directly to her bedroom.

'Mum's gone to have a chinwag with Mrs McAllister, so we're alone,' Lexa replied.

Cordelia blew her nose into a scrap of hanky, then used it to wipe away tears. She was in a terrible state, and knew it.

'Cordelia?'

'Not now.'

'What's wrong? You can tell me. Surely it's better if we talk?'

Maybe it would be, Cordelia thought, wiping away more tears. Lexa already knew about Joe anyway. But not that he'd gone to London.

'Come in then,' she called out in a quavering voice.

When Lexa was sitting on the bed beside her, Cordelia took a deep breath and launched into her story.

'I've noticed a big difference in you of late,' Pam said to Lexa, over her usual fag.

'Oh?'

'Aye. I have.'

'What sort of difference?'

Pam thought about it. 'You seem happier somehow. And more chipper.'

'Maybe she's got a fella she's not telling us about,' Tarantula probed. She had taken to joining them for a smoke during their morning break, a habit she had only recently taken up.

Lexa pretended innocence. 'I only wish there were,' she lied.

'I've noticed something different about you as well,' Tarantula went on.

'You're both imagining things,' Lexa declared, trying to fob them off.

'I don't think so,' Pam persisted, studying Lexa closely. 'You seem to be sort of . . . well, blooming.'

'Blooming!' Lexa exclaimed. 'I'm not a flower, you know.'

'You're not preggers, are you?' Tarantula queried, eyes

glinting at the prospect of the scandal that would cause.

'How can I be that without a chap?' Lexa smiled disarmingly. 'It does take two to tango, after all.'

'Unless you're lying,' Tarantula said, rather nastily.

'About what?'

'Having a fella.'

Lexa stared straight into Tarantula's eyes. 'Why on earth would I lie about not having a chap?'

'I dunno,' Tarantula admitted, shaking her head.

'Anyway.' Pam exhaled, and changed the subject.

Cordelia found Ginge and a young lad waiting for her when she arrived at the stall on Monday morning. The lad was well built, broad-shouldered, blue-eyed and, to Cordelia's relief, blond-haired, not red like his cousin Ginge.

'Cordelia, this is Kenny Smith. Kenny, this is Miss Stewart, who'll show you the ropes.'

The two of them shook hands, Cordelia immediately taking a shine to the young man.

'I'll leave the pair of you to it then,' Ginge declared, and strode away.

Chapter 17

'Well, what do you think?' William proudly asked, gesturing at the car parked outside Lexa's close.

'It's beautiful,' she gasped. 'Absolutely beautiful.'

'She's a Hornet in British racing green. She's got a 1,275cc engine, and goes like the proverbial clappers when you put your foot down. As you can see she's a two-seater.' He then began to describe the special gearbox, which meant absolutely nothing to Lexa.

'It really is a smasher,' she declared. 'So different from your other car.'

'Chalk and cheese.' William nodded. 'I took possession of her two days ago. And you shall have the privilege of being my first passenger. So climb in and we'll be off.'

He opened the door for her and she slid inside, thinking it rather a tight fit. There was no roomy space here.

'Where are we going?' she asked.

'I know a lovely little country pub where we might have a drink,' he replied.

Lexa was thrilled. At long last she was going to visit a

pub, something she'd wanted to do for a long time. 'Sounds wonderful,' she enthused.

'The pub is very old with lots of oak beams and tartan everywhere. The beer's awfully good, too.'

'No wine?' she teased.

''Fraid not. I have spoken to the landlord in the past but he's just not interested. Told me his customers simply wouldn't want to know. Not a proper drink, according to them. Something only gentlemen of dubious sexual orientation might buy.'

The penny dropped, and Lexa blushed bright red. She had heard of men like that, though she had never come across one, as far as she knew. 'I see,' she murmured.

William started the engine, engaged gear, and away they went. 'It'll take us about an hour to get there,' William informed her. 'So it's a decent drive there and back.'

Lexa listened to the throbbing of the engine, which was quite noisy. A certain vibration was something new, and rather exciting.

'By the by, my sister Kirsty is going to be there with her boyfriend Cameron who's a trainee doctor. I hope you don't mind?'

Lexa shook her head. 'Not at all.'

'Are you sure?'

'Of course.'

'Kirsty's dying to meet you.'

'You've told her about me then?'

William laughed. 'Don't forget she's my twin. We share all our secrets – always have. We don't keep anything from one another.'

The truth was, William's surprise announcement had rather thrown Lexa, who wished she'd had time to get used to the idea of meeting his sister. She could only hope everything would go all right.

'There's something I want to talk to you about,' she said.

'What's that?'

'The girls in the office are getting very nosy about you and me. They've guessed I'm seeing someone, which I've denied. But what happens if they find out, and that it's you?'

William frowned. 'How did they guess? Did you accidentally let something slip?'

'No, I haven't. They say I've changed recently, that I'm different. And they put it down to a boyfriend I'm not telling them about.'

He thought for a few moments. 'I would much prefer they didn't know it was me. It would become the talk of the building.'

'I honestly didn't let anything slip, William, I swear.'

He smiled at her. 'I believe you, Lexa. If you say you didn't, then you didn't.'

'Thank you.'

He patted her on the knee. 'Let's just see how things turn out, eh?'

She wondered what that meant. Would he break off their relationship if the news got out at work? She sincerely hoped not. It simply didn't bear thinking about.

The pub was called the Clansmen's Inn, and the inside was just as William had described. Lexa prayed her nervousness wasn't obvious as William steered her towards a table where a blonde-haired woman was deep in conversation with her male companion.

Introductions were made, and then William declared he'd get a round in. When he asked Lexa what she'd like she elected for a gin and tonic, which was what Kirsty was drinking.

It was a shock for Lexa to see just how alike William and Kirsty were. Different colour of hair, and different colour of eyes – Kirsty's were green – but apart from that they were two peas in a pod.

'Is it true you used to run a fruit and vegetable shop?' Kirsty asked Lexa.

Lexa nodded, wondering what was coming next. Some sort of putdown perhaps? 'With my sister.'

'How jolly interesting,' Kirsty enthused. 'Good for you.'

Lexa relaxed, hearing the sincerity in Kirsty's voice. Kirsty was genuinely impressed.

The evening was going to be all right.

'I liked your sister,' Lexa declared as they started the drive back to Glasgow.

'And she liked you too. I could tell.'

'Could you?'

'I keep reminding you she's my twin. I can read her like a book, and she me.'

'I thoroughly enjoyed myself, William. Thank you.'

'No, thank you.' William suddenly laughed. 'At least there wasn't a fight. Twice I've taken you out and there have been incidents. I have to apologise for that.'

'There's no need to apologise. They weren't your fault.'

'None the less.'

Lexa closed her eyes, and leaned back in her seat. It had been a perfect evening.

When they arrived at her close it was a good fifteen minutes before Lexa got out of the car and went upstairs with the broadest of smiles on her face.

Ginge came over to Cordelia's stall while Kenny was off getting tea. 'How's the lad doing?'

'Fine. Very helpful, and picks things up quickly. He's also good with the customers. Knows just how to chat to them. Flirts outrageously with the women, which goes down a real treat with them.'

Ginge grinned. 'Cheeky bugger. That's him all over. So you have no complaints?'

'None whatever. He's ideal for the job.'

'Right then. I'd better get back. No rest for the wicked, eh?'

Cordelia couldn't imagine Ginge being wicked. It simply wasn't in his nature.

It was about half an hour later when Cordelia spotted an extremely angry man bearing down on the stall. He was huge, certainly by Glasgow standards, well over six feet and built like the proverbial brick shithouse. She knew it just had to be Big Alec.

'Is Given around?' he snarled on reaching the stall.

Cordelia felt fear clutch at her insides. The man was terrifying. No wonder Joe had been so scared of him. 'No, he's not.'

'Then where is he? Or when's he coming back?'

Cordelia became aware that Kenny had come to stand by her side. Moreover, he was holding one of the claw hammers they used to prise open wooden boxes.

'You all right, Miss Stewart?' he asked quietly.

Bless him, Cordelia thought. But he'd stand no chance against the powerhouse that was Big Alec. None the less, she appreciated the fact he was there. 'I'm fine, Kenny.'

'Well?' Alec demanded, his voice a harsh grate. Veins were standing out on his neck.

'Are you Alec?'

'I am.'

'Joe's gone. Scarpered. He knew you'd come looking for him so sold his pitch and took off like a scalded cat.'

Alec frowned. 'Took off where?'

'London.'

'London!'

'Aye, that's right. Said if he stayed in Glasgow you'd hunt him down.'

'He was damn right about that,' Alec snarled. 'Have you his London address?'

Cordelia shook her head. 'Sorry. I haven't.'

Alec leaned into the stall, damaging some flowers in the process. 'Don't lie to me, bitch. You must have an address.'

'Watch the flowers,' Kenny said boldly. 'They cost money.'

Alec swivelled his gaze on to him. 'Shut the fuck up, son. Speak again and I'll take that hammer off you and stick it up your arse.'

Despite himself, Kenny flinched, but he didn't back off.

'I don't have one,' Cordelia stated firmly. 'He didn't

have an address when he left, and he hasn't been in touch since. But I can tell you he'll be looking for work in the London flower market, if there is such a place. If not, I'd try Covent Garden if I were you.'

Alec grunted, and stood upright. 'You know what he's done, don't you?'

'Made your wife pregnant.'

'Aye, that he has. The bastard. Just wait till I get hold of him. I'll rip his snivelling head off.'

Cordelia wanted to ask about Margy, but daren't. It was none of her business, after all.

A customer came up to the stall. 'See to that lady, Kenny,' Cordelia instructed. Kenny, after a searching look at Cordelia, did exactly that.

'What are you to Given?' Alec demanded.

'I was his assistant, nothing more. And now I work for the chap Joe sold the pitch to.'

Alec digested the information she'd given him. 'Sorry to trouble you then, miss. Nothing personal, you understand?'

'No offence taken, I assure you.'

Turning on his heel, Alec strode away.

Cordelia let out a sigh of relief, pleased that that was over. Alec had truly frightened her. When Kenny had finished dealing with the customer she thanked him for standing alongside her. Kenny, embarrassed, insisted it had been nothing.

Cordelia was impressed none the less. What he'd done had taken guts, and she reported as much to Ginge the next time they spoke.

*   *   *

'I'm afraid I'll have to cancel Saturday night,' William said to Lexa as he drove her home from the office.

Her disappointment was obvious. 'Why's that?'

'There's a wine conference held in London every year, and this year Father wants me to attend instead of him. Says it'll improve my knowledge of the trade, and also help me gain useful contacts. I'm sorry, Lexa. But I have to go.'

'What about Friday night?' she ventured to propose.

'I'm travelling down on the Friday, so that's out as well. However, we could go somewhere during the week. How about that?'

She smiled at him. 'Terrific.'

'Next Wednesday say?'

'Straight from work?'

'Best that way.'

'I'm looking forward to it.'

He matched her smile. 'Me too.' He briefly stroked her knee.

Lexa inwardly shivered with pleasure at his touch.

Cordelia was sitting on the edge of her bed thinking about Big Alec's visit to her stall. Why had she told him how he might find Joe? She needn't have done. She could have kept her mouth shut. Was it because she'd been hoping Alec might still give Joe the pasting he so richly deserved?

Confused, she shook her head. She still loved Joe even after what he'd done. Loved, and hated him too. It was a curious combination. One moment she wanted Joe back and to be hers. The next, she'd happily have watched Alec give him a good kicking.

Love. Hate. Opposite sides of the same coin.

How she missed him. Painfully so. An actual physical pain that clutched and squeezed her insides.

Every time she thought of Joe it was mental anguish in one form or another.

'I've had an idea, Lexa,' Alice announced.

'What's that, Mum?'

'You've been seeing William for quite some while now. Right?'

Lexa nodded.

'I think we should invite him to tea one night so he can get to know us better as a family.'

Lexa wasn't at all sure about that. 'I don't know,' she prevaricated.

'Not ashamed of us, are you?' Alice stared hard at her daughter.

'Of course not, Mum.'

'Then what's the problem?'

'There isn't one. I mean . . .' Lexa trailed off, not at all sure what she did mean. William for tea? 'Let me think about it,' she said slowly.

'You do that, darling. And let me know when you've made a decision. I think it would be lovely to have him here. We'd make an evening of it.'

On Saturday morning William went into the hotel dining room for breakfast. It had been late when he'd arrived at the hotel so, after a stiff drink at the bar, he'd gone straight to bed where he'd slept like a log. Now the conference lay before him.

He was studying the menu when, to his utter amazement, he saw Helen, his old girlfriend, enter the room.

Oh, Christ! he thought. What on earth was she doing here? More to the point, would she cause some sort of scene because of the letter he'd sent her breaking it off between them?

Helen was heading for an empty table when she spotted him. Her look of surprise was replaced by a smile as she changed direction.

William groaned inwardly, and rose to his feet as she came towards him.

'Well well well,' she said, reaching his table. 'May I join you?'

William gestured to a chair. 'Help yourself.'

'Thank you.' Helen sat and studied him. 'So how are you, William?'

'Tip top. Yourself?'

'Never better. May I ask what brings you to London?'

He explained about the conference. 'And you?'

'Mummy and I are here on a little shopping trip. Bond Street and all that.'

'I see.'

A waitress appeared, and they both ordered. When the waitress had gone Helen stared William straight in the eye. 'What you did to me wasn't very nice, now, was it?'

He dropped his gaze, uncertain what to reply.

'Was it, William?' Helen persisted.

He didn't answer, squirming inside.

'You could have at least told me face to face.'

'You were in Cannes.'

'You might have waited till I returned.'

He sucked in a deep breath. 'I suppose so,' he murmured.

'You took the easy way out. The coward's way out. I have to say, I was extremely upset. I was very fond of you, William, and thought we got on so well together.' She lowered her voice to almost a whisper. 'Especially in bed.'

He felt his neck flame. This was awful.

'So why?' she demanded. 'You didn't say in your letter. Only that you were breaking it off.'

William gritted his teeth. 'If you want the truth you're far too bossy and manipulative for me. That's why, in the end, I knew it wouldn't work between us. I didn't say so in the letter because I didn't want to hurt you.'

The waitress arrived back with tea and coffee, and they fell silent while the pots were placed on the table.

'Toast, madam?'

'Please.'

'And you, sir?'

'Please.'

'Is your mother joining us?' William enquired when the waitress had gone.

Helen gave a quick shake of her head. 'No. She never eats breakfast. Well, rarely, anyway. If she did want something she'd order room service.'

He'd forgotten just how beautiful Helen was, William reflected. How was it he used to think of her? Passionate, yet passionless at the same time. Yes, that was it.

'You *did* hurt me, though,' Helen said softly. 'Very much.'

'Then I'm sorry.'

'Are you really?' She gave him a long look.

'Yes, I am. I never realised you cared so much for me.'

For a moment Helen's eyes glittered, then the glitter was gone. 'It's all water under the bridge now anyway. Let's change the subject. Do you have someone new?'

'Yes, I do,' he admitted.

'Me too. His name's Anthony and he's a stockbroker. The family are filthy rich, own acres and acres of Perthshire which alone are worth a fortune. And your lady friend?'

'A modest background compared to your Anthony.'

'Her name?'

'Lexa Stewart.'

Helen frowned. 'What sort of name is that?'

'It's short for Alexandra.'

'I see. And how did you meet?'

William didn't have to answer for a few seconds as their toast arrived.

'Well?'

'She works for *Vins*,' he said.

Helen raised an eyebrow. 'Now I understand the modest background. One of the proles, I take it?'

'Don't be bitchy,' William snapped in reply. 'It doesn't suit you.'

Helen laughed gently. 'I stand reprimanded. I'm sure she's a lovely young lady. Must be to capture your attention.'

'And where did you meet Anthony?'

'At a party, actually. We hit it off straight away. He's terribly dashing. And frightfully clever. He makes me feel a proper ninny at times.'

William watched Helen reach for the coffee pot to fill his cup before filling her own with tea.

221

'I try to avoid taking coffee first thing in the morning,' she declared. 'It gives me heartburn.'

William smiled. 'I remember.'

'Do you remember any other things?' she asked, giving him the sweetest, and most innocent, of smiles.

'Yes,' he admitted.

'Such fond memories, eh?'

He didn't reply to that.

'Well, they are to me,' she added.

William tasted his coffee, wishing with all his heart he hadn't run into Helen. He made a mental note to skip breakfast altogether the following morning. Then he recalled Helen's mentioning room service. He'd opt for that.

'Now tell me all about your young lady,' Helen prompted.

At the first possible opportunity he escaped the dining room for the conference.

Chapter 18

'We usually go to the pub after we've packed up on a Saturday,' Cordelia told Kenny. 'By we I mean the stallholders. It's a sort of tradition. Want to come?'

He shook his head. 'I'm afraid I can't, Miss Stewart. I'm under age.'

'When are you eighteen?'

'In a few months' time.'

'Well, you look eighteen to me, so I don't see any problem. I'm sure no one will challenge you. What do you say now?'

His face cracked into a smile. 'You're on.'

'Let's just finish this lot, and then over we go.'

Cordelia found a table and told Kenny to sit while she went up to the bar. As a Saturday regular, and a stallholder, she'd become well known. Whereas women didn't normally go to the bar, it was quite accepted in the Hielan Laddie at this particular time.

Kenny was puffing away on a cigarette when she returned to their table carrying a dram and lemonade, and a pint of heavy which she placed in front of Kenny. He glanced around him. 'I like this place. It's smashing.'

'It's not the nicest of pubs. The decor, I mean. But you get used to it. And the staff are friendly, which is a bonus.'

'Is Ginge coming?' he queried.

'Probably. Why?'

Kenny shrugged. 'Just wondering.'

'Are you worried he'll be upset to find you here?'

Kenny shrugged again. 'He might be.'

'You leave Ginge to me. You're here at my invitation. Once he knows that you won't get a further peep of protest out of him, I promise you.'

Kenny hesitated, then asked, 'Can I say something?'

'Go ahead.'

'It's none of my business like, but Ginge fancies you rotten. I've heard him mention it on several occasions.'

'I know, Kenny. I'm well aware of the fact.'

'But you don't fancy him. Is that it?'

She nodded. 'He's a lovely man and I hold him dearly. But he just isn't for me.'

Kenny thought about it. 'Pity. You'd make a great couple.'

She didn't reply, as Ginge had just walked through the door. By the time he joined them she had started talking about something else.

'There's a note for you, Mr McLeod,' the receptionist told him as William collected his key after a full day at the conference.

'A note?' William queried in surprise.

'Yes, sir.' The receptionist retrieved an envelope from a pigeon hole and handed it over along with the key.

WILLIAM McLEOD had been scrawled on the front of the envelope, in writing which William instantly recognised as Helen's. Frowning, he opened the envelope and read the contents.

William, something has come up and I must speak to you right away. No matter the time, please come to my room, no. 126. I shall be waiting. Helen.

William had had lots of wine to drink during the course of the day, and was consequently somewhat befuddled, but the urgency of the message did not fail to strike him. What on earth was all this about? he wondered. What could possibly be so important? Should he go to her room as requested, or ignore the note? He was in two minds. Then curiosity got the better of him.

It only took Helen a few moments to answer his knock. 'Come in,' she invited.

The room was identical to his own, a double with a bathroom leading off. 'So what's this all about, Helen?' he asked, quite mystified.

She was wearing a pale-grey cashmere sweater and matching woollen skirt. Her slippers were blue, and oriental in design. 'Can I pour you a drink first?' She smiled, gesturing to an already opened bottle of champagne nestling in a silver bucket.

'That's kind. Thank you.'

He watched her pour, a host of memories flashing through his mind. 'Are you in some sort of trouble?' he asked as she handed him a flute three-quarters full.

'No, not really.'

'Then what's up? Why this mysterious late-night summons?'

'I needed to see you.'

'All right.' He nodded. 'Here I am.'

Crossing to her own drink, she picked it up and took a sip, her eyes boring into William's over the rim of her glass. 'I'll explain in a minute. But first I have to go to the lavatory. Do you mind?'

What a silly question, he thought. Why should he mind? 'Of course not.'

She replaced her glass, then glided from the room, leaving a strong whiff of scent mingled with cigarette smoke behind her. The bathroom door snicked quietly shut.

William shook his head in bafflement. He was tired, half drunk, and desperate for his bed. He could only hope this wouldn't take long, whatever it was.

In less than the promised minute the bathroom door reopened to reveal a stark naked Helen smiling at him.

To say William was taken aback would be an understatement. This was the last thing he'd expected. 'What are you doing?' he croaked.

'I never had the chance to say goodbye properly, and I thought I'd use the opportunity of our both being here in the same hotel to do so.'

William drew in a deep breath. He should leave, he thought. Get the hell out while the going was good. Instead he stood rooted to the spot, his eyes fixed on the gorgeousness before him.

She glided towards him, her breasts moving hypnotically from side to side, her bottom doing a little fandango of its own. She finally stopped only inches away.

'A final fling, William. For old times' sake? Surely you won't deny me?'

Reaching out she took hold of him, and gently squeezed. Smiling when she felt an almost instant reaction.

William was lost, and knew it. Naked like this, and beautiful as she was, what man in his right mind would turn her down?

'A last goodbye, eh? Where's the harm? None that I can think of. No one will ever find out, William. It'll be our little secret. One to remember, and cherish.'

Continuing to look into his eyes, she deftly began unbuttoning his flies.

Lexa lay in bed wondering how William had got on at his wine conference. Well, she hoped. It had been strange staying home on a Saturday night after being out for so many consecutive ones with him. Not to worry, though. She'd be seeing him on Wednesday, which wasn't so far away.

She pictured him in her mind. Dear, lovely William, whom she'd come to care so much about. And who she believed cared as much for her.

Looking back, life had been so dull and dreary before him, so colourless. But now . . . She sighed with contentment.

Snuggling down she closed her eyes, attempting to go to sleep. Eventually she did so, still thinking of William.

*   *   *

William came awake, briefly wondering where he was. Then the previous night's events came flooding back.

His head was pounding, his mouth as dry as the Sahara. Beside him Helen lay on her side, eyes closed, facing him.

What had he done! he thought in horror. But he was only too well aware of what he had done. Despite himself, he smiled at the memory. Christ, but she was something else. A tigress in bed one moment, a purring pussycat the next.

He had to get out of here, he decided. They'd said their farewells, as she'd called it. Now it was high time to hoof it.

He groaned when he came upright, thankful he had aspirins in his wash bag. Going into the bathroom, which smelt heavily of her perfume, he drank several tumblers of water before returning to the bedroom and swiftly dressing.

Halting at the door, he took one last look at the sleeping Helen, before exiting into the corridor and heading for his own room. She might be wild and wonderful in bed, but she still wasn't the woman for him.

It suddenly dawned on him that, if anybody, Lexa was. They simply suited. They were right for one another.

'Shite!' Kenny exclaimed, quickly clutching one hand with another. Blood started to seep through his fingers.

'What is it?' Cordelia queried in alarm.

'I've cut my hand.' The knife he'd been using to trim flower stalks had dropped to the ground, part of its blade stained red.

Cordelia hurried over. 'Here, let me see.' She frowned when he showed her the wound. 'That looks nasty,' she said.

'My own fucking fault. I was clumsy.' He was instantly contrite. 'I'm sorry, Miss Stewart. I didn't mean to swear like that.'

In other circumstances she might have laughed at his expression. 'It's all right, Kenny. You get used to bad language working in a place like this, I can assure you.'

'I'm sorry all the same. I shouldn't have used that word in front of a lady.'

A lady! She was hardly that, but she considered it flattering to be thought of as such.

'Right,' she declared, becoming businesslike. 'Let me get the first aid box and see what I can do.'

She fetched the box, placed it beside Kenny and opened it to reveal most items required for simple first aid.

'I'm just wondering if you should go to the hospital for some stitches,' she mused, examining the wound.

'It's not that bad, Miss Stewart. Honestly. It looks a lot worse than it is.'

'Are you sure?'

'Oh, aye. It's only a scratch really.'

Cordelia did what she could. She cleaned the wound, put antiseptic on it, covered it with a gauze pad, then tightly wrapped a bandage round it which she secured with several safety pins.

'How's that?' she queried.

'The pain's already eased. A proper nurse couldn't have done a better job.'

'Oh, I expect she could! But that'll have to do in the

meantime. When you get home have your mother change the bandage.'

His mother didn't have any bandages at home, but Kenny didn't tell Cordelia that.

'Now you have a sit down for a few minutes. Smoke a cigarette if you want.'

'I'm all right, Miss Stewart!' Kenny protested.

'I said sit down. You've had a bit of a shock, from which you need to recover. So do as you're told.'

He smiled, thinking her wonderful. 'Thank you, Miss Stewart. I appreciate you helping me.'

'The least I could do,' she replied dismissively.

Kenny sat, and lit up. She was a grand one, his Miss Stewart, he reflected. He'd fallen on his feet right enough coming to work for her. He couldn't have hoped for a better, or kinder, boss.

Lexa was in the best of humours when she arrived at work. It was Wednesday and she'd be seeing William that evening. She couldn't wait.

'There's a letter for you, Miss Stewart,' Mrs Sanderson announced reprovingly.

'A letter for me!' Lexa exclaimed in astonishment.

'For you, Miss Stewart. A *private* letter.' She tutted. 'It's simply not on to receive private mail. Not on at all. This is a place of business, I would remind you. All correspondence should be related to that, and nothing else.'

'I'm sorry, Mrs Sanderson,' Lexa apologised. 'I have absolutely no idea who would write to me here. It's certainly not at my instigation.'

Old pruneface snorted, and handed over the letter. Lexa immediately went to her desk and slit open the envelope while a curious Pam looked on. Tarantula had not yet put in an appearance.

The envelope contained three neatly written pages. Lexa started to read the first.

She had got halfway down the page when she went deathly white, and realised she felt sick. Gulping, she refolded the three pages and slipped them back into the envelope.

'Bad news?' Pam queried.

Lexa shook her head, but didn't reply, not trusting herself to speak. Averting her eyes, she picked up a file in front of her and pretended to study it. Her hands were shaking. Though, thank God, not enough to be noticeable. At the start of the morning break she hurried to the ladies' room where she locked herself in the cubicle. She sat, then took out the letter and read it from beginning to end. More slowly, she read it again.

'Lexa, are you all right in there?' Pam had come in search of her.

'I'm fine,' Lexa managed to croak.

'You don't sound it.'

'Well, I am.'

'Can I borrow one of your fags?' Lexa heard Tarantula ask.

'No. If I give you one I'll be leaving myself short.'

'Please, Pam,' Tarantula pleaded.

'I said no.'

'Meanie.'

'Meanie yourself. Now don't ask again.'

As she listened to this exchange Lexa found she was silently weeping.

William drew up alongside the tram stop where they'd arranged to meet as usual. Reaching across, he opened the door for her.

Lexa didn't get in. Instead she stared coldly at him. 'I have a question to ask you,' she told him in a level voice.

'Which is?'

'What was the name of your London hotel?'

'My London hotel?' he queried in surprise.

'That's right.'

'The Excelsior. Why?'

There it was, the proof and confirmation she required. Taking the letter from a pocket she threw it at him. 'That's why.' Then, turning on her heel, she strode hurriedly away.

William bent over and picked the letter up from the car floor, closing the passenger door at the same time. Glancing in the wing mirror he was just in time to see Lexa vanish round a corner.

He couldn't even begin to imagine what the problem was. But one thing was clear: Lexa had been extremely angry. Taking out the pages contained in the envelope, he began to read them.

'Oh, you bitch!' he exclaimed. 'You sodding bitch.'

The letter was from Helen, and it described in lurid, graphic detail their lovemaking on the previous Saturday night. It was all there. Absolutely everything. What she'd done to him. What he'd done to her. How he'd . . .

'Dear God,' William whispered. How could Helen do such a thing? Revenge, of course. She was getting back at him for breaking it off between them. No wonder Lexa had been so angry. He'd betrayed her. And now she knew he had.

William hung his head in shame.

'What are you doing home so early? I thought you were going out with William!' Alice exclaimed when Lexa came into the front room. 'I've nothing in for your tea. I wasn't expecting you.'

'That's all right, Mum. I'm not hungry.'

'And William?' Alice queried.

'I don't want to talk about him. At least not now.'

There must have been an argument of some sort, Alice thought, hoping it hadn't been too serious a one.

'I'm going through to my bedroom. And if you don't mind, I don't want to be disturbed,' Lexa said.

'Can I get you anything?'

Lexa shook her head, then made for her room, leaving a perplexed Alice staring after her.

Several hours later there was a quiet knock on Lexa's door. 'It's me, Cordelia. Can I come in?'

Lexa wiped tears from her eyes.

'I've got a cup of tea and a dram for you.'

Lexa felt she could use both. 'All right.'

Cordelia closed the door behind her, then came to sit on the edge of the bed beside her sister. 'You look in a right old state,' she said sympathetically. 'And you've been crying.'

Lexa didn't reply. Instead she took the dram from Cordelia and had a sip.

'Is it William?'

Lexa nodded, and took another sip.

'Want to talk about it?'

Lexa drew in a deep breath. Did she or didn't she? Maybe it would be best if she got it off her chest. 'William slept with his old girlfriend when he was in London.'

'Oh, dear,' Cordelia breathed. So this wasn't just an ordinary argument, or falling out, then. 'How do you know?'

'She sent me a letter describing everything they'd done together. The full nitty-gritty. When I asked William which hotel he'd stayed in his answer confirmed it was all true.' Lexa suddenly wailed, 'How could he do such a thing to me, Cordelia? How could he?'

Cordelia placed the cup of tea on the floor, and took Lexa into her arms, holding her tightly. She knew exactly what her sister was feeling, having gone through a similar experience with Joe Given. She couldn't have been more sympathetic or understanding.

'I'm beginning to think most men are proper bastards,' she told Lexa quietly.

'William certainly is.'

And Joe, Cordelia thought grimly.

'I had such high hopes for the pair of us. And now this.' Lexa began to shake all over, utterly distraught.

'Would you like another whisky, sis?'

'Please,' Lexa gulped.

Cordelia hurried off to refill her glass, only to be waylaid in the kitchen by Alice. 'What's going on?' she asked anxiously.

'It's up to Lexa to tell you, Mum. I shouldn't.'

'Oh, come on,' Alice urged. 'She's my daughter.'

Cordelia hesitated for a moment. 'Let's just say I doubt she'll be seeing William again.'

'Oh, dear,' Alice murmured. 'That bad, eh?'

'That bad,' Cordelia confirmed.

'Surely they can make it up in time?'

'Not a chance, in my opinion. Accept it, Mum. It's over between them.'

'He must have done something really awful to her.'

'He did. Something unforgivable. And if I were you I wouldn't try to bully it out of Lexa. She'll explain in her own good time.'

Alice sighed. This was a tragedy as far as she was concerned. William had been such a good prospect, and now this.

'Will she want something to eat? I could make her an omelette.'

'Just leave her be for now, Mum. I'm sure food's the last thing on her mind at the moment.'

Alice bit her lip. 'Is there anything I can do?'

'Maybe later. But not now.'

Cordelia refilled the glass and returned to the bedroom, closing the door again behind her.

'You didn't tell Mum, did you?' Lexa queried through her tears.

'No, I didn't.'

'I'd be so humiliated if she found out what's happened.'

'She won't find out from me, and that's a promise.'

The next day Lexa didn't go into work. By the time she returned the following Monday she'd managed to compose herself.

Her biggest dread now was running into William.

Chapter 19

Cordelia wondered where Kenny was. It was most unlike him to be late for work. She got on with unpacking and laying out the stall, assuming he'd put in an appearance before long.

But it was Ginge who did that. 'Kenny's been taken into hospital,' he announced. 'That wound of his became infected, really nastily so apparently, and his mother called an ambulance.'

Cordelia was immediately full of concern. 'I'm sorry to hear that. When did he go in?'

'Saturday afternoon.' It was now Monday morning. 'The doctors are afraid it might turn into septicaemia. Blood poisoning to you and me.'

'Oh, dear.' Cordelia knew people died from that. 'Which hospital was he taken to?'

'The Victoria Infirmary.' Not far from Mount Florida where the Stewarts lived.

'Have you seen him yet?'

'I'm going tomorrow night. His parents are going tonight. They're worried sick.'

'I'm not surprised. What about Kenny himself?'

'Well, he's not exactly happy, and that's a fact.'

'Is he in pain?'

'Quite a lot, I believe. But that was before the hospital. The staff have no doubt given him something for it by now.'

Cordelia had a quick think. 'Can I go along with you tomorrow night? You can come to our house for tea and we'll go straight from there.'

'There's an hour's visiting time and I've already arranged with his parents that I'll have the last half-hour. I don't see why you can't accompany me. Kenny would like that.'

'Thanks, Ginge. I've become fond of that boy. I'd hate to . . .' She broke off, having been about to say she'd hate to lose him.

'In the meanwhile I'll help you here,' Ginge declared, bending down and heaving a heavy wooden box on to a shoulder. 'Where do you want this?'

Kenny looked positively ghastly. His face was grey and there were dark rings under his eyes. He was attached to a saline drip, while the hand with the wound was heavily bandaged.

'Hello, Miss Stewart,' he croaked. 'My folks told me you were waiting outside the ward.'

'I've brought you some grapes.' She smiled, placing them on his bedside table. 'Don't eat them all at once.'

A thin smile lit up his face at the time-worn admonition.

'And I've brought you a couple of magazines,' Ginge

declared, laying them alongside Cordelia's grapes. Privately, however, now he'd seen Kenny he thought it would be some time before the lad was able to even glance through them.

'You have the chair, Cordelia,' Ginge said. Only one was provided.

'Thank you.'

'It's awfully good of the pair of you to come and visit,' Kenny said gratefully. 'Particularly you, Miss Stewart. I'm dead chuffed.'

'Of course I wanted to visit you,' Cordelia replied, 'especially as I'm afraid it might be my fault you're in here in the first place. I should have insisted you went to the hospital as soon as the accident happened.'

'Aye, well, it didn't seem too big a deal at the time.'

'How are you feeling?' Ginge asked.

'The truth?'

'The truth.'

'Terrible. Though a bit better than I did yesterday.'

'That's good.' Cordelia nodded. 'Let's hope you're on the road to recovery.'

'The specialist said it's now unlikely I'll get that septi thing. But they want to keep me in for a few days more to be on the safe side.'

'Septicaemia,' Cordelia reminded him. 'Blood poisoning.'

'How are you managing on the stall?' he asked. 'I can't wait to get back.'

'I'm managing just fine,' Cordelia told him. 'Ginge here has been a great help.'

'Aye well, it's my stall after all,' Ginge joked. 'It's in my interest to make sure it's business as usual.'

Cordelia shot him a glance, knowing that wasn't the

whole truth. Ginge would have helped even if he hadn't owned the stall.

They chatted away for the rest of their half-hour, then said their goodbyes. Kenny was desperately sorry to see them go, and Cordelia promised to come back again if he was kept in for more than the few days he'd mentioned.

'Do you fancy a drink?' Ginge asked as they left the infirmary.

'You mean a pub?'

Ginge shook his head. 'I only know of one round here and I wouldn't take even the roughest female there. And you're hardly that. No, there's a little hotel about ten minutes' walk away which is quite nice.'

'All right,' Cordelia agreed, deciding she would like a drink. As they walked she wondered if she should link arms with him, then decided it wasn't a good idea. It might give him the wrong impression.

In the bar, Cordelia lifted the glass Ginge had placed in front of her. 'Here's to Kenny and a swift recovery,' she toasted.

'Aye, Kenny and a swift recovery.' Ginge had a sip of his whisky, then a mouthful of beer. 'The trouble with this place is they only serve half pints,' he complained. 'They consider pints to be common.'

Cordelia grinned at that.

'As if I could be common,' Ginge joked. 'How far-fetched can you get?'

'I couldn't agree more,' Cordelia said solemnly, and they both laughed.

'So how come you know this area?' Cordelia queried. 'You live on the other side of Glasgow.'

'The answer to that's simple. I used to winch a lassie not far from here,' he explained. 'We used this bar quite a lot.'

'Was it serious?'

Ginge's expression became exactly that. 'It was on my part. But not on hers, apparently. She ditched me in the end.'

'I'm sorry,' Cordelia said sympathetically.

'Me too. She was a right cracker and no mistake. At least, I thought so.'

'What happened?'

Ginge thought for a moment. 'She simply wasn't all that keen. Left me when she met someone else she found more interesting. Or more handsome. She's married now with three weans.' He suddenly smiled. 'Saw her in the street a while back. To put it mildly, childbirth hadn't been too kind to her. She was the size of a house and looking dreadful. I felt quite sorry for her.'

'You don't seem to have much luck with women,' Cordelia mused, not unkindly.

Ginge shrugged. 'No, I don't. I always seem to fall for the wrong ones.'

Cordelia could only wonder if she was included in that. 'The right one will come along someday. You'll see.'

'Aye, maybe,' Ginge replied cynically. 'Though with a war looming who knows what might happen? I could be dead and buried this time next year.'

'Don't say that!' Cordelia admonished him sharply.

'Well, I might. Me and an awful lot of others. If the Germans march into Poland, and that looks highly likely, then that's that. The government is already talking about conscription, don't forget.'

Cordelia felt a cold stab of fear at his words. War was just too horrible to contemplate.

'I'll join up,' Ginge went on. 'Might as well. They'll probably just conscript me if I don't.'

'Oh, Ginge,' Cordelia murmured, appalled at the prospect.

'There again, maybe they won't want red-haired eejits,' he joked. 'There's always that possibility.'

'Daftie!' She smiled.

'It'll be the army for me if war does come. Don't fancy the navy – I'd hate to drown. And I certainly don't fancy the air force because I'm scared of heights.'

Cordelia shook her head. 'Can we change the subject? All this talk of war is depressing me.'

Ginge thought for a moment, then said, 'By the way, I have an address for Joe now. A proper one, that is, not the various bed and breakfasts he was staying in up until now. Do you want it so you can send him a letter?'

'Why would I wish to do that?' she snapped, shaken at the mention of Joe's name.

Ginge shrugged. 'I don't know. I just thought you might. You and he were quite pally, after all.'

More than that, Cordelia reflected. She'd been in love with him. Still was. 'Besides,' she said slowly, 'if Big Alec comes back I want to be able to tell the truth and say I still don't know where Joe is other than London. All right?'

'Fine. Suit yourself.'

Cordelia saw off the rest of her whisky. 'Will you go to the bar and get another round in while I nip to the toilet? I'm paying this time.'

'Of course.'

She laid some money on the table and hurried off. In the ladies' room she sank back against a wall. Joe bloody Given. She wished with all her heart she'd never set eyes on him.

Lexa finally snapped. 'Will you please stop going on about Bobby,' she snarled at an astonished Pam. 'It's Bobby this, Bobby that, non-stop Bobby Bobby Bobby. It's getting on my nerves.' Bobby was Pam's boyfriend, and she'd been seeing him for quite a while now.

'I'm sorry, Lexa,' Pam stuttered. 'I didn't realise I was annoying you.'

'Well, you are. All you ever talk about nowadays is Bobby. You're like a stuck gramophone.'

Pam had a puff on her cigarette, not knowing what to reply.

'Not jealous, are we?' Tarantula said nastily. 'You being the only one here without a chap.'

'Jealousy's got nothing to do with it,' Lexa retorted. She was lying, of course. Jealousy had everything to do with it. How she wished things had turned out differently between her and William. She was missing him terribly.

'Sez you.'

Lexa fought back the urge to slap Tarantula's face. Trust the bitch to put her finger on the truth. 'For a dwarf you've got a very large mouth, Angela. Large enough to get you into trouble one day,' she hissed.

Tarantula was outraged. 'I'm not a fucking dwarf!' she shrieked. 'Small maybe, but not a dwarf.'

'Sez you,' Lexa riposted, and swept from the ladies' before there could be any further exchange between them.

*   *   *

Alice answered the knock on the front door to find an obviously nervous William standing there.

'Hello, Mrs Stewart. Is Lexa home?'

Alice frowned. 'She is.'

'Then could I have a word, please?'

'I'll ask her.' And with that she closed the door again.

'I don't want to speak to him,' Lexa stated emphatically when Alice told her who'd come calling, and what he'd asked for.

'Are you sure, darling?'

Lexa glanced at her sister, who knew why she'd broken with William, but Cordelia gestured that she couldn't be any help in this situation. The decision had to be Lexa's.

'He looks awfully nervous,' Alice said. 'Coming here couldn't have been easy for him.'

I'll bet it wasn't, Lexa thought grimly. How could he have done what he did? How could he!

'Why not just have a word?' Alice suggested. 'Hear what he has to say. Surely that can't do any harm?'

For a brief moment Lexa was tempted. Perhaps he'd plead with her, beg her to go back with him. She'd enjoy that – even revel in it.

But it was a temptation she resisted. 'Tell him no, Mum. He can get on his bike as far as I'm concerned.'

Alice was disappointed. 'If you're absolutely certain?'

'I am.'

Alice took a deep breath. 'All right, then.'

She returned to the front door and opened it. William stared hopefully at her. 'I'm sorry,' she said.

William's face fell in disappointment. 'I understand.'

He nodded, and turned to trudge disconsolately down the stairs.

As he drove off he was unaware that Lexa was standing behind the net curtains in her room, watching him.

'That's decided it for me,' she announced a little later that evening. 'I'm going to get a new job.'

Cordelia focused on her sister. 'Doing what?'

'I've no idea. But I'll find something.'

'I thought you enjoyed being at *Vins*,' Alice protested. 'You've said so on many occasions.'

That was true enough, Lexa reflected. 'That was before I split up with William,' she said. 'Now I'm in a permanent state of anxiety that I might run into him, which would be awkward to say the least.' She paused for a few seconds. 'No, it's best I get out of there. For him as well as myself.'

'I think you're right,' Cordelia said. 'It's what I'd do in your position.'

'Would you?'

'Most certainly. I mean, there's no chance of the pair of you getting back together, I take it?'

Lexa shook her head. 'None whatsoever.'

'There you are then.'

'I'll start looking in the newspaper tomorrow and see what's going. There's bound to be something.'

Alice sighed. 'Such a handsome young man too. I just wish you'd tell me what went wrong between the two of you.'

Lexa simply couldn't imagine herself informing Alice that she'd broken with William because he'd shagged an old girlfriend while in London. Alice was her mother after all, and there were certain things you just didn't discuss with a parent.

Lexa tensed as William entered the office. Quickly she dropped her gaze so as not to make eye contact, the last thing she wanted to do. She was acutely aware of his presence as he walked over to Mrs Sanderson's desk.

He placed a piece of paper before the chief clerk. 'Would you be so kind as to have someone dig out all the details on this and have her bring them to me?'

'Certainly, Mr McLeod.'

'As soon as possible, please. A query has come up which I have to deal with urgently.'

'I understand, Mr McLeod.'

With a nod, he left the room.

Oh, please don't let her choose me, Lexa prayed. Not me.

'Miss Quigley, can you come over here?'

'Yes, Mrs Sanderson.'

Lexa let out a long sigh of relief. Thank you, God, she prayed. Oh, thank you.

This was becoming impossible, Lexa thought. She hadn't applied for a new job yet, even though there had been a few hopeful-looking ones in the newspaper. Well, she'd apply for the next one she spotted. It was high time she was out of here. Things simply couldn't continue as they were – the last few minutes had proved that.

Elspeth McLeod, William's mother, opened the door to the morning room to see a preoccupied William standing staring out of a window.

He'd lost weight recently, Elspeth reflected. Most

noticeably in the face, which had become almost gaunt. He'd been worrying her for some time now, though so far she hadn't said anything. It was time she did.

'William?'

He didn't respond.

'William?' she repeated, slightly louder.

He started out of his reverie. 'Sorry, Mother,' he apologised. 'I was miles away.'

'I could see that. Business?'

He shook his head. 'No.'

'A personal matter perhaps?'

He smiled. 'Perhaps.'

Elspeth crossed over and sank into a comfy chair, gesturing that William should do likewise. 'Now, what's worrying you?' she asked.

'What makes you think something's worrying me?' he prevaricated.

'You've been extremely moody lately. And you've lost weight. Are you ill?'

He considered making a joke, but didn't. 'Fit as a flea, Mater.'

'Then why are you losing weight?'

William shrugged. 'I don't know.'

Elspeth studied her son. He was lying. Or, to put it another way, hiding the truth from her. She knew him only too well. 'I've spoken to your father and he says there might be a young lady involved. Is that correct?'

William glanced away. 'I was seeing someone. But not any more.'

'I know I shouldn't pry, but will you tell me why? Is that what's bothering you?'

William sighed. 'Yes,' he finally admitted in a quiet voice.

'Did she give you up? Or you her?'

'Do we really have to go into this, Mother? I mean, my relationships are my concern and no one else's.'

'Not if they affect the way you behave at home.'

He sighed. 'Please don't take offence, but I don't need you, or anyone else, interfering.'

'So.' Elspeth smiled. 'She gave you up. And you didn't want that.'

'I never said so.'

'No?'

He glared at his mother, who could be so irritatingly right at times. It was infuriating.

'Did anything in particular cause the break-up?' Elspeth queried softly.

William was silent.

'I can't help if you don't tell me.'

Again he didn't reply.

'I see,' she murmured.

'I don't wish to be rude, Mother, but I have nothing further to say on the subject.'

'Very well.' Elspeth came to her feet. When she reached the door she hesitated, then turned to face him. 'Do you know what I think?'

'What?'

'That you're in love with this girl. If you are, then fight for her.'

William's jaw fell open. Was he in love with Lexa?

And in that split second he knew the answer.

Chapter 20

Lexa left the insurance company where she'd just been interviewed for a job certain she hadn't got it. Just as she hadn't landed the three previous ones she'd been interviewed for.

She knew the reason why. It was her own fault really. She simply couldn't summon up enough enthusiasm for them to take her on. There was no keenness on her part.

The company she'd just left had been terrible, in her opinion. For a start she hadn't liked the look of the employees, a miserable bunch who'd seemed to stare antagonistically at her as she'd passed by. As for the man who'd done the interviewing, she'd positively loathed him. And he'd have been her boss if she'd been hired.

Lexa took a deep breath, and finally faced the fact that she didn't really want to leave *Vins*. She was happy there, apart from the William thing.

None the less, she was going to have to leave, but not for a while yet. She'd had too many supposed sick days off recently to take another in the near future.

She'd do better in her next interview, she promised herself. Somehow she'd summon up the enthusiasm required to impress whoever interviewed her.

It was going to be hard. Very hard. But not as hard as leaving *Vins*.

'Kenny!' Cordelia exclaimed. 'It's wonderful to have you back. Ginge said you'd be turning up today.'

Kenny blushed. 'It's wonderful to be back, Miss Stewart. I've missed the stall.'

'You're fully fit, I take it?'

He raised what had been his damaged hand, and flexed it. 'Good as new. Except for a little scar, that is.'

Cordelia beamed at him, truly delighted at his return. 'First things first,' she declared. 'Here's some money. Two teas and two bacon sannies I think, eh?'

He accepted the cash. 'Coming right up.' He hesitated. 'There's just one thing.'

'Which is?'

'It's my birthday today. I was hoping you and Ginge would help me celebrate after work by having a drink with me?'

'You can count me in. I'll be looking forward to it all day,' she enthused.

He was pleased. 'Thank you, Miss Stewart. I was a bit hesitant in asking, you being the boss and all.'

'I hope I'm not that formidable?' she queried, laughing.

Kenny frowned. 'What does formidable mean?'

'That I'm not too stern or unapproachable.'

'Oh!' Kenny exclaimed. 'Not at all. You're lovely to work for. I couldn't have a better boss.'

Ginge put in an appearance. 'Everything all right?'

'Absolutely fine. We're going for a drink after work as it's Kenny's birthday. And, according to him, you're also invited.'

'I'll be there. Try to stop me.'

'I'll get those teas and sannies, Miss Stewart.' Kenny hurried off.

Ginge stared after his young cousin, his expression one of concern. He was thinking about the looming war, which Kenny was bound to be involved in, as he was himself. These were worrying times.

'So how does it feel to be eighteen?' Cordelia asked Kenny that evening in the Hielan Laddie.

'Not much different from being seventeen,' Kenny admitted. 'So far there's only a day in it, after all.'

Cordelia raised her glass. Kenny had bought the first round. 'Here's to you then. A big grown man that you now are.'

'Aye, here's to you, Kenny,' Ginge echoed. 'And I hope you have many birthdays to follow.'

Cordelia thought that a strange toast. Surely Kenny would have many birthdays to follow? She didn't realise what was going through Ginge's mind.

'Now that you are eighteen,' she said, 'I think we can dispense with formalities from now on. As from today you can call me Cordelia rather than Miss Stewart.'

Kenny's face broke into a huge smile. 'Can I really?'

'I just said so, didn't I?'

'Then I will . . . Cordelia.'

*   *   *

Alice switched off the wireless and turned to her two grim-faced daughters. 'That's it then,' she said soberly. 'War.' It had been inevitable since Germany invaded Poland two days earlier.

'We all knew it was coming,' Alice went on in the same solemn tone. 'But it's still a shock when it actually happens.'

Lexa shook her head. 'I can't believe it. I really can't. It's a nightmare.'

'A nightmare that's only just beginning,' Alice said. 'Everything's going to change from now on.'

Cordelia shivered as if someone had just walked over her grave. 'Dear God,' she whispered.

'I went through the Great War. The war that was supposed to end all wars,' Alice said quietly. 'But that'll be nothing compared to this one, you mark my words.'

'In what way, Mum?' Lexa queried.

'Aeroplanes for a start. During the Great War the Germans only managed to bomb southern England, and not too often at that. People were killed, but not many. This war will be quite different, according to what I've heard at the Labour Hall. The Germans will be able to bomb large parts of Britain, and that includes Glasgow.' She stopped for a few moments, her eyes large. 'Who knows? Perhaps even this very house?'

For the first time Lexa realised that she herself might be in mortal danger. She, Cordelia and Alice.

It was a chilling thought.

William was out making a delivery, his mind only half on the road. The other half was on Lexa.

Fight for her, his mother had said. But how? That was a question to which he so far didn't have an answer. If only he could come up with something. But to date he hadn't.

Damn Helen and her letter, he inwardly raged. And what a stroke of bad luck that she and he had been booked into the same hotel at the same time.

If only he hadn't gone to her room that night. If only he hadn't given in to temptation. If only she hadn't written that letter.

If only . . . if only . . . if only . . .

He didn't know it then, but an occasion was about to arise which would give him the opportunity to speak to Lexa. To try to make amends.

It was a storm straight from hell. Rain was sheeting down, while overhead thunder crashed and great jagged bolts of lightning split the sky.

A terrified Lexa was waiting for her tram, having just come from the office. She'd been frightened of thunder and lightning since she was a little girl, usually crouching under the table when they occurred. Now here she was, caught out in the open, with nowhere to hide. Her insides were heaving from fear.

'Terrible, isn't it?' a woman in the queue beside her commented.

Lexa nodded numbly.

'Holy Moses!' the woman exclaimed, at the loudest crash of thunder yet. It was followed seconds later by an incredible flash of lightning which momentarily lit up the entire sky.

Lexa closed her eyes, wishing with all her heart she was home, safe and dry. She opened them again, wondering where the tram was. It was late, ten or twelve minutes so. The storm must have held it up somehow, she decided. She turned her head away as the driving rain changed direction, now hammering against her. Rat-a-tat-tatting on her mac, like so many machine gun bullets.

She didn't hear the car approach, or stop just feet away.

'Lexa!'

She didn't hear her name being called.

'*Lexa!*'

She heard that. William was beckoning her to get in.

For the briefest of moments she hesitated, then ducked through the door William was holding open and sank gratefully on to the leather seat, closing the door behind her.

'Thank you,' she mumbled.

William engaged gear and drove off. 'I stopped because I remember you once telling me how frightened you are of thunder and lightning,' he said.

She glanced sideways at him. 'They don't frighten me. They absolutely terrify me. I was shaking in my shoes back there.'

William looked up at the sky, where more lightning was flickering. 'It's as bad a storm as I can remember.'

'Me too.'

At least they were talking again, he thought. That was something. 'How have you been?' he asked.

'Fine. And you?'

'All right,' he lied.

They drove on a little way in silence. William was

desperately trying to think of something to say; Lexa was just grateful to be out of the elements.

'It's terrible about the war,' he said eventually.

'Yes.'

'But we'll beat them in the end. You'll see.'

Lexa fervently hoped so.

She didn't know why she came out with it, but she did. 'I'm looking for another job.'

That jolted William. 'Why?'

'I should have thought it was obvious. Because of you and me. It's become . . . well, too difficult working together in the same building.'

'But I'm only there part of the time,' he protested. 'Mostly I'm out on the road.'

'None the less. It's best I leave.'

William took a deep breath. This was awful news. If she left he might never see her again. 'Please don't go, Lexa. Please?'

She bit her lip and didn't reply, taken aback by his tone of voice.

'Lexa?'

'Yes?'

'I know what I did was wrong. Terribly so. And how much it must have hurt you.'

'You're damn right it did,' she replied coldly.

'I can't tell you how sorry I am. Sorry from the bottom of my heart. It was a dreadful thing to do. Inexcusable. But please let me try to explain.'

She didn't try to stop him.

'I was drunk at the time. Not totally drunk, but fairly well oiled. Helen left a note at reception asking me to go to her room. It sounded urgent, and I went thinking she needed help of some sort. After a few minutes she vanished into the bathroom and came out naked.'

Lexa blinked in astonishment. 'She did what?'

'Went into the bathroom and came out starkers. Not a stitch on. I . . . Well, the truth is I simply gave in to temptation.'

Lexa tried to digest that. 'Did you arrange to meet her at this hotel?'

'No, I didn't,' William replied vehemently. 'It was purely coincidental that we were both staying there at the same time. I swear that's so.'

Coincidences did happen, Lexa reminded herself. 'As she mentioned being an ex-girlfriend I take it you'd slept with her before?'

William swallowed hard. 'Yes.'

'I see,' Lexa murmured, a little shocked. Nice girls simply didn't do that kind of thing. At least, not the ones she knew. It certainly wasn't how she'd been brought up.

'Can you forgive me, Lexa? I appreciate it's an awful lot to ask, but can you?'

She started at a boom of thunder which seemed to come from directly overhead. Without thinking she reached out and grasped him by the arm. There was still quite a distance to go, she realised. She wished the journey was over.

'Lexa?'

'What?'

'I asked if you could forgive me?'

'I'm sorry. I . . .' She trailed off, and removed her hand from his arm. 'Have you seen this Helen since?'

'No.'

'Are you sure?'

'I have absolutely no interest in her any more. And that's the gospel truth.'

Lexa decided to stick the knife in a little. 'What if she comes waltzing stark naked into your life again? Would you give in to temptation a second time?'

'I would not,' he declared firmly. 'There's nothing she could now do that would tempt me.'

'Not even if she had tassels on?' There was a hint of a teasing smile.

William grinned. 'Not even if she had tassels on.'

Could she forgive him? Lexa wondered. She knew enough to appreciate what a temptation a naked woman must be to a man, especially one throwing herself at him. 'Is Helen beautiful?' she asked lightly.

Christ, William thought. What a question. 'Yes,' he admitted. 'She is.'

'I somehow thought she was.' She wanted to ask if Helen was prettier than her, but was scared of the answer.

'There's one more thing you should know,' William said.

'Which is?'

'I've fallen in love with you.'

Lexa couldn't believe her ears. 'Say that again?'

He coughed. 'I've fallen in love with you.'

'And yet you slept with someone else?' she queried incredulously.

'That was before I realised I was in love with you.'

Was he lying? she wondered. It certainly didn't sound like a lie. In love with her? That changed everything. 'Are you?' was all she could think of to reply, now thoroughly confused.

'Yes, I am. Totally and utterly.'

She opened her mouth, then shut it again.

'Will you go out with me on Saturday night and we can discuss this further?'

Lexa shook her head. This was too much to take in all at once.

'Does that mean you won't?'

'No . . . no, it doesn't. I just . . . well, this is all so sudden. Coming out with that.'

'I'm sorry.'

Go out with him again? She'd made up her mind it was all over between them after what he'd done. And now this absolute bombshell!

'I need time to think,' she answered eventually. 'To come to terms with what you've just told me.'

'Of course. I understand.'

She closed her eyes when there was yet another enormous crash of thunder, followed shortly by a crack of lightning. She didn't open them again until William drew up outside her close.

'Have you decided yet?' he asked.

'I haven't, William.'

His spirits sank. She was going to say no, he was certain of it. And it was all his fault.

'I'll tell you what,' she said. 'You park here on Saturday night at seven. Give it to quarter past and if I haven't appeared then I've decided against going out with you. If I come down, then we will.'

He frowned. A strange arrangement, but . . . 'All right.'

She couldn't bring herself to look him directly in the face. 'Thank you for the lift. It's much appreciated.'

'My pleasure, Lexa.'

Then she was out of the car and running into the close mouth where she quickly vanished up the stairs.

Would she or wouldn't she appear? He had a three-day wait to find out. Three days he knew were going to seem like an eternity.

Lexa waited till the dishes were done after tea before whispering to Cordelia to join her in her bedroom. She wanted to discuss the latest developments without Alice's either overhearing or joining in.

'So, what's this all about?' Cordelia demanded, closing the bedroom door behind her.

Lexa told her what had happened, and then there were a few moments' silence between them.

'Do you believe him when he says he loves you?' Cordelia asked at last.

'I think so.'

'Then why are you hesitating?'

'Because he shagged another woman behind my back. That's why.'

Cordelia studied her sister. 'You have to remember that when he did that the pair of you were neither married nor engaged. Technically he was a free agent.'

Lexa hadn't thought of it that way.

'And on his own admission he was seduced by a naked woman. And a beautiful one at that. Given the circumstances, and the fact that he was half pissed, I doubt there are many men who would have resisted. There's an old saying, sis: when the cock's up, the mind's out.'

'Even though,' Lexa demurred. 'What would you do in my place?'

'Give him another chance. Be magnanimous. But the real question is, how do you feel about him?'

Lexa didn't answer.

'Well?'

'Let's just say I was extremely fond of him before that letter arrived. The letter destroyed everything.'

'Then you're playing right into this Helen's hands. I wouldn't be surprised if she didn't seduce him just so she could tell you. Maybe she wants him back, and knew he liked you too much to look at her without drastic action!'

Lexa wrung her hands. 'I don't know. I simply don't know.'

'Well, it's your decision. But as I said, if I was in your position I'd go.'

William glanced at his wristwatch. Dead on seven. To the very second.

The close mouth was empty. No sign yet of Lexa. He took heart from the fact that there was still fifteen minutes to go.

It was going to be a long wait.

'Made up your mind yet, darling?' Alice asked. Lexa had finally told her what was going on.

Lexa was dressed and made up, ready for the evening out with William. If she went.

She shook her head.

Alice sighed.

259

'Leave her alone, Mum,' Cordelia counselled. 'It's her choice.'

Alice sighed again.

That was it, a thoroughly dejected William concluded. The fifteen minutes were almost up. He waited until the last moment to be on the safe side. But no sign of Lexa.

He started the car and was about to drive off when suddenly she was there. Smiling, and looking unbelievably gorgeous.

He reached for the door handle to let her in.

Chapter 21

Cordelia thought she was imagining things, but she wasn't. It actually was Joe Given making his way through the crowd towards her.

'Hello, angel. How are you?' He was beaming when he reached the stall.

'What are you doing back in Glasgow?'

'Only here for a few days.' He tapped the side of his nose, and winked. 'On business, like.'

He'd changed, she thought. He appeared older, and somehow sleazy-looking. Shifty too. She could only wonder what this 'business' of his was. Probably something crooked.

'Aren't you worried about running into Big Alec?' she queried. 'He turned up here asking for you.'

'Naw, he's long since back at sea. I do have my contacts here, you know. And, as I said, I'm only in Glasgow for a couple of days.' He gestured towards Kenny, who was watching them. 'Who's that?'

'His name's Kenny Smith and he's Ginge's cousin. I needed help after you left and Kenny got the job.'

She indicated to Kenny that he should join them. 'Kenny, this is Joe Given who used to own this stall. Joe, Kenny.'

The two men shook hands.

'Pleased to meet you, son,' Joe declared. 'Ginge is an old pal of mine. Salt of the earth, that chap.'

Kenny hated being called son by someone other than his father. In addition, for some reason he'd taken an instant dislike to Joe. He too had picked up the impression of sleaziness. 'Pleased to meet you too,' he lied.

Joe turned again to Cordelia. 'I arrived in last night from Euston and booked into the Hielan Laddie. Why don't you come over and have a drink with me after you've packed up, eh?'

Cordelia wasn't at all sure that was a good idea.

'We can talk about old times and have a laugh. And don't worry if you're short, the drinks are on me. My treat.'

'I'll see how things go, Joe,' she prevaricated. 'Let's just leave it at that.'

'Suit yourself, doll. But I'll be in the bar anyway.' He rubbed his hands together. 'Now I'd better be getting along. People to see, deals to make.'

Cordelia found she was quite shaken after Joe had left them. That had certainly been a turn-up for the book. A little later she noticed that her hands were trembling. It didn't surprise her one little bit.

In the end curiosity got the better of her. Instead of heading home she crossed over to the pub, where she found Joe standing alone at the bar.

His face lit up when he saw her. 'You made it! I was hoping you would. Now, what'll you have?'

'A dram with lemonade.'

He pulled out a fat wallet from which he extracted a crisp white fiver.

'I see you're in the money,' she commented drily.

'Too right. Things are going well for me.'

Obviously, she thought.

Joe ordered himself another pint and dram, and the two of them went over to an empty table.

'There's a question I have to ask,' Cordelia said once she'd sat down. 'It's been bothering me ever since you left Glasgow.'

'And what's that, pussycat?'

Pussycat! He'd somehow made it sound obscene. 'What happened to Margy when Big Alec got back and found her pregnant. Do you know?'

'Oh, aye.' Joe nodded. 'He duffed her up, but not nearly as badly as he might have done. I imagine being in the pudding club saved her from that.'

'And the baby?'

'A wee boy, I believe.'

Cordelia had a sip of her whisky, eyeing Joe over the rim of her glass. She'd often wondered how she'd feel if she met up with him again, never really believing it would happen. Now she was about to find out.

'You look terrific, doll,' Joe enthused. 'A real picture.'

She smiled, but didn't reply.

'How's the stall doing?'

'Fine.'

Joe sighed. 'I sometimes miss the flower market, you

know. I enjoyed working there. Nostalgia, eh?'

'What are you up to now?' she asked, curious.

He laughed. 'Well, I'm sure as hell not selling flowers, and that's a fact. What I'm doing is far more lucrative.'

'Which is?'

He hesitated for a moment. 'I'm a representative for a small London firm.'

'Representing what?'

'The firm, of course,' he smiled.

'Don't play games with me, Joe,' she admonished. 'Selling just what exactly?'

'My my, you are nosy. But it's not important. Bulk paper if you must know.'

She stared into his eyes and knew he was lying in his teeth. She also knew that whatever the real answer was he wasn't going to give it to her.

'How nice,' she commented sarcastically.

Joe changed the subject.

Later, on the way home, she tried to work out her feelings. She'd met Joe Given again, and hadn't been impressed at all. Did she still love him? Was she still obsessed with the man?

No, on both counts. Which was rather a surprise. Nor did she hate him, either. Truth was, she'd rather pitied him.

They'd never have been right together, she knew that now. The Joe she'd fallen for didn't really exist. And probably never had. So why had she been in love with him in the first place? She had absolutely no idea. A fantasy figure, perhaps.

One thing was certain. She'd been lucky to have him get out of her life.

And she was truly thankful.

'What did you think of Joe Given?' she asked Kenny next morning.

He shrugged.

'Come on. Tell me?'

'I didn't take to him, Cordelia. Not at all. There's something slimy about him. He strikes me as the sort who'd sell his own granny if there was a quid in it. Why do you want to know?'

'Just curious, that's all.' That was true enough.

'He was your boss, then?'

'He was indeed.'

'So why did he move to London?'

Cordelia explained what had happened.

'Typical,' Kenny commented in disgust. 'Bloody typical. Just what I'd expect from his sort.'

It was a Monday morning when Pam breezed into the office, crossing directly to Lexa's desk and coming to a halt in front of it. She then placed her left arm over her breasts in a very obvious fashion.

Lexa's gaze was immediately drawn to the ring, her eyes flying wide open. 'You're engaged!' she exclaimed.

'On Saturday.' Pam laughed. 'Bobby and I decided last week, and bought this on Saturday.'

Immediately Tarantula joined them, and seconds later Mrs Sanderson.

'It's lovely,' Lexa declared, examining it. 'Congratulations!'

Tarantula was green with envy, but also managed to congratulate Pam, as indeed did an excited Mrs Sanderson.

'So when's the big day?' Lexa queried.

'Not for a while yet,' Pam replied. 'We need to save up first, and there is a war on. But as soon as we can.'

Lexa thought she'd never seen her friend look so happy.

'Pam – Miss Briers, that is – got engaged last Saturday,' Lexa announced to William as he was driving her home.

'Did she indeed?'

'She's over the moon. Kept breaking off work every few minutes to stare at her ring.'

'Is it nice?'

'Very nice.' Lexa sighed. 'I hope I get to attend the wedding. I'd enjoy that.'

'Perhaps they'll ask you.'

'We'll see.'

'How did Mrs Sanderson react?'

'I haven't seen her so excited since poor Lily got engaged. She was almost human.'

William couldn't help but laugh to hear the formidable Mrs Sanderson described in such a way.

Cordelia had never seen Ginge look so miserable and out of sorts. 'What's wrong with your face?' she demanded when he came up to the stall while Kenny was off getting teas.

'I've failed my bloody army medical, that's what's wrong,' he replied bitterly.

The fact that he'd already volunteered to join the army was news to Cordelia. 'What did they fail you on?'

'Asthma and a chest condition. They told me its name, but I can't remember it. Oh! And to top it all, I have that old classic, flat sodding feet.'

Cordelia was pleased Ginge had failed his medical, but wouldn't have dreamt of saying so. 'Did John volunteer?' John was Ginge's partner.

'Aye, yesterday. He was accepted and is now waiting to hear where, and when, he's to report for training. He thinks he's going into the Highland Light Infantry.'

'So what are you going to do about your stall if you're losing John?'

'I haven't really thought about that. We can share Kenny, I suppose. For the time being, anyway.'

'I'm sorry you didn't get in, Ginge,' she lied. 'Bad luck.'

'I'm going over for a gargle to try to buck myself up. Want to join me?'

Cordelia shook her head. 'I won't if you don't mind.'

'Then I'll drown my sorrows all on my ownsome. See you later, then.'

She watched him trudge away, a thoroughly dejected man. Then she noticed, for the first time ever, that he did walk a little strangely. It must be those flat feet.

'You haven't said, but I take it from your recent change of mood that it's all back on with your girl?' Elspeth McLeod probed.

William nodded. 'We made up.'

'Good. I'm delighted. Now when do I get to meet her? I presume it is serious between you?'

William was embarrassed, though he couldn't think why he should be. He averted his gaze. 'Yes, it is, Mother.'

'Then how about Sunday lunch? I'll ask Mrs Mack to do one of her specials.'

He considered the suggestion. If he had plans for himself and Lexa, and he did, though Lexa didn't know it yet, then it was best she met his mother sooner rather than later. She already knew his father, of course, though not socially. 'I'm out on the road for the next couple of days,' he replied eventually. 'But I'll speak to her next time I run her home.'

'Tell her not to be nervous. I may be your mother but that doesn't automatically turn me into a dragon,' Elspeth said lightly. 'She'll be made most welcome. I assure you.'

'Thanks, Mater.'

A smiling Elspeth left William to the evening newspaper he'd been so avidly reading.

They were crawling along, the journey from *Vins* to Mount Florida taking three to four times as long as it had done previously. All the street lamps had been turned off, and there were blackout curtains on every window. Even the car lights had been fitted with covers penetrated only by narrow slits to emit the weak beams.

'I thought we'd have had heavy bombing raids by now.' Lexa commented. 'At least that's what everyone predicted. But so far nothing.'

'I wouldn't complain if I were you,' William replied drily. 'Be thankful for small mercies. The bombing will come soon enough, you can count on it.'

'I am thankful, believe me.' Lexa shivered at the thought of what might lie ahead for Glasgow. It was a busy port and home to heavy industry, including shipbuilding. The yards were bound to be targeted by the enemy.

Lexa placed a hand on William's thigh, and squeezed. 'I so like being with you,' she said, smiling in the darkness.

'And I with you.'

'We make a good couple, don't you think?'

A couple? That's exactly what they were. 'I do love you, Lexa. I'll never tire of telling you that.'

She'd never said it to him before, but now she did. The time seemed right somehow. 'And I love you, darling.'

A surge of sheer joy swept through him. 'You do?'

'Oh, yes,' she breathed. 'Very much.'

Closing his eyes for a moment he offered up a silent prayer thanking God. She loved him! Taking the hand that was still resting on his leg, he raised it to his lips and kissed it.

'My mother would like to meet you,' he announced. 'She's asked you to Sunday lunch. What do you say? Will you come?'

Lexa was taken aback, not having been expecting such an invitation. 'What?'

'Sunday lunch. Mrs Mack, our cook, will do one of her specials for the occasion if you come.'

Lexa drew in a deep breath. She could hardly refuse. But the idea . . . well, scared her somewhat.

'Mother says to tell you you'll be made most welcome,' William added. 'So what do you say?'

'Will you pick me up?'

'Of course.'

'Then I'll be delighted to have lunch with you and

your parents.' As an afterthought, she said, 'Is there anything particular I should wear? Do I dress up?'

William laughed. 'Certainly not. It'll be completely informal. Just wear what you normally would on a Sunday.'

Lexa worried a nail. She'd have to think about this. She didn't want to get it wrong.

'Lunch!' Alice exclaimed. 'My my, you are getting your feet under the table. With such toffs too.'

'It's a bit scary, though, don't you think?'

'Can I give you a word of advice?' Cordelia asked.

'Go ahead.'

'Just be your normal, natural self. Try not to feel out of place, or awed, or anything like that. They might be monied but you're every bit as good as they are. We're all Jock Tamson's bairns, don't forget.'

Lexa smiled at that. It was true enough. They were all equal in the eyes of Jock Tamson – a Scottish name for God.

She nodded. 'I won't forget.'

Lexa was amazed to discover the McLeods employed a maid, though she shouldn't really have been if she'd thought about it. She wondered if there was a butler lurking somewhere, but it transpired there wasn't.

'Thank you, ma'am,' the maid said, taking Lexa's black woollen coat.

Ma'am! No one had ever called her that before. She had to struggle to keep a straight face.

William ushered her into what he referred to as the

drawing room where his parents were waiting, both standing and holding drinks.

'Father, you already know Lexa.'

Henry came forward and shook her hand. 'How nice to have you here, Lexa.'

'Thank you. I'm pleased to be here.'

After a great deal of discussion with Alice and Cordelia she'd finally settled for her skirt in Royal Stewart tartan, worn with an oatmeal-coloured roll-neck sweater and black shoes. To her delight Henry had on what appeared to be an old pair of trousers and a cardy with leather patches on the elbows, and she couldn't help but smile to see that Elspeth was sporting a skirt in the McLeod tartan and a pale-green roll-neck sweater. Snap! she thought gleefully. She'd got it dead right.

'And this is my mother,' William went on.

An elegant woman, Lexa noted. Slim, and extremely poised. The eyes were soft, and highly intelligent. That, and kind.

'I'm glad to meet you at last,' she said.

'And I to meet you, Mrs McLeod.'

'Would you care to join us in a drink?' Henry enquired.

A quick glance told her what Elspeth was having. She'd have the same. 'Sherry would be lovely.'

'William, will you do the honours?' Henry requested. 'And I think your mother could do with a top-up.'

'How did I do?' Lexa asked anxiously as they began the journey back to Mount Florida. 'I tried my best to mind my Ps and Qs.'

'It couldn't have gone better, Lexa, I promise you.'

'Do you think they liked me?'

'I'm absolutely certain of it.'

Lexa thought back to the meal, the main course of which had been a most delicious turbot. The pudding was a chocolate confection, while the starter had been smoked salmon.

She'd been asked a great many questions about herself, but in a friendly, not an inquisitorial, way. She'd asked a few questions of her own, thinking it was expected of her. She hadn't wanted to appear empty-headed. She did have a brain, after all, so why not show she had?

'Your mother was very nice,' she said.

'She really took to you. I could tell.'

Lexa suddenly giggled.

'What?'

'Here was me worried about what to wear, and I end up with a tartan skirt and roll-neck sweater same as your mum. I thought that was hysterical.'

William smiled. 'It was something of a coincidence.'

'And that wine we had! I know something about it now, and that one was out of this world!'

'Well, what else would you expect in a wine merchant's house? You'd have a fit if I told you what that cost a bottle.'

'Go on, William, tell me?' she coaxed. 'I'd love to know.'

She gasped when she heard. More than a month of her wages, she thought. Just for a bottle of wine! How the other half lived, right enough. She could just imagine Alice's reaction when she imparted that piece of information. The smelling salts might be required.

'Happy?' William asked.

'Oh, yes. And you?'

'Couldn't be happier.'

Lexa leaned back in her seat and closed her eyes. The lunch had been perfect. Happy? She was ecstatic.

William found his mother waiting for him when he returned. 'Well, Mater?'

'A charming girl. A little rough round the edges perhaps, but nothing that can't soon be smoothed away. You've chosen well, dear. I heartily approve. She'll be a great asset to the family in time.'

He might not have used the word, but William was ecstatic too.

Chapter 22

It was a terrible day for business, the teeming rain keeping customers away. In fact it was so bad that Cordelia was considering chucking it in and going home.

She had to smile, though, when she saw Ginge coming in her direction holding a lady's umbrella over his head. He looked ridiculous.

'How are you?' he asked on joining her.

'Wet. And you?'

'Bored out of my mind. Are you thinking what I'm thinking?'

'About going home?'

He nodded. 'Aye. It's a waste of time here in this weather.' He cast an eye skywards. 'I don't see any signs of it stopping, either. I'm certain this is in for the day.'

So was Cordelia. 'Start packing up, then,' she said to Kenny, who was hovering nearby.

'Right, Cordelia. I'll get to it.'

Was it her imagination or was there something of a new maturity about Kenny? she wondered. He'd certainly come a long way from the boy she'd first engaged.

'I had a letter this morning,' Ginge announced casually.

'Oh, aye?'

'From our old friend Joe Given. He's moved to Ireland. The south, that is.'

Which surprised Cordelia. 'Whatever for?'

'He didn't actually say. But knowing Joe I'd imagine he's gone there to escape the war. Joe isn't the sort to enlist. So he's getting out of it before there's a general call-up, which could happen any time, depending how things go.'

Cordelia shook her head. How typical of the man. Apart from everything else he was a coward into the bargain.

'I'm not impressed,' Ginge muttered darkly. 'But there we are.'

'Why did he write to you, anyway?'

'To give me his new address, for a start. He wants me to keep in touch and let him know what's going on round here. Who's doing what, and up to what, that kind of thing. Joe's always been one to keep his ear to the ground.'

What did she feel at the mention of his name? Nothing. Nothing at all, she decided. Joe had finally been exorcised from her heart and soul. He could jump off a cliff for all she now cared. The knowledge cheered her enormously.

'France!' Lexa exclaimed in alarm. 'But why?'

'Business, naturally. There are people I should see.'

Lexa didn't like the sound of that at all. It was far too dangerous in the current situation.

As though reading her thoughts, William said, 'I'll be safe enough, don't you worry.'

'But the Germans. What if they invade while you're there?'

William had to admit he wasn't entirely happy about it himself. But he and his father had discussed the proposed trip in depth, coming to the conclusion that there wasn't too much risk involved. They had agreed that at the first sign of any attempted invasion he'd get on the first possible ship back to England.

'The French have a defence system called the Maginot Line,' William explained. 'I'm not saying the Germans won't get through it, but if they do it'll take quite some time and effort. The French believe it's impregnable, and hopefully it is.'

Lexa gazed into his face, thinking how much she'd come to love this handsome man. 'Is it absolutely necessary you go?' she asked.

William shrugged. 'Not really. But if the Germans did conquer France it would be a long, long time before we could import wine again from there. This trip might be our last opportunity to increase our stock if the worst happens.' He smiled to see the concern in her eyes. Raising a hand, he gently stroked her cheek. 'It's only for about a week. I'll be home again before you know it.'

'It'll seem like an eternity to me, William. I shall be thinking and worrying about you every single minute.'

As it was dark outside, he leaned across and kissed her. A long, lingering kiss. A French kiss.

She sighed with contentment when it was finally over. But she tensed again when she remembered what they had been talking about. 'When are you off?'

'This Friday morning. That should give me plenty of time to get ready to start my business calls on Monday morning.'

'God, how I'll miss you,' she whispered.

'And I'll miss you. Terribly.'

She hated the idea of his going into possible danger. At least there was this Maginot Line thing to protect him. And then she forgot everything when he kissed her again.

A few days later she was on an internal errand for Mrs Sanderson, who'd sent her to get a fresh supply of carbon paper for the office, when she spotted Mr McLeod senior coming along the corridor towards her. It was the first time she'd seen him since having lunch with him and his wife.

He broke into a smile when he recognised her. 'Good morning, Miss Stewart,' he said as he came close.

'Good morning, Mr McLeod.'

As they passed each other he did something that was totally unexpected: he winked.

She was thrilled to bits. She truly had been accepted by the McLeods.

William was sitting outside a Parisian café having a cup of coffee and brandy. His experience of the city, and its inhabitants, to date was mixed.

There was a lot of fear about, and defiance. There was also a great deal of conversation about the Maginot Line, and how impregnable it was. The Parisians on the whole considered themselves safe from invasion, having as well a great belief in the ability of their army to protect them.

The morning's English newspaper that he'd been able to buy had carried the banner headline news that Britain had landed 158,000 men in France to fight alongside the French should it be necessary.

William had considered going down to the Languedoc, and decided against it. His instincts warned him that it might not be a good idea. If hostilities did break out between the French and the Germans he would be an awfully long way from home. No, best he stayed in Paris, with easy access to cross-Channel shipping.

He turned his face up towards the weak and watery sunshine to see a plane high in the sky. He couldn't tell if it was French or British, but found the sight of it re-assuring. He wondered what it would be like to be in a plane that high?

Wonderful, he decided. He continued to watch the aeroplane until it was finally lost to view.

'Worried about William?'

Lexa glanced over at her sister, and nodded. Alice was out at the Labour Hall with Mrs McAllister. 'It keeps preying on my mind that he's over there. I know nothing's happened, yet. But it could any day now, in which case he could be caught right in the middle of it.'

'I'm sure he'll be fine.'

'You don't know that.'

Cordelia sighed. 'I suppose not.'

'I've started saying a prayer for him every night when I go to bed. It helps me, if no one else.'

Cordelia came to her feet. 'How about a nice cup of tea? That might cheer you up.'

Lexa shook her head. 'Not for me, thanks.'

'Then how about a dram out the kitchen bottle?'

Again Lexa shook her head.

She really was worried, Cordelia thought. Had to be to refuse both a cup of tea and dram. 'When's William due back?'

'In a couple of days. That's if he doesn't stay longer than he intended.'

'Then let's hope they fly by, eh?'

Lexa couldn't have agreed more. She couldn't wait to know that William was back safe and sound.

'Can we have a quick drink after work? There's something I want to talk to you about.'

Cordelia regarded Kenny quizzically. 'Sounds important?'

'It is.'

'Can't you just tell me here and now?'

'I'd rather not, if you don't mind. I don't wish to be interrupted by customers, so I'd prefer doing it over a pint.'

Fair enough, she thought. And how mysterious. 'All right, you're on.'

He broke into a smile. 'Thanks.'

Now what was this all about? she wondered.

She found out later, when he laid a whisky and lemonade on the table in front of her and sat down opposite. 'Is it possible for me to have some time off tomorrow?' he said.

'Of course,' she replied, curious. Kenny had never before asked for time off.

'I'll come in first thing and unpack. Then if I could get away, say about ten o'clock?'

Cordelia nodded. 'Fine.'

Kenny suddenly became embarrassed. 'The thing is, you see, my brother Murray and I are going to enlist.'

Cordelia was quite shocked, though she supposed she should have seen it coming. 'Why not wait until you're called up? I imagine that will happen sooner rather than later.'

He sighed. 'Murray and I considered doing so. But in the end we decided we'd prefer to volunteer. We'll feel better about it that way.'

Cordelia failed to see why. But then, she told herself ruefully, she was a woman after all. 'Have you told Ginge about this?'

'No. But I will after the deed's done. If I told him now I know he'd only try to talk me out of it. Me and Murray. Ginge can be very protective. Too much so at times. He can also be extremely persuasive. Talk the knickers off a nun, that man.' He blushed when he realised what he'd just said. 'Sorry, Cordelia. That was rude.'

'Don't worry about it.' She laughed. 'I've heard a lot worse.'

'I'm going to miss you and the market,' Kenny said softly. 'An awful lot.'

'And I'll miss you, Kenny.'

He regarded her intently. 'Will you really?'

'Indeed I will. You've been an enormous help and support. And I hope we've become friends during your time on the stall.'

'I'd like to believe so as well, Cordelia. It's going to be

a terrible wrench. But Hitler and his Nazis have to be stopped, there's no two ways about it.'

'Yes,' she agreed. 'He has.' It suddenly dawned on her how difficult it was going to be to run the stall without Kenny doing the donkey work. It was something she'd have to discuss with Ginge.

'Are you in?' Cordelia asked when Kenny reappeared late the following afternoon.

'I'm in.'

She noticed he was flushed and sparkly-eyed. Well, no wonder, she thought. He'd just signed up and would soon be off to war. Her heart went out to him. She'd become fonder than she'd realised of Kenny Smith.

'What happens now?' she asked.

'I've to wait for a letter which'll come within the next fortnight. It'll inform me where to report, and when.'

Going to him, she kissed him on the forehead. 'There.' She smiled. 'That's for luck. Now, you'd better go and tell Ginge what you've done.'

'Aye,' Kenny agreed reluctantly. 'I suppose I'd better.'

Cordelia found there was a hint of a tear in her eye after he'd gone. She truly was going to miss him.

William strode into the office and had a brief conversation with Mrs Sanderson, and left again without looking at Lexa.

Relief flooded through her. She wondered whether he'd come into the office on purpose to let her know he was back, and decided to ask him on the way home that evening.

When he admitted that he had, she settled back in her seat with a contented sigh. 'Thank God was all I could think when I saw you,' she told him.

'Safe and sound, as promised.' He laughed. 'The whole thing was a doddle.'

She put a hand over his. 'Did you have any difficulties?'

'None whatsoever. Though I don't imagine I'll be going over there again for a while.'

'And was it a success?'

'Very much so. Providing the stock I bought arrives in Britain, that is. Got good prices too, which Father will be delighted about. How about you?'

'I worried every moment I was awake. Felt quite sick with it at times,' she replied.

He smiled, thinking how wonderful it was to love and be loved in return. It was simply the best feeling in the world. 'I've brought you a present,' he said. 'A very special one.'

'Oh! What is it?'

He laughed. 'A surprise.'

Perfume or scent, she thought. Bound to be. 'And when do I get this special present?'

'Once we've stopped outside your close.'

She almost wriggled with impatience, eager for their journey to be over. It seemed to her they were going even more slowly than usual, but at last William was drawing up to the kerb and switching off the ignition. He leaned back in his seat, hoping to hell he'd got this right and wasn't about to make a fool of himself.

'Well?' Lexa demanded.

'You do love me?'

'You know I do, William.'

'And I love you.'

'As you've often said.'

He groped in a coat pocket, then handed her a small box. 'That's for you,' he said huskily.

Lexa slowly opened it and could just make out the outline of the ring it contained.

'Wait a sec,' William said, and produced matches he'd brought along knowing how dark it would be inside the car, and that he couldn't put on the overhead light.

A match flared, and Lexa gasped at what was revealed. The ring was adorned by a single diamond which looked huge in the tiny flame.

'What does this mean, William?' she asked as the light died away.

'It means I want to marry you. If you accept then that's your engagement ring.'

'Oh, yes, William. Yes please,' she croaked.

'Then see if it fits.'

It almost did, but was slightly loose. 'No matter,' he replied when she told him. 'Any good jeweller will soon resize it for you.' Next moment she was in his arms, and they were kissing madly.

'Oh, William,' she breathed when the kissing finally stopped. 'I can't believe this.'

He laughed softly. 'Happy?'

'What do you think?'

'Shall we go upstairs and tell your mother and sister?'

'Not yet. I want to make this moment last.' And then they were kissing again, as eagerly and passionately as before.

It was a good twenty minutes before they finally got out the car.

'Engaged!' Alice exclaimed in delight.

'And there's the ring to prove it,' Lexa declared, holding out her hand and moving it so that the diamond sparkled, shooting out beams of white light.

'Look how big it is,' Alice marvelled, taking hold of Lexa's hand and staring at the stone. 'It's bigger than the Koh-i-noor.'

William laughed. 'Hardly.'

'Congratulations, sis,' Cordelia said, coming to Lexa and kissing her on the cheek. Then it was her turn to stare in awe at the diamond.

'William brought it from Paris. Didn't you, darling?'

He nodded.

'How romantic,' Alice enthused.

'It doesn't quite fit so I'll have to have it resized,' Lexa said. 'William says I can have it done at any good jewellers.'

'Why don't we tie some thread round the band in the meantime,' Alice suggested. 'That way it won't slip off.'

Lexa nodded. 'Good idea, Mum.'

'I'll fetch the thread while you, Cordelia, get the kitchen bottle. This calls for a celebration.'

Lexa beamed at William, who beamed back. Her lovely, lovely man. Now husband to be. She could have shouted for joy.

They waited till Alice had sorted the band with thread, assuring it was a snug fit, before lifting the drinks Cordelia had poured.

'To William and Lexa!' Alice toasted. 'May they have a long and happy life together. God bless them.' And she burst into tears.

'How wonderful,' Elspeth McLeod declared when she and Henry were given the news later that evening. 'I was certain something like this was in the wind.'

'I think we should have champagne on such an occasion,' Henry enthused after he'd congratulated William and Lexa. 'Can you lay out glasses, William, while I get some?'

'Of course, Pater.'

'It's a beautiful ring,' Elspeth observed, taking hold of Lexa's hand and examining it.

'I think it's absolutely gorgeous,' Lexa replied. 'I'm thrilled to bits.'

William hadn't stinted on it, Elspeth mused, thinking the ring must have cost a pretty penny. But she approved of that. It showed what he thought of Lexa.

'I say!' William exclaimed when Henry reappeared carrying a bottle. 'You really are pushing the boat out, Father.' For the champagne was vintage Krug.

'It's not every day my son gets engaged,' Henry pointed out. 'And to such a lovely girl too.'

Lexa blushed.

Henry expertly popped the cork, then filled the glasses and passed them round.

'To the happy couple!' he toasted.

It was the first time Lexa had ever drunk champagne, and she loved it. What they said was true, she thought. The bubbles really did get up your nose.

* * *

'I've decided what I'm going to do now Kenny's leaving,' Ginge announced to Cordelia in the Hielan Laddie.

'Which is?'

'Close down my stall. The pair of us will work together on yours.'

She hadn't expected that. 'I'd have thought you'd have taken on more staff.'

Ginge gave her a wry smile. 'It's not only finding, but keeping, new staff that would be the problem. There's a war on, don't forget, even if it doesn't seem like it at the moment. Things have already started to change, and that will only escalate as time goes on. All the able-bodied men will be gone before long, unless they're in jobs that give them exemption. And women will be going into factories and the like to help with the war effort. It happened in the last war and will happen again, mark my words.'

'So it's just to be the two of us, then?'

'Unless you object?'

'Why would I do that?'

He shrugged. 'You never know.'

Just the two of them, Cordelia mused. She did like Ginge, but she hoped he didn't have any aspirations towards her. It could ruin a good friendship if he did.

Chapter 23

It was the first time Lexa had worn her ring to the office, having now had it resized. She hadn't flashed it to the others when she arrived, preferring to wait until someone noticed. A whole hour had gone by and still no one had made any comment.

'What's that on your finger!' Tarantula exclaimed ten minutes later. 'Is it an engagement ring?'

Pam and Mrs Sanderson glanced across.

Lexa held up her left hand. 'Yes, it is actually.'

Tarantula's eyes widened. 'Will you look at the size of that diamond. It's bloody enormous!'

'Language, Miss Quigley,' Mrs Sanderson immediately admonished her. 'We'll have none of that here.'

'Sorry, Mrs Sanderson.'

Pam had now come over to Lexa's desk. 'Wow! That really is a corker.'

Mrs Sanderson hurried across, wanting to see and admire Lexa's ring for herself. She sucked in a deep breath when she got an eyeful.

'When did this happen?' Pam demanded.

'Last week.'

'And you haven't let on until now?'

'I had to have the ring resized. This is my first opportunity of wearing it.'

'Is it real?' Tarantula asked suspiciously, forehead creasing in doubt.

'Very much so.'

'Must have cost a fortune!'

'You've never even told us you were going out with anyone,' Pam said reproachfully.

'You've certainly kept it quiet,' Tarantula added.

Wait till they find out why, Lexa thought, inwardly smiling.

'So who's the lucky chap?' Pam asked. 'Must be a wealthy so and so to buy you a ring like that.'

'You actually know him,' Lexa said.

That baffled Pam. 'I do?'

'In fact you all know him.'

Lexa had to admit, Tarantula was quick off the mark in putting two and two together. No dummy she. 'It's Mr McLeod junior, isn't it?'

Lexa nodded.

'Dear me,' Mrs Sanderson breathed, visibly impressed, if not a little shocked.

'You told me he was only giving you a lift home that time I spotted the pair of you in his car,' Tarantula accused her.

Lexa smiled sweetly. 'I lied.'

Tarantula was consumed with envy. 'Of all the jammy luck,' she muttered.

'I've always fancied him,' Pam admitted, 'but I never thought he'd look at any of us.'

'You have Bobby,' Lexa reminded her.

'Aye, true enough,' Pam agreed. 'And a finer, or nicer, man never walked the earth.'

Lexa simply smiled.

'Well, congratulations, Miss Stewart,' Mrs Sanderson said. She too was envious. She would have died rather than admit it, but she also had a soft spot for William. She was a married woman, she reminded herself, and practically old enough to be his mother, but still . . .

'Have you fixed on a date yet?' Elspeth enquired. She and William were alone in the morning room.

'No, Mother.'

'Perhaps you should.'

'We've only just got engaged!' he protested.

'None the less, there is a war on. It might be better to get married sooner rather than later. Normally I'd suggest a longish engagement, but not in the circumstances.'

William studied his mother. 'You appreciate I'm bound to get called up before long?'

'I know,' she acknowledged sadly.

William rubbed his chin, deep in thought. His mother could well be right. It was something he'd have to think about, and discuss with Lexa. Bugger Hitler and his Nazis! They were making matters terribly inconvenient for him. Which hardly mattered in the scheme of things, he reflected ruefully.

Set a date? It would have to be fairly soon if they did.

* * *

'I'm pished,' Kenny declared. 'As a rat. Steamboats. Deid mockit.'

Cordelia looked into his bleary eyes and saw that that was true. She wasn't entirely sober herself. It was Kenny's last day on the stall and she and Ginge had taken him to the Hielan Laddie for what Ginge called a proper send-off.

'You don't say?' the latter commented sarcastically now. 'I wouldn't expect anything else after the amount of whisky and beer you've poured down your throat – it would be a miracle if you weren't.'

Kenny hiccuped.

'Are you enjoying yourself?' Cordelia asked with a smile.

'Oh aye, I'm having a rerr terr.' A great time.

'Well, Monday morning you'll be in Maryhill Barracks. A fully signed-up soldier. God help you,' Ginge said, wishing it was himself reporting for duty.

'What happens after your training?' Cordelia enquired.

Kenny shrugged. 'No idea.'

'Maybe they'll send you abroad,' Ginge speculated. 'Over to France perhaps to join the Tommies already there.'

'France,' Kenny mused. 'Don't the French nosh frogs and go around stinking of garlic?'

Cordelia laughed. 'I doubt our boys do either. I'm sure you'll be on ordinary army rations.'

'Bully beef and the like,' Ginge added.

'I like beef,' Kenny slurred. 'So that's all right then.'

'On the other hand they might send you to Africa.' Ginge was still speculating.

'Where the cannibals come from?'

'They're not all cannibals, Kenny,' Cordelia assured him. 'I doubt you'll have to worry about being eaten.'

'Or Arabia. Lots of camels in the desert. You'd probably get to ride one.'

'Camels,' Kenny muttered. 'I read somewhere they're awfully smelly. Real stinkers.'

Ginge finished his pint. 'Who's for another?'

'Not for me,' Cordelia told him hastily. 'I've had enough.'

'Rubbish, woman! This is a celebration, don't forget. You've got to keep your end up.'

Cordelia sighed, then decided she actually would like another drink. But if she did it would be a taxi home for her. 'All right,' she conceded. 'But this definitely is my last, celebration or not.'

'No need to ask you, Kenny, is there?'

'A pint and a hauf, Ginge. Thanks.'

'Coming up.' Ginge declared, and headed for the bar.

Kenny leaned across the table and placed a hand over Cordelia's. 'I have a favour to ask which I didn't want to say in front of Ginge,' he said.

'What's that?'

'If I do get sent away – Scotland, England or overseas – would you be a sort of pen pal for me?'

'Pen pal?'

'Aye, that's right. It would be lovely to hear from you and know what you're up to. That sort of thing. And I can write to you giving you my news. What do you say, Cordelia?'

She couldn't see why not. 'Of course I'll write to you, Kenny. It'll be my pleasure.'

His face broke into a huge grin. 'Ta. I appreciate that. You're an absolute diamond.'

Cordelia gently extricated her hand before Ginge returned.

Alice switched off the wireless, face flushed with excitement. 'The *Graf Spee* scuttled! That's one in the gob for those dirty Jerries. The rotten sods.'

'It's certainly good news, Mum,' Cordelia agreed.

'How long do you think this war will go on for?' Lexa asked thoughtfully.

'The last one lasted four years. Four long years,' Alice replied. 'And who knows? This one might go on for longer. It's entirely possible.'

Four years, Lexa reflected. A lifetime in many ways. What would happen to her and William during that time? She didn't really want to think about that. It was far too upsetting.

Ginge returned having been out and about round the market. 'That's another two stalls closed down,' he grimly announced to Cordelia. 'If this keeps up there'll be none of us left before you know it.'

She shook her head in despair. 'Do you really think it'll come to that?'

'Look at the facts. It's becoming harder and harder to get stock. Supplies from the Continent are getting patchier. As for the local stuff, I can see people being told to stop growing flowers and grow food instead. It's common sense when you think about it.'

'What's the answer, Ginge?'

'Your guess is as good as mine at this stage. Find other jobs, I suppose. What else can we do?'

Finish at the market? Cordelia thought. That would be terrible. Heartbreaking. But as Ginge said, it might just come to that.

'It's a bastard, isn't it?' Ginge smiled wryly.

Cordelia had to agree.

'Mother asked me recently if we were going to set a date,' William said as he was driving Lexa home from work.

She'd wondered when that subject was going to be mentioned. 'And are we?'

'That depends.'

'On what?'

He drove for a few seconds in silence before replying, 'There's a war on, and the brutal fact is people get killed in wars.'

Lexa went white.

'Right?'

She nodded in the darkness.

'I'm bound to be called up soon. There's no avoiding it. I'm only surprised it hasn't already happened, to tell you the truth. And when I do get my papers I'll have to go.'

'Maybe you'll fail the medical?' Lexa said hopefully.

'Not a chance. I'm fit as the proverbial flea. Years of rowing have seen to that. I'll pass all right, no doubt about it.'

Lexa couldn't bear to think of William going off to war, and not coming back. The very idea was too horrible for words. 'So, what do we do?' she asked.

'That's the big question. Get married now, or wait till after the war?'

Lexa was suddenly aware that her heart was pounding, while her throat had gone quite dry.

'What's your opinion?' he asked.

Lexa took her time in replying. 'I don't have one. I haven't really thought about it. And you?'

'I haven't decided either.'

'Am I intruding?'

William snapped out of his reverie. He was sitting at his father's study desk holding a glass of brandy, and had been staring into space.

'No, Father. You're not.'

Henry glanced from the brandy to the nearby green-shaded desk lamp, the only light switched on in the room. 'A period of reflection?' He smiled.

'Something like that.'

'Want to talk about it?'

Did he? William wasn't sure. There again, his father had always given him good advice. And he would be a sounding board, if nothing else. 'Please.'

Henry took a seat, and stared expectantly at his son. He was certain he knew what this was all about. And when William began to speak, he knew he was right.

'I don't know how we're expected to exist on what they're allowing us,' Alice complained bitterly. The leaflet in her hand explained that food rationing was coming in, and then proceeded to give details of what would be the weekly allowance per person.

'Four ounces of butter, twelve of sugar, four of bacon or ham. I mean, it's preposterous!'

'It'll get worse before it gets better,' Cordelia remarked.

'Bound to,' Lexa agreed.

'Well, there'll have to be a tightening of belts in this house,' Alice declared reluctantly. She was a woman who enjoyed her food. 'God knows how we're going to manage.'

'My guess is that's only the start. They'll be rationing all sorts before long.'

'Like what?' Lexa queried.

'Everything. You'll see.'

Alice slumped into a chair, still holding the leaflet. 'If only we hadn't been forced into selling the fruit and veg shop,' she sighed. 'At least we wouldn't have had any shortage with those.'

But I wouldn't have met William, Lexa thought.

'There is one good thing about all this,' Cordelia declared.

Alice frowned at her. 'Such as?'

'None of us will have to worry about going on a diet for a while. We'll be on an enforced one.'

Alice saw the funny side of that, and laughed. What Cordelia had just said couldn't be more true.

Returning from a delivery out in the country William pulled up close to the boundary fence of a small aerodrome. He had driven past it many times before without giving it undue attention: it had simply been there. There were several planes on the runway, though of what type he couldn't say other than that they appeared to be bombers of some sort. How deadly they looked, he reflected. Though purposeful too. He wondered which squadron they belonged to, and if they were operational.

As he watched, a flight crew appeared out of a group of huts, and approached one of the planes. He continued to stare in fascination as they climbed aboard and disappeared. Minutes later the engines were fired, and one by one the massive propellers began to turn. Even at that distance the noise was deafening as the plane started trundling down the runway, rapidly gaining speed. It took off, banking to the right as it continued to climb.

How thrilling, not to mention exhilarating, it must be to fly such a machine, William thought. What a simply wonderful experience.

He was smiling as he went on his way.

At dinner that evening, he knew it was time to tell his parents what he had decided to do. 'I've something to say to you both,' he announced, having taken a larger than usual gulp of his wine. 'I've come to a decision. Two, actually.'

For the space of a moment fear flashed in Elspeth's eyes, and then was gone. Carefully she placed her knife and fork on her plate, and glanced at Henry before focusing on her son. Somehow she managed to force a smile on to her face. 'And what are those, dear?'

William told them.

'January's such an awful month, don't you think?' Lexa said. She was making conversation as William had been unusually quiet during the journey so far. Quiet and brooding.

'I joined the RAF today. Signed on the dotted line. They'll be contacting me shortly about where I'm to be posted for training.'

Lexa was stunned. 'The RAF?' she croaked.

'That's right. I would have been conscripted anyway and decided I wanted the RAF rather than the army or navy. By signing up I got to make a choice, which I wouldn't have had otherwise.'

'I see,' she heard herself say.

'I wish things were different, Lexa. I desperately wish they were. But they aren't. It's as simple as that.'

Lexa took a deep breath. 'It's just a bit of a shock, that's all. So completely out of the blue.'

'You do understand, though, don't you?' he pleaded.

'Completely.'

'I don't think I'm cut out for the army, and the navy just doesn't appeal. The air force does. Flying an aeroplane must be a hundred times better than driving the Hornet, and I adore that.'

Lexa suddenly remembered Granny Stewart's prophecy. An important man would come into her life who had different-coloured eyes and had something to do with aeroplanes. Well, the prophecy had certainly come true, even if it had taken a while to happen.

'There's another thing,' William went on hesitantly.

'I'm listening.'

'I've given it a great deal of thought and I think it would be best to wait until the end of the war before we get married.'

That was another hammer blow.

'Lexa?'

'I heard you, William. You want to wait till the end of the war before getting married. That's plain enough.'

He could hear how upset she was, which upset him. 'I'm sorry. Truly I am.'

'Don't be. It's probably for the best,' she replied, rather stiffly, but with a choke in her voice.

'You see, Lexa, if the worst should happen, and there's always the possibility, I don't want to leave a young widow behind. It would be awful. At least that's how I see it. How about you?'

She ran a hand over her forehead, wishing she was home, locked away in her bedroom where she could succumb to the misery she was suffering.

'Lexa?'

Damn! she thought as she felt tears creep into her eyes. The last thing she wanted was to start crying. That wouldn't be fair on William.

'You've made your decision and we'll both have to stick to it,' she muttered. 'And yes, I do take your point.'

'Do you agree, though?'

'It would have been nice to be your wife, even if only for a short while,' she finally admitted.

William sighed. 'And what if I were to be killed? What then?'

'As you said, I'd be a young widow. One who'd lost the man she loved.'

This was turning out to be worse than he'd expected, William thought. But he knew he was making the right decision, for both of them. He was certain of it.

'I'm sorry,' he said again.

'How long before you have to report for training?'

'About a fortnight, I believe. Though where to I've no idea. It could be anywhere.'

'Anywhere,' she repeated sombrely.

They didn't speak again until they reached her close, where he stopped the car. For a few moments they sat in silence, and then he took her into his arms and kissed her.

It was a cold kiss. No fire or passion. Cold. When he released her she opened the door and got out, turning to close the door again. She tried to smile in the darkness, but couldn't. And when she tried to speak she couldn't do that either. Instead she just stood there staring at him through the glass of the window. Feeling more wretched than she'd ever done before in her life.

Turning on her heel, she walked away up the stairs, the tears she'd managed to hold back until then now streaming down her face.

Chapter 24

'Kenny!' Cordelia exclaimed when he suddenly turned up at the stall. 'This is a nice surprise.'

He beamed at her. 'I've finished training and got a week's leave. So I thought I'd better come and see you two.'

Ginge regarded the uniform Kenny was so proudly wearing. 'Couldn't you get a better fit?' he queried. 'Isn't it a bit big for you?'

Kenny laughed. 'They gave me this and told me to make the best of it. I'm hoping my mum will be able to take it in here and there.' To Cordelia, he said, 'Mum's a dab hand with a needle and thread. She's even got her own sewing machine. Though I have to admit, it did fall off the back of a lorry.'

Cordelia smiled. 'Forget the uniform. You look every inch the soldier, and that's a fact.'

A customer approached, and Ginge prepared to serve her. 'Why don't the pair of you go for a drink?' he suggested. 'I'll mind the shop while you do.'

'Cordelia?'

'Why not?' She took off her apron, and threw it over a nearby box. She didn't have to put on her coat as she was already wearing it, the weather being bitter. There had been a light fall of snow earlier that morning, although it had vanished now, except for the odd trace here and there.

On the way to the pub Cordelia hooked an arm round Kenny's. 'So how are you?'

'Pleased to be out and about again, I can tell you.'

'I'm sure.'

'This'll be my first pint since reporting in. Just watch it go down in double-quick time.'

Cordelia laughed, thinking how much she'd missed Kenny. She hadn't realised how close they'd become while he was working for her.

'Now, tell me all about it,' she demanded once they were ensconced in the Hielan Laddie with drinks in front of them.

'There's not a lot to tell, really. Most of the training is square-bashing. Up down, round about, with a sergeant major screaming at you. Then there are cleaning duties, and rifle practice. I like the rifle practice best. There's also bayonet drill.' He pulled a face. 'That's a bit scary. All I can ever think is if I'm close enough to Jerry to stab him, then he's close enough to stab me.'

Cordelia pulled a face to match his. 'Hm,' she muttered. 'Scary indeed.'

'The good side is I've become quite pally with a few of the lads. All Glaswegians like myself. It's comforting to know I'll have mates beside me, watching my back as

I'll be watching theirs, should we see action. Which is bound to happen sooner or later.' He stopped, then said, 'Now hold on a sec.'

Lifting his pint, he slowly drained it, and gave a huge sigh. 'Ah, that's better!'

'You weren't joking about the double-quick time,' she teased.

'Damn right I wasn't.' He came to his feet. 'Don't disappear while I get another.'

Cordelia studied him while he was at the bar. He'd lost weight, she could tell, even if his uniform was too big for him. And his posture had changed to become more military. There was also a new sense of strength and purpose about him. Yes, she thought. The army was certainly agreeing with Kenny.

'Now tell me what's been happening to you and the stall,' he said on his return.

'Nothing to me personally, though Ginge is worried we might have to close down eventually.'

Kenny frowned. 'Why?'

She explained, and Kenny nodded when she'd finished.

'It makes sense,' he said. 'I simply hadn't thought of that.'

'If we do close down then obviously I'll have to get another job, though God knows what. I haven't a clue what I'd do.'

'You'll think of something, Cordelia. Just don't forget I'll want to know when we start exchanging letters.'

She smiled, having almost forgotten about the pen pal bit. 'Any idea where you'll be posted to?'

'The rumour is France to link up with our troops already there. But so far it's only rumour.'

Cordelia had a sip of her whisky. A rumour she'd heard was that the sale of spirits was shortly to be curtailed. She had no idea why, and could only hope the rumour wasn't true.

'I've something to ask you,' Kenny said hesitantly.

She raised an eyebrow.

'I was wondering if you'd care to go out for a meal with me? One of my pals has recommended a restaurant called the Mirabelle where he worked as a sous chef before enlisting. He promised me the food's terribly good.'

A meal with Kenny? 'Restaurants are expensive,' she reminded him.

'I know that. And it won't be a problem. Trust me.'

Cordelia had a sudden thought, remembering her recently issued ration book. 'If we go we might need coupons,' she pointed out.

'Don't worry about that,' he assured her. 'I'll find out, and if we do need them I'll have enough for both of us.' He winked, which made her laugh.

'Like the sewing machine falling off a lorry?'

'Precisely.'

She couldn't help but think how grown up he'd become. Quite the dashing young man.

'So, what about it?' he demanded, authority in his voice.

'I'll be delighted to, Kenny.'

He was clearly pleased.

'Where is this Mirabelle?'

Kenny told her, and she realised she had vague recollections of passing it on several occasions.

'There's just one thing,' he said, his expression changing to one of concern. 'Ginge.'

'What about Ginge?'

'It may be tactful not to mention it to him.' Kenny hesitated, then went on, 'He's always been dead keen on you, Cordelia, and I don't want him to feel jealous or anything. Understand?'

They stayed chatting for quite some time before leaving the pub, and as they walked back to the stall Cordelia realised she was beginning to see Kenny in a rather new light.

Lexa glanced across at Pam, who was beavering away at her desk. Lucky old Pam, she thought. Her Bobby was in a reserved occupation, which meant he wouldn't be going into any of the armed services, and was therefore out of harm's way.

Her William, on the other hand, didn't have that advantage and would be very much in harm's way. Only a couple of days left before he was off, she reflected. She felt bad enough now, but that was when the real agony would begin.

'I've a confession to make,' Kenny said.

'What's that?'

He leaned across the table and whispered confidentially, 'I've never been in a proper restaurant before. Only a fish one.'

Cordelia had a sudden urge to giggle. Then she too leaned forward. 'Me neither. This is my first time.'

'Really?'

She nodded. 'Really.'

Kenny felt better when he heard that. Less gauche. They were on equal terms as far as the restaurant was concerned. 'More wine?' he offered, picking up the bottle of white he'd ordered.

'Please.'

He topped up her glass, and then his own. 'It's awfully kind of you to come out with me tonight, Cordelia,' he said quietly.

'Not at all. I'm enjoying myself.'

'Good. So am I. You haven't commented on my uniform yet. Hasn't Mum done a great job?'

'It certainly appears to fit a lot better.'

'I told you she was a dab hand with a needle and thread.'

'Not to mention a sewing machine,' Cordelia teased, her eyes twinkling.

'Not to mention,' Kenny agreed with a smile.

The next moment, to Cordelia's utter astonishment, Lexa and William came through the blackout curtains hanging over the door. What on earth were they doing here? Lexa had said nothing about the Mirabelle when they'd spoken earlier.

Lexa was equally astonished to spot her sister, and had a quick word with William after their coats had been taken away. She came over as William was shown to a table. 'Well, this is a coincidence,' she said when she reached them.

'Kenny, I'd like to introduce you to my sister Lexa. Lexa, this is Kenny Smith.'

Kenny rose and shook hands with Lexa. 'Pleased to meet you.' He smiled.

'Likewise. Cordelia has often mentioned you.'

'Has she!' Kenny exclaimed, chuffed.

'You never said you were coming here tonight,' Cordelia admonished her sister.

'I didn't know. William didn't say. You never mentioned it either.'

Cordelia shrugged. 'To be honest, I didn't see the point. It wasn't as if it was important or anything. Anyway, why don't you join us?'

Kenny's heart sank. He wanted Cordelia all to himself.

'Thanks for asking, sis, but as this is the last time I'll see William before he leaves I'd rather we stayed on our own if you don't mind.'

Cordelia held up a hand. 'I perfectly understand. You trot off now, and enjoy yourself.'

'Thanks, sis.'

A relieved Kenny again stood to say goodbye, and how nice it was to have met her. Lexa returned the compliment before walking away to rejoin William.

'You've met this William, then?' Kenny queried.

'Oh aye, he's been to the house. He and Lexa are engaged, you know.'

'No, I didn't.'

'William has enlisted, same as yourself. Only he's going into the RAF to train as a pilot. He'll probably be a very good as one as he's an excellent driver, I gather. At least, I presume that'll be the case.'

How lovely Cordelia was, Kenny was thinking. Such a beautiful face. As the expression went, he could have eaten her.

*   *   *

'Whitburn isn't that far away,' William was saying to Lexa. 'About halfway to Edinburgh. As I intend taking the Hornet with me I'm sure there'll be bags of opportunities for me to come back and see you.'

Lexa thought he was being somewhat overoptimistic. 'I can't see that happening,' she replied. 'Once you're at the aerodrome surely they'll keep you there.'

'It is a possibility.' William nodded. 'I'm only guessing about getting away. There again, it's still winter.'

Lexa frowned. 'What's that got to do with it?'

'Bad weather. There's bound to be lots of that and I can't believe we'll be expected to fly when there are storms raging, for example. Or if the visibility is awful.'

'What about desk work, though? Perhaps they'll use the periods of bad weather to make you do that. Surely there'll be lectures and the like? Stands to reason.'

'No doubt you're right.' He sighed. 'But I'm still hoping I'll be able to get away from time to time.'

'How's your veal?' Cordelia asked.

'Fine.' He wasn't really enjoying it. The sauce they'd put on the meat was far too rich for his liking. 'And your cutlets?'

'Lovely.'

'I shall remember this meal when I'm away,' he said quietly. 'I'll often think about it.'

'Is it that good?'

It wasn't the food he was talking about, but he was too shy to point that out to her. 'Oh, yes.' He smiled.

Cordelia glanced over at Lexa and William, who were deep in conversation. How much in love they were, she thought. It was blindingly obvious. She envied them in a way, wondering when her knight in shining armour would come riding along. If one ever did.

'I'm going to miss you terribly,' William said, gazing at Lexa.

'And I'll miss you. Every waking moment.'

'Damn this war!' he exclaimed through gritted teeth. 'What a mess it's making of everything. Us included. If only it had been otherwise.'

'But it isn't.' She smiled sadly.

'No, it isn't,' he agreed. Reaching across the table, he took her hand, and squeezed it. 'I do love you, Lexa.'

'And I love you.'

'Things will turn out all right in the end. You'll see.'

She only wished she could believe him.

It was time to go. Kenny had paid the bill, and left a tip. Cordelia slipped into her coat when the waiter brought it over.

'Should we say goodbye?' Kenny asked, indicating Lexa and William.

Cordelia considered for a moment. 'Better not. William might feel he has to offer me a lift home, which I don't want. It's their last night together for a while, after all. A wave will be enough.'

Outside, they plunged into blackout darkness. 'My tram stop's this way,' Cordelia declared, but Kenny held her back.

'I won't hear of that,' he said. 'You're having a taxi home. My treat.'

'But you've spent so much already,' Cordelia protested.

'Let me put it this way. It'll probably be some time before I'm again in the position to spend anything so the money side doesn't matter. All right?'

'All right,' she agreed. 'And thank you.'

'My pleasure, believe me.'

He was delighted when she put an arm through his as they headed for the nearest rank.

They found a taxi easily enough, Cordelia giving the driver her address while Kenny opened the door for her.

'Kenny, thanks again. It's been a wonderful evening.'

'Wonderful for me too.' He handed her a note for the fare.

He was so sweet, she thought. A lovely young man. 'Goodnight, then.'

'Goodnight, Cordelia. I'll write when I get a chance.'

'Do that. I'll certainly reply.'

She then surprised him by kissing him on the cheek, before slipping into the taxi and closing the door behind her.

A thoroughly elated Kenny was left touching the spot she'd kissed as the taxi moved off.

William drew the car up outside Lexa's close, and killed the engine. The moment they'd been dreading had finally arrived.

It had been a relatively quiet journey, the two of them only speaking intermittently, each preoccupied with their own thoughts.

'Here we are then,' Lexa said.

'Yes, here we are.'

'Oh, darling!' Lexa breathed, hating this.

'I promise you I'll do my best to get back whenever I can.'

'I'm sure you will.'

He gathered her into his arms, inhaling the sweet scent that was Lexa. Then they were kissing, and she was melting against him. One of his hands began moving up from her waist, but she neither protested nor cared, allowing him to do what she'd never before permitted, and loving it.

Neither could have said how long they sat there in the darkness, but when they broke apart for the last time Lexa's face was wet with tears, her make-up a ruin.

'Be careful, William. Please?'

'I will. You have my word on that.'

She took a deep breath, grabbed the door handle, and next second was out on the pavement. Then, heart thumping, she was hurrying up the stairs, unable to see where she was going through the tears that blinded her, and almost falling through the front door to find Alice anxiously awaiting her.

There was no need to ask how the parting had gone. It was obvious.

'Oh, Mum!' Lexa wailed.

'Come here, lass. Come here.'

Lexa needed no second bidding. Enveloped by her mother's arms she let herself go, her entire body shaking while the tears continued to flow.

Cordelia, who had been getting ready for bed, came into the room and took in the situation at a glance.

'Your sister's a wee bit upset,' Alice said, an understatement if ever there was one.

'Can I do anything?'

'Would you like a nice cup of tea, Lexa?' Alice asked.

Lexa was so overcome she couldn't reply.

'There there,' Alice muttered, stroking her hair, thinking how awful the parting must have been for her. 'Cordelia told me you both ended up in the same restaurant. Imagine that!'

Lexa said nothing.

'A real swanky place, too.'

'It was, Mum,' Lexa finally managed to say. Pulling herself free, she wiped her face with the flat of her hand.

'And you both enjoyed yourselves?' Alice was only too aware how trite that sounded.

Lexa nodded.

'Cordelia had a lovely time too, didn't you, darling?'

'Lovely,' Cordelia echoed, feeling terribly sorry for her sister.

'Oh, Christ,' Lexa swore, managing to pull herself somewhat together. 'What if I never see William again?'

'You musn't think like that,' Alice gently rebuked her. 'Of course you'll see him again.'

'He thinks he might be able to get home occasionally while he's training,' Lexa croaked. 'But what if he can't?'

'Only time will tell,' Alice replied. 'But in the meanwhile you'll just have to be brave and keep your chin up. Can you do that?'

Lexa, engulfed in misery, nodded. 'I'll try.'

'That's my girl. Now, what about that cup of tea I mentioned? I could make it black for you and add a wee splash of whisky. How about that?'

'Please, Mum.'

'In fact we'll all have it black with a splash of whisky. Just what the doctor ordered.' Alice hurried off to the kitchen.

Cordelia crossed to Lexa and put her arms round her. 'Oh, sis,' she whispered.

When Alice returned with the tea Lexa was something of her old self again.

Chapter 25

'There's a letter for you,' Alice announced.

Cordelia looked up from her breakfast, guessing straight away who it must be from. Nobody else would be writing to her, after all.

And she was right: it was from Kenny, the first she'd received. There were three pages written in pencil, containing a great many misspellings. Kenny, it seemed, was no scholar.

The rumour he'd heard had proved correct. He was now in France and had been in action twice, emerging unscathed on both occasions. Not everyone in his company had been so lucky. The food wasn't too bad, and to date he hadn't been obliged to eat any French muck which, when he'd come across it, had, without exception, stunk! He was still missing the market, but her and Ginge most of all. He was also missing the Hielan Laddie and often thought fondly of their Saturday afternoon sessions there. Fierce fighting was occurring a little further north than where he was at present, and there had been a lot of rain recently which was a pest. Could she please reply soonest as he was desperate to hear from her and about the goings-on in the market.

It was signed *Aye, Kenny*. Always, Kenny.

Cordelia read the letter twice, then returned it to its envelope. She'd noted the return address, an army one, and decided she'd write back that evening.

Mrs Sanderson came into the office and went straight to Lexa. 'Will you please go and see Mr McLeod senior, Miss Stewart? He wants you straight away.'

Lexa frowned. 'Did he say what for?'

'No, he didn't. And I certainly didn't ask. That would have been impertinent. Now off you go.'

'Yes, Mrs Sanderson.'

A few moments later, she was knocking on Mr McLeod's door.

'Come in!'

Lexa opened the door to see Mr McLeod behind his desk. At a gesture from him she closed the door behind her.

'You wanted to see me, sir?'

His somewhat stern expression softened, and his eyes twinkled. 'It seems you don't have a telephone at home, Lexa.'

'That's correct, sir.'

He waved a hand dismissively. 'No need for such formality when we're alone. Just call me Mr McLeod.'

'Yes . . . Mr McLeod.' What was all this about? she wondered. She quickly found out.

'I've just had a conversation with William, who's informed me he's coming home late tonight.'

Lexa was thrilled. William coming home! He'd managed it after all.

'Tomorrow being Saturday he suggests he meets you straight from work. How does that sound?'

'Oh, yes, please.' Lexa smiled.

'What we've agreed is that he should spend most of tomorrow with you, and all of Sunday with us. His mother will insist on that.'

Lexa nodded. She understood.

'However, I thought you might come to Sunday lunch so that you see as much of each other as you can. Is that agreeable to you?'

'Very much so, Mr McLeod.'

'William said to tell you he'll be waiting outside in the Hornet when you come out of work.' Henry paused, then went on, 'I could let you have the morning off, Lexa, but I feel that wouldn't set a very good example. I don't want you being thought to receive favourable treatment because you're engaged to my son. That wouldn't do at all.'

'I agree.' It was true, though she had to admit to herself that the extra hours with William would have been an added bonus.

'That's that then. So run along, Lexa, and we'll look forward to your company on Sunday.'

'As I will, Mr McLeod. Thank you.'

When she got back to the office she was regarded quizzically by the other three inhabitants, but offered no explanation as to why she'd been called to see the boss. Luckily the afternoon tea break had been and gone, so Tarantula had no opportunity of quizzing her about it, much to Lexa's relief.

*   *   *

315

There he was, waiting as promised. He beamed at her as she got into the Hornet, and pecked her on the lips. 'We'll get to the serious stuff later,' he promised, starting up the engine.

As they drove off Lexa saw Tarantula and Pam standing in the doorway. Tarantula was gaping, Pam smiling, and Lexa couldn't resist giving them a wave. Only Pam waving back.

'Oh, William,' she breathed. 'It's so good to see you again.'

'And you, Lexa.'

'I've missed you dreadfully.'

'And I've missed you.'

She snuggled up to him as closely as possible. 'Where are we going?'

'I thought we might have a drive down the coast to Largs. I know a café there which does the most fabulous fish and chips. How does that appeal?'

'Anything would appeal as long as I was with you,' she replied honestly.

He laughed. 'Same here. Me with you, that is.'

She gazed adoringly at him, wanting more of his kisses, and his arms round her. Later, she thought. She would just have to be patient. 'You're returning tomorrow night, I understand,' she said.

'That's right. As long as I'm back there before ten everything will be hunky dory.'

'And I'm to have you all day today?'

'Most of it anyway. I'll have to go home and change at some point, as will you.'

'Oh?'

'How would you like to go dancing tonight?'

'Love to.'

'Good. Then that's what we'll do. Trip the light fantastic.'

'Now tell me all about your training,' she demanded. 'I want to know everything.'

'Everything?' he teased.

'Absolutely.'

'It might bore you.'

'I don't care.'

William launched into an account of his life at Whitburn, and what the other chaps and instructors were like. According to him he was having a whale of a time. And he had taken to flying like a duck to water.

'You weren't exaggerating. These fish and chips are the best I've ever tasted.'

'Told you so.' He smiled. 'Have you been to Largs before?'

She shook her head.

'Then we'll have a walk round afterwards. Maybe even have a drink. The Marine Hotel has a lovely bar. Cosy too.' He suddenly looked away, remembering that the last time he'd been there was with Helen. A lifetime ago, it seemed now.

Lexa took a sip from the huge cup of tea she'd been given, thinking how wonderful the day was turning out to be. But then she'd known it would.

'Happy?' he asked.

'Delirious. And you?'

'The same.' Reaching across the table he touched her hand. 'I do love you, Lexa. And always will.'

317

'I love you too, William. And always will.'

He lifted his cup. 'To us!' he toasted.

'To us.'

When they left the café they strolled along the front, and William told her the Vikings had once landed there.

'How do you know so much about Largs?' she asked, curious.

'The Marine Hotel is a customer so I used to come here frequently. I also serviced a couple of restaurants in the town.' He stopped suddenly and stared skywards, having heard the distinctive roar of Merlin engines. 'Spitfires!' he exclaimed as a flight of three, in a V formation, passed rapidly overhead.

'Will you be flying one of those?'

He laughed. 'I'd certainly like to. But that's not down to me. It all depends on which squadron I'm posted to after I get my wings. I don't really have a choice in the matter. In fact, I don't have any choice at all.'

It was a question she didn't really want to ask. 'How long will it be before you get your wings, darling?'

'Hard to say. But if all goes according to plan then I would imagine the month after next. Possibly sooner if I do exceptionally well.'

The month after next, and possibly sooner! Her heart sank. 'Any idea where you'll be posted to?'

'None at all. But most of the chaps who've recently been reposted have been sent to aerodromes in the south of England. But you never know. I could stay in Scotland.'

Lexa fervently hoped that would be the case.

Later, on the way back to Glasgow, William slowed down, then turned the Hornet into a narrow track he'd spotted. He drove for several hundred yards till he found a suitable opening among the many trees surrounding them, where he pulled off the track, went on for a little way, and killed the engine.

'William?'

He twisted round and smiled at her. 'I promised you the serious stuff would come later. Well, now it's later.'

It wasn't very comfortable, but Lexa didn't care in the slightest.

Nor did William.

'How do I look?' Lexa's deep-blue dress had envelope shoulders, a high straight neckline and a slightly full bodice, with sleeves coming just to the elbow. Lexa thanked God she'd had the foresight to buy it some weeks previously for just such an eventuality. It was the first time Alice and Cordelia had seen it on.

Alice studied her daughter. 'Which dance hall are you going to?'

'The Plaza.'

'Hm,' Alice murmured. The Plaza was a rather posh establishment not usually frequented by the hoi polloi.

'Well, I think you look fabulous,' Cordelia declared, giving her verdict.

Alice had to admit she thought so too. 'You'll do,' she said. 'Are you wearing your black coat?'

Lexa nodded.

'That's the ticket.'

Lexa started when there was a knock on the front door. 'That'll be William!' she exclaimed. But it wasn't, it was Peggy McAllister wanting a word with Alice.

William arrived ten minutes later, and a few minutes after that, Lexa clutching her dancing shoes, they were clattering down the stairs on their night out.

'So how are Mr Watson and Mr Kirby getting on?' William enquired of his father over lunch the following day, naming the two retired gentlemen who had been taken on to replace him.

'Not too bad, actually,' Henry replied. 'They get the job done, albeit it takes them longer than it took you. But between the pair of them they make a fist of it.'

'Good.' William nodded. He glanced sideways at Lexa, and smiled. She smiled back, then looked up at the nearby grandfather clock, noting how quickly the time was slipping away. She realised she was being addressed by Mrs McLeod, and turned her attention back to William's mother, seeing that the older woman was just as aware of how rapidly the time was passing as she was.

It seemed only minutes later that the Hornet was drawing up outside her close. 'It was a lovely lunch, William. Thank you.'

He stroked her cheek. 'I'll get back here as soon as I can. I promise.'

'I know you will.'

'Perhaps next weekend, if I can wangle it.'

'You will take care, darling?'

He smiled. 'Don't you worry about me. I'll be safe enough. Now, Lexa, I really have to go.'

'I understand.'

'I love you.'

* * *

320

Ginge shook his head in despair. Trade was terrible and getting worse. Yet another stall had closed down earlier in the week.

'Boring, isn't it?' Cordelia said.

'You can say that again.'

He gazed about him, thinking that their stock of flowers was pathetic compared to what it had once been. It was simply getting harder and harder to get any stock at all.

'Tell you what, Cordelia, why don't you take the rest of the day off? I can manage fine by myself.'

'Are you sure, Ginge?'

'Of course I am. We've only had three customers so far, so we're hardly run off our feet.'

That was true enough. 'If you're absolutely certain?'

'I am. Now scoot.'

Taking him at his word, she scooted. Alice was surprised to see her back.

'What are you doing home so early?' she exclaimed.

Cordelia explained, and added, 'At this rate it won't be long before Ginge closes down our stall like the others who've already done so.'

'Well, let's hope it doesn't come to that. I know how much you like that job.'

'I do,' Cordelia agreed. 'But I have this horrible feeling I won't be in it for much longer.'

'Anyway, as you're here, you can help me by taking the washing down to the back court and pegging it out. And when you've finished that there are spuds to be peeled for tonight's tea.'

'All right, Mum.'

Cordelia found herself thinking of Kenny as she humped the washing downstairs. According to the papers things weren't going at all well in France. It was three weeks now since she'd last had a letter from him. She hoped he was all right.

'So how's the omelette?' William asked. It was the fourth time he'd managed to get home from Whitburn.

'Very nice.' She had a sip of wine, a bottle of Burgundy William had opened.

'Well I'm glad you like it, because it's one of the few things I can make.'

'I'm not surprised, having been brought up with a cook dancing in attendance,' she teased.

'Silver spoon, eh?'

'Something like that.'

'How about you?'

'Do you mean can I cook?'

'That's right.'

She shrugged. 'I have to admit Mum does most of it. But she has taught us a number of recipes, so let's just say I could get by if pushed.'

William topped up Lexa's glass, and then his own. 'Would you like to see round the place when you've finished? I'll gladly show you.'

They were alone in the house. Henry and Elspeth had gone through to an obligatory funeral in Edinburgh and given the staff the day off.

'I'd love to have the grand tour,' Lexa enthused.

'Female curiosity?'

'Of course. It's always interesting to see other people's

houses. And this one will be of particular interest being so large and posh.'

William laughed. 'Do you still consider me posh?'

She thought about it. 'Not as much as when I first met you. You're just William to me now.'

'Good.'

When they'd finished, and topped up their wine glasses again, Lexa followed him out of the kitchen and into several downstairs rooms which she'd never previously entered. Then he took her upstairs to the bedrooms, all sumptuously decorated with flowery wallpaper and imposing Victorian furniture.

'And this is mine,' he declared, throwing open the last door.

'It's a total tip,' she observed, going inside. 'You're very untidy.'

He shrugged. 'Guilty as charged.'

She gestured towards the double bed, which hadn't been made. Half of the top quilt was hanging down on to the floor. 'I'd have thought you'd have had a single.'

'I inherited that. And jolly comfortable it is too.'

Lexa saw a look come into his eyes, a look she'd come to recognise only too well.

He came to her and took her into his arms. 'I hadn't planned this, but now we're here, and in the house by ourselves, we should make the most of the fact.'

'I . . .' Her protest was stifled by his mouth. 'Oh, William,' she breathed when the kiss was over.

'We are engaged, Lexa. One day we'll be man and wife. Not to mention the fact that I'll soon be reposted God knows where. And then how long before I see you again?'

She stiffened as she felt him begin to undo the back of her dress. Before she knew it she was naked to the waist.

'I'm scared,' she whispered.

'Of what? It's only me.'

Moments later she was entirely naked, feeling totally vulnerable. Her heart was hammering.

'You're beautiful,' William said quietly, eyes shining. 'But I knew you would be.'

She watched in fascination as he took his clothes off. Then he took her hand and led her to the bed, where she quickly dived under the covers while he fumbled with something she knew must be a French letter, although she had never seen one before.

There was kissing and cuddling, and then her eyes opened wide as he entered her. She'd often wondered what it would be like, and now she was finding out.

'You must learn to relax,' William said when it was over.

'Wasn't I any good?' she queried in alarm.

He smiled. 'You were fine, Lexa. But too tensed up. We'll leave it a few minutes and then try again, shall we?'

The second time was a great success, and a surprise too for Lexa, who hadn't known women could experience what she just had. It was a glorious revelation.

Chapter 26

It was organised chaos. The place was called Dunkirk, and Kenny had never even heard of it until he arrived there the previous day. Now the entire British army in France, the British Expeditionary Force as it was known, was facing the seemingly impossible prospect of being evacuated with the Germans hard on their heels.

Kenny was standing waist high in water patiently waiting his turn to be taken on board one of the vast flotilla of ships, mainly small ones, that had flocked to the rescue. At that moment all he could think of was that he give anything for a fag, but he'd run out days ago.

Incredibly, a cockney voice belonging to a chap in the next line of men was singing loudly:

'I don't want to join the army,
I don't want to go to war.
I'd rather hang around
Piccadilly underground,
Living off the earnings of a high born lay . . . dee . . .'

Over to his left Kenny spotted some Stuka dive bombers screaming down from the sky. Their bombs were released to go plunging earthwards, and then the Stukas levelled out to machine-gun those on the beach.

'Bastards!' hissed Denny Malone, a pal, who was standing in front of him.

Kenny watched as those on the beach scrambled for cover, some falling like ninepins under the hail of fire, others simply blown to bits.

He glanced at the line of men ahead of him, the lead ones being picked up by what appeared to be a fishing boat. Further out a huge warship lay at anchor, its decks already crowded with troops.

The Stukas disappeared, but moments later a flight of fighter aircraft appeared to resume the strafing. And, to his horror, he realised they were coming straight at him.

Denny Malone keeled over as bullets ripped straight across his chest.

The next second Kenny was hit. He felt a searing pain, then lost consciousness, and pitched sideways into the water.

A grim-looking Alice switched off the wireless. The three of them had been listening to the news.

'Those poor lads,' Alice said, her voice laden with sympathy. The newsreader's account of what was happening at Dunkirk had been absolutely dreadful.

Cordelia was worried sick about Kenny, who she presumed was part of the evacuation. She offered up a silent prayer for his safety.

'Denmark, Norway, Holland, Belgium.' Alice shuddered. 'Where will it end?'

'What if they make it over here?' Lexa muttered, and a shiver ran down her spine.

'I would never have believed it possible,' Alice went on. 'But now . . . ?' She trailed off, and shook her head.

'God help us all,' Cordelia said quietly. Who knew what lay ahead? She doubted even Winston Churchill, the new Prime Minister, did.

The Old Mill was a typical English pub with oak beams, lots of brass, and prints on the walls. It was where all the lads in 105 Squadron came to drink.

William was sitting with Peter Blythe, his navigator, and each of them had a pint in front of him. To William's disgust he'd found on his first ever visit to the Mill that it didn't serve wine. Spirits were strictly rationed to one measure per night when available, which wasn't very often. When they were William always asked for brandy, but if that was off he'd have whisky. To his amusement Peter ordered gin and tonic, or gin and water when the tonic had run out. William considered gin and water an appalling combination.

'Heard from that popsy of yours recently?' Peter enquired languidly. He came from Devon, and like William had been privately educated. He had also rowed while at school, and had actually competed against William many years previously. When they discovered this fact a bond had been forged between the two men over and above that of flying together.

'I keep telling you, old chap, she's not a popsy, she's my fiancée,' William reprimanded his friend.

Peter shrugged. 'They're all popsies to me. Wives,

sweethearts, whatever, they're all popsies. Bless them.'

'You're incorrigible, you know.'

That made Peter laugh. 'The only way to be.' He glanced around the pub. 'Nothing doing in here tonight. But there again, there rarely is.' He let out a huge sigh of disappointment. Peter liked to think of himself as a ladies' man.

'Ops again tomorrow,' William said quietly, and frowned. The squadron was flying Blenheims, which he hated. They were obsolete, and he considered them death traps. 'I wish we'd hear something concrete about this new wonder aircraft we're supposedly being assigned.'

'Vague rumours, nothing more,' Peter said. 'All very frustrating.' He also couldn't wait to be rid of the damn Blenheims.

'I suppose it'll happen when it does,' William declared morosely.

'*If* it does,' Peter qualified.

William drained his pint and got up to get them both a refill. If he hadn't already had his single tot of brandy he'd have had another, and a large one at that.

It was a Saturday afternoon, and Cordelia and Ginge were having their usual Hielan Laddie session before going their separate ways.

'I've got some bad news, I'm afraid,' Ginge said.

'Oh, aye?' She guessed what was coming.

'I'll have to let you go, Cordelia. I'm sorry, but I'm simply not making enough to keep you on.'

There it was. As she'd feared. 'Business has been terrible.'

'I'll keep the stall on for a while, working it alone. But I don't see it lasting long.' He glanced at her, obviously embarrassed. 'Any idea what you'll do?'

She shook her head. 'No. I should have given it some thought, as I saw this coming, but I haven't. I'll soon get something, though. There are plenty of jobs around with so many men in the forces.'

Ginge smiled. 'I'll miss you.'

'And I'll miss you. But there you are – nothing lasts for ever.'

Ginge nodded his agreement, then reached into an inside jacket pocket to produce an envelope. 'This is for you,' he said. 'Call it severance pay.'

The flap of the envelope hadn't been stuck down, so Cordelia had a look to see what it contained. Fivers, lots of them. 'Bloody hell!' she exclaimed.

'It adds up to fifty quid.'

'I can't take that much!' Cordelia protested. 'Fifty quid is a small fortune.'

'Of course you can. You deserve it.' He smiled thinly. 'I want to see you right, and that's my way of doing so.'

'But Ginge . . .' She trailed off, lost for words.

'With that behind you you won't have to take the first job that comes along. You can bide your time until you find something that appeals.'

'I just don't know what to say.'

He looked away. 'Then don't say anything.'

She could hear the affection in his voice. Perhaps it was even more than that. 'Can you afford this amount?' she asked.

'I'm a single man, don't forget, with few outgoings. I've

tucked quite a bit away over the years. That's only a part of it, believe me.'

'Then thank you.'

'You're welcome, Cordelia. Anything for you.'

He rose abruptly as his emotions threatened to overwhelm him. 'I'll get another round in. Same again?'

She nodded.

Later, outside the pub, they said their goodbyes. He was startled when she kissed him on the cheek.

'All the best, Ginge. I mean that.'

'And you too.'

There was a moment's awkward pause, and than Ginge turned and walked swiftly away down the street. A lump came into Cordelia's throat as she headed in the opposite direction.

Out of a job. But plenty of money to see her through. She really was going to miss Ginge – possibly even more than she realised.

He'd been a good friend. But there had never been any chance of its being more than that.

'Do you mind if I join you, ladies?'

Alice recognised the speaker as a relative newcomer to the Labour Hall whose name was Mr Winning. 'Please do,' she replied politely.

Mr Winning placed his cup of tea on the table and sat down next to Alice. Peggy McAllister was on the other side.

'I'm Bill, by the way. Bill Winning.'

Alice introduced herself and Peggy, wondering what this was all about.

'I hope you don't mind me intruding, but I'm trying to get to know the other people who come here,' he explained.

That made sense to Alice. 'I've seen you here before,' she said.

'I don't get to come as often as I'd like because of shift work.'

'Oh?'

'I'm a policeman.'

A polisman! Well well well, Alice thought, eyeing him anew. She guessed him to be a little older than herself, and seemingly a pleasant enough man. The three of them chatted amiably until the tea break was over and then returned to the whist drive which had brought them there.

On the way home, Peggy commented, 'I think our new friend Mr Winning fancies you.'

Alice was shocked. 'Don't be daft! Why would he fancy me?'

'I saw the way he was looking at you. Concentrating far more on you than he did on me. I'm sure he was interested all right.'

'Nonsense!' Alice protested. 'I'm well past that sort of thing.'

'Why should you be?' Peggy argued. 'You're still a relatively young woman, and a bit of a looker, if I may say so. He wasn't wearing a wedding ring either. Did you notice?'

Alice hadn't. 'But I am.'

'Ah!' Peggy smiled. 'Maybe he enquired about you before coming over so knew you were a widow despite the ring.'

'You're imagining things, Peggy McAllister. Talking a load of hooey.'

'I know what I saw. You wait, he'll be asking to join us again before long.'

Alice discovered that she was quite flustered by what Peggy had had to say. Not that she believed a word of it. The idea was ridiculous.

'Christ!' William exclaimed as a solitary Bf109 opened fire on them. Where had that come from? It hadn't been there a moment ago. He immediately banked the Blenheim in an attempt to get away, knowing there would be no escape from the far faster, more manoeuvrable Messerschmitt, arguably the best of the German fighters.

The Bf109 was swiftly back in an attacking position, firing a second salvo which ripped into the Blenheim's tail and fuselage.

This was it, William thought. Another burst would finish them off. All he could wonder was whether they would blow up or spiral downwards to crash into the deck. He hoped they blew up. That would be quicker.

He was vaguely aware of a voice praying to God, and realised it was Peter. He was surprised, as he had not been aware that Peter was religious.

And then, to his amazement, the Bf109 shot past them. He actually saw the pilot staring at them. And then the fighter was gone, allowing them to continue on their way. It seemed Peter's prayer had worked.

Back at the airfield, they got out to stare at the bullet holes in the tail and fuselage.

'Why?' Peter asked in a hollow voice.

'Why what?'

'Didn't he finish us off?'

William shook his head. 'There's only one explanation I can think of: the bastard must have had at least one previous engagement, and when it came to our turn he simply ran out of ammo.'

A white-faced Peter turned away and threw up. And in the small hours of the following morning William sat bolt upright in bed, eyes starting, sweat pouring down his face. He'd been having a nightmare.

He'd been back flying the Blenheim with the Bf109 attacking. Only this time the Messerschmitt hadn't run out of ammunition.

'There's someone here to see you, Cordelia,' Lexa announced, having answered the knock on the front door.

'Kenny!' Cordelia exclaimed in delight when he entered the room, his left arm in a sling.

'Hello, Cordelia.' He smiled.

'You're wounded,' she said in alarm.

'Not badly, and it's well on the mend.'

She introduced him to her mother, and Kenny handed Alice the bottle wrapped in brown paper he'd been carrying.

'Whisky!' Alice enthused. 'A bottle of this is rarer than hen's teeth these days. Where on earth did you get it?'

Kenny gave her a wink. 'Let's just say I know a man who can lay hold of things other people can't.'

'You mean a spiv?'

'Something like that,' Kenny acknowledged.

Alice laughed, not minding in the least. 'Lexa, fetch

some glasses and we'll all have a tipple before I'm off.' It was one of her nights at the Labour Hall.

Cordelia was eager to hear all about France and Dunkirk, but had to contain her impatience for the moment. She was surprised at how pleased she was to see Kenny. There again, having thought and worried about him so much, maybe she shouldn't have been.

A little later Alice left the house, and Lexa, presuming Cordelia and Kenny wanted to be alone, tactfully took herself off to her bedroom.

'Another one?' Cordelia queried.

'If you don't mind.'

'Not at all. Now, why don't you sit down and tell me all about it? How long are you home for? And how did you get that wound?'

Kenny laughed. 'I don't know how long I'm home for, but it'll be quite some time. First of all this wound has to heal properly. And secondly the regiment has to be rebuilt.' A faraway look came into his eyes, and when he next spoke he'd dropped his voice. 'We lost a lot of men in France. Good lads all.'

'I'm so sorry,' she whispered.

'I copped a bullet at Dunkirk. But I was lucky – it went straight through just under my shoulder. One of my pals who was beside me was . . .' He broke off, and shook his head. 'Denny was killed. Let's just leave it at that.'

Cordelia gave him his refill. 'I thought a lot about you, Kenny. Every day, in fact.'

'Did you?' He was delighted.

'I did.'

'I thought about you all the time too. I'm sorry I didn't

write for a while, but it became impossible in the end.'

'Did you get my letters?' she asked.

He shook his head. 'Not for ages now. They're bound to be somewhere, but they didn't reach me. I didn't think you'd stopped writing, though. I knew better than that.'

She stared at him, thinking he was a young man no more. His youth was gone; France had seen to that. The person facing her was a fully grown adult, older than his years. War, death and whatever horrors he'd been through had irrevocably changed him.

'I went to the stall this afternoon,' Kenny went on. 'Ginge told me he'd had to let you go.'

'I've got a new job now,' Cordelia informed him. 'I'm a conductress on the trams.'

'A conductress! A far cry from the flower market.'

'It is that. But, like the flower market, I enjoy the work.'

Kenny pulled out a packet of cigarettes. 'Do you mind if I smoke?'

'Not at all. I'll get you an ashtray.'

He watched her as she left the room, thinking that his memory hadn't played tricks on him. She was as lovely as he remembered, if not lovelier.

When it was time for him to go, Cordelia saw him to the front door, where he hesitated.

'I was wondering if you'd care to come to the pictures with me on Saturday night? There's a film on I'd like to see.'

'And what's that?'

'*Ninotchka* with Greta Garbo. She's one of my favourites.'

'She's one of mine as well. I'd love to go with you. Where shall we meet?'

'In front of the Central Station at six?'

'I'll be there. That's a promise.'

'Goodnight then, Cordelia.'

'Goodnight, Kenny. Thanks for the whisky.'

'My pleasure.'

When he was gone she took a deep breath, thinking how much she'd enjoyed seeing him again, and the conversation they'd had.

She also felt strangely elated, and it had nothing whatsoever to do with the whisky she'd drunk.

'So what was that mysterious conversation with Bill Winning all about?' Peggy McAllister demanded as she and Alice made their way home from the Labour Hall.

'Nothing at all,' Alice replied vaguely.

'Oh, come on, I know what I saw. The pair of you were up to something, and no mistake.'

Alice blushed. 'Well, actually, he asked me to go to a tea dance with him.'

Peggy stopped dead in her tracks, forcing Alice to do the same. 'A tea dance?'

'That's right.'

'And what did you say?'

'That I'd think about it. That he'd caught me somewhat off guard and I needed time to consider his invitation.'

They resumed walking. 'I presume you'll take him up on his offer?'

'Well you presume wrong, Peggy. I meant exactly what I said. I'll think about it.'

'He's a fair-looking bloke, you know. And very mannerly. He's also got a good and steady job.'

'He only asked me out,' Alice replied sarcastically. 'Not to marry him.'

'You know what I think?'

'What?'

'He's on the lookout for a wife. I'm almost certain of it.'

That rocked Alice. 'Do you really think so?'

'I do.' Peggy nodded.

Dear me, Alice thought. Looking for a wife! That put a whole new complexion on things. If it was true.

Alice lay in the bath staring at herself. She wasn't in bad condition for a woman who'd had two children. Not bad condition at all. She had been carrying a bit too much weight, but that was now gone, thanks to rationing.

She'd have to get her roots done again shortly, she reminded herself. The white was beginning to show through, the white that was the result not of age, but of the loss of Jimmy.

Aye, Jimmy, she thought. How she still missed him. Dreadfully.

Chapter 27

'That was simply terrific,' Kenny enthused as they left the picture house. 'Wasn't Garbo wonderful?'

'She was indeed,' Cordelia agreed.

'In fact, I wouldn't mind going and seeing it a second time.'

Cordelia laughed. 'A glutton for punishment, eh?'

He grinned at her in the darkness of the blackout. 'You could say that.'

They started to walk towards Cordelia's tram stop. She was sad that the evening was almost over. There was something very comforting about being with Kenny. Comforting and relaxing.

'I had some good news yesterday,' he told her.

'Oh?'

'I'm being promoted to lance corporal.'

'That's fabulous!' she exclaimed. On the spur of the moment, she gave him a big hug. 'Congratulations.'

'Thanks, Cordelia.'

'I'm sure it's well deserved.'

'I thought . . . well, I thought we might celebrate. You and I, together.'

'I'd love to celebrate your promotion, Kenny. What do you have in mind?'

'How about we meet up Wednesday night in the Hielan Laddie? Go there for old times' sake? I'd enjoy that. We could sort of reminisce.'

She nodded. 'We had a few laughs there right enough.'

'So are you on?'

'Indeed I am.'

Cordelia slipped an arm through Kenny's, and kept it there till they reached her tram stop.

Alice stood looking down at Jimmy's grave, and the newer one next to it. Granny Stewart had died the previous year, having arranged soon after Jimmy's death to be buried next to her son.

Alice sighed, and closed her eyes. What should I do, Jimmy? she asked silently. I'm in a right two and eight about all this.

She knew in her heart of hearts what Jimmy's reply would have been. He'd have said that he was gone, but that didn't mean her life was over. God willing, she still had a long way to go yet.

Married again? If indeed that's what going out with Bill Winning led to. Was she prepared to go through with that? Or was Peggy wrong, and all Bill wanted was a little companionship?

Alice chapped Peggy's door and invited herself in for a cup of tea.

'Have you made your mind up yet?' Peggy asked as she filled the kettle. 'It's a fortnight since you were last at the Labour Hall. People are wondering if you're ill.'

'I'll be going with you tonight,' Alice told her.

Peggy glanced sideways at her friend. 'So you've made up your mind?'

Alice nodded.

'And?'

'I shall be turning down Bill's invitation.'

'But why?' Peggy demanded in exasperation.

'I just don't want to accept, that's all.'

'That isn't an excuse, Alice. You must have a reason. Don't you like him, is that it?'

'Oh, I like him well enough. He's very personable. Charming even.' She stopped to collect her thoughts. 'Jimmy and I were extremely close. I loved that man with all my heart, as he loved me. Losing him was the worst thing that's ever happened in my life. He's gone, but somehow he's still with me. Waiting. Can you understand that?'

There was a softness in Peggy's eyes when she replied. 'Aye, I can.'

'No one could replace him, Peggy. Or even begin to. He's my chap, and always will be. You see, I don't even want male companionship. Don't need it. I'm happy as I am, and that's the truth of it.'

Peggy studied her friend. 'Then you've made the right decision. I shan't mention the matter again.'

And Peggy never did.

'Tell me something,' Lexa said. 'Is he a good kisser?'

Cordelia glanced at her sister in astonishment. They were alone, Alice having gone to bed early because of a bad headache. 'Is who a good kisser?'

'Kenny, of course.'

Cordelia blushed, and looked away. 'I don't know,' she eventually replied.

That wasn't at all what Lexa had expected to hear. 'What do you mean, you don't know?'

'Exactly that.' This was making Cordelia feel extremely uncomfortable.

'But . . . how many times have you been out together?'

'Four. No, five.'

'And he hasn't kissed you? Has he even tried?'

'Drop it, Lexa. Please. I'm not in the mood.'

Lexa had no intention of dropping it. She was intrigued. 'Is there something wrong with him? Shy perhaps?'

'There's nothing wrong with him. And he certainly isn't shy. It's just . . .' She paused and took a deep breath. 'We're good friends, that's all.'

Lexa laughed. 'My bum!'

'Don't be so crude,' Cordelia admonished her.

'I've seen you getting ready to go out and meet him. All abuzz and excited. Nervous sometimes. And there's a look in your eyes that tells me you're going to see a man who's a lot more to you than simply a friend.'

With a shock Cordelia realised that what her sister said was true. That's exactly what she was like when going to meet Kenny. Heart a-flutter. Eager.

Was it because she'd made such a mistake with Joe Given that she'd held back, not wanting to repeat that mistake? Or was it because she'd first thought of Kenny as a young lad and had somehow never totally eradicated that original impression?

'Well?' Lexa demanded.

'Thanks, sis.' Cordelia smiled. 'You've made your point. And you're right. I've been incredibly stupid.'

'And Kenny?'

'We'll see. And let's leave it at that. Please?'

'All right. But let me know how things progress. I'm dying to know.'

'I promise.'

The following Sunday afternoon Cordelia and Kenny went for a walk in Queen's Park. After a while they sat on a bench and Kenny lit up.

It wasn't in Cordelia's nature to be forward, but in this instance she was going to force herself.

'Kenny, can I ask you a question?'

'Of course.'

'I'm a bit confused. What exactly is our relationship?'

He had a puff on his cigarette, staring intently at her. 'What do you mean?'

'We go out together, right?'

He nodded.

'So what are we? Friends, or more than that?' There, she'd said it.

'That depends,' he replied softly.

'On what?'

'How you actually think of me.'

She looked away, slightly embarrassed. 'I think I'd prefer to first of all hear what you think of *me*.' She had no intention of being possibly caught out by declaring herself before he did.

Kenny took his time in answering. 'I've been mad about you since shortly after joining the stall. In the days when I still called you Miss Stewart. The thing is, I never thought I stood a chance with you. And I suppose that notion has stayed.'

Cordelia felt a lump come into her throat. Had she known so all along? She wasn't sure.

'Shall I go on?' he ventured.

'Please do.'

'I started off being mad about you, and then one day, before I enlisted, I realised it had changed to love.'

Her heart leaped at that.

'I've never said or done anything about it because I still presumed I didn't stand a chance where you were concerned. If you just want us to be friends then I'll have to settle for that. Now it's your turn.'

'Do something for me, Kenny?'

'Name it.'

'Kiss me.'

He stared long and hard at her, threw the remains of his cigarette away, and took her into his arms.

'Oh, Kenny,' she whispered when the kiss was over. 'I've been such a fool in not seeing what was looking me straight in the face.'

He smiled. 'And what's been doing that?'

'Somewhere along the line, I don't know when, I fell in love with you too.'

He gazed deeply into her eyes. 'Are you certain about that?'

'As certain as certain.'

He took a deep breath. 'Then from now on you're my girl. My one and only.'

'And you're mine.'

'I think we've both been fools,' he said. 'But no more.'

'No more,' she echoed, feeling as though she was standing on top of the world.

Oh, this was right. So very, very right. 'I love you Kenny Smith,' she whispered, a hint of tears in her eyes.

'And I love you, Cordelia Stewart. For ever and a day.'

One kiss turned into two. Into three. Into four. When they finally left the park bench it was hand in hand, and each had a joyous spring in their step.

'Not spam fritters again!' Lexa complained, as Alice placed two of them in front of her.

'I'm sorry, but it's the best I can do, young lady. Trying to get any decent meat out of the butcher nowadays is almost impossible. Even mince is a rarity.'

Kenny glanced at Cordelia and smiled. He had been invited for tea.

'Do you mind spam fritters, Kenny?' Alice queried.

'Not at all, Mrs Stewart. You get used to all sorts in the army,' he replied, tongue in cheek.

Alice gave him a look, and turned again to Lexa. 'And if you're unhappy with those then just wait till tomorrow night. I have a real treat in store for you then.'

'What's that, Mum?' Lexa asked hopefully.

'Tripe and onions.'

Lexa almost gagged. She loathed tripe and the way it slithered slimily down the throat.

'So there!' Alice declared, and left them to fetch more fritters.

The look on Lexa's face made both Cordelia and Kenny, who now literally had his feet well under the table, burst out laughing.

'Ah, there you are, Lexa. Right on time. Come in, come in.'

Lexa closed the door behind her, wondering what was coming. She'd been instructed to report to Mr McLeod senior at five to three on the dot, and here she was.

Henry rose. 'I usually have a sherry round about now. Care to join me?'

'No thank you.'

'It's excellent sherry. I can highly recommend it.' He sighed. 'Before the war I always took it with a digestive biscuit. But no more, I'm afraid. Simply can't get hold of any these days, which is a great pity.'

She watched as he poured himself a schooner from a crystal decanter.

'Sure you won't change your mind?'

She shook her head. 'No thank you, Mr McLeod.'

He returned the decanter to the cupboard he'd taken it from, then tasted his sherry. 'Capital,' he pronounced. 'Absolutely first class.' He glanced at a wall clock, then checked the time against a half-hunter he wore.

'I must say you're looking well.' He beamed.

'Thank you.' What was going on? Had she been invited here just to make polite conversation? She doubted that.

The telephone on Henry's desk began to ring stridently.

Henry cleared his throat and laid his schooner down. Then he turned to Lexa. 'That's for you, my dear. I'll wait outside while you answer it.'

'Me?' she queried in astonishment.

'Yes. I think you can guess who's on the other end.'

'William,' she whispered to herself. It had to be. And it was.

'Lexa?'

'William?'

He laughed. 'Surprise, eh?'

'You can say that again.'

'I've got a spot of good news. The squadron is being relocated, and as a result I've got two weeks' leave. A whole fortnight! I'll be back in Glasgow the day after tomorrow.'

'Oh, William,' she breathed.

'Spoke to Pater earlier and made this arrangement to ring and speak to you. The other good news is he's agreed to shift your annual holiday to coincide with my being home, which means we can spend the fortnight together. Isn't that wonderful?'

'Absolutely,' she enthused, feeling quite giddy at this turn of events.

'Can't speak much longer, darling. Stay in Mount Florida the day after tomorrow and I'll come over when I can. All right?'

'All right,' she agreed happily.

'See you then.'

'See you then, William.'

There was a click, and the line went dead. She was smiling broadly as she cradled the phone.

346

'May I still have that sherry?' she asked when Henry re-entered his office.

'Of course you can.'

It was a celebration, after all.

'I've got an announcement to make,' Alice told them over tea.

'What's that, Mum?' Cordelia queried.

'I've decided to do my bit for the war effort and go to work. They're crying out for women to help.'

'But you haven't had a job since before we were born!' Lexa protested.

'What's that got to do with the price of fish? I'm fit and able. So it's only right I get off my backside and do something.'

Cordelia glanced at Lexa, then back at her mother. 'Do you have anything specific in mind?'

'Well, I don't fancy going into a factory, or anything to do with industry. So I thought I might become a tram conductress like yourself. If there are any jobs going, that is.'

Cordelia frowned. 'Are you sure, Mum? You're on your feet all shift, don't forget. It might not look all that much, but it really is pretty hard graft.'

'I'll manage just fine,' Alice declared. 'Don't you worry about me.'

'Then I'll have a word with the supervisor down at the depot,' Cordelia said, 'and see what can be arranged.'

'Good. I can start whenever they like.'

Well well, Cordelia thought. This was certainly a turn-up for the book.

Lexa was thinking exactly the same thing, not entirely

sure she approved. But once their mother had set her mind on something there was no stopping her.

'Oh my God!' Lexa gasped, and shook all over.

William waited a few moments, then gently disentangled himself. They were on the back seat of the Austin, which was parked in an out of the way area of the Linn Park golf course where he'd known they wouldn't be disturbed, and could be totally private.

'How was that?' he asked, tongue in cheek, already knowing the answer.

'How do you think?'

'Rather special, I'd say.'

'And some.' She pulled herself into a sitting position, her insides still pulsing. 'Cuddle me, William.'

He put his arms round her, and held her close. 'I hope we can do this at least a couple of times more before I have to go back,' he whispered.

So too did she, though she frowned at his mentioning having to go back. 'There are still ten days left,' she reminded him quietly. 'We'll make the best of them.'

'We certainly will if I have anything to do with it.' Detaching one arm, he reached up and stroked her hair. 'Happy?'

'I couldn't be more so. And you?'

'Bursting with it.'

He fumbled on the floor to find the bottle of wine he'd brought along. Pulling the cork free, he offered her the bottle. 'Like a slug?'

Lexa giggled. 'What a horrible expression. Slug! I thought those were things that crawled round gardens.'

He smiled in the darkness. 'That doesn't answer my question.'

Taking the bottle, she had a swallow, then another. 'How common, drinking from a bottle like this. My mother would have a fit if she saw me.'

'I imagine she would. Not only drinking from a bottle but with your knickers round an ankle and your skirt up to your bum.'

Lexa laughed. 'She wouldn't just have a fit, she'd have a frenzy and probably smack me half silly.'

He took the bottle from her and had a few swallows himself. 'It's useful having a father who's a wine merchant,' he said.

'I can't argue with that.'

He laid a hand on her bare thigh, then slid it higher, causing her to suck in a breath. 'The night's still young,' he said softly.

'What does that mean?'

'We don't have to be in a rush to leave. Do we?'

'No,' she agreed.

'Good.'

It was over an hour later before they finally headed back to the main road.

William halted Lexa outside a photographer's studio in Sauchiehall Street. 'Here we are,' he declared.

'Is this the surprise?'

'It is. I've booked an appointment for you to have your portrait done. I want one for my new billet down south where it shall be proudly displayed and no doubt make all the other chaps insanely jealous.'

'Oh, William.' She thought that was sweet.

'You've no objections, I take it?'

'Only one. More of a condition, really.'

He frowned. 'What's that?'

'I want a photograph of you for my bedroom. That way I can look at you every morning when I get up, and every night when I go to bed.'

He laughed. 'Agreed. Shall we go inside?' The door tinged as he opened it. 'You first.'

'Beauty before the beast, eh?'

Years later she recalled saying that, and shuddered at the memory.

'We both knew the day had to finally come,' Kenny said. 'And now it has.'

'Still no idea where the regiment's being posted to?'

He shook his head. 'None at all. It's all strictly hush-hush. There are all sorts of rumours flying about, mind. Any one of which could be right. There again, they could all be wrong.'

'Christ, I'll miss you,' Cordelia said, a choke in her voice.

'And I'll miss you. Like billy-o.'

How long before she saw him again? Cordelia wondered. It could be years. She refused to think he might not return, and that this could be their last time together. Refused point-blank to consider the possibility.

'I'll write to you when I can. Though it might be quite a while before I'm able to. In the meantime you're not to worry. Understand?'

Tears weren't very far away now. 'I understand, Kenny.'

350

'So, chin up, eh?'

She tried to smile, but couldn't.

There was a last kiss, and then he was gone. Striding away.

The tears that had been threatening now fell like rain.

It was months before the first letter arrived, the envelope containing a sprinkling of sand which Cordelia guessed was his way of telling her he was somewhere in the desert. Though she had no idea which one.

If he'd been allowed to say, the answer was Libya. And it was Rommel, the Desert Fox, whose forces they were facing.

Chapter 28

William, Peter Blythe and the rest of the squadron were waiting impatiently for the new wonder aeroplane they'd been promised, the first of which was scheduled to arrive at any moment.

'Listen!' Peter exclaimed, eyes bright with excitement.

Now William could hear the far-off drone of engines rapidly coming closer. He used a hand to shade his eyes as he stared in the direction from which the sound was emanating.

And then there she was. The Mosquito came storming in a few feet above the hangars, banking, and then coming in to land, William delighting in the marvellous crackling of its mighty Merlin engines.

They were all agog as the Mosquito taxied towards them, and William knew instinctively that this plane, as had been promised, was something special.

The Mosquito came to a halt, the engines killed. Moments later the hatch was opened, a ladder positioned, and down came suede shoes and yellow socks. Geoffrey de Havilland junior had arrived.

The squadron crowded round the aircraft, one or two of them whistling in admiration.

The Mossie, as it was to become known, was simply the most beautiful aircraft William had ever seen. It wasn't just its clean, streamlined, gracious profile – it seemed to be actually alive. With its slender fuselage, high cocked tail and those two superb engines it gave the impression it was holding itself back from leaping into the air.

'Wow!' William enthused, far more than just impressed. He couldn't wait to fly one himself.

'I wonder when the rest are getting here?' Peter mused.

'Search me. But I hope it's soon. I'm itching to take one of those up.' William glanced over to where de Havilland was deep in conversation with the station commander, Group Captain Battle, OBE, DFC and the squadron commanding officer, Wing Commander Peter Simmons, DFC.

'I've just fallen in love,' Peter Blythe declared, staring in awe at the Mosquito.

William laughed. 'That'll be a first.'

'Love it is, I assure you, old boy.'

There were many in the squadron who felt the same way about this brand-new bomber. And most of those who didn't there and then did so later.

Tarantula lit a cigarette and sucked smoke deep into her lungs. Pam produced a packet of five Willy Woodbines, and also lit up.

'Christ, it's getting harder and harder to get fags these days,' Tarantula complained bitterly after exhaling. 'I thought I was going to have to sell myself for this lot.'

'It is difficult,' Pam agreed. 'In fact it's so much trouble I might actually pack it in.'

Tarantula snorted, then turned her attention to Lexa, who was sipping tea. 'Heard from lover boy recently?' she queried, a hint of nastiness in her voice.

Lexa had come to loathe Tarantula, whom she considered common as muck. It wasn't that Tarantula came from a working-class background, but the way she behaved. And spoke.

'If you mean William, yes I have.'

'How's he doing?' Pam enquired, genuinely interested.

'Very well, according to him. He goes on and on about this new plane the squadron have. A Mosquito it's called. He thinks it's sensational.'

'What sort of plane is it?' Pam asked.

'A bomber. And it's made entirely of wood. Other than that I can't tell you anything. William hasn't mentioned any of the technical details – not that I would understand them if he did.'

'Has he shagged you yet?' Tarantula asked, the nastiness still in her voice.

Lexa was genuinely shocked at the question. 'No, he hasn't,' she lied immediately.

'Something wrong with him, is there?'

Lexa fought back the urge to slap her. How rude! It just wasn't the sort of thing one asked. Especially of someone who was only a work colleague. 'No there isn't.'

'You hope.' Tarantula suddenly laughed. 'If I was you I'd try him out before you get married. Men aren't all the same, you know. Some are flops in that department. Useless. You don't want to get landed with a bloke like that.'

Lexa was outraged. 'I've had enough of this conversation,' she declared. 'It's disgusting.'

'I'm only giving you good advice,' Tarantula protested.

Lexa eyed her with distaste, still wanting to smack her. Why, she hadn't even confided in Cordelia that she'd slept with William. That was strictly their business and no one else's.

Pam was listening to the exchange with a guilty expression on her face, not wishing to take part. 'That's me then,' she declared, stubbing out the remains of her cigarette, and preparing to leave the room.

Lexa laid her cup and saucer aside. She'd wash and dry them later. 'I'll come with you,' she said.

Tarantula shrugged. 'I was only trying to help,' she said in an offhand manner.

Like hell, Lexa thought, following Pam out the door.

Later, sitting behind her desk, she glanced over at Tarantula and inwardly smiled. If only you knew, she thought. Flop was the last word she'd use to describe William!

The weather had closed in over Swanton Morley where 105 Squadron was based. And as the same weather had been forecast for the next few days, precluding flying, the chaps had decided to have a thrash in the Officers' Mess.

William was drunk, staggeringly so – as indeed most of them were – and thoroughly enjoying himself. There was a shriek of laughter as a handful of machine-gun bullets, having been thrown on to a blazing fire in an adjoining room, exploded. Everyone thought it was hilarious. Pilot Officer Jensen was banging away on the old Joanna, as they called the piano, halfway through his repertoire of filthy rugby songs.

William collapsed into an armchair to try to catch his breath. God, this was good. A real lifter to counteract the extreme anxiety and gut-wrenching fear that, if he was honest, occurred during bombing raids. Terrifying ordeals from which not everyone returned.

'Are you asleep or dead?' a voice demanded.

William opened his eyes to find Peter swaying in front of him. 'Piss off,' he slurred.

'Indeed. But in the meantime would you care for another drink? I'm in the chair.'

William smiled at that. 'About time too, you tight-fisted bugger. It's the Scots who're supposed to be mean. Not you English.'

Peter pulled himself erect, and stopped swaying. 'Then I have news for you, laddie.'

'And what's that?'

'My maternal grandmother was Scots. From Fraserburgh.'

'Ahh!' William exhaled. 'That explains it then. Why you're so penny-pinching.'

Peter shook his head. 'You look pissed as a rat.'

'I am, old boy. As are you.'

Peter hiccuped. 'Sorry.'

'Accepted.'

Peter peered at his friend. 'So do you want another, or not?'

William thought about that. Not, he decided. Another and he might be throwing up. 'Later,' he replied. 'Right now I'm going to have a little snooze to help clear the head.'

'Suit yourself. But I'm going to have one. Damn right I am.' He lurched off.

William closed his eyes again, and within moments had drifted into a trouble-free sleep where there were no German fighters, no ack-ack and no fear of being killed.

A sleep that brought a smile to his face as he dreamt about Lexa. His darling, beautiful Lexa.

Alice looked over to where Bill Winning was chatting to Bella Ogilvy, a widow like herself. Bill had been courting Bella for some time now, and it was whispered by some who attended the Labour Hall that marriage was in the air.

If that was true then Peggy was right: Bill had been on the lookout for a wife. Well, he could do a lot worse than Bella, whom she'd always considered a very nice woman. Attractive, too.

Did she have any regrets about turning down Bill's invitation to the tea dance, and what it might have led to? The answer was no. None at all.

To have taken up Bill's invitation would somehow have been a betrayal of Jimmy's memory. And she wouldn't have betrayed Jimmy, or his memory, for all the world.

They were heading for Berlin in the first ever daylight raid on the city. And the weather was continuing to worsen, making William wonder if they'd have to abandon the mission.

'Bf109!' Peter suddenly shouted in warning.

William quickly spotted the fighter coming in fast on an intercept course. 'Shit!' he muttered. This was the second Bf109 they'd run into in the last twenty minutes. Luckily there was some heavy cloud directly ahead, which he headed for, praying he could get into it before the Jerry was upon them.

It was close, but they made it. Suddenly they were surrounded by cloud, obscuring them from the fighter. Safe – for now, anyway.

In the event the raid was abandoned because of weather conditions, and they set a new course for Hamburg, their secondary target. There they were again attacked by Bf109s, and William slipped into cloud cover at 16,000 feet, only dropping below that cover when they were over the Dutch coast.

Almost immediately they were attacked by two Fw190s. William evaded the first attack by going into a steep turn, only to find himself head on to the second Fw190 which fired a burst as they closed.

The Mosquito juddered as it was hit, but the controls still responded perfectly as William yet again climbed into cloud, and started for home. The cloud gave out just beyond the Dutch coast, so William descended to sea level and outran his pursuers, having the faster aircraft.

On arriving back at Swanton Morley a thoroughly shaken William went into his room and closed the door behind him. Sitting on his bed he raised his hands and stared at them. They were shaking almost uncontrollably.

That had been a near thing. Too bloody near. He'd seen two Mossies shot down over Hamburg, and another hit by ack-ack, blowing up in a huge fireball.

'Christ,' he muttered. 'Sweet Jesus Christ.'

He went to his chest of drawers and picked up the bottle of whisky standing on it. Putting the bottle to his mouth, he gulped and gulped and gulped.

'Fares, please!'

Ginge smiled on hearing that familiar voice. He'd been told Cordelia was working on the trams, but had thought it unlikely they'd run into one another.

'Fares, please!'

'Hello, Cordelia.'

'Ginge!' she exclaimed in surprise.

'I recognised your voice. How are you?'

'Mustn't grumble. There's a war on, after all.' She stared him up and down. 'I must say you're looking well.'

'So are you.'

'Where are you going?'

He named his destination.

'That'll be tuppence then.'

He handed over the money, and she noticed as he did so that he was wearing a wedding ring. 'Are you married now?'

He nodded. 'Her name's Marlene, and she's the best thing that's ever happened to me. She's ginger like myself.'

Cordelia found the idea amusing. 'When did all this happen?'

'Last year. We met at work, and it just sort of went from there. We get on like a house on fire.'

'I couldn't be more pleased for you, Ginge. Truly I couldn't.'

'There's a baby on the way too. So I'll be the proud dad when it arrives.'

'When's it due?'

'A couple of months, if all goes according to plan.' He hesitated, then said, 'I heard about you and Kenny. Good luck to the pair of you.'

'Thanks, Ginge,' she replied quietly, remembering how much he'd fancied her.

'Do you miss the flower market?' he asked.

'All the time. Though I enjoy this job well enough. It can be a bit of a laugh at times. They're a good bunch back at the depot. My mum's a conductress too, doing her bit for the war effort she calls it, and she enjoys it as well. Though she doesn't like it so much when she has to do late shifts, which don't bother me at all.'

'Have you heard from Kenny lately?'

'Only the other day. I've no idea where he is, but he assures me he's fine and well. They have been involved in some fierce fighting of late which he's come through without a scratch.' She took a deep breath. 'Which, please God, is how things continue.'

They arrived at another stop and several passengers came on board.

'You'll have to excuse me, Ginge,' she apologised.

'I understand. On you go. It's been great seeing you again, Cordelia.'

'And you, Ginge.'

To her disappointment she was upstairs when Ginge got

off, so they never got to say goodbye. Ginge happily married with a baby on the way. She really was delighted for him.

Peter had lost consciousness some time previously, and William had no idea whether he was alive or dead. Nor was he able to find out as he fought the bucking controls.

They'd been jumped by a fighter over the French coast, and riddled with several extended bursts that had done serious damage. William considered it a miracle he'd been able to nurse the Mosquito this far. If he'd been sensible he'd have baled out, but he refused to do that in case Peter was still alive.

Swanton Morley came into view, to William's profound relief. He even managed the semblance of a smile as he started his approach run. He vaguely noticed smoke coming from somewhere behind him, but put it out of his mind as he concentrated on landing.

There was the familiar bump as the plane made contact with the ground. Then it all went horribly wrong.

The undercarriage collapsed, and simultaneously a sudden wave of fire engulfed the cockpit. Fire that hideously hissed and crackled. Fire that . . .

Seemingly far away William could hear someone screaming. He did not realise it was himself.

'Here's the letter you've been waiting for.' Alice had just picked up the morning post from the front door.

At last! Lexa thought. It had been so long since the previous one she'd been frantic.

Forgetting her breakfast she hastily tore open the envelope

and scanned the single sheet of paper it contained. The colour drained from her face. 'Oh, my God!' she whispered.

'What is it?' Alice asked anxiously. It was obvious that something was terribly wrong.

'William's been involved in a crash and is now in hospital. He says he'll probably be in for some time, but I'm not to worry. He's having the very best of attention.' She glanced up at her mother. 'And that's it.'

Alice frowned. 'Doesn't he say what his injuries are?'

'No.'

How odd, Alice thought.

There was an address at the top right-hand corner of the sheet of paper. The hospital was in East Grinstead, wherever that was.

'I'll reply this evening,' Lexa said. He may have told her not to worry, but she was worried sick none the less.

Lexa and Pam were having their morning break. Tarantula was not present as she was off ill.

'That's awful news,' Pam said after Lexa had told her about the letter and its contents.

'The point is, he hasn't said how serious it is. That's what I can't understand.'

Pam couldn't either. 'He'll probably tell you in his next letter,' she declared, trying to buck Lexa up.

Yes, Lexa thought. That's probably what will happen. 'Just don't mention this to anyone, though, especially Tarantula.'

'I'll keep it under my hat. That's a promise.'

'Not until I know more, anyway.'

*   *   *

362

'It's two months now, Mum. What's stopping him writing?'

'I read something in the newspaper the other day which might explain it,' Alice replied slowly. 'Could it be he's depressed by his injuries? That happens, apparently. Not only in wartime, but peacetime too. A patient can get so depressed by their operation that they don't want to communicate with the outside world. Not even their nearest and dearest.'

'Hm,' Lexa murmured thoughtfully. That was a possibility.

Henry McLeod looked up from his desk and smiled. 'You wanted to see me, Lexa?'

'It's William. I've only had two letters since his crash, both short. And in neither does he say how badly he's hurt. Do you know?'

Henry sat back in his chair and studied Lexa. 'He did mention in one to us he'd been a bit mangled, but nothing that couldn't be put right in time. That's it, I'm afraid.'

Mangled? Lexa wondered what that meant.

'It's very like William to behave like this,' Henry went on. 'He's the stiff-upper-lip type. Not one to complain. So there you are,' he added in a breezy tone.

Lexa felt she'd just been dismissed. 'Thank you, Mr McLeod.'

'Glad I've been able to help.'

'I'll get back to work, then.'

'And so must I.' He picked up his pen and bent over the papers in front of him.

When Lexa had gone Henry laid his pen aside, rose,

went to where he kept the brandy decanter and poured himself a stiff one. He needed it.

The letters from William kept coming, but they were few and far between. And always short. Lexa began to feel she was corresponding with a stranger. Then, eight months after the first, the final one arrived.

Lexa read it in disbelief.

'Well?' Alice demanded.

Lexa opened her mouth, shut it. Then opened it again. 'William has broken off our engagement. He's met someone else. A nurse who's been looking after him. He's sorry, but . . . They intend to marry as soon as he's recovered, and before he returns to his squadron.'

'Oh, lassie,' Alice whispered.

Cordelia went to Lexa and put an arm round her shaking shoulders, unable to think of a single thing to say which might help.

Lexa felt as if she was crumpling in on herself, her mind numb. He'd found someone else! The man who'd sworn time and time again that he loved her. 'I can't go in to work today,' she sobbed. 'I couldn't face the girls in the office. Not after this.'

'Perfectly understandable,' Alice sympathised. 'I'll take time off as well. I don't want you to be left alone.' She looked at Cordelia. 'Will you make some kind of excuse for me down at the depot?'

'Of course, Mum. Leave that to me.'

For the rest of that day, and many days afterwards, Lexa was inconsolable.

*　　*　　*

Lexa laid an envelope and her engagement ring on Henry's desk. He didn't speak, merely stared guiltily at her.

'That's a letter of resignation,' she said in a flat voice. 'And the obvious.'

Henry sighed. 'I'll be sorry to lose you. I'm sure we all will. You've given us excellent service.'

It was a fortnight since William's letter breaking off their engagement had arrived, a fortnight during which she hadn't appeared in *Vins*. Until now.

'You obviously know why I'm resigning,' she said.

Henry nodded. 'I'm terribly sorry, Lexa. But won't you reconsider and stay?'

She almost laughed. 'Don't you realise what a humiliation it would be for me to face the others in my office after what William's done. Have you any idea?' Tarantula would have a field day, she thought grimly.

'I understand,' Henry murmured, his heart going out to her. 'But I think William would prefer it if you kept the ring. It is rather valuable, I believe.'

Lexa was outraged. 'Is that offer meant to be some sort of pay-off? Is that it?'

'No,' Henry replied hastily. 'I didn't mean it like that at all.'

Lexa nearly said, 'My arse!' but managed not to. She'd done what she'd come to do, and now it was time to go. 'Goodbye, Mr McLeod.'

'I'll have your money made up and sent to you. Is that all right?'

Why not? Lexa thought. She was entitled. 'Thank you,' she replied, her voice cold as charity.

'Lexa!' he called out when she was almost at the door.

She stopped, and turned to face him.

'I want you to know both my wife and I wanted you for our daughter-in-law.'

'Really?' she replied sarcastically.

Once outside Lexa walked away, never looking back, her heart filled with bitterness, and black despair.

Summer 1948

It was a Saturday afternoon and Lexa was in town shopping for a present for wee James, Cordelia and Kenny's little boy, who would be two years old in a couple of days. Kenny had come home safely from the war, and he and Cordelia had married at the earliest opportunity. They lived in Battlefield, not far from Mount Florida, and were ecstatically happy together.

'Lexa?'

She turned from the shop window she'd been looking into to stare in astonishment at the speaker. The resemblance was still incredibly marked. Well, they were twins, after all.

'Hello, Kirsty.' She smiled. 'It's been a long time.'

'I wasn't sure it was you for a moment. As you say, it's been a long time.' Kirsty was pushing a pram holding two babies, each sucking on a dummy. 'How are you?'

'Fine. Are you still nursing?'

Kirsty laughed. 'Not with this lot to look after. I gave up when I got married fourteen months ago.'

Lexa, still thrown by running into William's sister, bent over the pram and cooed. 'They're lovely,' she declared, warmth in her voice.

'Twins. A boy and a girl just like . . .' Kirsty trailed off in confusion, realising what she'd been about to say.

Something twisted in Lexa's stomach. Her expression became stony.

'And what about yourself?' Kirsty queried, blushing slightly. 'Have you any children?'

Lexa shook her head. 'I'm afraid not. I've never . . . well, I've never married, you see.'

Kirsty didn't know what to say to that.

'Anyway, it's been nice seeing you again,' Lexa said, suddenly wanting to get away as quickly as she could.

'And you.'

'Bye then.'

'Bye.'

Lexa left Kirsty, and hurried into the shop, though she had no intention of buying anything there. For the rest of that day she kept wondering if she should have asked after William, and how he was doing.

She finally came to the conclusion that it was best she hadn't. The answer she might have been given was probably one she wouldn't have wanted to hear.

It was Lexa's night for washing her hair, which she was just about to start – Alice across the landing having a chinwag with Mrs McAllister – when there was a knock on the front door. Perhaps Cordelia was making a surprise visit, she speculated as she went to answer it. But it wasn't Cordelia. To her utter amazement it was Elspeth McLeod.

'Hello, Lexa.' Elspeth smiled. 'Is it possible to have a word?'

'Of course,' Lexa stammered. 'Come in.'

Elspeth's gaze flicked round the room she was ushered into, noting how neat and tidy it was.

'This is unexpected to say the least,' Lexa said, having somewhat regained her composure.

'I hope I'm not disturbing you?'

'Not in the least. Take a seat. Would you like a cup of tea?'

'No thank you. But I will sit down.'

What in God's name was all this about? Lexa wondered, sitting opposite the older woman.

Elspeth cleared her throat. 'This is embarrassing, but there is something I have to ask you.'

'Go ahead.'

'Kirsty told me she ran into you last Saturday, and the pair of you had a brief conversation during which you mentioned you'd never married. Correct?'

Lexa flushed. 'That's correct.'

Elspeth took a deep breath. 'This is the embarrassing bit. But I have to ask. Your answer's important. Can you tell me why?'

'I never married?'

Elspeth nodded.

How rude! Lexa thought. How *bloody* rude. 'Isn't that my business, Mrs McLeod?'

'Yes, normally it would be. But honestly, it's terribly important. At least I believe so.'

Lexa stared long and hard at Elspeth, then dropped her gaze to stare at the floor. 'The opportunity simply never arose. There have been a few boyfriends along the way, but no one I could get serious about.'

'I see,' Elspeth murmured.

'Does that answer your question?'

'Perhaps. And there again, perhaps not.' Elspeth drew in another deep breath, then slowly exhaled. 'I'll put it bluntly, Lexa. Have you never married because you're still in love with William?'

This time Lexa flamed red. 'I don't see the point in all this,' she said angrily.

'Oh, there is a point,' Elspeth replied softly. 'There most certainly is. Otherwise I wouldn't be here, I assure you.'

There was silence between the two women for a few moments. Finally Elspeth let out a huge sigh. 'All right then, I'll go first. The letter William wrote you contained a lie. There never was anyone else. No nurse, in other words.'

Lexa was rocked to the core. 'No nurse?'

'He made her up as an excuse to break off your engagement.'

'But why?' Lexa demanded.

'Because of his injuries. His face was very badly burned during the crash. Actually, it wasn't exactly a crash. The plane went up in flames as William was landing it. It was a miracle he got out, but somehow he managed to, albeit he has no recollection of escaping the aircraft.'

Lexa was stunned. No nurse. Face badly burned.

'William was taken to the Queen Victoria Hospital in East Grinstead,' Elspeth went on, 'where a wonderful surgeon called McIndoe was pioneering a new technique called plastic surgery. Mr McIndoe performed miracles there, rebuilding noses, eyelids, and all sorts. But the miracles were limited; it was a pioneering technique, after all. Many of his patients have gone on to lead useful and productive lives even though badly disfigured.'

'Dear God,' Lexa whispered.

'William broke it off between you because he didn't want you landed with someone as disfigured as he was going to be. His other reasons were that he didn't want you marrying him out of pity, or because you felt obliged. So he invented his lie and sent you that letter.'

Lexa's mind was reeling as she tried to take it all in. 'Why are you telling me this now, after all these years?' she queried, her voice shaking.

'I'll come to that in a moment. After being discharged from hospital William resumed flying, and continued to do so till the end of the war. On leaving the RAF he returned home, and stayed with us for a while. He refused point-blank to take up his old job again. In fact he rarely left the house, and never socialised. Then one day he announced what his intentions were.'

Elspeth paused for breath before continuing. 'He moved to a place up north where there was a garage for sale. Bought the garage and set himself up as owner/mechanic. And that's where he's been ever since. Living alone and doing a job he adores. His reason for moving so far away was that no one would know him from before. In other words a fresh start, a new location and new people who couldn't compare him with what he'd once been. The move was a great success. Once the reason for his disfigurement became known he received lots of sympathy, but no one was patronising with it. That was acceptable to him, and what he'd hoped for.'

Elspeth stared Lexa straight in the eye. 'And there you have it. The full story. Except for one other thing. Henry and I were up there a few months back, and while William was at the garage I decided to strip his bed and do the washing. I'd been in his bedroom on previous occasions, but hadn't seen it. My guess is that William had put it away during our various stays. But on this occasion he clearly forgot. It was your picture, Lexa. Standing on his bedside table. I knew then, call it a mother's intuition if you will, that he's still in love with you. And that is why I came here tonight to ask if you're still in love with him.'

It took Lexa several moments to answer, being overcome with emotion. 'Yes,' she whispered. 'I never stopped loving him, and that is the real reason why I never married.'

'I thought that might be the case.' Elspeth nodded. 'William will be furious with me for telling you the truth, but ever since Saturday I've known I had to. You have the right to make the decision denied you in the past. What you do now, or choose not to do, is up to you.'

Elspeth opened the handbag she was carrying and produced a piece of paper. 'This is his address and phone number.' Coming to her feet, she placed the paper on the mantelpiece. 'I'd better go now. Henry's waiting downstairs in the car.'

Lexa rose too. 'I'll see you to the door.'

'Thank you.'

'And I appreciate your visit. What you've told me is a complete shock.'

'I understand,' Elspeth said, touching Lexa sympathetically on the shoulder. 'You've a lot to think about.'

After Elspeth had gone Lexa collapsed into a chair and cried her eyes out. When Alice came in a little later, it was sometime before she could make head or tail of the story her daughter sobbed out to her, but at last they were sitting at the table with a pot of tea in front of them and Lexa was able to marshal her thoughts.

'I just feel so bloody angry, Mum. He had no right to do what he did. No right at all.'

Alice regarded her daughter sympathetically. 'I'm sure he thought it was for the best.'

'Oh, no doubt! But that's not the point. He lied to me, cutting me right out of his life without a by your leave. That's just not fair.'

Alice sighed, agreeing with Lexa. 'And Mrs McLeod says he's still in love with you?'

Lexa nodded.

'And you're still in love with him?'

'Always will be, Mum. It's one of these things.'

'Even if he is badly disfigured? What if you go to him and find he now repulses you. What then?'

Lexa bit her lip, and didn't reply.

'If that had happened to Jimmy, your father, I know it wouldn't have affected how I felt about him. Even though he could be an old sod at times.' Alice's eyes took on a misty look. 'Jimmy was aye the one for me. No one else ever got a look in. For all his faults, and mine, we were sweethearts up until the day he died. True sweethearts. I'd have done anything for that man, and he for me.' She paused, then asked softly, 'Does that help at all?'

Lexa nodded again.

'Then I suggest that you go and see William.' Almost whispering, Alice added, 'Face to face.'

Lexa came to a halt outside William's garage, her heart thumping nineteen to the dozen. The big moment was almost upon her. Closing her eyes, she offered up a silent prayer. Then, steeling herself, she went inside.

Feet and ankles protruded from underneath a vehicle. William's she presumed.

'I'll be with you in a minute,' a muffled, yet so familiar, voice informed her.

She didn't reply. Just stood there, waiting.

It was more than a minute before the flat trolley William was lying on moved. Lexa braced herself, wondering, as she'd done so many times since Elspeth's visit, how bad his face actually was.

The trolley rattled out from beneath the vehicle, and William was fully revealed. His expression froze when he saw her, eyes widening with shock.

'Hello, William.' She smiled, but it was with an effort. If he was shocked, so too was she on being confronted with the reality of what Elspeth had told her.

'Lexa?'

'That's me.'

'But . . .' He trailed off, and came to his feet to wipe his oily hands on a rag that had been stuffed in one of his overall pockets.

He stared at her in consternation, eyes that had shown shock now registering nothing but pain.

'Your mother gave me this address,' she explained.

'She had no right to do that!' William exclaimed angrily. 'No bloody right at all. I never wanted to see you again.'

'Isn't it the other way round? You didn't want me to see you.'

'Well, would you blame me for that?' He was still angry.

'I don't know about blame, but I can understand why.'

'Can you?'

'It's not as awful as I imagined it might be,' Lexa declared softly. 'I was expecting worse.'

'Awful enough though, eh?' He gestured to his face. 'Look at me. Something straight out of a horror story.'

'Well, you certainly aren't a pretty boy any more, William. I can't deny that. But you're still William.'

'I don't want your pity,' he snapped. 'You can stuff that.'

'I didn't come to offer pity,' she replied quietly.

'No?'

'No.'

'Then what did you come for?'

'To talk to you.'

'About what?'

'Us.'

'There is no us,' he retorted bitterly. 'That ended a long time ago.'

'With a lie.'

He dropped his gaze to stare at the floor. 'What I did was for the best, Lexa. Believe me.'

Now it was her turn to be angry. 'It was nothing of the sort. What you did was selfish. Utterly *fucking* selfish.'

He stared at her in astonishment, never before having heard her swear, far less use that particular word. 'How do you make that out?'

'Don't you think I should have been allowed to make my own decision about what had happened? I was an adult, don't forget. One with a mind of her own.'

'It was for the best,' he repeated doggedly. 'I wanted to spare you. Let you off the hook.'

'Oh, William,' she whispered. 'How little you know about women. Or about me.'

He had no reply to that. 'So why did my mother give you my address?'

'Because she found out I'd never married. And she wanted to know why.'

He stared hard at her. 'And why's that?'

'Because I've never stopped loving you. Your mother also believes you still love me.'

'Nonsense.'

'Then why do you keep my photograph on your beside table?'

'Do I?' he blustered.

'Your mother saw it there when she last stayed with you.'

Again he had no reply. 'The pub will be open shortly,' he said, glancing at his watch. 'And I could certainly use a drink. We could go for a walk first. What do you say?'

'That sounds fine by me.'

'I'll get my jacket.'

His face was pretty gruesome, she thought. But not as gruesome as all that. Parts of the skin were a reddish inflamed colour, others a sort of shiny yellow. His nose wasn't as she remembered, and she guessed correctly that it had been rebuilt.

'Right,' he declared on returning, having changed out of his overalls. 'Let's go.'

She watched him lock up, and then he led her down the road towards the sea in the near distance. 'If we'd stayed there we wouldn't have been able to continue our conversation,' he explained. 'Customers would have been dropping by, and other locals stopping for a natter, I expect. They often do.'

'Popular, eh?'

He shrugged. 'It's a small place, Lexa, and people are friendly. I like both.'

'Not the same as Glasgow then?' she teased.

'Not the same at all.'

Within minutes they'd arrived at a long beach of golden sand which, with the summer sun beating down, was quite breathtaking. 'It's beautiful,' Lexa breathed.

'One of my favourite walks, if not my favourite. Just don't think of going for a swim, that's all. The water's permanently freezing.'

They went a little way in silence, then William said, 'It is good to see you again, Lexa. Even though I didn't want to.'

'And it's good to see you.'

'Despite the face?'

'Despite the face, William,' she stated firmly.

'I wish I could believe you.'

'Well, do. For it's true.'

'Do you remember . . .' he started after another few steps in silence. Within minutes they were sharing their recollections of past events, laughing at some of them, sighing at others. Such fond memories.

Eventually she came to a halt and turned to him. 'So, do you still love me?'

He nodded.

'And I still love you. Now, I want you to listen to what I have to say next. I fell in love with William the *man*. Not the pretty face, but *you*, what's inside you. Can you understand that?'

'I don't deserve this,' he said huskily.

Reaching up she gently put a hand on his cheek. 'I want you to do something.'

'What?'

'Kiss me.'

A hint of tears appeared in his eyes. 'Are you sure?'

'Just kiss me, damn it. Of course I'm sure.'

She sighed when the kiss was over. 'Nothing changed there, darling.'

Then she was back in his arms, this kiss deeper, longer and fiercely passionate.

She slid a hand into his as they resumed walking. Chattering away like the lovers they'd once been. And soon would be again.